Regret
and
Redemption

A Forever Inked Novel

Sabrina Wagner

Stay Connected!

**Want to be the first to learn book news, updates and more?
Sign up for my Newsletter.**

https://www.subscribepage.com/sabrinawagnernewsletter

**Want to know about my new releases and upcoming sales?
Stay connected on:**

Facebook~Instagram~Twitter~TikTok
Goodreads~BookBub~Amazon

**I'd love to hear from you.
Visit my website to connect with me.**

www.sabrinawagnerauthor.com

Books by Sabrina Wagner

Hearts Trilogy
Hearts on Fire
Shattered Hearts
Reviving my Heart

Wild Hearts Trilogy
Wild Hearts
Secrets of the Heart
Eternal Hearts

Forever Inked Novels
Tattooed Hearts: Tattooed Duet #1
Tattooed Souls: Tattooed Duet #2
Smoke and Mirrors
Regret and Redemption
Sin and Salvation

Vegas Love Series
What Happens in Vegas (Hot Vegas Nights)
Billionaire Bachelor in Vegas

About This Book

It was a one-night stand... sort of.

I'd never done the one-night stand thing before, but I threw caution to the wind and followed Chase home from the bar like a lost puppy. For once, I wanted to forget my responsibilities as a single mom and live on the wild side.

Chase made me feel beautiful and desired, but when our tryst ended abruptly, I tucked my tail between my legs and returned to my carefully planned life.

Women like me didn't get to have men like him.

I thought I'd never see the sexy tattoo artist again, so when I found him talking to my six-year-old daughter, my heart dropped to the floor.

♥♥♥♥

I'd never been able to say no to gorgeous women. Casual sex kept me happy. No strings and no commitments. My heart had nothing to do with it.

I'd been satisfied until an almost one-night stand had me wanting more.
We hadn't even gotten down to the dirty deed before she ran off in a flurry.

She had a daughter and there was no way I was ready for that. My past was proof enough.

I tried to forget about her, but Maggie was completely unforgettable, and I couldn't get the fiery redhead out of my mind.

When a chance encounter brought us back together, I knew one night would never be enough...
we had unfinished business.

Table of Contents

Prologue
Chapter 1: Chase
Chapter 2: Maggie
Chapter 3: Chase
Chapter 4: Maggie
Chapter 5: Chase
Chapter 6: Maggie
Chapter 7: Chase
Chapter 8: Maggie
Chapter 9: Chase
Chapter 10: Maggie
Chapter 11: Chase
Chapter 12: Maggie
Chapter 13: Chase
Chapter 14: Maggie
Chapter 15: Chase
Chapter 16: Maggie
Chapter 17: Chase
Chapter 18: Maggie
Chapter 19: Chase
Chapter 20: Maggie
Chapter 21: Chase
Chapter 22: Maggie
Chapter 23: Chase
Chapter 24: Maggie
Chapter 25: Chase
Chapter 26: Maggie
Chapter 27: Chase
Chapter 28: Maggie
Chapter 29: Chase

Chapter 30: Maggie
Chapter 31: Chase
Chapter 32: Maggie
Chapter 33: Chase
Chapter 34: Maggie
Chapter 35: Chase
Chapter 36: Maggie
Chapter 37: Chase
Chapter 38: Maggie
Chapter 39: Chase
Chapter 40: Maggie
Chapter 41: Chase
Chapter 42: Maggie
Chapter 43: Chase
Chapter 44: Maggie
Chapter 45: Maggie
Epilogue: Chase
Another Epilogue: Maggie

Dedication

To My Sister~

Although you have lost your battle,
you are not forgotten but loved and missed dearly.
You continue to inspire me every day.
Heaven has gained a beautiful angel.

"She made broken look beautiful
and strong look invincible
She walked with the Universe on her shoulders
and made it look like a pair of wings"
– Ariana Dancu

Prologue

We stumbled into his apartment, my arms around his neck and his around my waist. Our lips locked together in a crushing kiss.

I hadn't been on a real date in forever. Not that this qualified as a date. More like a random hookup with a hot guy from the bar. I'd never done the one-night stand thing before, but for once I was breaking my own rules. My carefully planned life could use a little shaking up, even if it was only for one night. If I was lucky, maybe two.

He was cute, his blond hair cut short on the sides with longer strands on top and a dimple on one side of his smile. He won me over with his boyish charm and sense of humor. He was exactly what I needed. Someone who didn't approach life too seriously, but more with a live-in-the-moment attitude.

I threw caution to the wind and followed him home like a lost puppy. The two martinis I drank at the bar didn't hurt either. I was barely buzzed, but my body hummed from his lips pressed against mine.

He led me to the couch and brought my body down on top of his. My purse fell carelessly to the floor with a thud.

Chase cupped my face in his hands. "You're so goddamn sexy, Maggie. Do you have any idea how bad I want you?"

I shook my head, my curls brushing the sides of my face. "I don't normally do things like this. I don't want you to think I'm easy. I'm not a slut."

He put a finger to my lips. "Shhhh. We're two consenting adults. This is a no-judgement zone." His hands ran up under my blouse along my ribs, his fingers brushing lightly along the underside of my breasts.

I wanted him to touch me. I hadn't been touched in so long. My back arched, pushing my breasts forward. "Please."

"Please what?" he teased.

"Touch me. I need it, Chase. Please, touch me," I begged. My voice sounded desperate to my own ears, and I cringed. I didn't want him to know how desperate I actually was.

His fingers gently pulled down the cups of my bra under my blouse and ran over my nipples. "Like this?"

My eyes rolled back, and I let out a breathy sigh. "Yes. Exactly like that." There was no hiding the desperation in my voice now. With the way he caressed me, I couldn't have cared less.

Chase wrapped his arms around me and flipped us over. My back crashed against the soft fabric of his couch. He inched my skirt up higher and leaned over me, his strong, lithe body between my legs. His fingers gripped the back of one thigh and brought it up around his waist as he pushed his hardness against my softness. "Do you feel how bad I want you, Maggie?"

I felt the length of him behind the rough denim of his jeans pressed against my silky panties. I was defenseless against him. "Yesss.". I wanted to forget for one night. Forget who I was. Forget my responsibilities. I wanted to live life on the edge. To indulge in this reckless behavior for one reason…. because tonight I could.

My hands ran through his shaggy hair and pulled his lips back to mine. Our tongues twisted together in a slow, seductive dance. When we pulled apart, Chase placed soft kisses on the corners of my mouth. He continued across my jaw, until he nibbled on my earlobe. The sensation sent shivers down my spine. I arched into him and dropped my head back, giving him access to my neck. Neck kisses were the best, especially when delivered by someone so unbelievably sexy.

He didn't disappoint.

Soft kisses trailed down the column of my neck and along my collarbone.

I grabbed the hem of his shirt and yanked it up his body. I needed to see more of him. I wanted to run my hands all over him.

The man kneeling between my legs stripped his shirt off, up and over his head it went, revealing his sculpted chest and washboard abs. He was inked in intricate designs I couldn't distinguish in the dim light. My fingers traced every indent and crevice along his torso and down to his hips, where the sexy V disappeared beneath the waistband of his jeans. His body was pure perfection, toned and tatted. My hands rubbed over his rock-hard erection straining against his zipper.

I wanted it inside me.

So bad.

I needed it.

Chase lowered down between my legs and kissed the sensitive skin behind my knee. My lady parts clenched in anticipation of what was to come. And if I had to guess, it would be me in the next few minutes. He peppered kisses along the inside of my thigh, as he pushed my skirt even higher, exposing my red, lace panties.

I thanked the sex goddesses I'd gone racier than the usual cotton ones that filled my drawers. My life was practical, and red lace panties weren't. They were one of the few pairs of sexy underwear I bought on a whim during my latest shopping spree. Victoria's Secret and I weren't good friends, but as Chase rubbed his finger over the lacy panel between my legs, I decided she and I should become better acquainted.

"You're soaked for me."

"Yes, and you're teasing me." I wanted nothing more than for his fingers to inch back the fabric and slip inside my panties. My muscles involuntarily clenched, and my hips bucked at the thought of him inside me.

"Not teasing," he growled. "I'm taking my time with you. We'll both get what we want by the end of the night. That's a promise."

God, this man, the way he touched me with a gentle caress like I was the most precious thing he'd ever had was killing me. I needed him. Now.

I leaned forward enough to reach the button on his jeans and pushed the metal through the hole. Chase grabbed my wrists and held them above my head. "Nuh-uh. Wait your turn, Red."

"Red?"

"Yes, Red... red hair, red panties. If I were a betting man, I'd wager your bra was red too."

He wasn't wrong. I gave him a seductive smile. "Guess you'll have to find out for yourself."

He shifted my wrists to one hand and trailed the other down my cleavage. He skillfully flicked the buttons open on my blouse one at a time until all of them were undone, then carefully pulled back the material exposing what was underneath. He sucked in a breath. "You're beautiful, Maggie."

I knew exactly what he was seeing. I'd examined myself in the mirror before going out tonight, trying to justify the exorbitant amount of money the lingerie set cost. The matching bra was sheer red lace. My nipples were clearly visible through the fabric and with how turned on I was, they were as hard as diamonds. The look on Chase's face told me the lace was worth every penny I'd spent.

3

He wasted no more time. Chase pulled back the cup of my bra and sucked my nipple into his mouth. His tongue played with the tip, while his teeth gently nipped at me. His hand slid up my thigh to the place I wanted him to touch me most. Two fingers slid inside my panties and pushed into my wet heat.

I threw my head back in ecstasy. Soft moans escaped my lips. I was so close to fully losing control. My body hummed and buzzed from his touch.

Buzzzz. Buzzzz.

I was completely under his spell. "More, Chase. More," I pleaded.

Buzzzz. Buzzzz.

When I realized the buzzing wasn't just my body, it was like a splash of cold water and the spell was broken. I gently pushed Chase back and reached for my purse where it had fallen to the floor.

He sat back on his heels, clearly agitated. "You're kidding me, right?"

Buzzzz. Buzzzz.

I fumbled to unzip my bag and reached for my phone. "I wish I was, but I have to get this." Chase got off the couch and headed for the kitchen as I answered. "Hello?"

"Hi, Maggie. I hate to disturb you. I know you don't get much time to yourself."

"It's fine, Jane. Is Ella all right?" I tried hard to hide the tinge of panic in my voice.

"She's fine, Maggie, but she had a nightmare, and I can't seem to console her. She's asking for you."

I stood from the couch and began straightening my skirt. "I'll be there in fifteen minutes. Let Ella know I'm on my way. Thank you for calling."

I started buttoning my blouse as Chase came back with a beer in his hand. "You're leaving?"

I sighed. "I'm so sorry. I have to. My daughter is at her first sleepover tonight, and she had a nightmare. I have to go get her." I carefully slipped my feet back into my heels.

Chase's eyebrows narrowed and one lifted high. "You have a kid?"

I'd seen that look before. This was the part where men bowed out. Having a child was a deal breaker for them, but Ella was the whole deal for me. I straightened my spine. "Yes. A six-year-old little girl. Her name is Ella and she's the light of my life."

4

He nodded. "Well, you better get going then. I'm disappointed, but I understand." Chase came over and kissed me chastely on the cheek. "You're a good mom. Go get your baby."

It was more than I got from most men. "Thank you. I really am sorry."

He walked me to the door and opened it for me to leave. "I'm sorry, too."

I hurried out to my car and headed off to get Ella. Chase hadn't asked for my phone number, but then again, I really hadn't expected him to. It wasn't a big surprise. I pushed down my disappointment and wiped the stray tear that ran down my cheek.

Damn!

I really liked this one. He was sweet and funny and good-looking. I thought for a brief second there were possibilities. But alas, it was the story of my life.

I pulled into the driveway a couple of blocks from my house and hurried up the walk. The door opened, and Jane held my daughter on her hip. Ella wiped the tears from her eyes and lit up when she saw me. "Momma!"

"I'm here, baby." Jane passed Ella to me and she clung to my neck. I took her backpack in my other hand. "Thank you for taking care of her. I'm sorry about this."

Jane waved me off. "It was no problem. The girls can try again another night."

I smiled at her. "Thanks again." I carried Ella down the drive and gently buckled her into her booster seat.

"Momma?"

"Yes, ladybug?"

"You look pretty. Did you go to a party?"

I smiled at her through the rearview mirror. "Kind of."

She kicked her feet back and forth. "Did they have games and balloons?"

"It wasn't that kind of party."

"What kind of party was it?" My baby girl was wide awake now.

I contemplated what to tell her. "The adult kind. It was actually boring." I hated lying to Ella, but it wasn't the first time and it certainly wouldn't be the last.

We pulled into our driveway and I carried Ella to her room. "Can I sleep with you tonight, Momma?"

I was hoping to be in Chase's bed tonight, but this was probably better in the long run. "Of course, you can." I turned and carried Ella to my bedroom across the hall. Pulling back the covers, I tucked her inside. "Give mommy a minute to change her clothes."

I went to the bathroom and took off my blouse and skirt. My red lace bra and panties mocked me in the mirror, as if they were saying *Better luck next time.* I stripped them off, dropped the lingerie in the hamper and grabbed my nightshirt and sleep shorts from the hook on the back of the door. Nothing sexy about them.

After brushing my teeth, I crawled in next to my baby and tugged her close. She curled into my arms and whispered, "I'm sorry I ruined your party."

I stroked her hair and blinked back my tears. "Oh, ladybug, you're more important than any party. I'll always be here when you need me."

And that was the truth. As much as I would have liked for my night with Chase to have ended differently, nothing was better than holding my baby girl in my arms.

Chapter 1
Chase

Running a hand through my hair, I sat on the edge of my bed and stared at the clock on the nightstand. The red numbers glared at me. Two twelve a.m. I glanced over my shoulder at the dark hair on the pillow and smooth skin that was barely covered by the sheet.

Becca had been a constant in my bed for over three years. We weren't serious. We were on again and off again. There'd been a lot of other women in my bed over the past several years too. I wasn't naïve enough to think the same wasn't true for Becca, but somehow, we always ended up tangled in the sheets again.

She'd become my regular hookup when I wasn't entertaining another one of God's most gorgeous creations. I had a healthy sexual appetite and so did Becca. We satisfied a need for each other. It was zero work, with all the benefits.

I liked her well enough. She was pretty, had big tits, and fucked like a dream… that was where it ended. We had amazing sexual chemistry but beyond that we didn't have a lot in common. I knew it was a dead-end relationship, if you could even call it that.

For more years than I was willing to admit, I'd been okay with it. I wasn't ready for anything serious. But now the steady stream of different women was getting old.

I hadn't always been a manwhore. Once upon a time, I was in a serious, committed relationship. Until I fucked it up. Since then, I hadn't trusted myself enough, or any woman, truth be told, to go through the heartbreak again. Casual sex kept my dick happy. My heart had nothing to do with it. But now…

Everyone at the tattoo parlor I worked at had coupled up. The owner, Zack, had gone to New York and brought back the beautiful Rissa. Now they were married with a baby. When Draven started to work at Forever Inked, I was glad to have another single guy around. Thought we'd hit the bars and seduce all the lovely ladies. That barely lasted a week before he was all over Layla. Now the two of them were shacked up and would likely be together for the long haul.

Something had to change. The problem was I hadn't found anyone who could keep the attention of more than my dick.

I chuckled to myself. That wasn't entirely true. There was the redhead from a few months ago. She was funny and smart and unbelievably sexy. We hadn't even gotten down to the dirty deed before she left in a flurry.

Chick had a kid and there was no way I was ready for that. I barely functioned as an adult as it was. I had no business being with a woman who had a daughter. It was a no-brainer.

Then why couldn't I get her out of my head?

She'd been playing on repeat in my fantasies for months. Maybe it was curiosity; the fact that I'd barely gotten a peek at what she hid under her clothes. Maybe it was her eyes; the way they crinkled when she laughed. Maybe it was the freckles that dusted across her cheeks and the impulse I had to run my finger over them. Maybe it was that she was way out of my league but didn't seem to care.

Whatever it was, it didn't really matter. I hadn't even gotten her number. The chances of seeing her again were slim at best, but she was there, just under my skin.

The sheets rustled behind me. "Come back to sleep, Chase."

I lay down with my hands behind my head and stared at the ceiling. "What are we doing, Becca?"

She curled into my side and threw her arm across my chest. "We *were* sleeping, but I'm ready to fuck again if you are."

I wrapped an arm around her back and sighed. "That's not what I was asking. I mean, where is this relationship going? Are we even in a relationship?"

Becca traced the tattoos on my chest. "Ugh! You said the R word. Do you want us to be?"

I shrugged. "I don't know. Don't you ever get tired of it? The bars? The clubs? The one-night stands that never lead to anything?"

She softly kissed my chest. "Yeah, but isn't that why we have each other? Kind of like a backup plan?"

"I think I want more," I admitted. "This isn't enough for me."

Becca let out a soft giggle. "Are you breaking up with me?"

I ran my hand through her hair. "It's not personal. We've never *really* been together. You've been with other people and so have I. What we have is…" I was lost for words to describe our non-relationship arrangement.

"Comfortable," she supplied.

"Exactly."

"I get it. I really do. I want to get married one day and have kids. I love you, Chase, but I also know that's not us. What we have is different. More of a friends with benefits situation."

My hands palmed her ass and pulled her astride me. "You're going to make someone really happy someday. It's just not how *our* story ends."

Becca kissed my chest, up my neck, and pressed her lips against mine. "Doesn't mean I want to give this up, but you're right. We need to. We need to see what else is out there for us."

"Let's make a deal," I suggested. "We need each other, we'll be there, but no sex. We have to do this cold turkey. Let's give it at least a month. Maybe two."

She nodded her head. "Agreed. But... I need to fuck you one more time. Call it a going-away present."

I laughed. "I think I can accommodate you. My dick is going to hate me after this. I should make him happy at least one more time before it becomes official."

"You have a relationship with your dick?"

"He's the only one who really understands me." I chuckled.

Becca and I fucked long and hard into the early hours of the morning. And when the sun came up... we went our separate ways.

Chapter 2
Maggie

"Momma, Momma!"

I heard my baby girl turning the doorknob to my bedroom. I looked to the side of my bed that was usually empty and sighed. *Crap! What had I done last night?* I pulled the sheet up to cover myself and pasted on a smile.

Ella stormed into the room and skidded to a halt at the edge of my bed, her messy red curls bouncing wildly. "Did you and Daddy have a sleepover?"

When Jeff brought Ella home last night, one glass of wine led to a second. And a third. Pretty soon the bottle was empty, and we opened another.

I was an idiot. Letting Jeff into the house was dumb enough. Letting him into my bed was beyond idiotic.

I hated what he'd done to me. But I was a woman. One who had needs that hadn't been satisfied in a long, long time.

I loved Ella beyond anything else, however, the woman in me had been put on the back burner for far too long. Sex was something Jeff and I had always gotten right. It was everything else that was messed up.

When I got pregnant with Ella in college, Jeff made it abundantly clear a pregnancy wasn't going to change his plans for the future. He had goals. He had dreams.

He acted as if I didn't.

I had dreams and goals too.

He disappeared for a time. Pretended what we created together didn't exist.

If it weren't for my parents and my brother, I don't know if I would have made it through. Showing up for my student teaching pregnant wasn't a high point in my life. Everyone assumed I was Mrs. Malone. I wasn't. I was Ms. Malone. Single and pregnant, just what every parent wanted for their child's teacher.

It was embarrassing and humiliating to answer the inevitable questions that accompanied my pregnancy. *What does your husband do?* I don't have one. *How long have you and your boyfriend been together?* We're not. *Where's the father?* Not with me.

I dodged every question with a smile on my face and bit my tongue to keep from disrespecting the father of my child.

I might have been single and pregnant, but I would never consider Ella a mistake. She was the light of my life. The greatest thing I had ever done. She was the best part of me and the best part of Jeff in one adorable package.

The night I went into labor, my dad called Jeff and gave him a piece of his mind. I don't know what he said, but by the time I was pushing Ella out, Jeff was by my side. I thought things would change between us.

They didn't.

Jeff and I had a love-hate relationship. I loved that he was there for Ella, even if it was less than part time. I hated that he wanted nothing to do with me. We could have been a family of three, but Jeff was too focused on his career as a financial advisor to be bothered.

I should have been happy he paid his child support on time, but I wanted more. I wanted him to be invested in our lives. He tried when it came to Ella. Me, not so much.

Except last night. Wine worked wonders. Every six months or so, we found ourselves back in bed together again.

It wasn't enough.

Not even close.

But once in a while, when I was feeling weak, he would sweep in and seduce me.

It was my own damn fault and I detested myself for it. The hold he had on me was ridiculous. He needed to step up or I needed to move on. It'd been six years. It was time.

I smiled at my baby girl and put a finger to my lips. "Shhhh…. Daddy's still sleeping. Go be a big girl and brush your teeth. We'll be out in a minute. How do pancakes sound?"

She clapped her hands together quietly. "I love pancakes. Can we have bacon too?"

"Absolutely. Go brush your teeth and we'll be out in a minute."

Ella took off down the hallway, her tiny feet pitter-pattering on the hardwood floor. I rolled over and nudged Jeff. "Hey, get up. Your daughter wants pancakes and is waiting for us."

He cracked a sleepy eye and rubbed a hand over his face. "Can't. I gotta get to the golf course. Guys and I are getting together one last time before it's too cold."

I let out a frustrated huff. It was so typical of him. He'd spend the night in my bed and then fly out the door in the morning barely glancing over his shoulder. "Are you serious right now? It's Saturday, and Ella wants to have breakfast with her dad. You can't stay and have a goddamn meal with her?"

Jeff rolled out of bed and pulled his pants on, "Don't give me shit about this, Mags. Ella and I had dinner together last night. She'll be fine."

I pulled on my robe and rolled my eyes. *Fine?* I didn't want my daughter to be *fine.* I didn't want her to have a dad that thought taking her to dinner once a week was *fine.* There was nothing I could do about him being a shitty father, but there were other things I had the power to change. "You know what, Jeff? I'm done. This," I pointed between the two of us, "isn't happening again. You can't breeze in and out of our lives whenever it suits you."

He pulled his shirt over his head and tucked it into his pants. "Don't be so dramatic, Mags. You act like you've got men banging down your door." He smirked. "We both know that's not true. So what if we fuck once in a while?" He came over and lifted my chin. "It's good for you and you like it."

I pushed his hand away from my face. "You think you're the only game in town? You're not. I don't need you." I pointed toward the hall where Ella had run off to brush her teeth. "But, she does! You need to spend more time with her. She needs more than a part-time father. God! You're barely even that!"

Jeff planted his hands on his hips. "I'm doing the best I can. I'm trying to make a career for myself. You knew I didn't want kids and you still ended up pregnant. This was never my plan."

It hadn't been my plan either, but I wouldn't change a damn thing. Ella was my whole world. Rage took over at the idea that she was anything less to Jeff. "Get the fuck out!"

"Mags."

I poked him in the chest with my finger. "I mean it. Get out! I'm done!"

Jeff slipped on his shoes and headed toward the door. "That fiery temper of yours is exactly what makes you such a great lay." He brushed by me, sweeping a kiss across my cheek.

I stood paralyzed by disbelief as he walked out of my house with a slam of the front door. Tiny feet pattered on the floor. "Where'd Daddy go? I thought we were having pancakes."

I took a deep breath, trying to suck the air back into my lungs. The lie rolled off my tongue easily as I picked up my daughter and plastered a smile on my face. "Your daddy had to go to work, but you and I can still have pancakes. You can help me mix the batter. I'll even let you put in the eggs."

Ella frowned. "Okay, but I really wanted Daddy to help."

I couldn't blame my girl for loving her father. I just wished he knew how much she adored him. He was missing out. One day he'd regret the time he didn't spend with her. Six years had gone by in the blink of an eye. At some point Ella would realize the type of man Jeff was, and by that time, it would be too late for him.

"Looks like it's just us girls today. How about we go get our nails painted?" I carried Ella into the kitchen and sat her on the island countertop. Our little house wasn't much, but I owned it and was proud of the home I'd made for the two of us.

Her little legs kicked excitedly. "Toes too?"

I pulled back and pretended to gasp. "Toes? Why on Earth would you want to paint your toes?" Grabbing ahold of her little feet, I began to tickle them.

Ella squealed. "Stop, Momma! That tickles way too much!"

I gave her feet a squeeze and kissed her on the forehead. "Why do you want your toes painted, ladybug?"

She pointed down at my feet. "So I can be just like you. We can be like twins." She giggled.

My toes always matched my fingernails. Right now, they were bright red.
Red.

I could barely think the word without thinking about Chase. He'd called me Red that night, referring to my hair and my panties. The same ones that now sat next to the matching lace bra at the bottom of my lingerie drawer, if you could call cotton underwear lingerie.

Jeff was an asshole, implying no one else wanted me. Chase seemed to want me just fine that night. Until he found out about Ella. Chances were I'd never see him again.

But for one night he made me feel wanted and desired. It was a feeling I wished I could get back.

"Toes are a definite yes."

Ella and I sat side by side in the massage chairs at the salon, our feet soaking in the warm, bubbling water. My fingers were painted a deep red, while Ella's were a light shade of pink. My daughter was so desperate to be grown up, but I wasn't ready for that. She had a lot of years before boys made empty promises and broke her heart. I just prayed one day she'd find a man that would treat her better than her father treated me.

The nail technicians lifted our feet from the hot water and began to dry them. I looked over at my daughter who was my mini-me in every way. "Are you having fun, ladybug?"

"The best, Momma. This is so much fun!" She threw her arms into the air and waved them around.

"I'm so glad. I think I know a little girl who's having a Halloween party at school in a few weeks. Do you know who that is?"

Ella pointed at herself. "Me! I'm having a Halloween party. I want to be a fairy princess, because fairies are magic, and princesses are beautiful. Can I? Please?"

I tapped my finger against my lips as if I were considering the idea. Lord knew, she'd get exactly what she wanted. "We'll see what we can do."

She clenched her hands together in front of her chest and begged. "Please, Momma."

The technician massaging my feet smiled at me. She knew I had no choice but to concede.

She was absolutely right. Really, there were no choices. Ella had me wrapped around her little finger since the day she was born, the day she became my reason for being.

When we left the salon, Ella and I headed to a Halloween store. One of those places that opened the end of August and closed the first week of November, left deserted as if it never existed to begin with and stood dark for the next nine months.

Ella dragged me to the costumes for little girls, instinctively knowing just where to look. Her face was set with determination as we passed vampire teeth, superhero capes, and cheerleading skirts. She skidded to a halt when she found exactly what she was looking for and stared at the wall in amazement. "They're beautiful, Momma."

I knew precisely what she was talking about. Pink, glittery fairy wings sparkled from high up on the wall, just out of her reach. She stretched her arms up high, her fingertips barely grazing the delicate wings.

I pulled them down, slyly glancing at the price tag, and cringed. It was almost criminal the way corporate America preyed on us. I didn't have a lot. I made a modest wage as a teacher, but it paled in comparison to what I could have made had I chose another profession. I hated to admit it, but Jeff's child support kept our heads above water. It allowed me to splurge on things like fairy princess costumes and mani-pedis for my daughter. That didn't mean I didn't have to be careful. I'd gladly go with less, so my daughter could have more.

Ella held her arms out so I could slip the wings over her small shoulders and fasten the elastic in place. She pulled a plastic silver tiara adorned with cheap jewels from the shelf, set it on her wild, red curls and then grabbed a fairy wand with streamers attached to the end. "How do I look?"

I brought a hand to my mouth trying to rein in my delight at her happiness. "Like the cutest fairy princess I've ever seen."

Two teeth were missing from her wide smile. "Really?"

I nodded my head. "Absolutely. Let's go find a mirror."

Ella skipped ahead of me, anxious to see herself. She turned a corner, out of my sight for only a few seconds, making my heart race. When I found her, it dropped to the floor.

My daughter twirled in front of the mirror, talking to the man next to her. "I'm gonna be a fairy princess for Halloween. Do you like my wings?"

He kneeled in front of her. His blond, shaggy hair that was longer on top fell over his forehead. "You look adorable. The best fairy princess I've ever seen." The dimple on one side of his smile made *him* adorable. He'd just made her day.

Ella swung her head in my direction. "I love it, Momma!" She waved her wand around carelessly, almost smacking him in the head with it.

His gorgeous aqua eyes met mine and recognition dawned on his face. "Red?"

Chapter 3
Chase

Red.

The one woman I hadn't been able to erase from my mind for the past few months stood a couple feet away with wide blue eyes. I had wondered if I'd recognize her should our paths ever cross again. But as I looked at her, I realized she was unforgettable.

A long mane of red curls fell down her back and over her shoulders, brushing across her breasts. Ones I had cupped and squeezed and sucked on that night. So soft and round and perfect.

Her red lingerie flashed through my mind. The lace so sheer it left nothing to the imagination.

She'd been so wet and ready for me. I remembered what it felt like to push my fingers deep inside her.

It'd been two weeks since Becca and I had gone our separate ways and I'd spent every minute of that time thinking about the one and only time I'd been with Red.

Red was totally unforgettable.

And I was a sick pervert.

I chastised myself for having those thoughts about our almost night together with her daughter standing in front of me.

The little girl was cute as a button. Wild, red curls like her mom and bright blue eyes. She was the reason Maggie had left that night. I realized it was the best reason in the world.

And me?

I didn't belong in that world. Memories from my past swirled around me like a cyclone, making me remember *her* when all I wanted to do was forget the mistakes I made. The accusations *she'd* hurled at me cut so deep they never fully healed. And all I did in the years that followed was prove her right.

16

"Chase?"

I snapped out of the past I was lost in and focused on the beautiful woman in front of me, "Hi, Red."

The little girl giggled. "Her name's not Red, silly. It's Maggie."

I tapped her on the nose. "I know that. You know what else I know?"

She put her little hands on her hips. "What?"

I cupped my hands by her ear like I was telling her a big secret and brought my voice real low. "I know your name is Ella."

Ella pulled back in shock, her eyes big and round. "How do you know that?"

Standing from my crouched position, I looked Red up and down. "Because your mom and I are friends."

Maggie cautiously stepped toward us, her arms wrapping protectively around her daughter. "We are?"

I tried to keep my amusement at bay. "Last time we saw each other I'd say we were pretty friendly."

A crimson blush crept up her neck and into her cheeks. "I didn't think I'd ever see you again."

"Me neither, but I'd be lying if I said I haven't thought about you."

Ella tugged at the bottom of her mom's shirt. "Who is he, Momma?"

Maggie cleared her throat. "Ummm, Ella, this is Chase. I met him at a party." She tried to be vague for the sake of the little girl.

Ella's eyes lit up. "I like parties. Was it a regular party or a grown-up party?"

This little girl's cuteness was off the charts. I gave her a wink. "Definitely a grown-up party."

She scowled. "I'm not allowed to go to grown-up parties. Momma says they're no fun anyway."

I mustered up the most serious look I could. "She's totally right. They're no fun at all."

Maggie rolled her eyes. "Yeah. Such a bore. I hope Ella never has to go to grown-up parties." The sarcasm in her voice was palpable.

My finger ran along the side of Maggie's face. "This party was an exception, though. One I thoroughly enjoyed and would like to revisit. Someday soon."

What the fuck was I doing? She had a kid.

Red's lips curled into a smile. "How soon?"

I pierced her with my eyes. "Very. We have unfinished business."

I turned and left her standing there with questions in her eyes.

17

Seeing Maggie made me want her even more, but meeting Ella reinforced all the reasons it was an awful idea.

"What the hell, man? You've been gone over an hour and show back up here with nothing?" Zack, my boss, didn't seem amused. He'd sent me to get Halloween decorations for Forever Inked. I showed back up empty-handed.

I stepped into his studio and fell into his tattooing chair. "Shit went sideways."

Zack crossed his arms over his chest. "What does that mean?"

"I got distracted."

Layla, one of my best friends and coworker, poked her head in the room. "He probably saw a squirrel and had to chase it. You know how much he likes getting a little tail."

I rolled my eyes. "Hardy-har-har. It means I ran into somebody I thought I'd never see again. It was unexpected to say the least."

Layla leaned against the door. "Who?"

I shot her an exasperated look. "The redhead."

She ambled inside and popped a squat on an empty stool. "The one with the little girl?"

I touched a finger to my nose and pointed at her. "Bingo."

Yeah, she knew exactly who I was talking about. She'd been the one to send me in her direction at the bar that night. Layla knew my insecurities. Knew I wasn't ready to date a girl with a kid. She just didn't know why.

"Did you meet her daughter?"

"Yeah."

"And how was it?"

I shrugged not knowing how to respond. The little girl was cute as a button. Almost an exact replica of her mother.

Zack pressed his fingers to his temple trying to catch up. "What are you two talking about?"

Layla glared at me in warning. If I didn't say something, she would.

"I kind of hooked up with this girl while you were in California. I thought it was a sure thing, but she up and left before we even got down to it. Turned out she had a kid."

18

"And?" Zack questioned. He clearly didn't comprehend the problem.

"She has a six-year-old daughter. Do you really think I'm equipped for that?"

"I don't understand," Zack admitted.

Layla added her two cents without being asked. "Chase doesn't think he's responsible enough to handle a woman with a child. He's scared."

I glared at her. "I'm not scared."

"The fuck you're not. Women are practically your religion. You worship each and every one of them and have never had a problem dipping your toe into their holy water a second, third, or even fourth time. Yet this girl, you haven't seen again even though you were smitten right off the bat."

"I didn't have her number," I defended. But when laid out like that, even I had to admit her version of the truth held water.

"You act as if I don't know you." Layla placed her hand on my leg. "You like her, but for some reason you don't think you're good enough."

She hit the nail on the head. "I'm not."

Layla probably knew me better than my family. We had worked together for over five years. I loved her like a sister, but until recently she'd been a mystery, never talked about her family or her past. When I found out about her abusive ex-husband who tried to kill her, I was shocked.

My past wasn't that traumatic, but I wasn't proud of it. My skeletons weren't something I wanted to offer up on a silver platter for everyone to judge. And after all this time, she had no idea about my life before working at Forever Inked. No one did. The mistakes I'd made were best left tucked in the back of a dark closet.

"I won't deny that I like her. A lot. But I'm not dad material. I can't be what that little girl needs."

"I call bullshit!" That came from Zack. "You think I was ready to be a father? I was scared to death. Rissa was engaged to my brother before he died. She was already pregnant with his kid when we got together. That was some scary shit, but I'll tell you what, I love Alexandria with all my heart. She's my daughter no matter what genetics say."

I scoffed. "That's different. You started from scratch. Maggie's daughter is already six, and I'm assuming she has a father."

"Maybe you're looking at this all backward. If Maggie's daughter has a father, then maybe those aren't the shoes you need to fill. Start by being a friend. Someone who can be there when she needs it but with less responsibility. Just start by having fun with her."

19

What Zack said actually made sense, but it didn't help to alleviate my worries.

I looked away from two of my best friends. "Doesn't matter. I pussed out. I didn't ask for her number. Again. The chances of seeing her are slim. It's going to take the stars aligning just right for us to connect and I don't see that happening."

Layla's jaw dropped and she cuffed me on the back of the head. "You're an idiot! How could you not get her number? Today was fate and you wasted it."

"Enough with the hair!" I rubbed at my head. "Didn't seem right. Trying to pick her up with her daughter clung to her side? It was just wrong."

Zack pressed me harder. "You really like this woman, don't you?"

I rolled my eyes and tried to seem nonchalant. "I don't even know her. It was one night. We had some drinks, talked, laughed. At the end of the night, I invited her back to my place. We messed around, and god... she's gorgeous and sexy. I wanted her bad and she wanted me."

"Yeah, most girls do. Must be your boyish charm," Layla chided.

Draven stuck his head through the door and joined the party, sporting a huge smirk. "I thought it was his rocking bod."

Layla snapped her fingers and pointed back at Draven. "You're right! I distinctly remember Chase saying women only wanted him for his body. He insisted it was a serious problem."

She was obviously taking the opportunity to rib me. Usually that shit didn't bother me, but today it sat sour in my stomach. "I think I liked you two better when you hated each other. Now that you're shacked up, all you do is team up against me."

Layla wrapped her arm around my shoulder. "Oh, Chase. That's not true at all. I picked on you plenty before Draven ever started working here." No matter how much she picked on me, I knew Layla always had my back. Just like I had hers.

Zack raised his hand. "I can attest to that. You two have bickered like brother and sister since day one."

"True," I huffed, "but I'm not really in the mood. I know I did the right thing by walking away, but I also feel like I missed my opportunity."

"Hold up." Zack crossed his arms over his chest. "Maybe not. You met her at The Locker, right? If she's into you, then it makes sense she'd go back there. It's the only way she could contact you."

I perked up. "You think so?"

Draven scratched at his scruffy chin. "Makes sense to me. What have you got to lose?"

"Nothing," Layla answered for me. "Looks like we're going out tonight." She pulled out her phone. "I'll contact Rissa and let her know the plan."

My heart raced at the thought of seeing Maggie again. "Tonight?"

"Yes, tonight. You have to strike while the iron's hot…or she's hot… or she's hot for you… or you're hot for her," Layla babbled while texting. "You know what I mean, while everyone's hot and bothered."

I groaned. "This seems like a recipe for disappointment. What are the chances she'd go there tonight?"

Draven clapped his hands together. "Guess we're gonna find out."

Chapter 4
Maggie

"You think he's going to show?" Roxy pushed her dark hair over one shoulder while sipping her martini.

The two of us were sitting at the sleek wooden bar inside The Locker. Roxy and I got hired at the same time. She taught fifth grade and I taught first. We bonded at our orientation and had been best friends ever since.

My finger skimmed around the edge of my own martini. I shrugged my shoulders. "It's a gut feeling. He said he wanted to see me again, he just didn't say when. Only," I gulped, "… soon. Do you think that meant tonight?" My eyes drifted toward the door for the umpteenth time. "Do you think I'm being overly optimistic?"

"Maybe," she sighed. "Be honest with me. What are you looking for with this guy? Is this about a quick fuck or something more?"

I cringed. Roxy never pulled any punches. Her blunt honesty was one of the things I loved about her, just not when it was directed at me. "I don't know. All I know is how he made me feel that night. He made me feel wanted and beautiful. He took his time with me. Jeff never does that."

One eyebrow shot up. "Speaking of Jeff…"

"Let's not."

"You still letting him into your bed?"

I dropped my head into my crossed arms atop the bar. "Last night. I was drinking. And desperate. And stupid."

She patted me on the back. "You're not stupid."

I gave her a scathing look. "But I'm desperate?"

Roxy lifted her martini to her lips. "Your words, not mine."

"Gah!"

She set her glass down in front of her. "I'm not judging. Jeff's a damn good-looking guy. I bet he does one hell of a horizontal mambo."

The way she pursed her lips together suggested she wanted all the dirty details, but I wasn't going there. To me, all sex was good, even if I didn't always cross the finish line. Jeff was decent between the sheets. It was the only reason I kept letting him back in. He just sucked at everything that didn't involve his P in my V, like having an actual relationship. "Sex was never our problem. Commitment was. Once he found out I was pregnant, everything changed."

"So, there's no chance of you two ever being together for real?"

"Zero, and I'm tired of thinking he might come around. I deserve better. Last night was the last time. My vagina is officially closed for business."

Roxy bumped my shoulder with hers. "Not closed, just more selective about its clientele."

I held my glass up. "Exactly." I threw back the rest of my drink and plucked out the olive. "Why do these always taste better in martinis?"

"I'm pretty sure everything tastes better soaked in vodka."

I popped it in my mouth. "True that." I motioned for the bartender to bring us another round.

The bar had gotten more crowded in the hour we'd been sitting there. The lights had dimmed, and the music had gotten louder. People streamed through the doors, ready to celebrate another Saturday night.

It was almost ten-thirty. My prospects of running into Chase dwindled with every minute that passed. I'd clearly read the signs wrong this afternoon. He wasn't going to show.

I tried not to let disappointment fill my chest, but I could still feel the burn on my skin where his fingers had run down my cheek. That single touch had scorched me from the inside out.

It confirmed my memory of that night was correct, not some illusion I had cooked up. I hadn't subconsciously enhanced the feeling of my body on fire. Flames engulfed me that night until the buzzing of my phone doused them down to mere embers. Embers that continued to burn for the last couple months, until Chase set them ablaze again today. The only thing I had exaggerated was my denial.

When I concocted this plan tonight it seemed like a good idea. Ella jumped up and down at the prospect of having a sleepover with Nanna and Papa. She'd raced around the house gathering her things and shoving them into her favorite backpack. A purple, sixty-dollar bag with Elsa from *Frozen* on it. I knew she would love it and so I shucked out the money. The look on her face when she opened the gift on her birthday was worth every penny.

Ella flew out of the car when I dropped her off. I was barely a second thought compared to baking cookies with her nanna. It made me feel a little less guilty I was dumping her at my parents' in hopes of finding the man who'd turned my insides to mush and my body into an inferno a few months ago.

But as the minutes ticked by my plan seemed stupid and yes… desperate. Thinking I could conjure him out of thin air because it's what I wanted was silly. I had a ninety-nine percent chance of going home alone to an empty house and an empty bed. The thought was depressing.

"Holy Mother of God! I think I've died and gone to heaven."

Roxy's exclamation pulled me from my pity party. "What?"

She motioned over my shoulder. "Geeza Louisa! Look what just walked in. Holy hotness."

I nonchalantly turned my head toward the door. Two gorgeous men walked in with equally gorgeous women hanging on their arms. Right behind them, was *him*. I gasped and focused back on my friend.

"Looks like one of those hotties is single," Roxy rambled. "I call dibs on that sinful piece of man meat. He's got my name written all over him. Mmmm…mmmm, delicious and all mine."

I grabbed her finger that was waving around in the air and pulled it back down to the bar. "That's him."

"Who him?"

I rolled my eyes. "*Him*. That's Chase."

Roxy's gaze flew back over my shoulder. "Sweet Jesus! Hell could set me on fire and I'd still feel like I was looking at an angel." She smirked. "Hopefully a fallen angel. No wonder you're so wound up."

"Shhh! You're making a scene," I whisper-shouted. Her eyes came back to mine and I continued my reprimand. "What's with all the religious spouting, anyway? You don't even go to church."

Roxy straightened her spine. "I'll have you know I was raised Baptist."

"Really?" I asked sarcastically. "And your mama taught you how to talk like that?"

She got a sly smile. "Hell no! The preacher's son did. Every time he came, he'd yell out *Sweet Jesus.*" She sighed. "God, I miss that boy." Her eyes glazed over as she reminisced.

I snapped my fingers in front of her face. "Hey! Focus!" Then I thought about what she said. "What happened to the preacher's son?"

"Oh! We got caught bumping uglies in his dad's office. I was asked not to come back. My mom is still pissed she had to change churches, but it was totally worth it."

I shook my head and laughed. "Did you ever see him again?"

"No. His dad sent him down to Georgia to live with his grandma. Damn shame! That boy was a fine piece of ass. He used to do this thing with his tongue… well, let's just say he had *me* shouting *Sweet Jesus* more than once."

"How old were you?"

"Sixteen. He was seventeen, but I swear he had the body and the skills of a twenty-five-year-old. Good times."

"Damn, girl! I knew you were wild but… just damn." I shifted in my seat and glanced over my shoulder. Chase was still there, sitting at a table with his friends, looking delectable. *Sweet Jesus!* I looked to Roxy for advice. "What do I do, oh wise one?"

She raised an eyebrow. "What do you want to do?"

My nerves ratcheted up about ten notches. "I'm not sure. I mean… do I go over there and just say hi or will that make me look overeager? Maybe I should just let him settle in and then like accidently bump into him when he goes to the bathroom or something," I rambled. "This is stupid! I'm a fucking train wreck."

Roxy put her hand on my arm. "Why don't you start by breathing. In through your nose, out through your mouth." She mimed. "Big breaths."

I closed my eyes and took a big breath in, then slowly blew it out. Then again. One more and I was back under control.

"Feel better?"

I pinched my thumb and forefinger about an inch apart. "Marginally."

"My advice… let him sit for a while. He's not going anywhere anytime soon. If you read him right, then he's waiting for you too and he has no idea you're here. A little anticipation will do him good."

I bit my lip. "Right. I'm going to be cool, calm and collected." My fingers tapped restlessly on the bar top. "How much anticipation?"

"Well, he only got a small sample of the goods last time. If I had to guess, his anticipation is already ramped up and he's currently at a low simmer. Give him another ten minutes and he'll be at a full boil."

"You think?" I turned my head to get another glimpse.

25

Roxy grabbed my chin and turned me back to her. "Do not look at him. It'll make you weak. Make him work for it." She pulled out her phone, set the timer, and tapped on the screen. "When this thing goes off, you're going to casually walk over to the bathroom. It'll take you close to his table without being obvious. There's no way he'll miss you."

I nodded resolutely. "I like that plan. I can do that." But within thirty seconds it became blatantly obvious I couldn't. I tapped on Roxy's phone screen. "How long is ten freaking minutes? Is this thing even working?"

She took her phone and turned it upside down. "It's working. Trust me. Why don't you sip that martini while we discuss this. What's the plan here? Are you going back to his place or are you taking him to yours?"

This I could answer. I'd already given it a lot of thought. "His place."

"Reasoning?"

"Easy. If Ella scared him off before, I highly doubt being surrounded by all her things will be conducive to a sexy night. Plus, Jeff was in my bed last night and that's just gross!"

She pursed her lips at me. "I'll give you a pass on the part about Jeff because I happen to agree, but back the truck up to Ella. What are you going to do? Stick her in a closet if it goes beyond tonight?"

I pulled back in shock. "Of course not. I just want one night where I'm not a mom. Where I'm a 28-year-old single woman spending the night with a cute guy. No bath to give. No bedtime story to read. No watching *Frozen* for the one thousand four hundred and fifty-sixth time."

"I get that, but what about after tonight?"

"I guess I'll find out. He'll either accept Ella as part of my life or he won't. If he doesn't, then I'll have one night to remember him by." I sighed. "Ella will always come first. No man will ever change that."

"How was he with her at the Halloween store?"

My face broke out into a huge smile. "Sweet. He even remembered her name."

"And he implied he wanted to see you again, so maybe he wasn't as scared off as you think."

A blast of short beeps went off on Roxy's phone.

I grabbed my purse from the back of the chair. "We're about to find out."

Chapter 5
Chase

She wasn't coming.

That much was clear. Every time the door opened, my eyes swung that way. Lots of pretty girls had come in, but none of them had long, red curls and alabaster skin. None of them were Red.

I picked up my phone off the table. "I think I'm gonna get outta here."

Draven lifted his brow. "You're giving up? We haven't even been here that long."

A dry laugh escaped me. "I'm not giving up. I'm facing reality. This whole idea was a shot in the dark. All of this was for nothing. I'm going home."

"You're not going to give it a chance?" Rissa questioned. "Come on, Chase. Aren't you the one who kept encouraging me to not give up on Zack?"

That was true. When shit went sideways with her and Zack, I was firmly in her corner. Zack needed a swift kick in the ass, and I was more than willing to give it. He was a stubborn bastard.

"This is different."

"How so?" Layla asked. "She needed us and now you need the favor returned."

"It's not like that," I huffed.

"Then how is it?" Rissa asked.

"I don't fucking know. Maybe I should just call Becca. We called it off a few weeks ago, but I know she's a sure thing." It was an awful idea, but she wouldn't say no if I called her.

"You like this girl?" Zack asked. "Or is it just the thrill of the chase? Pun intended," he teased.

"You're an asshole." *The thrill of the chase.* That was my usual MO, and everyone knew it. I ran a frustrated hand through my hair. "I think it's more, but I won't know until I see her again."

Rissa gently set her hand on my arm. "You'll have to excuse my husband. Zack obviously doesn't remember what it's like to want something but be afraid to go after it." She glared at him. "His reputation wasn't exactly stellar when we started out, but we made it anyway."

Zack sheepishly kissed her on the temple. "True story. When I met Rissa, my whole life changed. It took me a while to get my shit together. I'm sorry, Chase. I shouldn't be passing judgment. I've just never seen you this worked up over a girl before."

I gave him a nod. "It's fine."

Layla leaned back in her chair, crossing her arms. "You were a grumpy, stubborn ass, Zack."

Draven laughed into his fist.

Layla turned to her man and poked him in the chest. "And you weren't much better. You both needed a good woman to turn you around."

Draven wrapped his arm around Layla's shoulders. "Yeah? And what do you know about being a good woman? You're very, very bad," he said suggestively.

She scowled at him. "And you fucking love it. I'm the best thing that ever happened to you and you know it. Or would you rather still be getting blow jobs in the front seat of your car by some floozy?"

He nuzzled her neck. "No floozies, but my car is parked out back if you're up for it."

Rissa's eyes bulged as she held her hand over her mouth and spit out part of her drink. Zack gently tapped her on the back. She was so sweet and innocent. How she ever ended up part of this ragtag group, I'd never know. Zack was a lucky fucker.

Layla patted Draven on the chest. "Later, big boy. It's not always about you. Tonight we're here for Chase."

Rissa held up her drink. "And to help him find a good woman."

Everyone lifted their glasses and clinked them in the center of the table.

"To good friends," Zack toasted.

"And fine ass women," Draven added.

Layla tapped on my shoulder like a woodpecker. "Hey! Isn't that her?"

"Where?" My eyes quickly scanned the bar, looking for Red.

"By the bathroom."

I could only see the back of her, but I'd recognize her mane of hair and that tight ass anywhere.

Unforgettable.

Layla gave me a little shove. "Use your boyish charm on her."

"Fuck that. Show her your abs," Draven teased.

"You guys suck!"

"You know you love us." Layla blew me a kiss. "Go get her, tiger!"

Joking aside, one thing was for sure, I wasn't letting her get away from me this time. Tonight was my chance and I was taking it. Just me and her. I'd deal with the rest of my fucked-up issues tomorrow.

I left my friends and went after the woman who'd been occupying all the space in my head. For once in my life, I ignored the little voice from the past that continued to tell me I wasn't good enough for a woman like her.

Or her daughter.

Chapter 6
Maggie

I washed my hands and rubbed at the makeup under my eyes, fixing the slight smudge from my black eyeliner.

Breathe in. Breathe out.

I reached into my blouse and pulled the girls up. I wanted them to be front and center for Chase. I even let a little of the red lace peek out.

Breathe in. Breathe out.

A quick dash of lipstick and I was ready.

I was having sex tonight. And not the kind I had with Jeff, which was good but lacked the "*It*" factor.

If our previous encounter was any indication, Chase would make me feel cherished and desired. My body was amped up and ready to go. My panties were already damp just from thinking about it.

I wiped my hands on my black skinny jeans and let out one last cleansing breath.

It was showtime. I was as ready as I'd ever be.

The door swung open as a buxom blond came in. I squeezed past her and out into the hallway.

Suddenly, big hands grabbed around my waist from behind and flipped me around. Fear coursed through me as my back hit the wall. My wrists were held above my head in one hand and another rested gently on my hip. My body relaxed as the scent of familiar cologne filled my senses.

I was planning on nonchalantly walking by his table, but it seemed he had gotten the upper hand on me. *Literally.* Pure adrenaline and lust replaced my uneasiness.

I raised my head, looking into his aqua eyes. "Hi," I whispered.

He stared down at me. "Hi." That one word, those two little letters, was the sexiest sound I'd ever heard.

"Chase." His name came out breathlessly.

"Red." His mouth curved up on one side with that adorable dimple. "What are you doing here?"

I played innocent, gulping down any apprehension I'd had going into this harebrained scheme. "Having a drink with a friend. You?"

He evaded my question. "A guy friend?"

I ran my tongue over my bottom lip. "Not yet, but we are friends, right?"

"You wanna be my friend, Red?"

Why did every word he spoke sound like seduction? Make the place between my thighs throb? Make my nipples strain against the lace of my bra?

Chase was pure sex.

I pulled my bottom lip between my teeth and bit down hard. "Depends."

He quirked an eyebrow up. "It depends? On what?"

"How you kiss me," I challenged. Where my streak of bravery was coming from, I had no idea. Confidence had never been one of my strong suits. "I need to know if what I remember is real or if it was a fantasy I made up in my head." I craved the touch of his lips against mine.

He pressed his strong hips into my softness. My back was up against the wall and I felt his erection through the thin layer of my silk blouse. There was no mistaking that he wanted me as much as I wanted him. "This isn't proof enough? You need more?"

I wondered for a moment if I had bitten off more than I could chew. If I was in over my head. In a matter of seconds, I had become a pawn in the game I started. My plan had been to snag his attention, tease him, make him chase me. It was clear that my game had worked too well. He was the hunter, and I was his willing prey. A wide-eyed doe who succumbed to the big, bad, sexy wolf. When he pierced me with his eyes, I was helpless against him. Paralyzed by his aqua orbs and mesmerized by his masculinity. A strangled "yes" fell from my lips and a swarm of butterflies took up residence in my chest, fluttering their way down to my stomach. Was it anticipation or anxiety? Maybe a little of both. Although we were far from alone, the music faded into the background and all I could see was Chase.

He chuckled softly. "This is a first. Usually, I don't have to work this *hard* to make a *friend*. Only for you, Red."

My heart ratcheted as he brought my arms down around his neck and hung them loosely over his shoulders. His hands ran over the curve of my ass with enough pressure to pull me off-kilter and I stumbled into his chest.

On instinct, my fingers dug into his firm muscles. One strong arm wrapped around my waist while his other snaked up my back. His fingers threaded up under my hair to cradle my head. His warm breath whispered across my cheek. Our lips were mere inches apart. "I'm gonna kiss you now."

He said it as a warning. As if I might change my mind. There was no danger of that. His kiss had been the only thing I'd thought about since I'd seen him this afternoon. I was dying for it. "I'm waiting," I gasped breathlessly.

Without another word, he pulled me into him and pressed his lips to mine. Sparks traveled from the top of my spine down to my toes. His soft lips moved with a gentleness I hadn't expected. His tongue ran along the seam of my lips, begging for entrance. I had no choice but to open to him, twisting my tongue with his. His hard length pressed into my stomach. Need sparked inside me as the kiss deepened, increased in intensity and urgency. I couldn't get enough. My fingers twisted in his hair as I held on for dear life. It felt so good, so amazing, it set my soul and body on fire. The kiss seemed to last forever. No doubt, one of the most erotic experiences of my life.

I pressed my hands to his chest, trying to put some distance between us. "Holy shit."

His cocky smile never diminished. "Friends again? Because I'd really like another night with you."

I was a goner. Jeff had satisfied my needs over the years, but he had never set my soul on fire. Not like Chase. I realized in that moment that I had never been *truly* satisfied.

How sad was it that at twenty-eight I had never had phenomenal sex? I'd settled. No more. I wanted to know what it was like to be wanted. Desired. Fucked until I couldn't see right.

I had no doubt Chase could deliver on all accounts. His kiss was proof enough. "My memory was pretty accurate, but I'm not that easy," I said timidly. Memories of our last encounter swam through my head and I was almost embarrassed of how quickly I'd fallen to my back. "But… I might be persuaded if you buy me a drink."

His hand ran through my hair. "Something tells me there's nothing easy about you, Red. But I'm willing to work for it. One drink?"

"One cocktail and a whole lot more of that kiss you just gave me." The words tumbled from my lips without thought or care.

"Come meet my friends and I'll buy you that drink." He twirled a lock of my hair around his finger.

"Only if you meet mine." The thought of Roxy sitting alone at the bar made me sad, even if she knew what she signed up for by coming out with me tonight. "I left Roxy at the bar."

One brow shot up. "Roxy? Is that even her real name? Or is it Roxxaaanne?" he crooned the old Police song.

I laughed. "Roxanna. She's a sweetheart, but she'll pummel you if you sing that song to her. I've seen it happen. It wasn't pretty."

Chase pulled me even closer. "Duly noted. Don't piss off the best friend." His lips fluttered over mine. "Lead the way."

I held my hand out and he laced our fingers together as if we'd done it a million times. Roxy was already flirting with an older guy who had taken my abandoned seat at the bar. Or maybe he was flirting with her. Damn, she worked fast. Her head fell back in laughter at something he said that couldn't possibly have been as funny as she was making it out to be. Girl knew how to work a man, that's for sure. She reeled them in without any effort. Men naturally gravitated to her charm and beauty.

As we approached, Roxy tapped a finger against her lips as if she were trying to figure out a puzzle. "You leave to use the ladies' room and come back with a man. Did you get lost?" She was being coy, like we didn't plan the whole thing. And I kind of loved her for it.

I smiled and played along. "Funny thing. I was coming out of the bathroom and ran into Chase."

Roxy reached out her hand to him. "So, you're the mysterious man we're here to stalk. Nice to finally meet you, Chase."

What the hell? My cheeks burned red with mortification.

Chase grabbed ahold of her hand and brought it to his lips. "Pleasure to meet you, Roxy. Thank you for being Red's partner in crime."

I pulled Roxy's hand from his. "Some friend you turned out to be. You weren't supposed to blurt everything out. I'm seriously going to have to consider finding a new best friend."

"What? I'm just keeping it real. Besides, why do you think he's here?" She waved her hand at him carelessly. "You both had the same plan."

33

Chase's arms wrapped around my waist. "Guilty as charged." Then he leaned in close so only I could hear. "I couldn't get you out of my mind."

My heart did a little flutter in my chest. "Same."

The guy sitting in my chair turned to face us and held out his hand. "Hi. I'm Stevin, with an i." He was an older man, decked out in a dress shirt and tie. His hair was meticulously gelled and his eyebrows manicured. He was way too old for Roxy, by at least twenty years, but she had always been an old-man magnet. Older guys loved her. There wasn't anywhere we could go without one sidling up next to her.

Chase lifted a brow but grasped his hand in a firm shake. "Chase, spelled the normal way."

I gave Roxy a look. Was this guy for real? Any guy who needed to introduce himself with the spelling of his name was not for her. Not to mention he could be her father. Just... *Ewwww*. "We were going to sit at a table. Want to come with?" I figured the least I could do was give her an out.

Roxy grabbed her phone off the bar. "You know, I might. It was nice to meet you, Stevin with an i, but my friends are calling. Maybe some other time?"

"Sure. I'm here every Wednesday and Saturday. We'll catch up later." He planted a kiss on her cheek that for some reason disgusted me.

I pulled Roxy from the barstool and followed Chase to the table where we'd seen his friends. I needed to put as much distance as possible between Roxy and Stevin with an i.

When we got to the table, Chase pulled up two extra chairs for Roxy and me.

The gorgeous woman with jet-black hair and black-lined cat eyes took the two of us in. "Damn, Chase, you're good. Two?"

The raven-haired giant of a man who sat next to her let out a low laugh. "He must have showed them his abs. Works every time."

It was an inside joke I wasn't privy to. I tried not to let the remark affect me, but the implication was clear. Chase was a ladies' man. *Maybe this was a mistake.* I shook the thought from my head. It was only for tonight. That's what I had set out for, which didn't make me much better.

The fact that we were sitting having a drink and not running to his bed made me feel a tad less slutty. Because after that kiss we shared... *damn.* It would have been so easy to lose all my senses and follow him home without passing GO.

He draped his arm over the back of my chair, letting his fingers glide up and down my arm in a soothing motion that put me more at ease. "This is Maggie." He pecked a kiss to my cheek. "And this is her friend, Roxy. We just saved her from the king of douchebags."

"Which I thoroughly appreciate. What can I say? Old guys love me." Roxy held up her drink.

Chase continued with the introductions, he pointed at the dark-haired couple. "The evil twins are Layla and Draven."

Layla reached her hand across the table. "Nice to meet you and we're not really twins or the fact that we share a bed would be totally gross."

"So would this." Draven gave Layla a searing kiss that I felt embarrassed to watch. There was no shame in his show of affection for her. *I want that.* I wanted someone to kiss me like I was their whole world.

"They're unabashedly in love," Chase explained. He gestured to the blond guy who had his arm wrapped around a beautiful blond with long curly locks much like mine. "That's Zack. He owns Forever Inked where we all work. And that's his wife, the beautiful Rissa, who should have been mine."

Zack wrapped Rissa tighter in his arms while she gave us a little wave. "He wishes. Chase never had a chance with my girl."

"You own the tattoo parlor?" Roxy asked. Zack nodded. "Well, that explains all the ink." She motioned around the table. "Sexy as hell, by the way."

Roxy rambled on about the tattoo she wanted to get, but I couldn't take my eyes off Rissa. Something was familiar about her, like I knew her from somewhere, but I couldn't place it. Chase leaned close to my ear. "What's wrong?"

I tried to shake the feeling from my head, but I couldn't. "Nothing. Rissa just looks familiar."

He let out a little chuckle. "Give it some time. You'll figure it out."

I gave him a puzzled look. "What does that mean?"

"I'll tell you later," he whispered.

I wasn't satisfied. "Do you work at Forever Inked too, Rissa?"

She held a hand to her chest. "Oh, goodness no. I don't have that kind of talent. I used to bartend here, but now I'm mom to an almost seven-month-old baby girl. Sometimes I help with the books, but for the most part, Alexandria keeps me busy."

"Don't listen to her, she's got plenty of talent. Just not at drawing," Layla said cryptically.

Rissa waved her off. "Enough about me. Tell us about you. What do you do, Maggie?"

They were all super attractive and had cool jobs. I felt like the nerdy girl trying to fit in with the popular kids. It was sort of the story of my life. I always had friends back in high school, but I was not part of the "in" crowd. They were risk-takers who went out smoking, drinking and partying every weekend, while I stayed home to study for my chemistry test. It didn't matter that I was twenty-eight, right now I felt like I was a teenager again.

I swallowed down my apprehension. I worked damn hard for what I'd become, and I was going to own it. Cool or not. "Roxy and I are both teachers. I spend my entire day surrounded by first graders. Then I go home to my own daughter, who just turned six in August."

"You must have a lot of patience," Layla commented. "I was an art teacher back in Oregon. Draven and I are buying the building next to Forever Inked so I can set up an art studio for kids." She smiled sweetly at Draven. "It'll give me the best of both worlds. I can still tattoo and teach art. Once it's up and running, it would be a great place for a field trip."

She couldn't have surprised me more if she tried. I would have never pegged her for a teacher. "You'll have to keep me in the loop. Because that sounds great. Are you sure you'd be up for twenty-five little people? At one time? They can be a lot to handle."

"Absolutely. It's just in the beginning phases, so probably not until the end of the school year."

Rissa leaned forward. "Do you have a picture of your daughter?"

Ella wasn't supposed to be the focus of the night, but what could I do? She was the most important person in my life. Rissa was a mom too, so she clearly understood. I reached into my purse and pulled out my phone, scrolling through my recent pictures. I choose the one from her birthday party. Ella proudly wore a tiara as she blew out the candles on her cake.

I held it up for Rissa to see. "Oh my god! Can you say 'mini- me'? She looks just like you, Maggie. Absolutely adorable!"

My phone was passed around the table with my baby girl on full display. It made me self-conscious.

"It must be hard being a single mom," Zack commented.

I wasn't sure if he was fishing, but I wasn't going to give up any details about my relationship with Jeff. "My parents and brother have been a godsend. I'm not sure what I would have done without them. They're the reason I get to have nights like tonight. When it comes to baking cookies with Grandma, I can't compete."

"Is she staying the whole night with them?" Chase asked quietly.

I nodded. "I'm all yours. If you want me."

He nipped at my earlobe. "I want. Very much so."

Tingles ran down my spine and settled low between my thighs. "Then I guess it's settled."

After another round of drinks, Roxy excused herself, making sure I was good catching a ride with Chase. Maybe it was stupid not to have a car or an exit plan, but that was what Uber was for if it came to that.

We said our goodbyes to his friends and Chase led me out the door with his hand on my back. I remembered that he drove a truck the night I followed him home, but I didn't see it anywhere. "Where are you parked?"

"Behind the shop. It's about a block down." He stared down at my tall, black boots. "You okay to walk in those? I can pull my truck up."

"Actually, they're pretty comfortable. I'll be fine." The last thing I wanted Chase to think was that I was some kind of princess who needed to be pampered. There was only one princess in my house, and I sure as hell wasn't her. I hadn't been spoiled or pampered in a long, long time. "I can walk."

The late September air was cool against my skin, causing it to breakout in goose bumps. I wrapped my arms around myself. Chase slung his arm over my shoulder. "Where's your coat?"

"It was warm earlier. I didn't think to bring one."

He pulled me closer. "It's not much farther. I'll keep you warm."

And he did. It wasn't so much his arm around me, although his body blocked me from the wind and the chill in the air. It was more the fact that he cared about me being cold.

We walked to the glass entrance door of a large brick building, with a neon sign that read Forever Inked in fancy script. Chase pulled a set of keys from his pocket and unlocked the door, ushering me inside. "This is where I work." He punched a code into the alarm. "I have a sweatshirt in my studio you can wear."

I followed him into a small room with a black, leather chair in the center. The walls were adorned with framed drawings, some done in black and white, and others in vibrant colors. The contrast in the drawings floored me. Some portrayed death, with skulls and grim reapers, but there was a beauty to them. In the way the lines flowed together, the balance of light and dark. Others were... breathtaking. A leopard with stunning eyes, a butterfly that looked like it could fly off the page, and a phoenix rising from the ashes. Each one had the same signature scrawled in the corner. "Did you draw all of these?"

"I did." Chase held out his sweatshirt for me to stick my arms through. He turned me around and zipped up the front.

"God, Chase, you're so talented." The random thought of getting a tattoo ran through my head when I realized I may not ever see him after tonight. For all intents and purposes, this was a hookup.

Tonight was nothing but a do-over for both of us. An itch that needed to be scratched. After we had sex, that itch would go away. We were using each other with no promises of anything beyond tonight.

I'd never done this before. The last time I was with Chase was the first time I'd considered having a one-night stand. The few guys I'd slept with over the years I'd at least dated for a while. Ella never met any of them. I'd kept my private life away from my daughter. The only man she'd ever known me with was her dad, Jeff.

That needed to change, but it wouldn't be with Chase. This was one night only and I was going to enjoy the hell out of it.

"You okay?" Chase asked, pulling me out of my own head. "You changing your mind?" He stroked my cheek and pushed my hair behind my ear.

"I'm not changing my mind. I know what I want tonight."

His arms wrapped low around my waist, pulling me flush to his body. "And what's that?"

"You. I want you, Chase."

His fingers danced along my collarbone and down the cleavage exposed by my blouse. We were cheek to cheek, his breath hot in my ear, "I haven't been able to stop thinking about you and finishing what we started. Let's get out of here."

"Please."

He led me out the back door to where his big, black truck was parked and opened the door for me. After helping me inside, Chase ran around and hopped in. He grabbed my hand and pulled it to his mouth, kissing the back of it. A sweet gesture that made me feel like I was more than a one night deal to him, even if I knew better.

The ride to his apartment was quick. Before I knew it, we were stumbling through the door. A sense of déjà vu overwhelmed me. My eyes immediately homed in on the couch where Chase had slid his long fingers inside me. My thighs clenched and the place between tingled with anticipation.

"Uh-uh. No couch tonight. I want you in my bed so it's harder for you to escape. I'll tie you to it if I have to."

"You won't, unless that's something you're into." My hand ran down his hard chest, frantic to get his shirt off and feel his skin against mine. "I promise I won't escape."

His hands skimmed down my back, cupping my ass. He lifted me like I was a feather and my legs wrapped around his waist. Jeff had never picked me up. He always complained that it would hurt his back. I mean, I wasn't a skinny twig, but I wasn't some cow either. I had curves that Jeff obviously liked, or he wouldn't have slept with me in the first place. For years I convinced myself it was me that was the problem. If I'd just lost some weight or hadn't skipped that yoga class, maybe I would be more desirable to Jeff. But as Chase carried me to his bedroom, I realized how wrong I'd been. I wasn't the problem.

He set me on his king-size bed, and I instinctively checked out his room. Definitely a bachelor pad, done in dark woods, blues and grays. I wondered how many other women had sat where I was right now.

I pushed the thought away.

This was what I wanted. I couldn't judge him for doing the same thing. Especially when my own sheets still had the smell of Jeff's cologne on them. Yeah, those were coming off tomorrow. It would be my first priority.

Chase leaned me back on the bed, covering my body with his. Our lips crashed together with lust and desire. His hands wove through my hair, as I wrapped my arms around his neck.

"God, Maggie, you're all I've thought about. Tell me you're wearing red under these sexy as hell clothes."

I smiled at him shyly. "I may have remembered how fond you were of red when I chose my lingerie tonight."

He groaned deep in his chest. A sexy sound that made me giggle, even though I wasn't a giggler. Something about Chase made me feel more carefree than the responsible mom I usually was. I liked the feeling.

He twined his fingers with mine and brought them up over my head. "I never thought I'd see you again. I think today was destiny telling us we had unfinished business." His lips skated down the side of my face, along the column of my neck and to the valley of my breasts. Holding my wrists in one hand, Chase used the other to unbutton my black blouse. With each button he released, he planted kisses down my body. When the last one was free, he pushed the fabric apart. "I love red on you. So damn beautiful."

I pushed my hips up into him. His long, thick erection pressed between my legs. "I aim to please. I want to finish what we started, Chase. I want you to fuck me." The bold words spewed from my lips before I could stop them. I felt the flush in my cheeks before the embarrassment registered in my brain.

"Oh, that's definitely on the agenda, but not before I get a taste of you. I'm gonna make you come so hard it stops all the wheels spinning in that pretty little head of yours. You'll forget everything but the pleasure I give you."

"Promise?" I whispered.

"Yes, Red. Let's start with getting you naked." Chase slipped to the edge of the bed and kneeled between my legs. "These sexy boots will be the first to go."

I propped myself up on my elbows and watched as he slowly slid the zipper down one of my knee-high boots, slipped it off my foot and tossed it over his shoulder. Then he did the same to the other. He made taking my boots off so damn arousing.

"Next to go will be these jeans." His fingers deftly worked the button and pulled the zipper down. I lifted my hips so he could shimmy them off my legs. In one smooth motion, my jeans joined my boots somewhere on the other side of the room.

I let my blouse fall off my shoulders, tossing it to the side. The only thing left was the red lingerie that mocked me months ago. Chase's eyes roamed up and down my body, taking in every curve that was on display.

"You're gorgeous, Maggie. I don't even know where to start with you."

"How 'bout you start with your clothes. The playing field feels a little uneven here."

He gave a sideways smile, that damn dimple denting his cheek. "You want a striptease, Red?"

I bit my lip and nodded. "It only seems fair."

"Who said anything about fair?" He started unbuttoning his shirt from the bottom. "I mean, it's hardly fair that all I've been able to think about is red lace and what lies beneath it." The shirt fell off his shoulders onto the floor, revealing a myriad of artwork that covered his chest and arms. Too many to catalog or appreciate at the moment. He toed off his white Converse and then started on his jeans. The fly fell open and I peeked at the unmistakable bulge straining against his black briefs. "Do you think it's fair that I've had a hard-on for you for months? That all I've been able to think about is being inside you?"

I swallowed down the lump in my throat. "You have?"

He slid his jeans down his legs and kicked them to the side. "Does it look like I'm lying?" His hand rubbed against his long length hidden beneath his boxer briefs. "I'm not a liar." Chase cradled his hands under my back, moving me farther up the bed.

My legs spread to accommodate his lean, strong body as he kneeled between them. His hands found mine and he threaded our fingers together, lifting them to the pillow above my head as I lay back.

His eyes never left mine. Even in the dim light of the room, they were a brilliant aqua. Mesmerizing. Captivating. And I was afraid I was going to get lost in them. That I could get lost in this man.

It didn't matter that I didn't know him. What mattered was the way he made me feel. Like my heart would beat out of my chest. Like my breath was imprisoned in my lungs. My voice lodged in my throat.

"Are you nervous, Red?"

"A little."

"Why?"

"We hardly know each other. I told you before, I don't do things like this."

"Have sex with strangers? We're not strangers anymore. I know everything I need to know about you." His voice was deep and sexy, yet soft and reassuring.

"Be careful with me, Chase," I whispered. I was sure this man could wreck me.

"Don't you worry about that. I'm going to take care of you. Do you trust me?"

Trust? For tonight? Yes. Beyond that? It didn't matter.

Before I could answer, Chase's lips were on mine, coaxing them apart to slip his tongue inside. Our tongues twisted in the most delicate way. Lazy and unhurried. This was the kiss of a lover not a one-night stand. He swept away all my insecurities with that kiss. A soft mewl escaped from me.

"I want those sounds from you all night long. Can't wait to hear what you sound like when you come on my tongue."

Well, fuck me! At this rate, all he would have to do is keep talking and I'd be coming in no time at all.

Kisses swept down my neck and between my breasts. A flick of his tongue. A brush of his lips. My back arched into his touch, dying to get closer, to have him take me in his mouth.

Our hands were still connected when his teeth gently bit my nipple through the lace, then sucked away the sting.

"Oh god," I gasped.

He let go of my hands and braced himself above me, his shaggy hair falling over his eyes. "God has nothing to do with it, Red. I try to keep him out of my bedroom as much as possible because I'm sure he wouldn't approve of what I'm going to do to you."

I was speechless. This man. If he delivered on half the promises his mouth made, I would walk away a happy woman.

Resting on his knees between my legs, Chase reached behind my back and unclasped my bra. He brought it to his face and breathed in the scent. "Smells like you. All sweet with a hint of sin, because that's exactly what your body was made for. Sin." He cupped my breasts in his big hands, brushing his thumbs over the tips. "All this creamy, smooth skin. Totally pure except for these freckles on your chest that lead to the most amazing tits I've ever seen." Without warning he ravaged them, kneading and sucking and kissing.

My hands grasped his sculpted shoulders, his muscles rippling under my fingertips. I ran my hands down his back and squeezed his ass. It was tight and firm under my hands. Pure perfection.

Chase growled. "Gonna eat your pretty pussy now. Bet it's just as sweet as the rest of you." He backed down the bed, hooking his fingers in my panties and dragging them down my legs. Placing his hands on my knees, he gently spread my legs apart.

I felt self-conscious and exposed as Chase gazed at the place between my legs. I was so wet for him it was almost embarrassing.

He started with a finger, running it through my slit and up to my clit. His thumb started rubbing small circles. It felt so good, but it wasn't nearly enough. A moan slipped from my lips. "You're teasing me."

"Not teasing you, Red. Taking my time with you. I want to enjoy every minute with you. I want to make it good for you."

Oh! And then it was, "Aaahhhh" and "Ooohhhh" as he tenderly kissed the inside of my knee and up my thigh, all the while his thumb continuing to rub me in the most delicious way.

Chase's tongue ran along the apex of my legs, so close to my center that I shook with need. He licked at my opening, spearing me with his tongue. Then he replaced his thumb with his mouth, flicking his tongue over my clit before sucking it long and hard.

"Fuck, Chase. What are you doing to me? That feels so good." My hips lifted toward his mouth, trying desperately to get closer.

"You taste so sweet. Come on my face, Red."

I grabbed the back of his head and pushed him into me. No way was I going to let him stop to talk, even if his words turned me on. I much preferred the other things his mouth could do.

Chase licked and flicked and sucked until I was teetering on the edge of ecstasy. Just when I thought I couldn't take anymore, he pushed his fingers inside me, crooking them just right to hit my sweet spot. My body began to tighten until it was almost painful. All my muscles contracted and I let go. A stream of incoherent words spewed from my mouth as my head flew back and my body spasmed like never before. "OhmyfuckshitsogoodneverhaveI...aaahhh!"

Chase chuckled from between my legs and wiped his mouth with the back of his hand. "That good, huh?"

When blood flowed back to my brain and my senses started to return, all I could muster was, "Jesus Christ, Chase."

He slipped his boxers down his legs and his enormous cock sprang free. It was long and thick and hard, reaching almost to his belly button. Chase reached into his nightstand drawer and pulled out a string of condoms. Ripping one from the strip with his teeth, he made quick work of opening it and rolling it over his length. "And just think, we haven't even gotten to the good part yet."

I blinked rapidly. "That was amazing."

He shook his head slightly with his smile turned up on one side. "Oh, darling, we've just begun. Consider that a preview."

He crawled over me like a panther stalking his prey.

I wasn't worried what Chase would do to my body, but I had a feeling my heart was going to leave here damaged tonight. "Be gentle with me."

"I'm gonna take care of you, Red." Then he tenderly kissed my lips. "Your pleasure is my pleasure. If you're not getting off, then neither am I. Are you ready for me?"

"Yes."

Chase nudged his head at my entrance. "Are you sure?"

I'd come this far, there was no way I was backing out now. Not with how he'd just made me feel. "Yes, I'm sure. I need you inside me."

He pushed in slowly, stretching me in the most delicious way. When he was all the way in, Chase's eyes locked with mine, as he held his body above me. I don't know that I had ever felt so full before. Jeff seemed like a boy compared to Chase, who was without doubt all man.

He ran a finger down the side of my face. "Are you good?" His concern for me was sweet, considering this was a one-time thing.

I copied his motion, running my finger along the side of his face. "I'm perfect. You're perfect. Will you please fuck me now?"

"Only since you asked so nicely." He pulled back and pushed back in slowly. There was no hurry. No rush. He was making it last. Drawing out our pleasure. "You feel amazing, Red." His eyes held mine as he moved. In and out, pushing a little harder, a little deeper, a little faster each time. It felt phenomenal. Each stroke pushed me closer to another orgasm. He leaned forward, so each thrust rubbed against my clit. I wrapped my legs around his waist, locking them behind his back, and pushed up to increase the sensation. "God, you're killing me, Red. You keep doing that and I won't last long."

He pulled out and flipped me over. With an arm around my waist, Chase hiked me up to my knees and leaned over my back. Soft kisses caressed my shoulder and neck. "You look perfect like this."

He gently pushed into me from behind and let out a little moan of his own. Each thrust was deeper and harder. My eyes rolled back as my head dropped between my arms. It felt so good. I wanted more of what he was giving me. This was a hundred times better than what I'd gotten last night. "Don't stop, Chase. Please, don't stop!"

"Give me another one, Red. Come for me again." He reached a hand between my legs and thrummed my clit. I could feel the ache growing stronger. It reached epic proportions between his fingers working their magic on the outside and his cock stroking me on the inside.

Nothing could have prepared me for the orgasm Chase delivered. I bit my lip hard enough to draw blood when he pushed me over the edge. A strangled cry that I tried to contain escaped as I came. I was sure I would have collapsed had Chase not been holding me up.

He grasped my hips tighter and began to fuck me harder. "That's it, baby, squeeze my cock with your pussy. I'm so damn close." With a few more thrusts, he roared his release, my name tumbling from his lips, then slowed his pace until he rested inside of me. Featherlight kisses crept up my spine to my neck. "You're incredible," he panted in my ear.

Not pulling out, he wrapped his big arms around my body and rolled us to the side, so my back was nestled into his hard chest. We were hot and sweaty, but none of that mattered in the moment. I felt cherished and cared for with his body wrapped around mine.

He buried his head in my hair. "Hey, stranger."

I turned my head and smiled up at him. "Hey."

His fingers twirled through my strands. "Have I mentioned how much I like your hair? I couldn't stop thinking about it."

I laughed. "Yeah. I'm sure it was the hair that you couldn't get out of your mind."

That dimpled smile quirked up on one side. "Seems lately I'm a fan of everything red." He held my hand up in his, "Red fingers and toes included."

"I couldn't stop thinking about you either. I'm glad I took a chance tonight."

"Me too. After seeing you today I knew I needed a taste." He unwrapped himself from me. "I'll be back in a minute."

A taste? I chuckled to myself. The only one I was fooling was myself when I thought he might actually be interested in me. I needed to remember what this was. Sex. And only sex. A not so random hookup. His itch had been scratched and so had mine. It was time to go.

I didn't have much experience with this, but overstaying my welcome seemed like a Hookup 101 no-no. Pushing back the tangled sheets, I scanned the room for my bra and panties. They were nowhere to be found.

Just great.

They had to be here somewhere. I started picking up our clothes that were strewn around the room, shaking them out like I was looking for one of Ella's missing socks.

I eyed the space under the bed. With my luck that's where my underwear were. The trick was to look underneath without putting myself in some weird position that put my hoo-ha on display. I carefully knelt next to the bed, tucking my knees beneath me and peered underneath, which was surprisingly clutter-free and clean. Much better than the scene under my own bed.

"Did you lose something?"

I startled, smacking my head on the rail of the bed. "Ouch!" I winced at the pain. That fucking hurt.

Chase was right by my side, rubbing the spot on my head that collided with his bed. "Jeez, Red, are you okay? What are you doing?"

Finally, I spotted a bit of red lace that was hidden by the comforter. Stretching my arm under the bed, I managed to snag them. "Looking for these." I held up my panties and dangled them in his face. Chase had his boxer briefs back on. *Great. I was crouching tiger while he was hidden dragon.*

He helped me to my feet and handed me a warm washcloth. "I thought you might want to clean up."

I graciously took it and gathered the rest of my clothes from the floor, clutching them to my chest. "Thanks. I'll just go in the bathroom and get dressed."

He quirked an eyebrow. "You're not leaving are you?"

I bit my lip nervously. "I… ummm…just assumed…"

Chase took the clothes from my arms and replaced them with a T-shirt he pulled from his dresser. "Stay. You can wear this." He must have seen the worry in my eyes. "I don't want you to leave yet. I'll take you home in the morning. Please, stay." He ran the back of his fingers down the side of my face.

I shuffled awkwardly from foot to foot, trying to cover myself with his shirt. "I thought this was…"

He put a finger to my lips to stop me. "Shhhh… I don't know what this is, but I know I don't want you to go." He turned me around and gave my bottom a little smack. "Hurry back."

Alrighty then.

I hurried to the bathroom and cleaned myself up. Chase's black Forever Inked shirt was about ten sizes too big for me and it fell halfway down my thighs. A quick look in the mirror confirmed what I already knew. My cheeks were flushed, my eyes shined, and my hair was wild. I looked thoroughly fucked, like a woman who had just had the best sex of her life. And that's exactly how I felt… completely satisfied.

When I went back to the bedroom Chase had folded the covers back and was partially tucked underneath, leaning against the headboard. I needed a moment to take in the beauty of him. Sculpted chest and chiseled abs covered in colorful art that continued down his arms. His hair was cropped close on the sides and longer on top. It flopped over his forehead, giving him a boyish charm. He had a slight five o'clock shadow covering his angular jaw that only amplified the bad boy vibe he gave off.

I had no idea what he was doing with me. Maggie Malone was about as far from a bad girl as you could get. It didn't make sense. I was nothing like his friends from the bar.

"There you are. I thought maybe you snuck out the bathroom window."

I motioned down at his shirt that dwarfed me. "That would have taken my walk of shame to a whole new level. You stole my clothes. I didn't have much choice but to stay." I tried to sound annoyed but failed miserably when my lips curled up into a smirk.

"That *was* my master plan. You look cute in my shirt." He patted the space beside him on the bed, then reached over on the nightstand and grabbed a pint of ice cream with two spoons sticking out. He held it up to me. "Peace offering?" His aqua eyes pierced me.

I crawled up next to him on the bed. "Now how am I supposed to resist ice cream?" I checked out the label. "Chocolate chip cookie dough? You really know the way to a girl's heart, don't you?"

"Whatever it takes. I'm not beyond bribery." He dipped one of the spoons into the creamy goodness and held it just out of my reach. "So, you'll stay?"

"You drive a hard bargain, but I can't resist ice cream." I grabbed his hand and pulled the spoon toward my mouth. It melted on my tongue. Heavenly.

He laughed as his thumb came up to wipe the bit that dripped down my chin. He sucked it off and my heart raced. Chase had a way of looking sexy even when he wasn't trying.

I leaned back against the headboard next to him and covered my legs with the sheets and comforter. "Soooo, your friends were nice." I scrambled for something to get my mind off Chase sucking the ice cream from his thumb.

He dipped the spoon back into the container and handed another scoop to me. Then he reached for his own spoon. "They're more family than friends, but yeah, they're the best." I could see the genuine admiration in his eyes. "We've been through a lot together."

"How long have you worked for Zack?"

"Layla and I got hired around the same time. I guess it's been a little over five years."

"And Zack's wife? I swear I've seen Rissa before."

Chase chuckled. "You probably have. Ever go on Facebook or Instagram?"

I crinkled up my nose. "Yeah, it's practically mandatory these days."

"Yeah, I guess it is." He laughed. "And you listen to the radio?"

"Of course. And?" I prodded.

"You know that song "Broken Wings"? That's her. She's Rissa Black. Her debut album is releasing in a few weeks."

My eyes about popped out of my head. I loved that song. I'd seen the promos for the album all over social media. "That's Zack's wife?"

"Yep, lucky bastard. Sweet as sugar, voice of an angel, and not too hard on the eyes."

I bumped his shoulder with mine. "Sounds like you have a little crush on her."

"Nah, she and Zack are perfect together. She's great. Even though she's the youngest of the group, Rissa likes to mother hen all of us. Even Draven, and trust me, that's some funny shit when she sets him straight. Dude looks like a five-year-old who got scolded for putting his hand in the cookie jar."

"That's hard to imagine. He's intimidating."

"I wouldn't fuck with him, but deep down he's a softy, especially for Layla." There was a faraway look in his eyes when he talked about his friends.

"Sounds like they're good friends to have. What made you want to do tattooing?"

He shoveled another scoop into his mouth, "I always liked drawing and art as a kid. I doodled all over every assignment I was given. It made my teachers crazy. My mom gave up on painting my bedroom when I was about twelve. Every time she painted over the graffiti on my walls, I'd draw on them again. After a while she gave into it and to this day my old room has walls covered in my artwork."

"That's kinda cool that she just accepted it as part of who you are. Your mom and dad must be proud that you made your art into a career."

Chase's demeanor changed. "It's not what my dad wanted for me. I put my parents through a lot when I was younger. My dad died before I could prove to him that I could make something of myself."

I smacked my hand up over my mouth. "I'm so sorry. I didn't know."

He bumped his shoulder into mine. "Don't worry about it, I made peace with it a long time ago. Besides, we're strangers. We're not supposed to know anything about each other yet."

"True, but I still feel bad for sticking my foot in my mouth."

He shrugged. "Let's talk about you."

I pushed my hair behind my ear. "What do you want to know?"

"Tell me about Ella's dad."

My heart caught in my throat. "Wow. Going there already?"

He held up my hand and laced our fingers together. "No ring, so I'm assuming you're not together."

I let out a sigh. "No, we're not together."

"Divorced?"

"Never married. We dated in college." I shook my head. "Not even sure I could call what we did dating. We messed around. A Lot. When he found out I was pregnant, he took off. I didn't see him again until the day Ella was born."

"So, he's part of your life now?"

I waved my hand back and forth. "Sort of? He tries to be there for Ella, although I'd like him to try a little harder. Me? He's not so interested in. We get along, but it's complicated."

"Complicated how?"

I wasn't sure how much I wanted to reveal. But considering I probably wouldn't see Chase after tonight, I told the truth. "I guess I always thought I'd be married when I got pregnant. All I ever wanted was a family, but Jeff, that's his name, wasn't and isn't interested in a family. He's more focused on his career. So, for the most part it's just Ella and me. We do okay for ourselves. My parents are a big help and so is my brother, but I don't like to depend on them too much."

"That sucks, I guess. But his loss is my gain tonight."

"I suppose it is." If Jeff weren't such a dick to me, I wouldn't be here with Chase right now, wearing his shirt and sharing ice cream in bed.

"How often does he see Ella?"

"He takes her to dinner every Friday. Occasionally there will be something else, but I guess I should be grateful he sees her at all."

"And you?"

"And me what?"

"Do you have feelings for him?" he prodded.

This was getting personal and fast. It really wasn't any of Chase's business. "Why are you so interested?"

"Just trying to get to know the stranger in my bed sharing ice cream with me. You don't have to answer."

I thought about that. Why was I hemming and hawing about telling Chase the personal details of my life? Hadn't I just told Jeff this morning that we were done? In the back of my mind, I had been holding out hope that Jeff would come around, but the way he treated me today had made things crystal clear. Jeff was Ella's father. Nothing more. Nor would he ever be. I was a quick and easy fuck for him. I deserved better, even if it was only a wild romp in the sheets with a sexy stranger. "You want the truth?"

"Yes. I want to know who you are."

"I used to love him, but now I tolerate him. Jeff will always be part of my life. He's the father of my daughter and because of that I owe him at least that much. Since Ella's been born, we've slept together on and off. Not so much because I loved him, but because I'm a single woman who has needs. It satisfied those needs without disrupting Ella's life, but we're done. He'll never be the man I wanted him to be. If I don't start putting myself first, Ella will graduate from high school and I'll have spent that entire time waiting on someone who doesn't give a damn about me."

Chase lifted an eyebrow. "That sounds harsh."

I tilted my head to the side. "The truth usually is." I couldn't help but laugh. "Okay, I know that was a little much for a one-night stand, but god it felt good admitting it."

"What makes you think this is a one-night stand?" He lifted a spoonful of ice cream to my lips.

I eagerly accepted and moaned as the sweetness hit my tongue. "It isn't?"

Chase dropped the spoon back into the almost empty container. "Look, I don't know what this is, but let's not be so quick to put a label on it. There was a reason both of us showed up at The Locker tonight. Let's enjoy the night together and see where it goes."

The fact that he wasn't putting a kibosh to everything felt good, like maybe there was hope for something more. Chase had an easygoing personality that relaxed me. I didn't have enough moments like this in my life. "Okay, we'll see where it goes."

"Now that that's settled, let's deal with the next item on the agenda. As much as I like seeing you in my shirt," he grabbed the hem of his tee and slipped it up over my head, "I like you better without it."

Chase brought me to pleasure again and again, and when he had thoroughly fucked me, he wrapped me in his arms with my back to his chest. He pressed a kiss to my shoulder and whispered, "I don't think one night is going to be enough with you."

My body warmed in a way it hadn't for a man in a very long time. I squeezed his hand that was weaved with mine. "Me neither."

Soon a soft snore vibrated against my ear. How men could fall asleep so fast I'd never know. My mind always raced when I lay in bed, even more so now that I was in someone else's bed.

I wondered how this man would fit into Ella's life. Or if he would even want to. Ella had never known me with anyone but her father. Would she accept Chase into our lives?

My mind spun with possibilities when a soft buzz filled the room. Both our phones rested on the bedside table and one of them was going off. I would have liked to ignore it, but that little voice in my head wouldn't let me. My parents were more than capable of taking care of Ella… but what if?

I stealthily twisted out of Chase's arms and sat on the edge of the bed. I picked up my phone and checked for missed calls or texts. Seeing none I set it back down.

His phone buzzed again. It was after two in the morning. Who would be texting him? It was none of my business, but curiosity got the best of me and I lifted it into my palm. I knew what I was about to do was wrong, but my fingers had a mind of their own. Two new messages had come in, both from the same person.

Becca: You busy?

Becca: I'm horny and I miss you! My bed misses you.

The messages slapped me back into reality. I set the phone back down. "Shit!"

All of my what ifs and wonderings had been for nothing. I glanced over my shoulder at the beautiful man beside me. It had been a great night, but that's all it was. One night.

I quickly pulled up my Uber app and ordered a car. Within the next seven minutes this would be nothing but a sweet memory. Gathering my clothes from the floor, I took them into the front room to get dressed. I didn't want to risk waking Chase and having to explain my escape in the middle of the night. Finding a pen and paper on the counter, I scribbled a quick note and set it next to his coffee maker.

Headlights glared across the front window signaling my ride had arrived. I took one last look around the room and picked up my purse from the couch. Irrational sadness crept into my chest and filled it, causing an emptiness that made no sense.

I snuck out the door, letting it click quietly behind me, then rushed down the stairs to my waiting ride, leaving Chase and all my silly fantasies behind.

Chapter 7
Chase

She left.

Snuck out like a thief in the night.

All that was left of her was the smell of perfume on my sheets and the note she left by the coffee maker.

Thanx for a great night! xoxo ~Red

I didn't realize how much I'd wanted her to stay until I found her gone.

It was for the best. She had a daughter. She wanted a family.

That wasn't me.

Then why did it bother me that she left? Didn't even leave a phone number.

I took a shower, almost hating to wash the remnants of Red from my skin. She was different than any woman I'd ever been with. Soft and innocent on the outside, she was a first grade teacher for God's sake. She spent her days caring for and nurturing six and seven-year-olds, preparing them for life by teaching them how to read and do basic math. Then she went home to one of the cutest little girls I'd ever seen, with minimal help from anyone else. She was the epitome of sweet and pure.

It was one of the things that turned me on most last night. There was a nervousness about her. A quiet but tentative trusting. She wasn't sure about giving in to a stranger, but once she did, she was beautiful. The way Red's body responded to mine was exquisite. Each kiss and stroke of my tongue had her writhing and moaning beneath me.

There was also a bit of wild inside Red that had been dying to break free. A part of her that needed to escape from her carefully planned life. Last night I'd seen a glimpse of it.

She should be with a lawyer or a banker or an engineer. A guy like me would only taint her. I'd bet anything that her ex didn't have a single tattoo and the thought of marring his perfect skin disgusted him.

If he only knew who was inside Maggie last night.

I laughed at the picture of him in my head. Some pencil-dick suit with a stick so far up his ass it tickled his tonsils. Dress shirt and tie with a Catholic boy haircut. Golfed with the guys and drank scotch while bragging about his latest financial investment.

The worst part was that she deserved someone like him—not that exact version—but someone who could provide a stable life for her and Ella. Maggie needed someone who would step up to the plate and take care of her and her daughter. I'd proven time and time again that I was a selfish bastard.

The hot shower did nothing to relieve the disappointment of waking up alone. I grabbed my phone and checked it for messages before heading to my mom's house for our family's weekly Sunday breakfast. There were two messages, both from Becca. She'd wanted to hook up last night. It had only been two weeks since we parted ways and already she was caving. It would have been easy to give her a call, but I was the one who put this in motion. I had to stand my ground… at least until I had more answers about Maggie.

I wanted more than a regular hookup. I wanted what Zack and Rissa had. What Draven and Layla had. I was tired of being the lone wolf surrounded by a pack. Don't get me wrong, I loved my days as a lone wolf. The hunt was part of what made me tick.

Maybe that's what it was about Red. The hunt. I'd had her last night, but she slipped through my fingers… from my bed… without a trace. I had no way to contact her even if I wanted to. My contact list was filled with chicks I'd hooked up with. Dozens of names, minus the unforgettable redhead I'd sunk into last night.

I cataloged all the things I knew about her:

Long red hair. *Gorgeous.*

Blue eyes. *Mesmerizing.*

Plump cherry lips. *Totally kissable.*

Great rack. *Ka-ching!*

Luscious ass. *Double ka-ching!*

First grade teacher. *Super sweet.*

Douchebag ex. *Stupid fuck!*

Six-year-old daughter. *Slam on the brakes!*

It was like an awful car crash I couldn't avoid. You know the one. It's a sunny day and you're rocking out to your favorite jams on the radio. The light just turned yellow and you have plenty of time to go through the intersection, but the person in the opposite lane assumes you're going to stop. You see it happening before it even registers in your brain. The oncoming car is making a left turn right in front of you and there's nothing you can do but slam on the brakes. At that point it's too late. You've just T-boned them and all the airbags are going off in your car, but even they can't stop the damage that's already been done.

I had a choice to make. Either go through the yellow light that warned me I was entering a danger zone or slam on the brakes before entering the intersection and play it safe. Maggie would make her turn and continue driving without us ever crossing paths again.

I'd been in this situation before and the crash almost killed us both. We'd both walked away broken and battered. I didn't know about *her*, but my wounds were deep and still hadn't healed.

I'd like to think I learned from my mistakes, but the way Red invaded my mind I wasn't quite sure that was true.

The smell of bacon permeated the air. Eating breakfast at my mom's every week was a recipe for a heart attack. She was born and raised in Alabama. Breakfast was a full-blown affair with fried potatoes, biscuits, eggs, bacon, and pancakes. It was a wonder all of us weren't morbidly obese. I battled it with lots of cardio and weightlifting, burning even more calories with my horizontal workouts.

Mom was busy cooking up a storm and Grams was helping. Grams had moved in after my dad died. She'd been living alone in Alabama for years and it made sense at the time. She liked being home with her only daughter and decided to stay.

I sidled up next to mom and gave her a kiss on the cheek. "Smells amazing and I'm starved."

"Then you came to the right place. Get yourself some juice and have a seat. Breakfast will be ready soon." She pecked me back.

Gram stepped away from the stove, wiping her hands on a dish towel. She opened her arms wide. "There's my favorite grandson. Give me a hug."

I leaned down and wrapped her small body in my big arms, laughing. "I'm your only grandson."

"And therefore, my favorite." She winked at me.

"Don't make his head any bigger than it already is," my sister, Amber, scolded as she walked in carrying my three-year-old nephew. "He already thinks he's God's gift to women."

I grabbed Theo from her arms. "Someone's got to teach this little man how to pick up chicks. Right, dude?" I held up my hand for him to high-five.

Theo gave it a slap. "Chickies smell. Tay eat and poop and peck." He bobbed his little head forward imitating the chickens.

"You tell him, Theo." Then Amber leaned in close to me. "Stop trying to corrupt my son. I'm in no hurry for him to grow up."

I rolled my eyes. "Where's Dave?"

Amber sighed. "He's in Chicago for some IT conference. I hate when he goes away for business." She tickled Theo's tummy. "This little guy's a lot of work."

"I's not work, Mommy. I's big." Theo held his arms out wide.

Amber tapped him on the nose. "Not big enough to hang out with your Uncle Chase."

Her words smacked me in the chest like a Mack truck. Even my sister knew I wasn't responsible enough to be trusted with a child. "Maybe one day, big guy." I set my nephew on the ground and he ran into the other room to find Grandma's secret stash of toys.

I grabbed some glasses from the cupboard and began filling them with orange juice. "I'm not a total fuckup, Amber."

"Language," mom reminded, while nodding to Grams.

Grams huffed. "I've heard that word before, may have even used it a few times." She gave me a wink. My grandma always had a soft spot for me, and I'd be lying if I said she wasn't my favorite too. We shared a special connection that not many people ever got to experience.

"Don't be so touchy," my sister retorted. "I wasn't implying you were, but let's face it, you're a free spirit. I don't think childcare is your forte."

I loved my sister, but sometimes she was oblivious of the things she said. One might even say she was a bitch. How we came from the same parents was a mystery to me.

"Come on, now." My mother tried to calm the storm that was brewing. "Let's all sit and eat while the food is hot."

I helped mom bring everything to the table then settled into my usual seat next to Grams while Amber wrestled Theo away from the toy trucks in the other room.

We'd barely started eating when Grams rested her hand on top of mine. "Seriously, Chase, you need to meet yourself a nice girl."

I gave her a smirk. "Trust me, Grams, I meet lots of nice girls." My philandering ways weren't a secret to anyone.

She smacked me with her napkin. "I'm sure you do, you're a handsome boy. I meant one you'd be willing to bring around. Maybe settle down with."

I stuffed my mouth with a piece of bacon because no one could expect you to answer when your mouth was full of bacon. That was a given. "Working on it," I mumbled.

Mom's fork clanked on her plate. "Chase Crawford Montgomery, are you seeing someone?"

Full name. *Fuck!* I hated my full name. It made me sound like some hillbilly born and raised in the sticks. Mom's Alabama roots ran deep, right down to the naming of her children. Crawford had been my dad's name, but he'd had enough sense to go by Ford. No one could ever take you seriously with a name like Crawford.

I gulped down my entire glass of juice. Again, with the full mouth thing. I couldn't be expected to give more than a one-word answer. "Maybe." Once my mom got a whiff of anything juicy, she was like a bloodhound sniffing out the details. It was a little something I liked to call *The Betty Louise Inquisition*.

"Well, hallelujah! Who is she?" mom prodded.

"It's nothing, Mom. Seriously, we've only gone out once. Well, twice if you want to get technical."

Amber's ears perked up, but she was surprisingly silent.

"Don't keep us waiting." Grams nudged me with her shoulder. "What's her name? What's she like?"

"It's nothing," I insisted. "I barely know her, but she's cool."

"What's her name? What does she do?" Mom kept it up.

It wasn't every day that I mentioned one of my hookups. I kept my sex life private. No one wanted their mom or grandma to know that they got more ass than a toilet seat. The fact I mentioned Red should have been my first clue that I wanted her to be more.

"Her name is Maggie and she's a teacher. She's really pretty and sweet. I like her a lot."

Grams patted my hand again. "Sounds promising."

Amber couldn't help but rain on my parade. "What's she doing with you?"

I shot her a dirty look but held my tongue out of respect for everyone else at the table.

"Oh, I know!" Amber clasped her hands over Theo's ears. "S-E-X."

I pretended to scratch the side of my head using my middle finger. My sister was a real piece of work. "It's more than that," I spat.

"Of course it is." My mom shot Amber a scowl, warning her to hold her tongue.

"Honestly, I don't know her that well." I shrugged my shoulders. "We just clicked."

"I'm sure she's a nice girl. When are you going to see her again?" mom asked.

Now that was the question. When and how would I see Maggie again? "I'm not sure. We're taking it slow," I lied.

"Do you even know her last name? Know anything besides her bra size?" Amber picked at the invisible scars Maggie had unknowingly brought to the surface.

I threw my napkin on the table. "What's your problem?"

"You're my problem! You walk around like you don't have a care in the world. You blew the best thing that ever happened to you and pretend like it doesn't matter."

That was enough. Amber and I had been tap dancing around this for years. It was bound to come to a head at some point. I just wished we didn't have an audience when it did. I stood up abruptly, my chair crashing to the ground in the process. "Fuck you, Amber!" I pointed to my chest. "It matters to me! Not a single day goes by that I don't think about it. I know she was your best friend and you lost her because of me, but what am I supposed to do? Do you want me to pay for it the rest of my life? 'Cuz, trust me, I haven't forgotten any of it, but I can't go back and fix it. What's done is done!"

"You didn't even try, did you?" she accused.

I flipped her the middle finger. "Fuck you! It was too late to make things right!"

I picked the chair up from where it had fallen and grabbed my coat from the floor. My mom had tears in her eyes and Grams sat silent. "I'm sorry. I can't be here right now."

"Chase?" my mom pleaded.

"I… I just can't. I need some space to breathe. I'm sorry I ruined breakfast. It wasn't my intention."

Grams grabbed my hand as I stormed from the kitchen. "We know. You're okay. It's going to be okay."

"For Christ's sake, quit babying him. He needs to grow the hell up!"

"Amber, that's enough!" mom yelled.

I'd rarely seen my mom lose it like that. Since my dad died, all she wanted was for us to be a normal, happy family. We weren't. The divide between Amber and me was far and wide. I couldn't dwell on it.

57

I rushed out to my truck and headed to the one place that always gave me peace. I unlocked the door and entered the security code. In my studio, no one would bother me. It was just pens and paper and my emotions.

My hands worked furiously and began drawing before my mind could keep up. Dark lines covered the page. A woman with long, curly hair and vibrant eyes appeared before me. The thing was… she looked more like Red than Meredith. What the hell was wrong with me?

I crumbled up the paper and tossed it toward the trash can, missing by a mile.

I was so off, and my mind was even further gone. Meredith should have been the first thing I thought of, but Red permeated my brain. What the hell?

Draven crept quietly into my space. "I heard the alarm beeping. What are you doing here so early?" He and Layla lived upstairs, and he was always on alert. Draven picked up the crumpled paper and smoothed it out. "Woman problems?"

"Something like that."

"How was your date?"

"Amazing. She's amazing."

"So, why are you holed up like it was the worst thing that ever happened to you?"

"Ghosts. You ever have something in your past that kept you from moving on? Kept you from really being happy?"

Draven laughed. "Only my whole fucking life. Until I met Layla, I never thought I deserved it. Then I came here, and everything changed. My whole fucking life came into focus."

"How did you know she was the one? You'd been with tons of girls, what made her so different?" Draven's past wasn't exactly a secret. It was known about inside these walls that sheltered all of us from the outside world. The walls of Forever Inked protected all our secrets. It was one of the things that made us so close. Made us a family.

He shrugged. "From day one I couldn't get her out of my goddamn head. She was all I could think about, even when she was pissing me off."

Maggie had consumed my mind since the first night I met her. "But you left her behind and went back to New York." Layla had been heartbroken when he up and left without a word. She'd become a shadow of herself while they were apart.

"I was fucking miserable. I thought I was doing what was best for Layla. Once I realized I couldn't live without her, there were no more choices for me. I had to have her. Almost losing her was the hardest thing I've ever done."

I thought about Draven's admission, but I couldn't wrap my head around it. "Maggie deserves better than me. If I fuck it up, it won't just affect her. It'll affect her daughter too."

Draven patted me on the shoulder. "That's true, but why don't you let Maggie make that decision." He scratched his scruffy face with his index finger. "What makes you think you'll fuck it up?"

I gave him a self-deprecating laugh. "Have you met me?"

"Actually, I have, and I think you're a decent guy. Don't sell yourself short."

Becca and I sat at the bar in The Locker. She was on her second beer while I nursed my first. I had agreed to meet with her, because despite everything, Becca and I were friends, and I missed my friend.

"I met someone," I said nonchalantly, as I lifted the warm beer to my lips.

She quirked an eyebrow at me. "You did?"

I nodded. "I'm not sure where it's going, but I want to find out." I finished off the bottle and motioned to Lou, the owner, to bring me another.

"Is that why you didn't text me back the other night?"

"Yeah. I was conked out by the time you messaged me, but we were together." Lou grabbed my empty and placed another in front of me. "Are you pissed?"

Becca picked at the label on her bottle. "No. It's what we agreed to. I've been on a few dates, but nothing has really panned out. Guys are jerks."

I tapped my bottle to hers. "Yes, we are. King of the jerks sitting right next to you."

She shrugged. "You're like turkey jerky though. It's so good, you don't even realize you're not getting the real thing."

I paused mid-sip. "What the hell does that mean?"

She began cracking up. "I don't even know. All I know is that when I'm with you, turkey doesn't seem so bad. You're like premium turkey or some shit."

Becca was nuts. "Thanks, I guess. That was a compliment, right?"

"Yep. Let's just say that if things don't work out with whatever her name is, you can gobble me up all night. I like your stuffing."

I couldn't control my laughter. "What the fuck are we even talking about right now? Are you saying I have a turkey dick?" I held my fingers up, mimicking the size of a turkey's dick. I assumed it was small, but maybe I was misinformed.

She held her hands up in surrender. "Hey, I've got no complaints. Maybe you're like a super turkey or something. Actually, maybe you're not a turkey at all. Maybe you're an ostrich in turkey clothing."

I ran my hand through my too-long hair. "This is the weirdest conversation I've ever had. If you wanted to compare me to an animal, I could think of a few others that would be more appropriate."

She slapped me on the shoulder. "Nope, I like ostrich. You're like an ostrich stud. Do ostrich farmers have ostrich studs? Because you'd make an excellent one."

This was out of control hilarious. "Fuck if I know. Are there such things as ostrich farms?"

She waved her hand around in the air. "Of course, where do you think baby ostriches come from?"

It was official. Becca was definitely nuts.

Chapter 8
Maggie

"So, you just left?"

I poured myself a cup of coffee, adding lots of cream and sugar to avoid eye contact with Roxy. "Uh-huh." The teachers' lounge was the last place we should have been discussing my love life. The first rule of working in a school was that there were no secrets. I could swear the walls had ears. I didn't need people knowing my business. Ella could accidently hear something, and I didn't need her knowing her mom was a tramp. Not that she knew what a tramp was, but still.

Roxy leaned in close, afraid the walls would hear. "And how was the sex?"

I looked up at the ceiling and sighed. "Magical. Phenomenal. Mind-blowing. It was everything I dreamed it would be."

"Damn, girl. You should see your face right now. I think you're still in postorgasmic bliss. Why in the world did you leave? You could have gone for round two in the morning."

"It would have been round four, not that I was counting." I smiled sheepishly, pushing my hair over my ear. "Anyway, after he fell asleep, his phone buzzed on the nightstand. I may have accidently checked his text and saw it was from another woman."

She quirked her eyebrow up. "Accidently?"

I rubbed my hands over my face. "So maybe it was accidently on purpose. It doesn't matter. It reminded me of what the night was supposed to be, a one-time thing. He doesn't have my number and I don't have his, so it's over."

"But you know where he works."

"It's irrelevant. I had my fun, now it's time to get back to reality. A guy like Chase isn't interested in being saddled with a kid." I shrugged. "Ella and I are a package deal, so why bother."

Roxy scoffed at me. "Because the man has stamina and he's a hot piece of ass. Nuff said."

I shook my head and laughed. "That's all true, but…gah! It was really a great night and I don't just mean the sex. He was sweet and thoughtful and well, I'm afraid I would get attached. I don't know if I'm ready for that kind of heartbreak after everything I've been through with Jeff. And what if Ella's not ready for me to have another man in my life?"

"And what if she is? She knows you and Jeff aren't together."

"Does she? I let him into my bed on Friday. What kind of message am I sending her?" I was a bad mom. Ella should have always come first, and Saturday I dumped her at my parents for a chance to hook up with a guy. That wasn't the kind of mom I wanted to be.

"I'm not saying you should have sleepovers with Chase or anyone else for that matter but give yourself a chance to be happy."

I frowned at her. "I am happy."

She hugged me tight. "I know you are, but I think you could be happier. Promise me you'll start taking care of you."

"Of course I will," I lied.

Being with Chase was a night I wouldn't soon forget, but I needed to. My life wasn't conducive to dating. The chances of me meeting someone else were zero to none. Single men didn't hang out at Ella's dance studio or Brownie meetings and lately that was the extent of my social life. The rare nights out, like the night I'd met Chase, were few and far between. My nights were spent reading fairy tales, watching Disney movies, giving Ella a bath, and having a glass of wine after tucking my sweet girl into bed.

I had a feeling Chase's nights were a little more exciting than mine.

I closed down my computer and walked down to the gym to get Ella. I wasn't thrilled about leaving her in our school's childcare program at the end of the day, but I didn't have much choice. I needed the time to get things done in my classroom. There weren't any other reasonable alternatives. At least I was close if she needed me, and it was usually less than an hour.

My girl was trying her hardest to dribble a basketball, but it kept getting away from her. I watched as she chased the damn ball halfway across the gym, her little legs trying to catch up. A boy in her class tried to swipe it away from her, but she checked him with her shoulder and grabbed it. I didn't condone aggressive behavior, but I was proud of my girl for holding her own.

I waved at Ella across the gym. "Time to go, ladybug!"

She dropped the ball and ran over to me. I scooped her up in my arms. "How was your day?"

"The best! I had tacos for lunch, and we got to do painting after recess."

I set her down and wrapped her hand in mine as we walked out to my car. "That sounds like a great day. What do you want for dinner tonight?" I fastened Ella into her booster seat, placing her backpack on the floorboard. She was getting too big for the booster, but the mom in me didn't want to admit it.

"Can we have McDonald's?" she sang from the back seat.

Fast food was something I tried to keep to a minimum. "Not tonight. How about chicken?"

Ella made a face and stuck out her tongue. "We have chicken all the time. Daddy takes me to McDonald's."

I forced down a groan. Of course he did. It was quick and easy. "Well, maybe he'll take you on Friday. Tonight we're having chicken and green beans."

"Yuck! Why did you even ask me?"

I internally laughed. "I thought you liked chicken. Besides it's good for you." I smiled at her in the rearview mirror.

"I just decided I hate chicken," she complained.

I resisted the urge to roll my eyes. It was going to be one of those nights. "You don't hate chicken."

"I do now," she sassed. Ella stared out the window watching the trees fly by as I made our way home. Her lip was tucked between her teeth. Something was bothering her, and it wasn't chicken. "What are you thinking about, ladybug?"

She looked at me in the mirror and our eyes met. "Andy, in my class, said his parents are divorced. What's divorced mean?"

How did you explain adult relationships to a six-year-old? I settled on, "It means they're not married anymore, and they don't live together."

"Are you and Daddy divorced?"

This was a conversation I was hoping to avoid, but with Ella starting school, I knew she would have questions. I'd kept her naïve about my relationship with Jeff for six years. It was time for the truth. "Your dad and I aren't divorced. We never got married."

I could see her wheels turning. "Andy said when a mommy and daddy get married, they have kids. So, if you weren't married, how did you have me?"

Who the hell was this Andy kid? I wanted to wring his neck. "That's not always how it works, but yes, when people get married, they usually have kids."

"So how did you have me?" Ella persisted.

Ugh! She wasn't going to give it up.

"It's complicated," I said. "Your dad and I spent a lot of time together and boom… we had you. It was the best thing that ever happened to me." I figured that should be enough to appease her, but it wasn't.

"So, you and Daddy weren't married? Why not?"

Damn, this couldn't get much worse. "We just weren't. It doesn't matter. Your daddy and I love you very much."

Ella thought about that for a while. "So, do you love Daddy?"

I decided to be honest with her. "I did, but not anymore. That doesn't mean that we don't both love you."

"Andy said his dad has a girlfriend. Does my daddy have a girlfriend?"

Ella's questions broke my heart. I couldn't lie to her. "I don't know. But if he does, I'm sure she'll be wonderful." The white lie I just told my daughter sank down into my stomach. I couldn't imagine another woman taking my place. I was sure Jeff had slept with other women. I just thanked God that he hadn't introduced any of them to our daughter.

My thoughts wandered to Chase. I didn't want another woman in Ella's life, but that wasn't really fair. Eventually, Jeff and I would have to come to an understanding in regard to dating. I just hoped Ella wouldn't have to pay the price for our mistakes. My daughter deserved more than the mess we were.

"Do you have a boyfriend?" she persisted.

"No, Ella. Mommy doesn't have time for a boyfriend."

"What about Chase?"

My heart caught in my throat. "Who?"

Ella grinned at me in the mirror. "The man at the costume store. He knew my name. I think he liked you. Why did he call you Red?"

Red.

That's what he'd called me in front of my daughter. I'd never had a man give me a nickname, something that was just for me.

I shook my head and ignored her question. "He's just a friend, ladybug."

Ella kicked her feet into the back of my seat. "He said I was the best fairy princess he'd ever seen. I like him." She smiled brightly.

Well, damn. That made two of us.

Midway through the week, the principal came to my door and peeked her head in during my math lesson. The students were scattered around the room creating patterns with beads, blocks, and buttons. There were lots of busy hands working and loud chatter filled the air.

Joey Nichols saw her first. "Ms. Jacobs is here!" he shouted out.

Every set of eyes in the classroom fell on her. If she was trying to be sneaky, she'd have to do better than that with a bunch of six-year-olds.

"I see that, Joey. Thank you." I gave him a wink and a thumbs-up. Turning my attention to the door I addressed the principal. "Hi, Ms. Jacobs. Come on in. What can I do for you?"

For a woman who was usually no-nonsense, she looked unusually perky. She continued to stand outside the door. "I was just in the office and something arrived for you. It looked important, so I thought I should bring it down right away."

Why didn't she just say what it was? Ms. Jacobs was a quirky woman, but her behavior was odd, even for her. I searched my memory trying to think if I had ordered anything recently. Nothing came to mind. Curiosity got the best of me and I moved in her direction. "What is it?"

She bent over and picked something up from the floor that was just out of view. She spun on her heels and thrust a big box at me. "Looks like someone has an admirer."

It wasn't just any box. It was from a floral shop. I rolled my eyes. "Very unlikely. It's probably from Ella's dad. We had a disagreement the other morning." Disagreement my ass. Maybe telling him to get the fuck out had finally hit home.

I took the large box from her hands, smiling sweetly. "Thank you, Ms. Jacobs." It was just like Jeff to say something nasty, then think he could buy his way out of it. From the size of the box, I'd say this time it cost him a pretty penny.

Ms. Jacobs frowned. "Aren't you going to open it?" She seemed way too invested in my delivery.

"Yes, of course." I carried the package to my desk with Ms. Jacobs right on my heels. She grabbed a pair of scissors from my Best Teacher mug and snipped the plastic straps that held the box together. I didn't need her help. "Thank you," I smiled.

She clapped her hands together excitedly. "I can't wait to see it!" Unfortunately, she wasn't the only one.

My desk was now surrounded by twenty-five little people who were also curious. "Is it from your husband?" Joey asked.

Sarah Meyers elbowed him in the ribs. "She doesn't have a husband, silly. It's probably from her boyfriend."

Joey's eyes went big. "Do you have a boyfriend, Ms. Malone?"

Nothing like being put on the spot in front of your boss and a class full of Nosy Nellies. "No, Joey, I don't have a boyfriend, but I do have friends that are boys."

"What's the difference?" Tonya asked. "Do you kiss them still? My mom kisses our neighbor, Mr. Riley, but not in front of Mrs. Riley. They're friends. Is it like that?"

I smacked myself in the head. Once they got going it was nearly impossible to stop the inquisition, and honestly, I didn't think Tonya's mother would be too happy about her daughter's loose lips. "That's enough questions. Who wants to see what's in the box?" I asked, diverting their attention.

Twenty-five hands shot in the air with a chorus of, "Me, me, me." Ms. Jacobs didn't say anything, but she didn't have to with the shit-eating grin on her face. *Seriously, what was up with this woman?*

Once the top was lifted off the box, a huge bouquet of beautiful wildflowers spilled out. Roses, daisies, lilies, alstroemeria, and some flowers I didn't even know the name of overflowed my desk in the brightest colors I had ever seen.

"Who are they from?" Sarah asked. Their little voices chattered with their guesses.

Ms. Jacobs reached over me and snatched the card from the arrangement.

I don't think so! I plucked the card from her fingers with a smile. "Thank you." Stepping back from the chaos, I slipped the card from the envelope and read it. *Oh Lord!* Quickly stuffing it back in the envelope, I slipped it into my pocket.

"Well?" my boss asked.

Searching my mind for an answer, I finally settled on, "They're from my brother. He's sweet like that."

Ms. Jacobs looked thoroughly disappointed. "Oh, well that was nice of him. My brother has never sent me flowers at work."

I gave her a little shrug. "What can I say? I guess I lucked out in the brother department."

"I would say so. Enjoy the rest of your day." She waved at the kids as she left my room.

She was deflated, but I sure as hell wasn't going to give anyone around here something else to talk about. My lie was totally justified.

"Yuck!" Joey spat. "I'm never sending my sister flowers. She'll think I like her or something. Girls are gross."

I let out a little huff. *You'll change your mind one day, kid.*

"Uncle Patty!" Ella ran to the door when my brother walked in. "I love the flowers you got for Momma!"

He scooped her up in his arms and kissed her on the head while giving me a questioning look. "You did?"

Ella's arms began to fling around as she talked. "Yep! Their so big and pretty. Momma put them on the kitchen counter so we can look at them all the time."

Carrying Ella, Patrick followed me further into the house to the kitchen where I was making our dinner. "My, those are pretty! Nothing is too good for my girls."

Ella's eyes widened. "They're for me too?"

"Of course." Patrick played along. "Pretty flowers for my favorite girls."

Ella gave him a tight squeeze. "Thank you, Uncle Patty!"

"You're welcome," he said, putting her down.

"Go wash your hands for dinner, ladybug," I instructed.

"Okay." Her feet pitter-pattered down the hall to the bathroom.

Patrick quirked his eyebrow at me.

I held my hand up. "Don't start."

"Somebody has a boyfriend, somebody has a boyfriend," he singsonged.

"What? Are you five? You sound like one of my kids at school."

Patty ran his hand through his hair. When we were kids it was bright red like mine, but over the years it had changed to more of a brown color. "Who is he and when do I get to meet him?"

"It's not like that. I met him at the bar, and we clicked." I continued stirring the spaghetti sauce on the stove. I knew he was going to get all up in my shit.

He motioned to the flowers. "You slept with him."

I threw my hands in the air, flinging a little of the sauce onto my white cupboards. "So what? I'm allowed to have some fun. All I ever get to do is work and be a mom. Sometimes I want to be a woman. Is that all right with you?"

My brother held his hands up in surrender. "It's fine. You deserve it. I just don't want to see you with another fucktard like Jeff."

"Don't call him that. Ella could hear you," I said, as I wiped the red mess from my cabinets.

"I call a spade a spade. The guy's an asshole."

Throwing the cloth into the sink, I huffed. "He is, but Ella doesn't know that yet. He's her dad and she loves him."

"He doesn't deserve her," he grumbled.

"Where's Brian tonight?" I changed the subject.

"He's working late. Has a dinner meeting with clients."

I pulled the garlic bread from the oven. "You two have been dating for a while now. Must be serious." Although I'd known since we were teenagers, my brother finally came out in college. By looking at him, you'd never know he was gay. He was way more Will Truman than Jack McFarland. Patty was a good-looking guy, who wore a suit to work every day. He kept his body in shape and was never at a loss for company. Brian had been the best thing that ever happened to him. My brother finally seemed settled. I was ecstatic; all we ever wanted for each other was to be happy.

"I'm thinking about asking him to move in with me."

"Wow! That's a big step."

He grabbed the plates from the counter and started to set the table for the three of us. "I know. Talk me out of it."

After setting the noodles on the table, I placed my hand on his shoulder. "Why would I do that?"

"Because it's too fast, right? I don't even know if he's ready to move in together. I'm just being impulsive."

I kissed him on the cheek. "Impulsive is the last thing I would ever call you. Being with Brian is not impulsive. He's good to you, Mom looks at him like another son, and he adores Ella."

"You're not helping."

"Yes, I am. You just don't want to admit that maybe he's the one."

Ella scurried into the room and hopped on Patty's lap. "Who's the one?"

My brother hugged her tight. "You. You're the light of my life."

"Is that why you sent me flowers?"

"Sure is, ladybug. You're my girl." He tickled Ella's chubby belly and she giggled.

My heart swelled. I wished Ella had a man in her life that would make her giggle like that on a regular basis.

I just wondered if the man who sent me flowers today would be up for the challenge.

Chapter 9
Chase

I hadn't heard from Red all day. Maybe the flowers were a mistake, but what woman didn't like flowers? Or maybe it was the note I enclosed that she didn't like. *I should have tied you to the bed. I won't be making that mistake next time. I want to see you again.* I signed my name and left my phone number. The ball was in her court.

If I didn't hear from her… fuck, what if she didn't call? She had to have gotten the delivery hours ago. Red was all I could think about while at work. Even tattooing Cassandra's ass couldn't distract me from thinking about Maggie. And Cassandra's ass was a thing of glory. On any other day, I would have jumped at the offers she was throwing my way. But today, I just wasn't into it.

I tossed my keys on the small table by the door inside my apartment and headed to the fridge for a beer. I took it out to the balcony and sat in one of the two patio chairs, checking my phone for missed calls. Again, there was nothing. Just a message from my mom, begging me to make things right with Amber.

Yeah, that wasn't going to happen. Maybe I shouldn't have jumped down her throat, but she was out of line. If anyone needed to apologize it was my bitch of a sister.

I propped my feet on the railing and drained half the bottle in one gulp. One wasn't going to be enough tonight.

A soft thud broke me out of my thoughts. Not My Cat stared up at me and let out a loud meow. He was a big ol' striped tomcat. His ear was clipped, and I was pretty sure he didn't belong to anyone but seemed to have taken a liking to me. He jumped up on my balcony almost every night. Little crapper was agile, that was for sure.

I reached down and scratched him between the ears. "Out on the prowl again? I feel your pain, dude. I could go for some pussy myself."

He put his front paws on my chair and stretched before hopping onto my lap. I rubbed his back. "What is your fascination with me? I'm just a single cat on the prowl like you." I chuckled. "Yeah, I guess we have a lot in common."

He meowed again and rubbed his body into my hand, purring loudly.

"I don't know why I put up with you. You know you're not my cat, right?" I reached down and grabbed the container of treats I had bought for him. After sprinkling some on the balcony, he jumped down and began to eat. "I think you're using me. It's cool, dude. Talking to you is better than talking to myself."

He flicked his tail in the air showing me his ass. It was a clear *fuck off* if I'd ever seen one. "I see how you are." I flipped him the bird. "Back atcha, buddy."

I drained the rest of my beer and opened the slider to get another one. Not My Cat pranced his fuzzy butt right inside. "Now you're crossing the line, mister. This is my place, not yours."

He hopped on the kitchen counter and started meowing like crazy. "What? Are you hungry? Treats aren't enough for you?" I grabbed him around the middle and set him on the floor. "You're a pain in the ass, you know that?" I started opening cupboards searching for something that would be suitable for a cat. I found a can of tuna and opened it up for him. The smell sent him into a frenzy, rubbing against my legs and yowling up a storm. "Be patient. You're lucky I'm even sharing this with you. It was supposed to be my lunch tomorrow." I took the can and placed it on the balcony. Not My Cat trotted out after me and started feasting. He was as happy as a pig in shit. "Good night, cat dude." I shut the door and left him out there.

At least someone was going to bed happy tonight.

That second beer was calling my name. I popped the top off another one and plopped on the couch to channel surf. Football highlights from Sunday played on *ESPN.* I liked football as much as the next guy, but rarely had the time to sit down and watch. Anytime a group of guys got together this time of year, football was sure to be a topic. Guy code insisted I at least be updated with the highlights, so I could contribute to the conversation without getting my man card revoked.

I played ball back in high school before I fucked everything up. Meredith and I had been hot and heavy during school and the years that followed. She was the same age as my sister, just a year younger than me. I really thought back then the two of us would go the distance. Get married, have a cute little house, two or three kids and a dog. Only part of that dream started to materialize and then I fucked it all up.

71

When she left, I didn't even go after her. I was heartbroken. She was pissed and had every right to be. I knew she was better off without me.

Meredith was the last time I'd had a serious relationship. Everything since then had been casual. I loved women but kept it to just sex. Sex was simple. Sex was uncomplicated. Sex didn't include heartbreak. I wasn't a dick about it; the women I slept with knew what it was and we both walked away more than satisfied. Honestly, no one had given me that fluttery feeling in my chest since Meredith.

The crowd was wild, cheering as the clock ticked down. My feet flew across the turf headed for the end zone. I was so close. I caught sight of a red jersey in my peripheral and used everything I had to barrel forward. The impact of the defensive tackle hurled me into the end zone. I nestled the ball to my chest with an iron grip, scoring us the winning touchdown.

His body crushed mine, but all I could hear was the roar of the crowd. "Get off me, man!"

The player rolled to the side and stood. He reached down a hand and pulled me to my feet. "Great game, asshole."

I gave him a chin up. "You too."

I thrust the ball into the air, proclaiming victory.

My team and coaches charged at me with chest bumps and congratulations. Another game, another victory.

I was on cloud nine by the time I left the locker room. The only thing that could have gotten me higher was the sweet little blond who was waiting outside for me.

Meredith leapt into my arms and I swung her around. "I'm so proud of you. You were amazing tonight!"

I set her on the ground and devoured her mouth. It was a little much for high school, but then again, with Meredith I was always a little too much. "You wanna celebrate with me?"

She smiled coyly. "Do you really need to ask? I think you need an extra reward tonight."

"Oh yeah? What did you have in mind?" I swooped her up in my arms and carried her toward my car. It was an old, piece of shit Monte Carlo with a big back seat.

She hung on to me tightly. "I was hoping you could score another touchdown."

"You're my favorite end zone, baby."

She giggled as I unlocked the door and set her gently on the seat. "Hurry, Chase! Watching you made me horny as hell."

Well, shit! I raced around and hopped behind the steering wheel. My tires squealed as we sped out of the parking lot to our special spot. She rolled down her window and stuck half her body out. Meredith's long, blond hair blew in the breeze as she screamed. "I Love Chase Montgomery! Do you hear that world? I love him!"

I tugged on her arm, pulling her back inside the vehicle. "You're crazy, baby! You know that?"

She wrapped her arms around my neck and pressed her lips to my cheek. "Crazy in love with you."

It was only a few minutes until I pulled down the deserted road that backed up to an abandoned barn that should have long since been torn down. It was our special place. Far enough from the road that we wouldn't attract attention and totally secluded.

Meredith climbed over the seat into the back without being told and I followed right behind her, groping her ass in the process. Her clothes came off in a flurry and she leaned back against the door, one foot propped up on the seat. "See anything you like?"

"Only my biggest fantasy come true." We were each other's firsts and I planned on making her my last. She was every wet dream I'd ever had come to life. I was totally, irrevocably in love with Meredith.

I spent the night deep inside her, both of us coming again and again. When we were as satisfied as two teenagers could be, Meredith had lain between my legs with her head resting upon my chest. My arms protectively wrapped around her small body. I kissed her on the top of her head. "I'm gonna marry you one day. I'm gonna take care of you forever and ever. You'll always be my baby."

My phone vibrated on my leg and lit up with an unknown number. My heart beat out of control with anticipation as I tried to rid my mind of Meredith. The unknown number had to be Maggie. My finger paused over the green button as I prepared myself for her sweet voice. I accepted the call with a swipe of my thumb. "Hello."

"Hi, stranger." There was a slight pause, "Ummm… I mean, this is Maggie… from the other night."

The way she doubted herself was adorable. I couldn't help the low laugh that escaped me. "I knew who it was. You're pretty unforgettable, Red. You got my flowers?"

"Yes. Thank you. They're beautiful," she said. "You caused quite the commotion in room 101 today."

I cringed. "That wasn't my intention."

She laughed. "It would have been fine if my nosy principal hadn't brought the box to my classroom. She and twenty-five little people were very intrigued."

"Yikes! I'm sorry." I thought about the message I'd written her. "Shit. You didn't open the card in front of them, did you?"

"Actually, I did. Lucky for you I'm a quick thinker. As far as they know, the flowers were from my brother."

This relationship hadn't even started yet and I was already fucking it up. "I'm sorry. I guess I wasn't thinking about the kids. I'm not good at this stuff."

"Stop apologizing. It was super sweet. Thank you."

"You're welcome."

"I only have one question, Chase. How did you find me?"

"You mean since you didn't leave a phone number? It wasn't easy. You mentioned you worked for Utica Schools, so I searched the websites for their elementary schools. The *Meet Our Staff* pages were very helpful. It took a few tries, but eventually, I came across a beautiful, redheaded first-grade teacher named Ms. Maggie Malone."

"Well, aren't you industrious?"

"I can be when it's worth it. Imagine my surprise, expecting to wake up next to a sexy woman with a mane of red hair only to find my sheets cold and empty. Why'd you run, Maggie?"

"I didn't run."

"Yes, you did. Did I do something to upset you?"

"No, Chase. You were perfect. Everything was perfect. I just… ugh… this is going to sound stupid."

"Just tell me, Red. If everything was perfect, why did you run? I thought we had a good time."

"We did. It was too good, and… well… I didn't want you to think I was expecting more. I was trying to make it easier on both of us."

"Uh-huh. Too good? I didn't think there was such a thing as too good. What if I *want* more than just one night with you?"

"Then I would say you're crazy. My life is complicated, Chase. Why would a guy like you want to get involved with a woman like me? I have a daughter, which is why I couldn't call you until now. She finally fell asleep. Dating me won't be like dating other women."

My hackles went up. "What do you mean… a guy like me?"

Maggie let out a sigh. "You know what I mean. You're single, good-looking, thoughtful, sweet. You can have anyone you want. I'm sure there is a long list of women who would be happy to go out with you. Women that don't have a child for you to deal with. You don't need that kind of baggage."

I relaxed back into the couch. It wasn't that she thought I wasn't good enough; she was doubting my interest in her. "Ella's not baggage. She's an extension of you and from what I saw, she's pretty great. I've never dated anyone with a kid before, so I'll be honest with you, I'll probably mess up. But if you can deal with the fact that I have no idea what I'm doing when it comes to kids, I'd like to try."

"Why?"

"Because I like you, Maggie. I had a great time with you, and I don't mean just the sex, although that was phenomenal."

"It was phenomenal," she agreed.

"So, Miss Maggie Malone, would you go out on a date with me?"

"I would love to."

I let out a breath of relief. Since she had Ella, I knew I would need to work around her schedule. "Great! What works for you?"

She paused and I thought for a moment that we got disconnected. "Friday night? Say 5:15 until 7:45?"

I choked back my surprise. "Wow! That's very…specific. I was hoping for a little more time with you."

Maggie sighed. "I know. I'm sorry. It's just that Friday is when Ella's dad takes her to dinner from five until eight. She's never met anyone I've dated. I kind of want to keep it that way for now."

"Ever?" Jeez, Ella was six. My instincts about Maggie being a mama bear were spot on.

"Never. God, this is embarrassing. Honestly, I haven't dated much at all and I didn't want to introduce Ella to any of them. I can't parade men in and out of her life. I don't want to be that kind of mom. Most guys decided on the first date they didn't want to be with a woman who had a child anyway, so there was really no point."

Now it was my turn to sigh, but Maggie was right for being protective of her daughter. I wouldn't want Ella around me either. If our time was limited, dinner and a fuck were out. There would only be time for one or the other. "I get it Maggie. Text me your address and I'll pick you up for dinner. You'll be back in plenty of time for Ella's drop-off."

"I'm sorry, Chase. This is the way it has to be until we know where this is going. If you want to change your mind, I'll understand."

Sure, I was disappointed but if I really wanted to see Maggie, I had to play by her rules. Chances were, she'd decide I wasn't good enough for her child, but I was willing to take the leap. "I'm not changing my mind, Red. Besides, I'm pretty sure you swiped one of my shirts when you were here."

She laughed. "Yeah, I did. Do you want it back?"

I figured that's where my shirt had gone. "Nah. It looks better on you anyway, especially with nothing underneath."

"Hmmmm. What should I wear for Friday? And I'm not wearing that shirt with nothing underneath." She laughed.

"I'm a casual kind of guy. Wear those sexy jeans and boots again. They make your ass look amazing."

"Well, crap. You're making me blush."

"Give me another night alone with you and I'll do more than that." Images of our last night together seared my mind and began to make my jeans a little tighter.

"Ummm… that's definitely something to look forward to."

Draven popped his head into my studio the next day. "Did she get the flowers?"

I ran my hand through my shaggy hair. "Yeah, but I messed up."

Draven furrowed his eyebrows. "How so?"

"They went to her classroom and the card wasn't exactly school appropriate. I didn't even think about it when I wrote it. Luckily, no one else saw the card. But still, I felt like an ass."

He shrugged. "It could have been worse. Lesson learned. Next time you'll be more aware. So, inappropriateness aside, did she like the flowers?"

"She did. We've got a date tomorrow night."

My friend quirked an eyebrow at me. "You don't seem very excited about it."

I dropped the pen in my hand and let out a huff. "No, I totally am. It's just… she doesn't want her daughter to know we're going out. It's like a big secret. I have to pick Maggie up after Ella leaves with her dad and have her back before eight. It's different is all. I'm used to spending the whole evening with a woman, not just dinner." I scratched at the stubble on my chin. "Actually, I don't usually do dinner at all." *How fucked up was that?*

Draven sat on the chair in my studio. "Well, at least she didn't say no. Layla fought me tooth and nail about taking her out. I took her to mini-golf on our first date." He pointed to himself. "Do I look like a mini-golf kind of guy?"

I leaned back and laughed. "I bet she kicked your ass too."

His head tilted to the side. "You know she did. Tore me up one side and down the other. I had no choice but to redeem myself on the go-kart track."

I scanned his body from head to toe. Draven was a big dude. "You even fit in a go-kart?"

"Yeah, I fit. But, damn, you should have seen her ass bending over in those jeans that night."

He had a dopey look on his face, and I couldn't resist. "Yeah, I been looking at Layla's ass for five years. I know just what jeans you're talking about."

That dopey look disappeared lightening quick and his eyes narrowed. "You shouldn't be staring at my girl's ass. It's not cool."

I couldn't help bursting out in laughter. "Don't get your dick in a twist. I'm totally fucking with you. You know Layla's like a sister to me."

He didn't look so sure. Draven and Layla had only been together a few months. "You guys never…." He paused, not wanting to say the words.

I gave him a blank stare just to fuck with him some more. "What?"

Draven grimaced and let out a little growl. "You know?"

"What?"

"You know what I'm asking," He growled again, deeper this time like he was seriously considering ripping out my jugular.

The gig was up. I liked my life a little too much and knew when not to push it too far. "Nah, man. No offense, but I like my women a little more demure. Layla kind of scares the shit out of me, and I'm not too much of a man to admit it. She needed someone like you to tame all her… shall I say, intensity?"

Now it was his turn to chuckle. "You don't gotta tiptoe around it. We both know she can be batshit crazy, but it's kinda why I love her. She's a wild contradiction. Soft as a kitten one minute and fierce as a tiger the next."

"Exaaactly." I nodded. "I like a little 'bad' in my girls," I finger quoted. "But when I say bad, I mean wild in bed bad, not stab me in my sleep bad."

Draven quirked an eyebrow. "And Maggie?"

"She's definitely got an inner bad girl waiting to break free. I just don't know if she's ready to admit it. She's got a daughter," I stated the obvious.

"You knew this was going to be different when you decided to pursue her. Keep it casual and give it some time. If she's not down with it, then you move on. But if she is…" He waggled his eyebrows suggestively.

"True." I scratched my head. "I think I'm gonna take her up to The Creek for dinner at the Italian Bistro and then over to the gazebo. They always have a band on Friday night. Like you said, keep it casual."

"See. You got this." He cuffed me on the shoulder.

I checked my appointments for the next day. "Do you think you can take my four o'clock appointment tomorrow?"

"My schedule is clear. Who is it?"

I chuckled. "Cassandra. I started a tat on her ass yesterday, but she wussed out on the coloring. I'm supposed to finish it tomorrow. Honestly, I think she just wanted to see me again."

"Are you out of your mind? Layla will kill me if I get anywhere near Cassandra's ass. That thing is lethal. Reschedule with her. If things don't go well on your date, there will always be Cassandra's ass."

Chapter 10
Maggie

"Are you going out, Momma?"

I sat in front of my vanity and applied one last coat of mascara. "Yep. I'm going to dinner, ladybug. Just like you and Daddy."

"On a date?" Ella asked innocently, looking at me through the mirror.

Ever since our talk in the car, Ella had been asking me about having a boyfriend.

"With a friend," I answered vaguely, while swiping some blush over her tiny cheeks. "Now you look just like me."

"Are you going to dinner with Roxy?" she asked while checking her reflection.

I hooked my earrings through my ears. "Not tonight. With a different friend."

"Is it Chase?"

My baby seemed to be obsessed with the man she met at the costume store. I didn't want to lie to her. "Yes. I'm going out to dinner with Chase."

"Is it a date?"

I brushed Ella's hair behind her ear. "Do you even know what a date is?"

"Yep. Andy said his mom goes on dates."

Again, with this Andy kid. "And what did he tell you about dates?"

"That you hold hands, and the boy buys you stuff and if the girl likes it, she'll kiss the boy. And then bam," she smacked her little hands together, "they're boyfriend and girlfriend." Ella smiled, showing me her missing teeth. She was very proud of herself, thinking she had it all figured out.

I hugged her tight, wishing I could keep her naïve to the world of adults. "It's a little more complicated than that. Chase and I are just friends."

"Are you gonna be boyfriend and girlfriend?"

"I don't know, ladybug. How would you feel about that?" This was new territory for me, and I wasn't sure how to navigate it.

Ella shrugged her shoulders. "Would he read me stories and take me to McDonald's?"

I laughed at how simple it was in her world. "Probably."

"Then I'm okay with it." She ran off to put her shoes on for her weekly trip to her favorite place. Sadly, it was the chicken nuggets and playscape that got her so excited, not her dad.

A few minutes later, Jeff pulled in the driveway and honked his horn. He couldn't even be bothered to come to the door for his daughter. I took Ella's hand in mine. "How about we keep my dinner with Chase a secret? You know, it'll be a girl thing."

"I'm a good secret keeper."

"I know you are." I hooked my pinky with hers. "You're my favorite girl. I love you."

"Love you too, Momma!"

I gave her a kiss before she ran out the door to her father. Jeff got out of the car and helped Ella into the back seat. I waved goodbye and watched the man I used to love drive away with my baby.

I was a terrible mom. What kind of mom asked a six-year-old to keep a secret? I had no idea how Jeff would react to me going out on a date. It was ridiculous to be worried. Chances were he wouldn't give two shits. He'd proven as much to me last weekend. I just wanted to know what this was between Chase and me before Jeff got all up in my business.

I put Jeff out of my mind and finished prepping for my date, spritzing on some perfume and applying lip gloss. I fluffed my hair in the mirror and declared myself ready. The last time I was on a date was over a year ago, with Jeremy. All he did was talk about himself and going to the gym. Dodged a bullet with that one.

The doorbell rang. I rushed through the hallway picking up Ella's toys and tossing them into a big basket next to the couch. I should have cleaned up earlier but was preoccupied with explaining what a date was to my child. Tripping over her backpack, I kicked it aside and fumbled my way to the door.

Breathe in, breathe out.

I open the door for Chase. "Hey."

He held out a single red rose. "Hello, beautiful."

I took the flower from him. "Thank you. Ready to go?"

Chase stepped inside uninvited. "Not yet." He wrapped one arm around my waist as the other slid up my neck and into my hair cupping the back of my head.

80

Chase pressed his mouth to mine and ran his tongue along the seam of my lips. I opened for him and he slipped his tongue inside, kissing me in the most erotic way. When he was finished, he pulled back and gazed into my eyes. "Now I'm ready."

I licked my bruised lips, trying to recover from his kiss. "I should…uh…put this in some water," I stuttered, while holding up the rose. I quickly turned and headed for the kitchen. I grabbed a bud vase from the cabinet over the stove and filled it with water, then stuck the flower inside.

Chase leaned against the island in the kitchen. "I like your house. Very homey feeling."

I cringed as I looked at it through Chase's eyes. There was no doubt a little girl lived here. Evidence was everywhere, from the tiny shoes next to the door to the *Frozen* lunchbox on the counter to the stuffed dog sitting on the couch. "It's not much, but it's more than enough for us."

He looked out the kitchen window, where Ella's swing set stood. "Great yard. Reminds me of the house I grew up in."

I smiled. "Where'd you grow up?"

"Here. I've never moved more than five miles from that house." He gave the swing set another look. "Wish I would have had one of those growing up."

"My dad and brother put it up for Ella before she was even big enough to use it. She loves the damn thing."

Chase grabbed me by the belt loops and pulled me into his chest. "You ready for dinner?"

I stared into his aqua eyes. "I'm starving."

He pushed his hips into mine. "Me too, but let's talk about dinner. I hope you like Italian. I made us reservations, so if we leave now, we should be right on time."

With the way Chase made me feel, dinner was the last thing on my mind. I wanted him to hoist me up on the kitchen counter and… "Then we should go."

It would have been so easy to skip dinner and head right to the bedroom, but if I wanted to see if Chase and I could be anything beyond bedmates, we needed to leave and quickly. I grabbed my purse off the table and headed out.

Chase was a perfect gentleman, opening doors and pulling out my chair. When the pretty waitress came to take our order, never once did Chase flirt with her or stare at the ample cleavage she proudly displayed.

"So…" I began, "tell me about Chase. I don't know anything about you besides you're extremely talented as an artist and have excellent stalker skills."

He gave me a wink and a smile that dimpled on one side. "I think you know a little more than that."

I certainly did. And now all I could think about was the steamy night we spent together. "Touché."

He reached over and ran his fingers along my cheek. "You're blushing again."

I waved a hand in front of my face. "Am I? It got hot in here all of a sudden."

Chase smirked at me. "It's not hot in here, Red. That's all you."

If I thought it was hot before, it just went up another ten degrees.

Seeing my discomfort, he straightened up in his chair very seriously. "So, what do you want to know?"

I took a sip of my Merlot. "Let's start with your last name. My stalker skills are not quite up there with yours."

"Ahhh... didn't look me up on the Forever Inked website, huh? Great thing, the internet. It wouldn't have mattered because Zack only lists our first names anyway. He respects our privacy. Some of our clients can be a little wacky."

I rolled my hand to get him moving along. "And your last name is...?"

"Montgomery"

I let that rattle around in my head a little. *Chase Montgomery. Maggie Montgomery.* It had a nice ring to it. Not as great as Malone, but then again, I wouldn't have to change my monogram. *Whoa!* Where did that thought come from?

I struggled to put myself back on level ground. "Southern roots?"

He chuckled. "My mom and dad were both born and bred in Alabama. They moved up here when my mom was pregnant with me. My dad got a job at Chrysler. Then my grandma moved in with us after my dad passed away. Grams is the sweetest darn thing ever. Southern through and through."

I laughed at his enthusiasm. "She sounds great."

Chase's face softened. "She's the best. I'm lucky to still have her."

I continued my inquisition. "Pets?"

"Nada, unless you count Not My Cat."

I choked on my wine. "Excuse me?"

"Big tomcat that comes around all the time. He's not mine, but I feed him. He's cool." Chase grabbed his beer and took a swig. "So, tell me more about Maggie."

"You already know the most important parts of me. There isn't much else. I go to work and I'm a mom. My life isn't that exciting."

The waitress delivered our entrees, giving me an out from really answering the question. My life was boring compared to his and it was the last thing I wanted to delve into. No one really wanted to hear the ins and outs of being a single mom.

When she left, Chase continued to prod. "I don't believe you. I saw something in you the other night. You're like the Catholic school girl who goes wild with a little freedom."

My insides churned. He wasn't wrong. "Maybe." I swirled around the wine in my glass, trying to formulate my thoughts. "I used to be wild and spontaneous, but that ended the day I found out I was pregnant. I didn't have any choice but to grow up fast, because it wasn't just about me anymore. I had this tiny little person depending on me for everything and what I wanted didn't matter anymore. The only thing that mattered was her."

Chase cocked his head at me. "What do you miss most since you've had Ella?"

No one had ever asked me that question before. I pondered my answer carefully. "Spontaneity and…" I covered my face with my hands. "You're going to think this is stupid."

He pulled my hands from my face and gave me that dimpled grin. "Then you definitely have to tell me."

I was embarrassed to say it, but there was no way Chase would let me back down now. "Dancing. I haven't been dancing in years."

"That's not stupid. You might be surprised, but I'm a pretty decent dancer."

I laughed. "You mean dancing, or bumping and grinding?"

He waved me off. "Ah, tomato tomahto. It's all the same. Dancing is just sex standing up."

"You would say that. Yeah, I loved clubbing and I miss that too, but I meant real dancing. You know, leotards and tights. I started taking lessons when I was three. By the time I hit elementary school, my mom enrolled me in every class she could: ballet, jazz, lyrical, hip-hop. God, I used to love being on the stage, even in college."

Chase sat back in his chair and studied me. "You should see your face right now. You're practically glowing."

"It was a big part of my life for a long time."

"I would have liked to have seen that. Could you do that thing where you put your leg up next to your head?"

"Yeah." I chuckled. "I was pretty flexible back then."

He leaned forward, placing his elbows on the table. "Damn. Think you can still do it?"

I rolled my eyes at his absurdity. "Doubtful. It was a while ago. I'm lucky if I make it to a yoga class once a month."

He waggled his eyebrows. "I know a way we can practice limbering you up."

I tossed my napkin at his head. "Get out of here, you goofball."

Chase caught the napkin in one hand. "Just saying."

Bantering with Chase was fun. He was so easygoing, and the conversation flowed effortlessly. It was like the two of us had known each other for years instead of days.

I just wondered how many days we had together before he decided a woman with a child was too much for him. If my dating history was any indication, it would be sooner rather than later.

Our days together were numbered. It was only a matter of time.

Chapter 11
Chase

After dinner, Maggie and I strolled through the outdoor mall hand in hand. Being with her felt natural. I was learning her quirks and what made her tick.

Of course I wanted to take her to bed, but it wasn't at the forefront of my mind. I enjoyed just spending time with her like this, our hands swinging between us.

Music echoed in the air and I steered us toward the gazebo. The band covered old favorites that were sure to be a hit with any crowd. Families and couples surrounded the gazebo listening and swaying to the music.

An elderly couple sat on one of the benches holding hands. I wondered how long they had been together. They were both wrinkled and gray, but the way the man looked at the woman couldn't be missed. He adored her and thought she hung the moon.

Maggie noticed them too. "That's sweet. Don't you think?"

I agreed. "They're cute together. I wonder how long they've been married."

"My guess is a long time. Did you think you'd still be single at almost thirty? Ever consider getting married before?"

Maggie's questions caught me off guard. Memories flooded my head, "Once. I thought she was the one. We were engaged, but it didn't work out."

My hands covered Meredith's eyes as I led her to my bedroom. I'd put a lot of thought into Sweetest Day this year.

"Chase, what did you do?" She tugged at my hands.

I kept them tight over her eyes. "Stop, you're going to ruin the surprise. Just go with it. Trust me for once."

"Fine, but all I got you was a card. I didn't know we were doing gifts this year."

I stopped when we got to the threshold of my bedroom. "You don't have to get me a gift. You give me yourself and that's more than I deserve. It's like getting a gift every day." I removed my hands from her eyes. "Happy Sweetest Day!"

Meredith took in the room before her. I had transformed it into a love nest just for us. Candles flickered on every surface and red rose petals covered the bed. "You did all this for me?"

"I'd do anything for you, baby."

She wandered into the room, her fingers brushing over the dresser as she went. "This is amazing, Chase. I love you."

I reached into my front pocket, palmed the ring I'd bought her and dropped to one knee. I took her hand in mine. "Meredith, you're the love of my life."

Her free hand shot up to cover her mouth. "Oh my god!"

"I know we're young, but I know I want to be with you forever. Will you marry me?"

She crashed into my arms and I fell back onto the bedroom floor. "Yes! Yes, I'll marry you." The tiny ring I bought slipped from my hand and clinked on the hardwood floor. She deserved better, but it was all I could afford.

Meredith crushed her lips to mine. We were a mess of hands and lips and tongues. We made love right there on the bedroom floor. When we slowed down, I swiped the ring from the floor and slipped it on her finger. "Move in with me. I promise to take care of you. Let me start now."

"What happened?"

I was lost in my own head, "What?"

Maggie squeezed my hand, "I asked what happened. To the girl?"

I struggled about how to explain without giving away the gory details. "We were young, and I was stupid. She left me and never looked back."

She eyed me with sympathy. "I'm sorry."

"Don't be. It was my own fault." I shrugged it off.

"When was the last time you saw her?"

I counted back in my head. "Over seven years ago." It was hard to believe so much time had gone by.

"Where'd she go?"

"I don't know. She made it clear that she was done with me and I respected that."

"Huh. You never looked her up on Facebook or Instagram? You were never curious?"

"Nope." Sure, I was curious, but the things that happened couldn't be changed. If I looked her up, I would just break my own heart again. I couldn't take the chance of seeing her with another man, happily living the life that should have been ours. Nope. I wasn't going there.

Instead, I focused on the woman in front of me. She wasn't Meredith, but she was the best thing that had come into my life in a very long time. The band started to play Van Morrison's "Brown Eyed Girl" and I pulled her out into the crowd of people. "Dance with me?"

"Here?"

I held her one hand in mine and wrapped my other arm around her waist, pulling her snug to my chest. "Yes, here. You said you missed dancing, so now's your chance. I know how to do more than bump and grind, Miss Malone."

She rested her free hand on my shoulder. "Is that right, Mr. Montgomery?"

"Uh-huh." I started moving her to the music. We weren't the only ones dancing, other couples joined us and a few young kids bopped around the edges of the patio.

We hammed it up, singing at the top of our lungs, not caring what anybody thought. I twirled her under my arm and soon we found a rhythm that was all ours. At the end of the song, I dipped her low and finished with a kiss. The bystanders hooted and hollered in encouragement.

I pulled Maggie out of the dip and into my chest. Her cheeks were flushed, and she was out of breath. "Oh my god! That was so much fun!"

My arm wrapped around her shoulder as I led her off the patio. "Come on, I'll get you a hot chocolate before I take you home."

"What time is it?"

"Quarter after seven."

"Already. I can't believe how fast this night went."

I pecked her on the forehead. "Don't worry. I'll get you home in plenty of time, Cinderella."

Maggie frowned. "Does it make me a bad mom that I don't want our night to end?"

I bopped her on the nose with my index finger. "Nope. It means you had fun and maybe you'll go out with me again."

"You mean I haven't scared you away yet?"

I shook my head. "Not even close."

I bought us hot chocolates and we sipped them on the way home. We pulled up in front of her house at 7:42. I met her in front of my truck and took ahold of her hand as I walked her to the door.

She pulled out her key and stuck it in the lock. "Thank you for taking me out tonight. I had a great time."

"It was my pleasure." I wasn't letting her get away without one last kiss. I pinned her against the door, caging her in with my arms. "When can I see you again?"

Her eyes locked on mine. "Soon. I'll call you."

That was all I needed. I pressed my hips to hers, making sure she knew how she affected me. "I'll be waiting." With that, I devoured her lips one last time before I said goodbye. I slowly backed away. "See you soon, Red."

I hopped into my truck and watched as she let herself into the house. Once she was safe inside, I backed out of the driveway. As I pulled away a black BMW pulled into the place my truck had just vacated. I slowed a bit, and watched Ella jump out of the back seat. A hint of jealousy crept into my chest. He would always have something I didn't have with Maggie. A connection. That connection being Ella. She tied them together no matter what Maggie felt for Jeff.

Chapter 12
Maggie

Ella had just finished her ballet class and I promised to take her for a Slurpee afterward. I was headed toward the 7-Eleven when an indicator light flashed on my dashboard. My left rear tire was losing pressure and fast. "Goddamnit!"

"You said a bad word, Momma." Ella frowned at me from the back seat.

"Yes, I did!" I steered the car into the closest driveway, which happened to be a crappy gas station and of course wasn't a service station. I pulled to the side by the air pumps. I needed to get us home. That was my main priority. "Stay in the car, Ella. Momma has to put air in our tire."

"What happened?" she asked.

"I'm not sure, just stay in the car." I hopped out and inspected my tire. It was as flat as my chest back in seventh grade. *What the hell?* This was the last thing I needed today. Trying to stay optimistic, I popped my quarters into the air compressor and slipped the hose over the tire valve. I heard the hiss instantly. As fast as the air was going in, it was coming out. There was no way I was going to inflate the tire.

I popped the trunk and pulled up the cover that hid my spare tire. I stared at the tire and the jack. Who was I kidding? I had no idea how to change a flat tire. I could call my dad, but my parents were in Traverse City for their anniversary. I mentally ticked my dad off my list of emergency contacts. Next was my brother, but he worked in the city and it would take him at least an hour to get here. As a last ditch effort, I called Jeff. It rang and rang until his voicemail picked up, *This is Jeff. Please leave your name and I'll get back to you as soon as I can.* I left a frustrated message. "It's Maggie. Your daughter and I are stranded. Answer your goddamn phone." I stabbed at the end button. *Just fucking great!*

Ella opened her door and hopped out in her leotard and tutu, inspecting the tire with me.

"I told you to stay in the car."

"That's a flatty," she pointed out the obvious.

I took a deep breath, determined not to take my frustration out on her. "I know. I called your dad, but he didn't pick up."

Ella shrugged. "So, call your boyfriend."

I looked at her like she'd sprouted a second head. "What boyfriend?"

She kicked at the tire. "Chase. He'll help us."

I don't know when my little girl had gotten so smart, but it wasn't a half-bad idea. "He's not my boyfriend," I stressed.

Ella rolled her eyes at me. "He took you to dinner. He'll help us."

Shit! I didn't want to be the girl who needed to be saved, but my options were limited. "Fine, but he's not my boyfriend. He's just a friend."

"Can he fix our flatty?"

Honestly, I didn't know. "I hope so." I dialed Chase's number and waited while it rang and rang.

I had just about given up hope when he answered. "Hey, Red."

"Hi, Chase. What are you doing?"

"I'm between appointments. What's up, beautiful?"

I hesitated before asking, "Do you know how to change a flat tire? Ella and I are stranded."

"Sure. Where are you?"

I sent a thank you up to the heavens. "The Mobile station at 23 and VanDyke. If you're busy I'll find someone else. I just…"

"Stop, Red. I'll be there in ten minutes. Hold tight. I'm coming."

"Thank you. I was going to call my brother, but he's an hour away."

"I'm already out the door. It's not a problem. I'm happy to help." I heard his keys jingle and the sound of his truck starting. "Are you off the road?"

"Yeah. I managed to pull into the gas station. I tried to fill the tire with air, but it just keeps leaking out," I explained.

"Don't worry, Red. We'll get it handled. I'll be there soon." The call disconnected and I wasn't sure if I should laugh or cry.

A flat tire shouldn't have been something that tilted my world off its axis, but it did. I didn't like being helpless and that's how I felt. I took pride in taking care of myself and Ella. I was pissed at Jeff. If he was any kind of father, I could have depended on him to help us. But as usual he fell short.

Ella stared up at me with her big blue eyes. "Is Chase coming?"

I held out my hand to her and she put her tiny hand in mine. "He is. Come on, ladybug, maybe they have Slurpees inside." We walked into the gas station and luckily, they had a slushie machine. "Do you want cherry or Coke?"

"Cherry, please."

I filled a small cup with the frozen drink and stuck a straw in it. "I'm sorry we're stuck here, ladybug. Chase should be here soon."

She shrugged her shoulders. "Shit happens."

I threw my hand up over my mouth to cover my giggle. "Ellanora Riley, where did you learn to talk like that?"

She rolled her eyes. "I've heard you say it a million times."

Damnit! She wasn't wrong. I wasn't as careful as I should have been with my language. "Well, just because I say it doesn't mean it's okay for you to say it. You shouldn't say *shit.* It's a grown-up word."

She rolled her eyes again. "I'm growing up, Momma. I'm in kindergarten now."

I closed my eyes and let out a measured breath. She was only six. The teenage years were going to be a joy. I could already hear my mother telling me it was karma. "Kindergarten is not old enough to use swear words and if you talk like that at school Ms. Jacobs will have you in the office so fast your head will spin."

She headed toward the check-out counter. "I know I can't say it at school, but we're in a gas station. Nobody cares."

She had me there. I scoped out the teenage cashier who was more interested in her phone than the customers. She wouldn't give a shit that my six-year-old was swearing. I decided to let it go. There were bigger fish to fry, like getting my tire fixed.

After paying for the slushie we walked back out to the car. "Hey, ladybug?"

"Yeah?"

"How about you not say anything to Chase about being my boyfriend. We're just friends, okay?" I was afraid Ella was going to scare him off before we even started. "And don't get attached. I don't know how much he'll be around."

"You mean like Daddy?" she asked sipping her drink.

My heart broke for her. She deserved better. I took her over to the parking block next to my car and sat us down. I pushed her curly hair over her ear. "You know Daddy loves you, right?"

"He has to because he's my dad. Isn't that the rules?"

I pressed my lips together, trying to figure out how to explain things to her. "You're right, it should be the rules, but it isn't. Daddy loves you because you're his baby girl. You should have seen his face on the day you were born. He fell in love with you right away."

"But he didn't fall in love with you?"

I shook my head. "Nope."

"Is that why you didn't get married?"

"Yeah, I guess so."

"What about Chase? He could love you. Then you wouldn't have to be alone all the time."

I hugged Ella tight and my words caught in my throat. "I'm not alone. I have you and that's all that matters."

I was saved from saying anything else when Chase's big, black truck pulled into the lot. He hopped out and walked over to us.

I stood and shoved my hands in my pockets. I didn't want to give Ella the wrong idea by giving him a hug. "Hey. Thanks for coming. We really appreciate it."

He mirrored my gesture. "It's no problem. I couldn't leave a fairy princess to be stranded at a gas station." He kneeled in front of Ella. "Where are your wings, pretty girl?"

She put one hand on her hip and held her drink with the other. "That's just for Halloween. I'm not a real fairy princess, silly. Today I'm a ballerina." She did an awkward twirl and almost tipped herself over.

Chase grabbed her by the hips to steady her before she toppled to the ground. "Be careful."

"I'm still learning that twirl thing. It's not as easy as it looks. My dance teacher says I gotta practice every day or I'm gonna get a bruised butt."

Chase couldn't contain his laughter. "Then I guess you better listen to her because nobody wants a bruised butt."

"I only fell three times today," she said, holding up her fingers. "She said that's called progress."

If I didn't stop her, Ella would talk Chase's ear off. "Okay, ladybug, Chase doesn't want to hear about your bruised butt. He's here to help us with our tire, remember?"

Ella scrunched her nose up. "It's a flatty."

"Yeah? Let's see." He walked over to my car and checked out the tire. "It's a flatty all right." Then he looked at the tire in my trunk. "I can change it, but that spare isn't meant to drive on permanently. It'll get you to the tire shop, but you'll need a new one."

I ran a hand over my face. It was another extra cost I really didn't need to incur, but what choice did I have? "Okay" I sighed.

Chase went to work pulling out the spare and the jack. "There's a shop about a mile up the road. I'll follow you and they should be able to get this fixed in no time. They might even be able to repair it instead of replace it."

"Sounds like a plan. Thank you."

"You don't have to keep thanking me. I don't mind." Chase used the tire iron to loosen the lug nuts, then jacked up my car and replaced the tire within a few minutes.

Once the spare was in place, Chase followed us to the tire shop. The three of us walked into a very crowded waiting area. "Let me go talk to the guy," Chase said, before taking my keys and going to the counter.

It was nice to have someone handle this for me instead of having to do it myself.

He chatted with the mechanic for a few minutes and then came back to us. "I've got good news and bad news. They can fix your tire, but it's a two hour wait."

I sank down into an empty chair and plopped Ella on my lap. "It is what it is. Thanks for your help. We've got it from here."

"I'm hungry, Momma."

"You just had a slushie. You'll be fine," I snapped at Ella.

"That was because I was thirsty from dance, but now I'm hungry," she whined.

I pulled out my phone and checked the time. It was way past lunch. "Maybe we can walk somewhere. There's got to be something to eat around here."

"I'm not leaving you here alone," Chase piped up. "I've got an appointment soon, but I have an idea. Let me make a quick call." He pulled out his phone and walked around the corner. When he returned, he knelt in front of Ella. "How do you feel about a pizza party?"

She waved her hands around excitedly. "I love pizza! Pepperoni is my favorite, but none of those green peppers Momma likes. They taste yucky."

"Got it. Pepperoni only." Chase took Ella's hand and started walking her toward the door.

"Ah… hello?" *Where was he going with my child?* "Anyone mind filling me in on what's going on here?" I was a little concerned that my daughter would so willingly go with Chase, even though she barely knew him.

Ella looked at me like it was obvious. "Weren't you listening? We're having a pizza party."

"Yeah, I got that much. Chase, can I talk to you for a minute?"

Chase strolled back to me. "What's up?"

I knew he didn't have experience dealing with kids, so I tried my best to be patient. "Here's the problem... I'm the mom, so I kind of need to know the plan."

He hung his head like a scolded puppy. "I fucked up again, didn't I?"

It wasn't my goal to make him feel bad, but he had to know the ground rules. I softened my voice. "No, you didn't fuck up, just fill me in."

He sighed. "I have an appointment in a half hour, but I didn't want to leave you here alone. I called the shop and Zack said it would be fine if you two hung out there. I've got a bunch of art stuff Ella can play with and Rissa said she'd order pizza. When your car is ready, I'll bring you back to pick it up. I thought it was a good idea, but I guess I should have asked you first."

His plan was actually really sweet and well thought out. I leaned in and kissed him on the cheek. "Thank you. I think Ella would really enjoy that. Are you sure we won't be in the way?"

"Positive. Zack's become a big softy since his daughter was born and Rissa... well, she's Rissa. You'll see what I mean once you get to know her."

"Is it weird that I'm a little starstruck, knowing we're having pizza with Rissa Black?" I asked as I grabbed Ella's hand.

"Nah. I get it. But to us, she's just Rissa. I don't think the fame has really hit her yet."

Ella reached for Chase's hand and she swung herself between us. "Are we getting pizza now?"

It warmed my heart that she had taken so easily to Chase, even if it was a little scary. "Yes, ladybug, but first we have to get your booster seat."

She huffed. "But I'm big now."

"Not that big," I reminded her.

She looked to Chase for help. He shook his head. "Don't look at me. Your mom is the boss."

"Dang it! Your supposed to be on my side," Ella complained.

He picked Ella up and settled her on his hip. "We're both on your side, princess bug. We want you to be safe."

I smiled as I pulled Ella's booster from my back seat. Chase was a fast learner, and he was wonderful with my daughter. He'd even come up with his own nickname for her.

Chase opened the back door of his truck for me and I secured Ella's seat in place. He sat her in the truck and buckled her in tight. After we shut Ella inside, he said, "You'll have to show me how to do that."

I gave him a wink. "It's not hard. You'll be an expert in no time."

We both hopped into the truck and Ella continued to complain about the booster. "You guys both suck. I hate this seat. I thought Chase was going to be cool, but he's not."

That was enough. Turning in my seat, I lost it with her. "Ellanora, I know you're tired and hungry, but if you say *shit* or *suck* one more time, I'm going to totally lose it with you. Chase was nice enough to come help us and you're being rude. Apologize right now!"

She cowered in her seat. "Sorry for being rude, Chase."

He peeked at her in the rearview mirror. "Apology accepted. We just want you to be safe, we're not trying to be mean."

I was embarrassed about Ella's outburst and mine. "I'm sorry you had to see that."

He grabbed my hand over the console. "It's fine." Then he gave me that sideways smile with one dimple. "Remind me not to get on your bad side."

"It's not my best side, but this day has not gone as planned. I didn't want to inconvenience you and you've been great. I really appreciate it."

He picked up my hand and kissed the back of it. "It's not an inconvenience. If anything, I wish I didn't have to work and I could take the two of you out to eat. I'm just trying to make the best of a bad situation."

Chase pulled into the back lot of Forever Inked. I turned to my sullen girl. "I'm sorry I yelled at you. I love you."

She pursed her lips. "I'm sorry I said you suck. I love you too."

We got out of the truck and Chase already had Ella out of her seat before I could make it around to her side. She held his hand as he led us inside the back entrance. I followed behind them, not knowing what to expect. All I remembered was the beautiful people I had seen at the bar and it was a little intimidating.

When we got inside there was a table set up outside the back office. Markers, colored pencils, and a stack of paper were set up in front of a name card that said *Ella*. My daughter saw her name right away and ran to the seat with her name in front of it. "Is this for me?"

Chase kneeled beside her. "I thought you might like to draw while you were waiting for the pizza."

My girl was clearly excited. "I love drawing. Where did you get all these markers?"

"That's what I do. I draw, but not on paper. I draw on people's skin." He rubbed her arm.

Her eyes popped out. "Can you draw on my skin?"

Chase laughed. "I have someone else waiting, but when I'm done, I'm sure we can come up with something."

"Can you draw me a ladybug? Momma always calls me ladybug," she said excitedly.

"I can." Chase stood and faced me. "Are you going to be okay here? My client just walked in. It'll only take an hour or so."

I took both his hands in mine. "It's perfect. Thank you. Go do what you need to do."

Chase gave me a kiss on the cheek and left to meet with his client, a big, burly guy that honestly was a little scary looking. I sat down next to Ella who was busy creating a masterpiece. "Are you okay?"

"Look at all these markers! My teacher never lets us use markers because they're messy, but I'm a pro."

I looked at the picture she was drawing of herself and a dog. We didn't have a dog, but Ella was always begging for a pet. I considered a dog for about three seconds. Our life was hectic enough, we didn't need to add a dog to the mix. I studied her picture. "Don't forget his tail."

"Oh yeah, I forgot." She quickly drew a long tail that looked more like poop coming out of his butt.

"That's better," I encouraged.

She continued working, poking her tongue out to the side, when Rissa walked in. She was just as beautiful as I remembered from the bar. "Did someone order a pepperoni pizza?"

Ella raised her hand like she was at school. "Me! I like pepperoni pizza as long as it doesn't have those green things on it."

Rissa raised the top of the box and peeked inside. "No green things. This must be yours."

I stood and met her halfway to the table. She was a normal person, I reminded myself. "Hi, Rissa. I don't know if you remember me, but I'm Maggie and this little girl is Ella."

She winked at me. "Course I remember. You're the woman who has Chase's panties in a knot. And that is your beautiful daughter. I remember her from the picture. She's your spitting image."

I was caught off guard. "Thank you. For everything."

She patted me on the arm. "Don't mention it. Chase is family and now you are too."

I must have made a face because she went on. "This place is special. They took me under their wing when they had no reason to. We're one big, dysfunctional family. There isn't a thing I wouldn't do for Chase or anyone else here. If you're important to Chase, then your important to all of us."

I felt the heat creep up my neck. "I'm not sure we're at that point yet. I mean, it's very new and my daughter and I are a package deal. It scares most men away."

"I know all about package deals," she said cryptically. Then she nodded toward Ella. "He called and had me set this up for her. First time he's ever done something like that, and he seems happy. Chase is a good guy he just needs a good woman to steer him in the right direction."

"And you think that woman is me?"

"I think you should give it a chance." She walked over to Ella and started to compliment her artwork. The two of them began chatting like they were old friends.

Zack came out of his office carrying an adorable baby girl. "Hi, Maggie."

I gave him a little wave. "Hi, Zack. Thank you for letting us crash here while my car is being fixed."

"Clarissa wouldn't have it any other way. She's the saint among us sinners."

I quickly surmised that Clarissa was Rissa. Rissa Black. I tucked away my inner fangirl and reached for my wallet. "How much do I owe you for the pizza?"

He put his hand on my arm. "Nothing. It's our pleasure. I had Clarissa get enough for everyone. We all need to eat."

I wasn't comfortable with someone else paying for Ella and me. "Let me give you something."

He shook his head. "Not a chance." He motioned to Rissa and Ella laughing. "That's all the payment I need. She's adorable by the way."

"Don't let the toothless smile fool you. She's full of piss and vinegar."

He bopped the baby in his arms on the nose with his finger. "So is this one, but I wouldn't trade her for the world."

Talking to Chase's friends was easier than I thought it would be. "Me neither."

The dark-haired couple from the bar emerged from the back hall, arms wrapped around each other. Zack reintroduced them to me, even though I clearly remembered them as Draven and Layla. I couldn't forget them because they were the epitome of what love looked like, even if it was a little dark and scary.

Draven clapped his hands together. "I smell lunch."

Layla smacked him on the chest. "You just ate."

He smirked at her. "No, I just had dessert. I'm ready for food now." It was a clear sexual innuendo and I found it erotic. This whole place oozed sex.

Zack frowned. "Can you two behave? We have company and we don't want to scare her off."

I held up my hand in protest, "It's fine. A little dirty talk won't scare me off that easily." *Lie.* These people intimidated the hell out of me. "We've invaded your space, not the other way around."

"Oh, I like her. She'll fit in just fine around here." Layla laughed. I couldn't see how that was true. I was as different from these people as apples were from bananas. She bumped my hip as she walked by. "You're exactly what Chase needs. Pretty, classy, sassy, and a whole lot sexy."

I wasn't sure how to take that, but I smiled anyway. "We're just friends," I said as a reminder to myself. Everyone here was acting as if we were more.

"For now." Layla disappeared into another room and returned with a stack of plates and napkins. She set them on the table. "Dig in, everybody."

I watched as Draven leaned over the table to get his pizza. His facial features were sharp, and his body looked like it had been sculpted from stone. Ella's eyes went wide as she took him in from head to toe. "You're really big."

His face melted into a smile as he took in my daughter and knelt next to her. "And you're really small."

"I'm only six. I'll grow." She poked at his bulging, tattooed arm. "You look like a coloring book. Where did you get all these?"

My brother had a couple of tattoos and so did his partner, Brian, but not like the people in this room. Their arms were covered in artwork and if I had to guess, so were the rest of their bodies. I tried to see Chase's friends through Ella's eyes. I thought it might scare her a little, but she seemed more curious than anything.

Draven laughed at her innocence. "What? You don't have any tattoos?"

She straightened up in her chair and pointed to her own tiny arm. "I got one right here at the fair, but it washed off. Are yours going to wash off?"

He shook his head. "Nope. They're there forever."

"I wish mine was forever, but the butterfly's head came off. Momma said it was time for it to go to butterfly heaven."

"Maybe when you get big you can get a real butterfly tattoo," Draven suggested.

Her face lit up. "Really?"

And that was my cue to interrupt. "Let's not be putting any ideas in her head just yet." I ruffled her hair. "You're too little to think about getting a tattoo, ladybug."

She crossed her arms over her chest. "I'm always too little for everything. I can't wait to get big."

I knew that day was going to come sooner than I'd be ready for. "Sorry, kiddo. You know what you're not too little for?"

"What?" she huffed.

"Pizza. Are you still hungry?"

"I'm always hungry for pizza. It's my favorite!" she exclaimed. And just like that, all thoughts of her getting a tattoo vanished.

Thank God!

Chapter 13
Chase

When I dropped Maggie off at her car, she thanked me profusely. It wasn't necessary. I was glad to spend time with her and Ella, even if the circumstances weren't ideal. Actually, I hardly got to spend any time with her at all. Unfortunately, Clyde's tattoo took longer than anticipated and I only got to spend about ten minutes with them before Maggie's car was ready. It was just enough time to draw a ladybug on Ella's arm with a Sharpie. Ella was thrilled and wasted no time walking around and showing everyone her new "tattoo".

I was hoping Maggie would invite me over later, but that didn't happen. So now I was sitting on my balcony like a sad sap, drinking a beer, and thinking about the woman with fiery hair that had my insides all twisted up. Before Maggie, I would have been sitting in a bar, turning on the charm in hopes of picking someone up for the night. Now, she was the only woman I wanted to spend time with. I hadn't done monogamy since Meredith and forgot what it felt like. And honestly, it felt a little pathetic, sitting around hoping Maggie would call.

I watched as Not My Cat walked along the narrow ledge of my apartment building, stretched his paws forward to the railing and hopped down onto the balcony. "Back for more, huh?"

He sat patiently at my feet and let out a loud meow. I stared down at him and he stared back at me, daring me to look away. We sat that way for a while, stuck in a staring contest until my eyes started to cross. I shook my head, blinking my eyes and straightening out my vision. "Damn, you're good at that."

He let out another loud meow, declaring himself the winner of our odd standoff.

"Yeah, yeah, I know what you want." I reached behind me, grabbed the container of treats, and sprinkled some on the ground for him.

My phone buzzed with a text alert. I snatched it off the table, instantly disappointed it wasn't Maggie.

Mom: *Are you coming over for breakfast tomorrow?*
Me: *No*

Irritated, I set my phone aside only to have it start ringing. I should have known my one word answer wasn't going to suffice. I picked it up and took my frustration out on her. "I'm not coming."

My mom sighed. "Why not?"

Really? My mom was a smart lady, she already knew why. "I need a break."

She huffed. "A break? From your family? From your mother who carried you for nine months and your sweet grandmother who might not be around that much longer? She's old, you know."

God, she laid it on thick. One thing my mom was good at was a guilt trip. "There's nothing wrong with Grams. She'll probably outlive all of us. I'll stop by one day after work." I hoped that would satisfy her nagging, but I was wrong.

"Your Grams hasn't been feeling well. She'd really like to see you."

That was a lie. "I talked to her yesterday. She did a Zumba class at the senior center and went to lunch with the ladies from church. Seemed she was feeling just fine."

"Well, she might have overdone it. She was moving slow all day. She's not a spring chicken anymore. I'd hate for you to have regrets about not seeing her one last time."

I rolled my eyes. "Oh jeez, Mom. Grams is not dying. I don't want to see Amber. End of story."

"Why not?"

"I'm sorry, were you not there to witness the shit show last week? I'm sick of her stabbing at me every little chance she gets. I'm done putting up with her crap."

"Amber feels bad about what happened. You should give her another chance."

My mother clearly lived in a fantasy world. "No, she doesn't. She's been doing it for years. I've given her lots of chances. I'm done. Unless it's an apology coming from her lips, I don't want to talk to her."

"Ever?"

I raked a hand through my hair. "I don't know. Not for a while."

"You're breaking my heart, Chase. I already lost your father. I don't want to lose you too."

She was so dramatic. Using my dad's death was an all-time low. I sighed. "You're not losing me. I promise to come by another night."

She perked up. "Will you bring your new girlfriend?"

I should have never said anything about Maggie. Grams and mom were desperate for me to settle down. All I'd done was plant a seed for them to water. "She's really busy. I'll see what I can do. And to be honest, I'm not sure we're at that point yet."

My mom kept prodding. "Not at a point to meet your family? What kind of girl doesn't have time to meet her boyfriend's family? What is she so busy doing?"

For Christ's sake! "Will you promise not to freak out if I tell you?" I knew exactly how my mother was going to react to Ella.

"I don't freak out, Chase. Wait! She's not a stripper is she?"

I rolled my eyes. "Oh my god, Mom, no! She's not a stripper. She's a teacher. I told you that."

"Yeah, but they don't make much money. Are you sure she's not moonlighting?"

"Pretty damn sure, yeah."

"Then what's she doing that you think I'll freak out about?"

I cringed because I knew what was going to come next. "She's busy being a mom. She has a six-year-old daughter."

"I'm gonna be a grandma again? Oh my goodness! I have to tell Grams. She'll be so excited!"

And that right there was why I didn't want to tell her. She would have me married off in no time and planning sleepovers with her new granddaughter. "Mom, stop! That's a long way off. I don't want you to get overexcited. Maggie and I haven't even decided what our relationship is yet. We're still figuring it out. I don't want you to get attached to Ella or worse yet have Ella get attached to you. She's still getting used to me. That's why Maggie and I are taking it slow."

"Oh," she said dejectedly, like I'd just rained all over her parade. "I guess that makes sense. But you'll still come by, even without her?"

"Yes. I promise."

"And when you figure out your relationship, I'll get to meet Maggie and her daughter?"

"If and when that time comes, yes."

"Okay, but I expect to see you this week," she persisted.

"Scouts honor."

"You were barely a Boy Scout, Chase. I ran all over town getting your uniform and guidebook and you quit two weeks later. Said you just wanted to go to the cider mill because you liked the doughnuts…"

"Goodbye, Mom. Love you." I disconnected the call and slumped back in the chair. Talking to my mom was more exhausting than running a 5K.

Not My Cat must have gotten bored because he'd disappeared sometime during my mother's inquisition, probably in search of someone else's free handout that had less drama.

It was just me again and I wasn't ready to hit the sack yet. I called Draven to see if he wanted to get a drink.

He answered with a grunt and was breathing hard. Layla squealed in the background. "Are you having sex right now?"

He grunted again. "Yeah. What's up?"

I swear those two were like rabbits. And not just regular rabbits, Energizer bunny rabbits. "Why would you answer the phone while having sex?"

"Layla said it might be important. Is it?"

"Nah, dude. I just wanted to see if you wanted to get a drink with me. I'll catch you another time."

"Hold up!" He mumbled something to Layla in the background. "We'll meet you in twenty minutes." Grunt. "Better make it thirty."

Shaking my head, I hung up the phone. I should have been shocked by that exchange, but not much fazed me when it came to those two anymore. Bright side was I had drinking buddies. Trying not to think about them fucking only minutes before, that was a daily challenge at work. Knowing my hand only got a reprieve once in the last three weeks made the challenge even more difficult. The last time I'd had this little sex was my junior year of high school.

My phone hadn't made a sound since I'd been sitting at the bar. I'd doodled on half a dozen napkins waiting for Draven and Layla to arrive. The pictures in front of me all had a common theme: a curvy body, a beautiful face, and long wavy hair.

"Gonna have to start charging you for those. Napkins ain't cheap," Lou, the owner, teased.

I flipped the pen in my hand and pointed it at him. "I'll take another beer, old man."

He grabbed a beer from the cooler, popped the top and slid it in front of me. "You flying solo tonight?"

I heard Layla's laugh as they stumbled through the door. I hiked a thumb over my shoulder. "They're my date."

He quirked an eyebrow at me.

"Sad, I know, but I was desperate."

He let out a low whistle. "You could do worse." He started pouring their drinks before they even made it to the bar and placed them in front of the stools next to me. It was an advantage of being regulars at The Locker.

Draven clapped me on the shoulder. "Where's your girl?"

"At home." I pouted.

"And why aren't you with her?" Layla asked.

"Because I wasn't invited." God, I sounded like a kid who was left out of a kickball game. "Thanks for coming."

Layla kissed me on the cheek. "Friends don't let friends drink alone, even when they were in the middle of some hot, freaky sex."

I huffed out a laugh. "I have a feeling all of your sex is hot and freaky."

"And yours isn't?"

I tugged at the front of my shirt. "I use a little thing called finesse. I'm more the sexual healing type of guy." I rolled my chest down to my hips and let out a deep moan. "Chicks love it."

Layla's smile tilted up on one side. "I bet they do."

"Dude, that even got me hot." Draven fanned himself.

I picked up my pen and chucked it at his head. "Get the fuck outta here."

The three of us were laughing and my mood was definitely lifting. All I'd been able to think about was Maggie and what I was missing out on tonight. I didn't care if we spent the night playing Candyland with Ella, I just wanted to be with them.

Them.

It was the first time I had thought about being with Maggie and Ella together. That little girl was quickly winning my heart. The way she willingly took my hand and wrapped her arms around my neck when I picked her up. She was so damn excited about the ladybug I drew on her arm. It was nothing to me, but it was everything to her. And what was more, was the look on Maggie's face seeing her daughter so happy.

Seeing my girls smiling, made me happy.

My girls.

Could it really be that easy? Could I fit into their life so effortlessly? I thought being around Ella would be hard for me, but today wasn't hard at all. It felt natural. Like it was meant to be.

I turned to my friends who were flirting like they hadn't just been in bed together. "Am I crazy?"

Draven choked on his vodka tonic. "That's a loaded question. You'll have to be a little more specific."

I let out a slow breath. "Maggie and Ella. Am I crazy for thinking I can make things work with them?"

Layla swirled the straw in her Jack and Coke. "I think the fact you're asking about both of them is a good sign. I watched Maggie with her daughter today. If you don't bond with Ella, you've got no chance with her Momma."

"The question is," Draven tapped his fingers on the bar, "are you ready for an instant family? That little girl is damn cute, and she's got spunk. You were good with her today."

Draven's compliment gave me hope that maybe I wasn't crazy. "It was good, wasn't it?"

Layla put her hand over mine. "Yeah, it was. Maggie's great. For as long as I've known you, you've had a revolving door of women dropping at your feet and none of them gave you the spark I saw today. Not even Becca."

"Becca was comfortable. We were never serious. But Maggie… I think she could be the one. Is that stupid? I mean, it's too soon to fall in love with her isn't it?"

"Sometimes you just know." Draven looked at Layla with complete adoration. "I was too stubborn to admit it but looking back it happened the first night I took her out."

I laughed remembering how Layla could rile him up with a simple look. "I think I knew it before you did. You two just clicked."

Layla's small body hugged him around the waist. "Still do. Draven's the best thing that ever happened to me."

The phone I abandoned on the bar started to ring. I took a deep breath before looking at the screen. My heart immediately went into overdrive when I saw her name on the screen. "Hey, Red."

I plugged one ear with my finger and walked toward the door so I could hear her better. "Hey. I just wanted to say thanks again for today. You were a life saver."

I stepped out onto the sidewalk. "You've already thanked me about a million times. I was happy to help."

"Yeah, but I don't think you know how much it means to me that you were there for us. Ella can't stop talking about you. She refused to wash her arm in the tub. She was afraid her tattoo would wash off."

"You tell her if it does, I'll draw her another one."

"I'll tell her in the morning. She conked out a little bit ago." Maggie hesitated. "I... ummm... was wondering if you'd want to come over."

She caught me off guard. I wasn't expecting her to ask. "Now?"

"Yes. No. It was a dumb idea. It's Saturday night. You probably already have plans. You're probably out right now."

I'm sure she'd heard the noise from the bar in the background when I first answered. "I'm just hanging out with Draven and Layla. I can come over."

"Are you sure? I don't want to pull you away from your friends."

"I'm positive. I'd much rather spend my night with you, if you'll have me."

"Yeah, I'd like that."

"I'll see you soon, Red."

I pumped my fist in the air and walked back in the bar. I hung my arms over my friends' shoulders. "Sorry to desert you, but my woman wants me to come over." *My woman.* It felt good to say. I laid my credit card on the bar. "Drinks are on me."

I pulled up in Maggie's driveway and cut the lights on my truck. I didn't want to risk waking Ella. Checking my hair one last time in the mirror and popping a mint in my mouth, I hopped out and headed toward her porch. The door flew open before I even had a chance to knock.

Surrounded by the backlight of the house, she was a vision. Black yoga pants molded to her legs and an oversized blue sweater that matched her eyes slouched off one shoulder. Her hair was tied up on top of her head, the curls falling down to surround her face. She looked casual and beautiful.

Most women would have primped before asking a guy to come over. I loved that Maggie was comfortable as she was. There wasn't one thing she needed to do to impress me. She was perfect without trying.

She opened the screen for me. "Sorry I called so late. Ella wouldn't go to sleep."

I cradled the back of her head in my hand. "I'm just glad you called at all." I pressed my lips to hers and Maggie's arms immediately went over my shoulders pulling me in closer. I kissed her like I hadn't seen her in weeks instead of hours. Everything else melted away when she was in my arms.

When I pulled back from the kiss, she looked up at me with her big, blue eyes. "Hi."

"Hi."

She unwound her arms from my shoulders. "Do you want something to drink?"

Drinking wasn't on my mind. The only thing I could think about was getting her out of that sweater. "Sure."

I followed her to the kitchen. She opened the fridge and held up a beer. "This okay?"

I took it from her hand and twisted off the top. "It's perfect." Something told me she wasn't a beer drinker, yet she had a full six-pack sitting in her refrigerator. "You drink these?"

The blush she always got when she was nervous crept up her neck. "I stopped at the store on the way home. Maybe it was wishful thinking." Maggie picked up her half-empty wine glass from the counter and took a sip.

"You don't have to be wishful. I'm always ready to spend time with you, Red."

"Hmmm..." she hummed into her wine glass.

I stepped forward, backing her into the counter. In one quick movement, I lifted her to sit on the flat surface. She let out a quiet gasp and wrapped her legs around my waist, her bare feet hooking together behind my back.

"Hmmm... so that's what this is like."

"What what's like?" I asked, just inches from her face.

Maggie cinched her legs tighter around my waist. "To have a man here. In my kitchen. Someone who's not my brother or my dad."

I ran a finger down her neck and over her exposed shoulder. "Oh, sweetheart, I ain't your Daddy or your brother. There's nothing pure about what I'm thinking I'd like to do to you."

"You can't stay the night," she said. "I'm not sure Ella is ready for that."

"It's still early. I'll be gone way before Ella wakes up."

107

"True. Will you be able to stay quiet?"

I smirked at her. "The real question is, will you?"

Maggie blushed again. "I… you might have to put a pillow over my face."

"That's going to be difficult if my head is between your legs." I laughed.

She groaned. "How is it that everything you say turns me on?"

I cocked my head to the side. "Are you turned on, Red? "

She slowly nodded her head while biting her lip.

I loved getting her riled up and decided to kick it up a notch. My cheek pressed to hers as I whispered in her ear, "I'm going to kiss you and lick you and taste you on my tongue. And after you come, I'm going to fuck you long and hard until you come again all over my cock."

Her breathing quickened as she squirmed on the counter, clenching her thighs, trying to relieve the ache. In a bold move, Maggie's hands flew to the button and zipper of my jeans. She had them undone in seconds. Her small hand wrapped around my cock, stroking me up and down, her thumb spreading the precum over the head. "Jesus Christ, woman. That feels amazing."

Maggie leaned forward and whispered back to me. "I want to taste you tonight too."

That was it. All my restraint snapped in an instant. My hands slid under her ass and lifted her from the counter, carrying her toward the hallway I assumed led to her bedroom.

"All the way at the end, on the right," she answered my unasked question.

When we entered her room, I gently closed the door and turned the lock. If Ella did wake up, I didn't want her to walk in on us.

The moon illuminated her room, shooting slivers of light through the blinds. If I hadn't been hard as a rock, I might have checked out something besides her bed, but my focus was on Maggie. All I could think about was her lips wrapped around my cock.

Her legs unlocked from around me and I lowered her bare feet to the floor. "I've been thinking about this since last night."

A growl erupted from my throat as she sank to her knees in front of me. I stood perfectly still and let her lead. The first thing she did was untie my Converse. I lifted one foot then the other as she took my shoes off. Then she slipped her fingers in the waistband of my jeans, dragging them down my legs to my ankles. I kicked them aside, leaving me in just my black boxer briefs and Henley. Maggie's hands caressed my legs from my ankles to my thighs.

108

I couldn't remember the last time a woman had taken such care undressing me. Maggie worked at an agonizingly slow pace. Every second she made me wait was like anticipating that perfect Christmas gift you'd snuck a peek at under the tree. You already knew it was going to be amazing.

Maggie's hands skimmed up my sides under my shirt. She rolled to the balls of her feet, standing and tugging my shirt up my chest. Impatiently, I yanked the damn thing over my head and threw it to the floor.

She stood in front of me totally clothed, her finger tapping on my lips. "Someone's anxious."

I sucked that finger into my mouth and released it with a pop. "Very."

"You were a good boy today and good boys get rewarded." Her fingers grazed down my chest and over my nipples. It wasn't something that usually turned me on, but my skin tingled under her touch. So soft. So sensual.

Sinking back to her knees, Maggie grabbed my ass under my boxer briefs and gave it a squeeze. She moaned softly when she peeled them down and my cock sprang free. Her soft hands wrapped around me, rubbing my length up and down in firm, gentle strokes. Then came her tongue. It licked a wet trail from root to tip, swirling around the head like it was her favorite lollipop. It was all a tease. She was testing my restraint and I wasn't sure how much longer I could hold out. I wanted to take ahold of her hair and shove my cock in her mouth. I was so hard it was becoming painful. A hiss of air filled my lungs and I let it out slowly.

Maggie peered up at me through her lashes. "You all right up there?"

"I think you know exactly how I am right now."

She smirked at me and lowered her head down over my cock, humming her answer. The vibrations went right to my balls that pulled tight to my body. If she kept that up, I wouldn't last more than another minute. Maybe less.

Playtime was over.

My hands went to the back of her head, applying just enough pressure not to choke her. "Don't tease me, Red."

Maggie bobbed her head up and down, her tongue stroking me like I'd never felt. Her cheeks sucked in as she worked like a Hoover to bring me to the brink of orgasm. Her fingers massaged my balls and that sensitive spot behind them most women ignored. Within seconds the base of my spine began to tingle, I was going to blow. And soon.

I drew in a ragged breath and tapped her on the head. "Red, I'm gonna come. Like. Now."

She kept going, not heeding my warning.

F
U
C
K!

Everything pulled tight and sparks shot through every part of me. My muscles convulsed from my fingers down to my toes. "Fuckfuckfuck," I murmured as the pressure released. Pleasure coursed through me, my eyes rolled back, and my legs nearly gave out. I came hard, shooting cum down her throat. Maggie's mouth never stopped as she sucked every last drop from my cock and just when I thought it was over, another burst shot from me The pleasure zapped every last bit of energy from my body. It could have been one long orgasm or the mythical double orgasm. Whatever it was, I couldn't stand any longer. My body swayed and I fell back onto the bed, slipping out of her mouth.

My chest heaved and my brain fogged.

Maggie climbed up my body and straddled me. She giggled. "Payback's a bitch, huh?"

I lifted my head from the mattress. "Is that what that was? 'Cuz I'd say payback's a goddess and she just blew my mind."

She leaned down and pressed her lips to mine. "You must really be out of it because that wasn't your mind I was blowing."

I loved her dirty thoughts. I loved her dirty mouth. Maybe it was just lust. I wasn't sure what I was feeling. I gripped the bottom of her sweater and ripped it over her head. "You tease me with this body. You tease me with this mouth. Are you a tease, Red, or is this real?"

"It's as real as I can give right now. I need to know… are you for real? Or is this just a fantasy I've built up in my head. I can't be careless. It's not just my heart on the line. There's a little girl sleeping in the other room who's depending on me to be smart. But around you, I forget who I am. I forget it's not just me. If it's just sex, let's enjoy it, but if it's more I need to know. I need to know if we can depend on you."

"I'm all in, Red. I want this with you."

What in the hell was I thinking?

I'd just made a promise I didn't know how to keep. *Be a man she can depend on?* God, I could barely depend on myself, let alone be there for anyone else to depend on. Red had me all twisted up inside, saying things I shouldn't.

Maggie leaned over me, pushing her breasts together. "Can I tell you a secret?" she whispered.

I struggled to keep my eyes off her tits and on her face. Straining forward, I whispered back, "Depends. Is it illegal? I'm pretty sure Draven would help us hide a dead body. He's got connections." It was a joke, but there was more truth to it than I'd admit.

Her eyes popped. "No!" She shook her head as if clearing the thought from her mind. "Just… no. Exactly what kind of people do you hang out with?"

I placed my hands in hers. "Relax. I was just yanking your chain. What's the secret?"

"My daughter is quite taken with you."

My eyebrows shot up. "She doesn't even know me."

Maggie shrugged her shoulders. "Ever since the costume store, you're all she can talk about. You made quite the impression. Today you solidified it."

"I was just being myself. I didn't do anything special."

"I know, but that's kind of what makes it great."

This was getting real and fast. My anxiety spiked. Although I was a mess of nerves on the inside, I couldn't let it show on the outside. "Well, I do have a way with the ladies."

Maggie tapped her fingers on my chest. "Aren't you full of yourself? If we do this, there won't be any other ladies, right?"

I twined my fingers with hers. "I haven't slept with anyone else in weeks. You have nothing to worry about."

Her throat bobbed. "Weeks? Why not?"

"I've been with a lot of women. More than would be acceptable to admit and I'm not going to lie, I loved every minute of it. But I want more than a revolving door of women. I want to find my person and all I've thought about is you. And Ella."

She held me captive with her thighs. "And Ella? Don't bullshit me. I can take it. I'm a big girl. I don't believe in fairy tales. That went out the window a long time ago."

"Red, I want to be the man you can depend on. Give me a chance." The words I was spewing scared the shit out of me. I wasn't that man, as much as I pretended to be. I was a scared rabbit and I needed to be fearless. Strong. I couldn't let my past dictate my future. I wouldn't fuck up this time.

"Where are we going?"

"Don't worry about it," I told Meredith.

She shifted in her seat. "Don't tell me not to worry. We're heading south of 8 Mile and that worries me. Nothing good happens down here, Chase."

Meredith was in her last semester at the university, going full-time to become a nurse. I promised her I would take care of her and I would, no matter what I had to do. I had willingly put my degree in graphic arts on the backburner so she could complete hers. I needed money, not a fancy piece of paper to hang on the wall. I certainly wasn't going to tell her I'd made this trip many times in the last several months since I'd taken the job at the garage. It was the only thing that let me take care of her the way she deserved.

I had planned on leaving Meredith at home today, but she practically jumped in the car when I said I had errands to run, saying she needed new scrubs for school.

I stroked her arm with my fingers. "I have to drop something off for a guy at work. Consider it a side job."

"What kind of job? I don't like this."

"It's not a big deal. I won't let anything happen to you."

The farther south we went, the shittier the neighborhood became. We were officially in Detroit. I checked my phone one last time. Another right and we would be there. I pulled up in a driveway sandwiched between two houses that had seen better days. Their windows had plywood covering them, there was trash piled up on the curb and the landscape was way overgrown. Damn. This was worse than my other drops. The cash was good though. I was getting paid a cool hundred for basically doing nothing. A couple of trips like this a week made a huge difference in our finances.

I patted Meredith on the leg. "Sit tight and lock the doors."

Meredith's eyes went wide. "Are you shitting me right now? You're going in there," she pointed at the house, "and leaving me in the car? You're out of your fucking mind!"

I let out a sigh. "Fine, you can come with, but you gotta be cool." I flipped up the center console and pulled out the bag of weed.

"What the fuck, Chase? You're dealing drugs?"

She was so dramatic. It was a little weed. Okay, a lot of weed, but the guy at the garage where I worked as a mechanic was paying me well for making the delivery. I stuck the bag in the front of my jeans. "Are you gonna be cool?"

Meredith threw her hands in the air. "Sure. Why not? If we get caught it'll just be jail time. Do you know what it's like in prison?"

I scratched my head. "Not really."

"Me neither and I'd rather not find out. This is fucking dumb, Chase. Promise me this is the last time. I want you to quit your job at the garage and get a real job. Do you understand me?"

Sure. It was only the job that paid our bills. I promised I'd take care of her and I would. If that meant doing some shady shit, I'd do it. It was only weed. It wasn't like I was dealing meth or coke. "Sure, baby. This is the first and last time. I promise."

Chapter 14
Maggie

"Momma, why is your door locked?" I heard the twisting of the knob and my eyes popped open in panic.

"Hold on a minute, ladybug." I nudged Chase who was sound asleep beside me. "Get up!" I whispered urgently.

He groaned and rolled over.

I grabbed my robe from the back of the chair and threw it on, wrapping the tie around my waist. I rushed to the door and cracked it open. My baby girl stood there with her wild morning hair. "Why was your door locked?"

"I must have done it accidently. I'll be out in a minute."

She pushed her small hand against the door. "Can I snuggle in your bed before breakfast?"

I kept the door in place. "Not today. Go turn on cartoons and I'll cuddle with you on the couch."

Ella pouted. "Fine." She huffed off toward the front room.

I shut the door, ran back to Chase, and gave him a hard shove. "Chase, get up. You need to go. Now!" The last thing I wanted was for Ella to find Chase sleeping in my bed.

He reached up and pulled me into the sheets with him. "God, you're beautiful in the morning."

I swatted his hands away. "We overslept. You gotta go." Crawling over his body, I rushed to the window and slid it up.

He threw the covers back showing me everything God had given him. "Are you serious?"

I rushed around picking up his clothes from the floor and threw them at him. "As a heart attack. Ella's already up. In about two minutes she'll be pounding on the door again."

Chase quickly pulled his pants on. "I haven't crawled out a girl's window since I was seventeen."

"I'm so sorry."

"Nah, it's fine." He finished dressing and pulled me into his arms. "I'll call you later?"

A little fist pounded on the door. "Momma, are you coming out? You're missing our favorite show."

"Just one more minute, ladybug," I called over my shoulder.

Chase squeezed my butt. "Later?"

I smiled up at him. "Yes. Definitely. Now go."

He gave me a searing kiss and crawled out the window. Had I been wearing panties they would have been a lost cause. That man sure knew how to kiss. I held my hand to my tingling lips and then an awful thought crossed my mind. I held my hand away from my mouth and breathed into it. "Crap." I hadn't noticed his morning breath, so maybe mine went unnoticed too. I had been more focused on his kiss than anything else.

I watched as he jogged out to his truck and jumped inside. Quickly shutting the window, I raced to the door and opened it, only to have Ella staring up at me, hands propped up on her hips. "What were you doing?"

My mind raced to come up with a reasonable answer when the doorbell rang. Ella's attention was immediately diverted, and she ran toward the sound.

"Don't you dare open that door, little lady," I called after her. Who in the hell would be here? It was barely eight o'clock. Jeff never showed up except for Fridays and Patty wasn't much of an early riser on Sunday.

Ella waited impatiently for me while I spied through the peephole. *You've got to be kidding me.*

I tugged open the door and smiled. "What a surprise! I thought we were going to talk *later*."

Ella jumped up and down on her bare feet. "Chase! What are you doing here? Did you come to see me?"

He patted down some hair that was sticking up on his head. "Well, I woke up this morning and I had a great idea. I thought what better way to start the day than with my two favorite girls."

I glared at him. "You did, did you?"

He gave me a conspiratorial smirk. "Yep. It nearly knocked me right out of bed. And I thought princess bug here might like pancakes." He gave Ella a serious look. "Do you like pancakes? 'Cuz I can make a mean pancake."

Ella grabbed him by the hand and pulled him inside. "I love pancakes! Can I help?"

He picked her up and carried her to the kitchen. "Of course you can help. I'll need a good assistant."

Ella hugged him around the neck. "I can crack the eggs and stir. I'm a good stirrer."

I threw my hands up in the air. "Sure, come on in." Chase and Ella were so busy chatting they barely noticed me as I followed behind.

One minute I was kicking him out the window the next he was standing in my kitchen pulling eggs from the fridge. That man… I wasn't sure what to make of him. Ella directed from her seat on the counter, telling Chase where to find everything. I couldn't do anything but watch. This is what Ella had always wanted from her father and he'd disappointed her time and time again. It was a little much, a little too fast, but there was no denying the joy on my daughter's face.

I stepped behind him to the coffee maker. "You want coffee?"

He wrapped his arms around me from behind and nuzzled my neck. "I'd love some. This is nice."

It sure as hell was. "Mmhmm…" I hummed.

"Are you mad?"

I twisted my lips to the side. "Did you see the smile on that little girl's face? How could I possibly be mad?"

"Why don't you go get dressed. I got this."

I pulled two mugs from the cupboard. "You sure about that?"

"Positive." He turned to Ella and held out his fist to her. "We got this, right?"

Ella bumped her tiny fist into his. "Yep."

"Now blow it up, girl." Chase showed Ella how to explode her hand open and they repeated the action until she had it down perfect.

"All right, you two. I'm going to go brush my teeth and put on some clothes. If you need me…" I pointed down the hall toward the bedroom. I don't know why I bothered. The two of them weren't listening to me at all.

I shut the door to my room and plopped down on the bed. I was conflicted about the events of the morning. If this didn't last, Ella was going to be crushed. I picked up the phone and called Roxy.

"Hello," she answered with a grumble. "It's barely eight. Why the hell are you waking me up?"

"Yeah, sorry about that. I need you to talk me off a cliff."

"What's going on? Is it Jeff?"

I lay back on my pillow, inhaling Chase's cologne. "Not even close. Do you know who's standing in my kitchen right now making pancakes with Ella? Chase. That's who."

She chuckled. "I thought you weren't doing sleepovers."

I rolled my eyes. "Yeah, me too. He stayed over and I pushed him out my bedroom window this morning. Then, instead of going home he showed up at my front door."

Roxy laughed hysterically on the other end. I held the phone away from my ear to dull the sound. This was not a laughing matter.

"Are you done?" I asked.

She snorted into the phone. "Sorry, sorry. You kicked that grown ass man out your window? What are you? Sixteen?"

"Apparently. What should I do?"

"About?"

I huffed. "Chase. In my kitchen."

"I guess I don't see the problem. You've got a hot guy in your kitchen making your daughter breakfast. I wish I had that problem. What's he wearing?"

"Okay, you know what? You're no help at all."

"The only problem I see is that you're letting Ella have all the fun. Instead of enjoying it, you're locked in your room brooding."

She had me pegged perfectly. I rubbed at the crease in my forehead. "I am not brooding. I'm just... I don't know."

"Stop fretting and get your ass out there. Bye, Maggie...love ya!" her voice droned off as she disconnected.

I threw my phone on the bed. That was useless. I rubbed my temples and tried to relax. Roxy was right, I was brooding. Every possible outcome of this situation ran through my mind on fast forward.

Chase.

Was in my kitchen.

Making pancakes with Ella.

Ella was smiling and happy.

She was okay.

She was more than okay.

She was ecstatic.

Just go with it. This is what you wanted.

But what if it didn't work out?

What if in a few days or a few weeks Chase was nothing but a memory.

I would be crushed.

Ella would be crushed.

How would I explain it to her?

After giving myself a pep talk, I got dressed, combed my hair, applied a little makeup, and brushed my teeth. It was a nice change getting myself ready without a tiny shadow following me around.

I sauntered back into the kitchen and Chase handed me a cup of coffee. "Morning, beautiful. Feel better?"

I took the coffee. "I will once I've had my caffeine." I surveyed the kitchen. "How's it going out here?"

Ella hopped down off the chair she was standing on. "Chase is making me Mickey Mouse pancakes. See the ears?" She pointed at the pan where the pancakes were cooking.

Chase pulled her hand away from the hot stove. "Careful, princess bug."

I was amazed at how good he was with her. "I see. Should we set the table?" I reached into the cupboard and pulled down three plates. Ella took them to the table while I got forks and napkins. Chase pulled butter and syrup from the fridge and handed them to Ella. We were a little team of three. It almost felt like we were… dare I think it… a *family*. My heart swelled and my eyes filled with tears as I took everything in.

"Hey, what's wrong?" Chase cradled my face in his hand, wiping a tear with his thumb before it fell down my cheek.

My words got stuck in my throat. "Nothing. Everything is perfect. Breakfast is perfect. My daughter is perfect. You're perfect."

He pressed a kiss to the corner of my lips. "I'm not perfect, but I'm trying."

"You're doing great."

Ella squeezed her body between us. "Are you two boyfriend and girlfriend now?"

Chase looked at me expectantly, silently asking me for direction.

I kneeled in front of Ella. "Well, what would you think about that?"

She shrugged her shoulders. "Will Chase make pancakes with us and stuff?"

I looked to Chase for verification. I didn't want to speak on his behalf because this had to be a little scary for him.

He kneeled next to me and talked to Ella. "Do you want me to? Are you cool with me hanging out with you and your mom?"

She got a serious look on her face. "Can we go to McDonald's, because that's my favorite place?"

Chase laughed. "That's up to your mom because she's the boss, but I think we can work that out."

She shrugged. "Okay, you two can be boyfriend and girlfriend. Can we eat now? I'm starving." Ella ran to her seat and waited for her pancakes.

"I guess that's it then," Chase said.

"So… you're officially my boyfriend?" I asked, tapping on his chest.

He wrapped his arms around me. "I guess I am. Are you ready for pancakes?"

I was. I was ready for pancakes and whatever this crazy ride had in store for me.

Chase helped me wash the dishes while Ella went to brush her teeth and get dressed. Taking the plastic bowl from my hand to dry, he bumped me with his hip. "I was thinking, since it's almost Halloween, that maybe we could take Ella to the pumpkin patch today."

"You don't have to work?"

He finished drying the bowl and set it on the counter. "Not today. What do you think? There's a place up in Romeo where we can get cider and doughnuts, go on a hayride, and they have goats."

"Goats?" I asked, lifting an eyebrow.

"Yes, goats. And Ella can feed them. Has she ever fed a goat before?"

I handed him the griddle I just finished washing. "I can't say that she has, but I think she would love it. Are you sure that's what you want to do on your day off? You're not sick of us yet?"

He tapped me on the butt with the griddle. "I wouldn't be a very good boyfriend if I was sick of you already. Are you sick of me?"

I took the pan and placed it in the cupboard with the rest. "It's not that."

Chase crossed his arms and leaned back against the counter. "Then what is it? I'm not getting a warm, fuzzy feeling here. Last night you were all in."

I mirrored his stance against the opposite counter. "I'm scared."

His jaw stiffened. "Of what?"

I let out a sigh. "Everything. You. Me. Ella. What if you decide we're not what you want? That this is too much, too fast? I'm feeling things I haven't felt in a very long time. What if we do this and it all ends up in broken hearts?"

Chase stepped forward and held my face in his hands. "I'm scared too. I can't promise you forever. I can't even guarantee six months. I don't know what I'm doing or if I'm good enough, but it feels right. The only thing I know is that if we don't try, we'll never know what could be. It's a leap of faith. Jump with me, take a chance on us."

He was right. We had no idea where today would lead us, my past should have been proof enough. I thought by now Jeff and I would be married and have another child. The dream I'd been holding on to was like a poof of smoke in the wind. I couldn't change that, but the future was wide open. I placed my hands over his. "You'll hold my hand when we jump?"

"Every single time, Red. Every. Single. Time." He kissed me tenderly and pressed his forehead against mine. "We gonna do this?"

I bit my lip and nodded. "Yes. Yes, I'll jump with you." We sealed the deal with a passionate kiss that had me leaning back over the kitchen island.

"Ewwww! Are you guys gonna kiss all the time now that you're boyfriend and girlfriend?"

We broke apart laughing at Ella's intrusion. I glanced at Chase. "You sure?"

"Absolutely."

I looked at my daughter. "What in the world are you wearing?"

She shrugged her shoulders. "What? I look good."

I usually picked out Ella's clothes, but with the distraction in my kitchen she'd been left to her own devices. She had on striped leggings and a polka dot shirt. "You don't match."

"Yes, I do." Ella pointed to a stripe in her pants. "There's pink here," then she pointed to one of the polka dots, "and here."

Chase snickered behind me. I gave him the evil eye. "Not helping."

"How about this?" he suggested. "You let your mom help you find something to wear and then I'll take you both to the pumpkin patch."

Ella considered his proposal. "Can I get a really big pumpkin?" She held her arms out wide.

All I could picture was those pumpkins on pallets that weighed six hundred pounds. Ella could talk her uncle and grandpa into just about anything. It was how she ended up with the pink Barbie jeep parked in my shed. My girl was excellent at persuasion and Chase was a fresh victim.

Chase bargained with her. "A medium pumpkin, cider and doughnuts, and…" he tapped the counter doing a drumroll, "…goats."

And just like that he had her. "Goats! I love goats! Do they bite?"

He plucked at her leggings. "They might nibble on these, but if you wore jeans, I think you'd be safe. Farm animals can be finicky."

Ella grabbed my hand and practically dragged me to her room. "Come on, Momma. We gotta get dressed for the farm."

I turned over my shoulder and mouthed *thank you.*

He gave me a thumbs-up.

Once in Ella's room, I searched for a clean pair of jeans while she scrounged around in her closet. She backed out holding up a pair of pink cowboy boots. My mom had bought them on a whim and honestly Ella had only worn them a couple times.

"I think those would be perfect." I pulled a plaid shirt and her jean jacket out of the closet and tossed them on the bed. "This will be much better for the farm. Get dressed while I go change."

I left Ella and sauntered across the hall to my own room. I changed into jeans, boots and a similar plaid shirt. I checked my hair and makeup, then spritzed on a little perfume. By the time I finished, Chase and Ella were waiting for me by the door.

"Momma!" she shouted. "Chase says I'm the cutest cowgirl he's ever seen and I'm gonna be safe from the goats."

"Did he now?"

He eyed me up and down. "I may have to amend that statement." He pulled me in close and kissed me on the cheek, whispering, "You look hot."

Ella pushed the screen door open and ran toward Chase's truck. "Here we come, goats!" She was so excited that she didn't even complain about her booster seat.

Chase wanted to make a quick pit stop at his place so he could change. I suspected he needed to brush his teeth too, although he must have been popping mints because his breath was fresh. I had almost forgotten he hadn't been home since last night.

When we arrived at his apartment Chase threw his keys on the table. "Give me fifteen minutes. I'm gonna jump in the shower real quick. The TV remote is on the coffee table. Make yourself at home."

I flipped on the television for Ella, then wandered around his apartment. I'd been here twice, but never spent any time taking it all in. The only parts I was well acquainted with were the couch, bedroom, and bathroom. Across from the couch, a bookshelf held a variety of books and half a dozen pictures. There was a photo of him with his coworkers at a bar. In another he was really little, maybe five or six, holding up a fish with his dad. Chase and his family stared back at me from all the captured memories. He hadn't changed much over the years. He still had that adorable dimple and shaggy blond hair.

Behind the other pictures was a black frame shoved way in the back, almost as if he didn't want to see it but couldn't get rid of it either. I carefully moved the other photos aside to get a better look. It was a prom picture. A younger version of Chase dressed in a tuxedo held a beautiful blond under a glittery arch adorned with blue and white balloons. She leaned her head into Chase's chest and his arms were wrapped around her waist. It was sweet. There was no denying they were in love. I wondered if it was the girl he had once been engaged to that left him. It wasn't my business, but I was curious.

The shower turned off and I quickly rearranged the pictures on the shelf. He didn't need to know I was nosing through his things. I lifted a book from the shelf and started thumbing through the pages. It was filled with pictures Chase had drawn, each one signed at the bottom like the ones I'd seen in his studio. His work was truly amazing.

A distinct scratching sound interrupted my snooping. Ella heard it too and jumped off the couch. "What's that?"

I returned the book to its rightful place. "I don't know."

Ella followed the sound and pointed toward the far side of the room. "It's coming from over there."

I followed her past the dining room table to the sliding glass door.

Ella dropped to her knees in front of the door. "Look, Momma! He's so cute. Can I open the door?" A big brown tabby cat stared back at her.

"I don't think that would be a good idea."

Ella held her hand up to the window. He placed his paw on the opposite side of the glass and let out a loud meow.

"I think he's hungry. Pleeeease, Momma." She moved her hand up and down on the glass and the cat followed with his paw.

My girl loved animals and had no fear when it came to cats and dogs; a trait that made me a nervous mom on more than one occasion. "Ella, we don't have anything to feed him. Besides, he might have fleas or a disease. What if he bites you?"

Ella scrunched up her nose. "He's not going to bite me. Look, he's playing. I bet Chase has something he can eat. Let's go look!" She stood up and started running toward the kitchen.

I caught her around the waist. "This isn't our house. You're not rummaging around in Chase's cupboards."

"But he's hungry," she complained.

Chase emerged from his room looking fresh and clean. His hair was still damp, and he'd changed into a plaid button-down to match ours. "Who's hungry? You couldn't possibly be hungry after all those pancakes you ate for breakfast."

"Not me, Chase. Him." She pointed toward the slider. "We gotta get him some food."

Chase followed her finger with his eyes. He smiled. "That's Not My Cat."

The tabby pawed at the window and let out another long, loud meow.

Ella ran back to the glass. "But he's hungry." She talked to the cat through the glass. "Don't worry, Mr. Cat. We're gonna feed you."

I let out a sigh. "Ladybug, leave him alone."

Chase kissed me on the temple. "It's fine." He opened the slider and scooped the cat into his arms. The cat immediately started purring when Chase rubbed his head. He kneeled in front of Ella. "His name is Not My Cat. You can pet him."

Ella ran her hand down the cat's back. "That's a weird name," she said.

Chase shrugged. "Yeah, I guess it is, but he's not my cat so that's what I call him."

"Who does he belong to?"

"I don't know. I don't think he belongs to anyone, but he visits me almost every day."

"Can we feed him?"

"Hold out your arms. You can hold him while I get some tuna," Chase instructed.

Ella held out her arms and Chase carefully wrapped them around the cat. "Like this?" The cat looked huge in her tiny arms.

"Tight, but not too tight. Just snuggle him."

I crossed my arms nervously. "Do you think that's a good idea? What if he bites her?"

"He won't." Chase walked to the kitchen seemingly unworried, with Ella on his heels trying to juggle the massive amount of fur in her arms.

The cat put his face right next to hers and my heart lurched in my chest. How could Chase not be worried about this?

Ella started laughing. "He's tickling me with his whiskers."

Chase patted him on the head. "Be a good boy, big guy." He pulled a can of tuna from his cupboard and drained the excess water. Using a fork, he fluffed it up and the cat went crazy trying to wiggle out of my daughter's grasp. "Let him down. He'll follow us outside."

Ella did as she was told and followed them out to the balcony. Not My Cat feasted while Ella and Chase rubbed his back. Seeing the two of them together sharing this moment warmed my heart. It was amazing that a man I barely knew a week ago could have such an impact on my daughter's life.

This is the way it always should have been. Ella had been robbed of these moments far too long by a man who didn't appreciate the gift he was given the day she was born. It made me sad for the both of them. One day Jeff would regret how little time he spent with Ella; that another man was getting the best part of her.

Chapter 15
Chase

I stared through the rearview mirror at the wild, little redhead asleep in her booster. "I think she finally conked out."

Maggie relaxed back into her seat. "It's about time. She's been going full-speed since early this morning."

I reached for her hand across the seat and twined my fingers with hers. "I had a great day. Thank you for sharing it with me."

Maggie squeezed my hand and leaned into me, resting her head on my shoulder. "I should be the one thanking you. You're so good with her. I thought she was going to breakdown when that goat ripped the whole cone of food from her hand, but there you were helping her with the next one. She's going to remember today for a very long time."

I kissed her temple. "And what about her Momma? Did you have a good time today?"

She peered up at me from under her long lashes. "The best. I don't want the day to end and I definitely don't want to go to work tomorrow."

The feeling was mutual. We'd been living in a little bubble since last night. It was about to burst, and I wasn't ready for that quite yet. I wanted to spend as much time with Maggie as possible. The feeling was all consuming. "I wanna stay with you tonight." Before she could protest, I added, "I promise I'll be gone in the morning. I won't disrupt your routine. I just want to lie with you and hold you in my arms, Red."

Maggie smirked. "Just hold me?"

I cocked my head from side to side. "Maybe some other stuff too."

She playfully swatted my chest. "That's what I thought." Maggie straightened in her seat. "You can stay, but I have things that have to get done tonight."

"Like what? Maybe I can help."

She started ticking things off on her fingers. "Dinner, laundry, give Ella a bath, do homework with her, make lunches for the both of us…"

I grabbed her fingers. "I can help. I know how to do laundry."

She laughed. "I'm sure you do, but I'm not letting you wash my underwear."

"Are they red lace? Black?" My eyebrows waggled up and down.

"They're very basic. Believe it or not I don't have drawers full of Victoria's Secret lingerie. That was special for you. I'm a single mom. I haven't really had a need for anything fancy. Nobody cares what I wear under my clothes."

She'd had herself trapped in the single mom box for way too long. She didn't realize how beautiful she was. Her ex had done a real number on her. "You know what I think?"

Maggie raised an eyebrow. "No, but I'm sure you're going to tell me."

"I think you're a gorgeous woman who deserves to pamper herself. You should always feel sexy because you are. You spend so much time taking care of everyone else that you don't take care of yourself. I'm fine with cotton granny panties, but you deserve satin and lace."

She crossed her arms. "They're not granny panties."

I winked at her. "I bet they look good on you. With that ass and those long legs, how could they not?"

Maggie glanced at Ella to make sure she wasn't listening. "They're just cotton bikinis. Why are we even talking about my underwear?"

"Laundry."

"Right. I'll do the laundry. Maybe you can help Ella with her homework. I'm sure she'd love that."

I nodded. "I can do homework."

We pulled up in the driveway and I looked back at Ella. "Should we wake her?"

"Yeah, but she's not going to like it. If we don't though, she'll never go to sleep tonight."

That would put a major kink in my plans for later. I hopped out of the truck. "I got her." I opened Ella's door and unbuckled her. "Wake up, princess bug." Her eyes fluttered open and she reached out for me. I lifted her from the seat and her arms wrapped around my neck, her head resting on my shoulder. I rubbed her back gently as I carried her to the porch.

Maggie opened the door. "Set her on the couch."

Keeping her in my arms, I sat and continued to stroke her back. "Time to open those pretty eyes, baby girl."

She lifted her head, squinting at me and put it back on my shoulder.

"Your Momma said you have homework to do and I'm going to help you. What do you think about that?"

"No homework," she mumbled.

I chuckled. "The boss says it's not a choice, but we can watch TV for a little bit first." I reached for the remote and clicked the television on. Flipping through the channels I settled on *Animal Planet*. A bunch of furry little critters ran around in the dirt chasing each other. "What are those things?"

Ella peeked at the screen from her place on my lap. "They're meerkats."

I knew what they were, but I wanted to keep Ella engaged on the show so she wouldn't go back to sleep. "What's a meerkat?"

She frowned at me. "Haven't you ever seen *The Lion King?*"

I scratched my chin. "Can't say that I have." Disney movies had never been my thing. I knew the basics—Cinderella, Sleeping Beauty, Pinocchio, maybe a few more—but other than that I'd never had a reason to keep up. I had a feeling with Ella in my life that was about to change.

"You've never seen *The Lion King*?" she asked with wide eyes. Ella scrambled off my lap and rustled around in the cabinet under the TV. After some searching, she emerged holding the movie in her hand. "You have to see this. It's soooo good. Do you want to watch it with me?"

I couldn't say no, but I wasn't going to let her sidetrack me. I leaned forward and clapped my hands together. "Let's make a deal. First we do homework and then we can watch the movie."

"Fine. But you have to do math with me and listen to me read."

"I'm good with that. You want to grow up to be as smart as your mom, don't you?"

Ella rolled her eyes at me. "Whatever. We get to watch *The Lion King*, right?"

"Absolutely." I was rocking this whole dad thing, even if I wasn't her dad.

Maggie walked by with a basketful of laundry. "Everything okay?"

I gave her my best confident smile. "Perfect. It's all under control."

She gave me a sideways glance. "Uh-huh. Sure it is."

Maggie had enough stress without worrying about me. I was going to prove to her I could handle anything Ella threw my way. "We're fine. Homework is next on our agenda. You worry about washing your granny panties and don't worry about us."

She glared at me. "Not granny panties. Focus on the homework."

127

I waved her off. "I guess we'll see later."

She continued with the laundry. "Not if you keep that up!"

I looked at Ella. "We better get started on that homework or we're gonna be in trouble with the boss."

She seemed totally unaffected. "Meh. I'm always in trouble."

I highly doubted that. "Let's not risk it. Go get your stuff and I'll meet you at the table."

Ella trudged off to get her backpack. She brought it to the table and pulled out her math workbook. "This stuff is easy. It's like they think we're babies. All I need you to do is read the directions."

Turned out Ella was a whiz at math. She added with ease, counting on her fingers and reciting the numbers aloud. We finished the math in less than twenty minutes. Then it was time for reading. Ella ran to her room and brought back a book. "We can read this. It's one of my favorites." She held up *The Best Nest.* Then she grabbed my hand and dragged me to the couch. Ella plopped on my lap and opened the book.

Maggie was clanking around pots and pans in the kitchen. "How are you two doing?"

Ella yelled over my shoulder. "I finished my math, now I'm going to read and then we can watch *The Lion King.*"

"After dinner and a bath, then you can watch the movie," Maggie answered.

"She's really a buzzkill," Ella grumped.

I barely held in my laughter. "Where did you learn that word?"

She shrugged. "My dad. That's what he said about my mom."

Suddenly it wasn't so funny. "Well, you shouldn't say it. It's not very nice."

"Now you're being a buzzkill."

She wasn't my daughter, and I had no right to discipline her, but I couldn't listen to her repeat her father's words. "Ella," I said sternly.

She looked at me sheepishly. "Sorry, Chase. I won't say it anymore."

I felt sort of bad for scolding her, but she had to know those weren't kind words to say about her mother. "Apology accepted." I pecked her on the forehead. "Now I want to hear you read."

She put her little finger on the first word and began to read. Ella was a good reader and added her two cents on every page to narrate the story. I had to help her with a word here and there, but for the most part she did it herself.

On the last page, she pointed to the baby bird that had popped out of an egg. "See Mr. and Mrs. Bird got married and they had a baby, 'cuz that's what happens when you get married, except my mom and dad didn't get married because he didn't love her enough, so I don't know how I got borned, but now you're my mom's boyfriend so maybe you could love her and get married and then you could have a baby, 'cuz I always wanted to have a baby brother or sister." When Ella finally stopped to take a breath, she smiled up at me with her toothless smile.

I froze, because that was a lot of information to take in all at once. How did we go from a day at the pumpkin patch to having a baby? I mean, I guess if things worked out that was where everything would go… eventually. But, damn… talk about a buzzkill. It was a little much, a little fast. This was exactly why Maggie wanted to wait for Ella to spend time with me. I'd royally fucked up by ringing her doorbell this morning instead of going home like I was supposed to.

My wheels spun as she stared at me waiting for a response. I had to say something, but what?

Maggie's voice rang out, "Dinner's ready." It was the most beautiful sound I'd ever heard.

Ella sprang off my lap and rushed to the kitchen.

I lingered on the couch for another moment. My skin felt too tight and my chest seized. It was suddenly too warm in the house. Dampness beaded on my forehead. A panic attack was hitting me… hard. I concentrated on breathing. *Air in. Air out.* I continued the measured breaths hoping the tightness would subside.

I'd gotten home from work late. The apartment was quiet and dark. Meredith started working at the hospital a couple of months ago and sometimes she had to stay past her shift, but she should have been home by now.

"Meredith?"

The apartment was totally silent.

I threw my keys on the table and went in search of her. There was light shining out from under the bathroom door. A quiet sob escaped from inside.

I knocked lightly. "Baby, are you okay?"

When she didn't answer, I twisted the knob and pushed the door open.

Meredith was curled up next to the tub with her knees against her chest. Her head rested on her bent knees. Another sob echoed into the small space.

I knelt before her. "Baby, what's wrong?"

She lifted her head. Tears rolled down her cheeks from her red-rimmed eyes. I'd rarely seen Meredith cry. She was tough as nails. It had to be something huge to bring this kind of emotion out of her.

"Meredith?"

She reached under her legs and pulled out a white stick. I took it from her and immediately saw the plus sign in the little window.

"You're pregnant?" I asked, even though I was holding the evidence in my hand.

She waved her hand at the stick. "Apparently."

I rubbed her back. "Why are you so upset? We're getting married. It'll be okay." We hadn't planned on having a baby yet, but I knew what I wanted with her and a baby was definitely on the agenda.

"Why am I upset? We're not ready for a baby. I just finished school and started working. You haven't finished your degree yet. We're barely making it as it is. The last thing we need right now is a baby."

Everything she said was true, but a baby with Meredith was everything I had ever wanted. "So, what if we do things a little out of order?"

She pointed at her chest. "I'm not ready. I don't want a baby right now. Yeah, maybe in a couple of years, but now? I can't do this!"

She was emotional and I was getting pissed. How could she not want our baby? Getting mad at her wasn't going to help the situation. All I could do was reassure her everything was going to work out.

I sat down next to Meredith and wrapped my arms around her small body. "Everything is going to be okay. I promised I'd take care of you and I will. I'll be right by your side the entire time. I'll go to every doctor appointment and I'll get a better job. We can do this."

"Promise me you'll be there, Chase. Promise me. I can't do this by myself."

I kissed the top of her head. "I promise. I'll do whatever it takes. You can always count on me. You know that. Me and you, baby. Together forever. That's the way it's always been and that's the way it will always be."

A hand on my shoulder snapped me back to the here and now. "Are you coming?"

"Yeah. Sorry. I just needed a minute."

Maggie frowned at me. "Are you feeling okay? You look flushed." She pressed her hand to my head.

I grabbed her hand and kissed her palm. "I'm fine. I just got lightheaded for a moment. I think I need to eat," I lied.

She smiled sweetly. "Come sit with us. I made enchiladas and cornbread. I hope you like Mexican."

After dinner and Ella's bath, the three of us cuddled on the couch and watched *The Lion King.* Maggie was curled into my side and Ella was snuggled into hers. About twenty minutes into the movie, Ella's eyes began to droop. She was fighting like hell, but sleep was winning.

Maggie whispered, "Ten more minutes and she'll be out."

I looked at the clock. It was just past eight. I was ready for some alone time with Maggie.

As predicted, Ella was a corpse within a few minutes. Maggie slunk out from under my arm and lifted her from the couch. Ella wrapped herself around her mom as she carried her away.

I stretched and headed to the kitchen. I helped myself to a beer and poured Maggie a glass of wine. After Ella's long-winded dissertation on marriage and babies I needed a drink. I couldn't get her words out of my head. They kept spinning around on repeat. Every mistake I'd made swirled into the mix. It resulted in a huge clusterfuck inside my head.

I needed to pull it together. That was the past. Maggie wasn't Meredith and I wasn't the same guy I was back then. Or maybe I was. It was hard to tell since I'd never really let anyone in since Meredith. What if I was the same stupid guy who made the same stupid mistakes? The cost would be much higher this time.

After tonight I would pull back a little. Give them some space. Give myself some space. I didn't want Ella to have unrealistic expectations. If I broke that little girl's heart, it would be worse than if I'd broken my own.

Maggie reappeared from tucking Ella in. I handed her the glass of wine and she took a long sip. "This is exactly what I needed. Has it been a long day or is it just me?"

"It's been a long day," I confirmed. "I don't know how you keep up with it all by yourself."

She hopped up on the counter and dangled her legs. "Some days are easier than others. I never really had a choice."

I ran my fingers down the side of her face. "You're doing a great job."

She blew at a piece of hair that had escaped her clip. "Some days I wonder. Since she started school it's gotten harder. I kept her so sheltered from my relationship with Jeff. All she knew was he was her dad, and I was her mom. Now she's asking all kinds of questions about marriage, divorce, and where babies come from. I'm not ready for that talk yet. For God's sake, she's only six."

It was like she was pulling thoughts right out of my head. Maybe if Maggie and I talked about this it wouldn't be so scary. That would be the adult thing to do and it was time I stepped up to the plate of adulting. "Did she say something about us?"

Maggie shook her head and took another sip of wine. "It was nothing."

That was a lie. I cocked my head at her. "Clearly it was something."

"I don't want to scare you," she whispered.

I lifted her chin with my finger. "I'll tell you a secret. I'm already scared to death. Just tell me."

She placed her wine glass on the counter and sighed. "She wanted to know if we were getting married because…"

"She wants us to have a baby," I finished.

Her eyes widened. "Yes. How did you know?"

All the anxiety I'd been holding in came out in a rush of laughter. "She already told me."

Maggie looked up at the ceiling. "Oh Lord! I'm so sorry." She buried her head in my shoulder in embarrassment.

The tightness in my chest drifted away. "Hey, at least we're on the same page now. 'Cuz holding that in was making me crazy. Not that I would be opposed to it, but…"

"It's a little soon to have that discussion? Agreed."

My hands slid under Maggie's ass and her legs wrapped around my waist. "So, we're not getting married or having babies anytime soon, but we can do other things."

Her lips met mine in a gentle kiss. "What kind of things?" she asked coyly.

This playful, sweet, innocent side of her was what turned me on most. When she tucked away her mom side and let out her inner minx. My jeans tightened at the thought of having her underneath me and showing her what sexual healing really was. I lifted her from the counter and carried her toward the bedroom. "Are we doing a show and tell? Because I'd much rather show you than tell you."

She hummed her approval. "I'm a big advocate of showing, although I might like a little dirty talk too."

I locked her bedroom door behind us. "That can be arranged. A little show and a little tell." I set her on the bed. "Let's start with showing." I started unbuttoning her shirt and she started on mine. Our hands got tangled together in our frantic efforts. When we were finally unbuttoned, both shirts were tossed aside in a forgotten heap on the floor.

Maggie's bra was pink satin. It didn't reveal as much as the red lace, but it pushed her breasts together creating mind-blowing cleavage. It was just as sexy, if not sexier than the red lace, alluding to what was underneath without giving away the best parts.

I stared at her in awe. "If you only knew what I wanted to do to you."

Maggie's eyes hooded. "Tell me."

I slowly shook my head back and forth. "Uh-uh. More showing first. I want to see what's underneath those jeans and then I'll tell you everything, Red."

She smirked at me. "You drive a hard bargain, Mr. Montgomery. You better make the showing worth my while." Her hands worked the button of her jeans and she slid them down her long legs.

She definitely wasn't wearing granny panties. They were black, cotton bikinis with little pink hearts that matched her bra. So freakin' cute and absolutely sexy. God, she turned me on.

Maggie leaned back on her elbows, bending one leg on the mattress. My eyes roamed her body from head to toe. Her ex was an idiot. "Damn, woman."

"That the best you can do?" she teased. "I expected more from you."

All I could think about was how my jeans were too tight and the things I wanted to do to her. There were so many choices I didn't know where to start. My fingers deftly worked my jeans open. They were off in a flash and I crawled up her body.

Hovering over her, I released the clip from her hair and whispered in her ear. "You were right."

Maggie's red mane fell down around her shoulders. She arched her body into mine, "About?"

I hooked my finger in the side of her panties. "These. They're cute as hell and sexy as fuck." My lips trailed down her neck to that delicate spot that met her shoulder. "I can't wait to take them off. I want to eat your pussy, suck on your clit, make you come all over my tongue, and then I'm gonna fuck you like you've never been fucked before, Red."

She whimpered. "Oh god." Her fingers clenched my shoulders, her nails digging into the skin, and she lifted her hips to mine. The only thing that separated us was two thin layers of cotton. Our arousal permeated the room. It was so thick you could feel the air crackle around us.

One hand scraped down my back beneath my boxer briefs. She gripped my ass and pulled me closer, forcing my cock to be buried in all her softness. Maggie was like a cat in heat rubbing against me. Her hips moved wildly, dry humping me and bringing me dangerously close to coming before I even got inside her. "You're a bad girl." I pulled back. "Slow down or I'm gonna blow."

"But it's so good I can't help myself."

I pulled the straps of her bra down her shoulders. "That may be, but I can make it so much better. When I come, it's going to be deep inside you." I worked down one cup of her bra, until her nipple popped out. It was rosy pink and beautiful. My tongue circled it and lapped at the peak. Then I blew a stream of cool air over the path I'd made with my tongue. Instantly, her nipple hardened.

Maggie shivered beneath me. Her eyes fluttered and rolled back.

I gave her other breast the same treatment. By the time I was finished, she was trembling.

She reached behind her back and released the clasp, tossing her bra to the side. I took both her breasts in my hands and squeezed them together. "You have the best tits." I sucked one into my mouth and then the other, giving each one the proper attention it deserved.

When I finished worshiping her tits, I kissed down her stomach to the top of her cute panties. "I like these. They're definitely not granny panties."

She giggled. "Told you. They may not be sexy but…"

I raised a finger to her lips. "Shhh. They are." I slid them down her legs and threw them to the floor with the rest of her clothes. My hands worked their way back up and settled on her thighs. "Open for me. Let me see you."

Her feet slid up the mattress and her thighs fell apart. Instinctually, Red's hips lifted, silently asking for the pleasure I was about to deliver. I spread her legs wider. "So gorgeous." The tip of my finger slid easily through her arousal. "So wet for me. Do you know how hard that gets me? Knowing you want me to touch you, to lick you, to fuck you?"

She gasped. "No more telling. Show me."

That was all the permission I needed. Her legs were over my shoulders and my hands firmly beneath her ass when I took my first taste. I dove in without hesitation.

Some men didn't like giving oral. They didn't like the taste or the smell. They were more interested in the main event and getting their rocks off.

But I loved everything about women. I loved the way they smelled. I loved the unique taste every woman had. I loved seeing her come undone. I loved knowing I made her heart race and her pussy wet. I loved giving pleasure as much as I loved taking it.

Women were complicated creatures, but I'd spent a lot of time perfecting my skills. Sex wasn't about just sticking my dick in and pumping away. Truly amazing sex started with oral and ended with earth-shattering orgasms. Multiple orgasms. It was worth the time and effort to see the bliss on her face when the deed was done. Every woman deserved to feel spectacular. Making Red come was my mission.

She was already quivering, and I'd barely begun. The sweetness of her essence covered my tongue and lips. I ate her pretty pussy with the voraciousness of a starved man. Because I was. I was starving for everything that was Red.

Maggie threw her arm over her face, stifling a moan that escaped her lips. She writhed on the bed, telling me to keep going with her hips as they pressed into my face. There was no danger of me stopping because I wouldn't stop until we were both totally spent.

My tongue licked up through her slit until it found the tiny treasure that was swollen with need. I tickled her clit with the tip of my tongue until her breathing became shallow and ragged. I kissed with my lips. I licked with my tongue. And yes… I nipped with my teeth. And when she was hovering on the edge of ecstasy and her body was about to break, I sucked her clit between my lips and slid two fingers inside her, curling them to find her G-spot.

Maggie reached for the pillow and held it over her face as her body spasmed out of control. Muffled sounds spilled out beneath the pillow. "Chase! Fuckfuckfuck! Jesus Christ!"

And that right there was why I loved giving oral. I pulled the pillow from Red's face. Her eyes were glassy, her cheeks were flushed, and her hair was a mess, but she was beautiful. Wrecked and beautiful.

"That was intense," she gasped.

I stripped off my boxer briefs and reached for a condom. "It's about to get a whole lot more intense. I can't wait to get inside you."

She took the foil package from my hand. "I haven't got to touch you yet. Allow me."

I was barely holding it together. My cock was hard as steel and begging for release. When Red's soft hand wrapped around me, I hissed in a strained breath. My little minx stroked me up and down, playing with me... tempting me... to lose control. I knew what she was doing. Turnabout was fair play. I'd driven her to the brink before I'd let her come and now it was my turn. She teased me with her thumb, rubbing the precum all over my shaft, her hand continuing to move in slow strokes. It was torture. Torture I'd take from her anytime, anyplace.

"How bad do you want me?" she whispered.

I ripped the condom from her hand and rolled it down my cock. "You're about to find out." Grabbing her wrists, I pinned them above her head and slid into her nice and slow. Did I want to slam into her hard and fast? Absolutely! But this wasn't just about me. It was about us.

Every time I entered Red, I was amazed at how good it felt. So tight. So wet. So perfect. I savored it for a moment, just basking in everything that was her.

Maggie let out a contented sigh.

I pinned her with my eyes. "You okay?"

"Mmmm... better than okay. You feel so good inside me."

I smirked at her. "It feels good to be inside you." And then I started to move. Slow and sure. Rolling my hips to draw out the pleasure for both of us. She moved with me, meeting me thrust for thrust.

Maggie mewled beneath me. "Feels so good. Never been..."

"Fucked like this before?" I finished for her. My hips pushed further, rotating to get even deeper. I hitched one of her legs up against my side. I couldn't get deep enough.

"You. Only you have ever made me feel like this."

I knew what she meant. I felt it too, but I wasn't sure if it was the sex or something more. There was a connection between us. It was more than physical. When I was inside Maggie, I got an ache in my chest that had nothing to do with my dick.

I didn't want to think about what that meant. I didn't want to think at all.

Red clung to my shoulders. "Flip us over."

In one smooth move I was on my back. Maggie used my chest for leverage as she rode me. Her hips rocked forward and back, her tits gently bouncing with the movement. It was a beautiful sight.

I reached down to where we were connected and rubbed my thumb over her clit.

She closed her eyes and dropped her head back. "Oh god." She picked up the pace, raking her nails across my chest. At this rate, I was going to come soon, and I wanted to make it last.

I sat up and wrapped my arms around her body, one hand skimming up the back of her neck and into her hair. With some quick repositioning I was on my knees and she was on my lap, my cock still buried deep inside her. We moved as one, grinding into each other at a slow, leisurely pace. Her breasts rubbed against my chest seductively.

It was more than fucking. It was more than sex. It was our souls connecting, melting together as one. The ache in my chest grew, filling all the empty space. Consuming me.

"I'm gonna come, Chase. So hard."

I picked up the pace so we would fall over the edge together. I pumped my cock into her hard and fast. My balls tightened and my spine tingled.

Red let out a little yelp and her pussy tightened around my dick, squeezing and releasing in quick succession. My body was electrified. I came long and hard, thrusting until every last bit of cum had been milked from me.

Maggie's head collapsed against my chest. I held her to me like she was the most precious thing in the world.

All I wanted was to keep her close.

I didn't want to let go.

I didn't want to lose this feeling.

Ever.

Chapter 16
Maggie

My alarm blared its shrill reminder that it was time to start a new day. I looked to my right, only to find the sheets cold and empty.

I'd fallen asleep wrapped in Chase's arms, my head on his chest. I'd felt warm and content.

He promised he'd leave, and he had. So why was I disappointed? Why did I feel an emptiness inside me, when he'd only done what I'd made him promise to do?

It was irrational. It was stupid. But deep down I knew what it was. Last night he'd made me feel loved and I hadn't felt that in so long. He hadn't said the words and neither had I. It was too soon for love. My head got the message, but my heart had other ideas.

I rubbed at the ache in my chest. I didn't have time to dwell on my heart. I needed a strong dose of caffeine and a shower. I lifted the sheet and sniffed… yeah, definitely a shower.

The red numbers on my alarm clock glared at me. I had exactly forty-five minutes before I had to wake Ella for school. I clambered out of bed and started the coffee maker, then headed to the shower. I let the hot water run over me, erasing the evidence of last night. After washing my hair, I squirted some body wash on my bath sponge and scrubbed it over my skin. I took the time to shave my legs and all my intimate parts, something I hadn't bothered much with before I'd run back into Chase.

Before him, my nights were predictable. There was a ninety-nine point ninety-nine percent chance that I'd crawl into bed alone. Now, I wasn't sure what the nights would bring. Better to be prepared than caught without my lady parts in pristine condition. When I ran the sponge between my legs, there was a soreness that reminded me how I'd spent my last two nights. It made me miss him more.

I'd only known him a week. None of it made sense.

It had to be the endorphins that had me feeling this way. That was the only explanation.

And with my daughter sound asleep in her bedroom, it wasn't something I could contemplate.

I pulled myself together, woke Ella, made her breakfast, and got her dressed for school. We rushed to the car, as was our usual, and Ella hopped into the back seat.

She buckled herself in and kicked her legs. "Where did Chase go?"

I peered at her through the rearview mirror. "Home, ladybug."

"Did he have to take care of Not My Cat?"

I chuckled. "Maybe."

"Is he coming over tonight?"

I frowned. "I don't know. He has his own apartment and things to do." This was so new, and it would be silly of me to have any expectations. Yes, we had decided to give this whole thing a go, but I wasn't really sure what that meant. He had his life and I had mine. It wasn't like they were going to magically mesh together. This wasn't one of Ella's Disney movies. This was real life. We both had responsibilities and obligations. Spending every night together would be unrealistic and unhealthy.

Ella looked out the window and then met my eyes in the mirror. "But he's your boyfriend. He can live with us. He can even bring Not My Cat. I can make him a bed in my room and maybe Not My Cat would like that. We could buy him toys."

Clearly my daughter needed a lesson in reality. We'd watched one too many princess movies together. Somewhere along the line I'd led her to believe all the Disney fluff was real. I believed that princes did exist, but they were few and far between. Chase wasn't our prince, and he wasn't going to charge into our lives and save us. Besides, we didn't need saving. We were doing quite fine on our own. It wasn't responsible for me to let her think life was a fairy tale.

I hated crushing her hopes, but I needed to be real with my daughter. "That's not the way things work, ladybug. Just because Chase and I are dating doesn't mean he's going to live with us. We'll spend time with him, but he has his home, and we have ours. We won't see him every day."

"You mean like Daddy?"

Shit! How could I explain this to a six-year-old? I sighed. "Your dad has his own life. He only comes to see you. He's not my boyfriend, so it's different."

"Because he doesn't love you? He only loves me?"

Why did that question cause a lump in my throat? I'd tried with Jeff. I really had. No matter what I'd done, it was never enough. I'd given up on him, but he'd given up on me a long time ago. That reality still hurt. "Yeah."

I didn't need Jeff. I didn't even want him anymore, but the rejection stung. I hated I was even giving him space in my brain. I felt guilty. After the night Chase and I spent together, Ella's father should have been the last thing on my mind, but my wild little redhead would tie us together forever. I'd never be able to escape Jeff. He'd always be lingering in the background, a permanent part of my life.

Roxy slunk into my classroom before school started, shutting the door behind her. "Spill!"

I kept checking the spelling papers in front of me. "About?"

She grabbed the marker from my hand, leaving a streak of green across my palm. "Don't play coy with me Miss Chase-is-in-my-kitchen-and-I-don't-know-what-to-do."

I shrugged my shoulders.

"So, I guess you figured out what to do with him." She tapped her high-heeled foot.

I picked up the spelling papers and arranged them in a neat pile on the corner of my desk. "I did."

She waved the green marker around in frustration. "And?"

I kept a straight face. "He made us breakfast, then took us to the pumpkin patch." I tapped my finger to my lips. "Oh, and he did homework with Ella."

She was waiting for more juicy details. "That's it?"

I couldn't keep the charade up any longer. My face split into a shit-eating grin. "Did I mention the multiple orgasms that nearly made me black out? I'm pretty sure at one point I lost consciousness."

She slapped me on the shoulder. "You bitch! You were holding out on me. Oral or penetration?"

I held my hands up in surrender. "Would you be jealous if I said both?"

She slumped back against my desk, propping herself on the corner. "Ugh! Yes. Super jealous. It's that good?"

"Good would be the understatement of the year. Mind-blowing. Earth-shattering. World-altering. Those would all be better descriptions. His tongue is a deadly weapon, not to mention…" I motioned down toward my nether region.

"His cock. He's got a huge cock, doesn't he?" she asked on an exasperated sigh.

I nodded. "And he knows how to use it. Fuck, that man is talented."

Roxy huffed. "Now you're just bragging. But please give me all the details, and I don't mean the SparkNotes version. I'm living vicariously through you. I've been in a bit of a dry spell and I'm horny as hell."

"Seriously? This is the first time since I've known you that my sexual escapades have been better than yours." I pushed my palms toward the ceiling. "Woot, woot!" She flipped me the bird as the warning bell rang. "Sorry, no time for the gory details."

Roxy rolled her eyes. "Excellent. I'll go spend my day with a bunch of prepubescent children who think sex is getting to second base." She mimed stabbing herself in the heart. "Sad thing is I'd settle for second base right now. I think my fifth-graders are getting more action than I am."

It was a sick and twisted sentiment. Sadly, these kids were way more knowledgeable about sex than we'd been at their age. The internet had changed everything. They were doing things we hadn't done until high school, and those who weren't faked it because they didn't want to be left out.

I pouted out my lip. "I'm sorry."

She huffed. "I might actually believe you if you weren't glowing."

I straightened out my face the best I could. "This better?"

"Pfft! Now you just look constipated."

"Thank God. I don't think I could have kept that up all day." I sagged with relief.

My phone pinged several times with incoming texts. I swiped it off my desk and opened my messages.

Chase: Good morning, beautiful. Leaving you last night sucked ass.
Chase: Now I'm thinking about sucking your ass.
Chase: I meant your ass cheeks, not your actual ass.
Chase: Unless you're into that then… okay probably not.
Chase: But I would do it if that's what turns you on.
Chase: Have a great day. Call me later.
Chase: Say hi to Ella for me.

I laughed out loud and Roxy practically ripped the phone from my hands. "Awww. Isn't that sweet…," she scrunched up her nose, "and gross… but sweet."

I texted him back.

Me: I missed waking up with you. And no. I don't think so??? TTYL.

Roxy peered over my shoulder. "Question mark, question mark, question mark? You got a kinky side I don't know about?"

I tucked my phone in my pocket. "Let's just say he makes me want to try new things. I've never done that before."

She steered me toward the door. "And for good reason. Fingers, toys and cocks? Yes. Tongues? No way in hell."

"Now who's showing their kinky side?"

Roxy rolled her eyes at me. "Like that was a secret. Trust me on this one."

We walked down to the gym to pick up our students. "Are you speaking from experience?"

"Yes. It's awkward. And then they expect you to do it back. No thank you. I'd rather French kiss a baboon."

Chapter 17
Chase

Red: I don't think so???

I laughed at the question marks. I could practically see the blush creeping up her neck and into her cheeks while standing in her classroom. Pretty sure that kind of kink wasn't up either of our alleys. Both figuratively and literally.

My truck pulled up in front of her house. It felt weird being here when no one was home. I trekked along the side of her house to the back where I'd seen the shed. Pulling the doors open, I inspected the inside. It was neat and organized. A motorized pink Barbie jeep took up a large portion of the floor space. I bet Ella loved riding around the yard in that thing.

Tucked behind the Jeep was what I was looking for. I was an expert in lawn maintenance. Since my dad had died, I'd religiously done all the yard work at my mom's house. Maggie's yard wasn't overgrown by any means, but the leaves were starting to pile up. She already had enough to do without worrying about fall cleanup.

I maneuvered the lawn mower out of the shed, checked the gas and started it. Sucking the leaves up was much easier and quicker than raking. I'm sure Maggie was quite capable of handling her own yard work, but the man in me couldn't stand the thought of her pushing a mower back and forth across the yard or worse yet, spending the hours it would take her to rake. If I could take one thing off her plate, I'd do it gladly.

Maybe I was being presumptuous. Maybe I should have asked her first. I hoped I wasn't overstepping, but it wasn't like I let myself into her house to wash her not-so-granny panties. Surely, she'd appreciate my effort and the thought behind it. If I wanted to be a man she could depend on, this was a step in the right direction.

In a little over an hour the lawn was cut and free of leaves. I lined the bags up neatly along the side of the garage to be taken out on collection day and tucked the mower back into the shed. When Maggie came home, it would be one less thing on her to-do list.

Seeing it was still early, I decided to make a stop at my mom's house. Better to get it out of the way than have her blowing up my phone with texts and calls. As an added bonus, Amber wouldn't be there. I should have let her comments roll off my back like usual, but I couldn't let it go. Amber and Meredith had been thick as thieves all through school and the years after. When Meredith left me, she left Amber too. That had been the breaking point for Amber and me. She lost her best friend, but I lost so much more. I lost my whole life. Every dream I ever had was shattered by the circumstances of our separation.

Since then, I'd worked hard to rebuild my life. To be a better man. I'd tried to atone for the mistakes I'd made, but Amber wouldn't let me move forward. She continually reminded me of what a fuckup I was. I was done with her shit. I couldn't change the past, but I sure as hell could change my future. It was time.

I was ready for the twenty questions my mom and Grams were going to throw at me. Problem was, I only had a handful of answers. I didn't know anything about Maggie's family. All I knew about her ex was he sounded like a giant douche canoe who didn't appreciate the gifts he was given. Everything I'd learned about Red, I'd learned in a week. It wasn't much but it was enough to know I wanted her in my life.

"Hello?" I called out when I stepped through the front door.

"In here," my mom called back from the family room.

I should have known. *The Price is Right* was Grams' favorite show. She watched it religiously, even if she complained it wasn't the same without Bob Barker. Grams was damn good at it too. It was her dream to sit in the audience and hear her name followed by the words *Come On Down!* It'd been the same since I was a kid.

I walked into the family room to find Grams sitting in her recliner with a pad of paper and a red pen. "What did you win today?"

She consulted her notes. "A widescreen TV, a new refrigerator, and a Mustang convertible."

"Nice." If Grams actually ever got on the show she'd clean up.

My mom popped up from her seat on the couch and wrapped me in a hug. "Come in the kitchen, I'll make you lunch. Grams is bidding on the showcase. She's trying to win a trip to Tahiti."

I chuckled. "Of course she is." I followed my mom to the kitchen and sat at the table.

She started pulling things from the fridge. "I have leftover lasagna, some chicken, or I can make you a sandwich."

I hardly ever got homecooked meals and my mom was a great cook. "I'll take the lasagna. Is there any garlic bread?"

She dangled a Ziploc bag in front of my face. "What's lasagna without garlic bread?" She popped my food into the microwave and set the timer. "To what do I owe the pleasure of seeing my firstborn on a Monday morning?"

I'd promised her I would come over, but the truth was, I was a mamma's boy at heart. "I missed you." Ever since my dad died unexpectedly from a heart attack, I made sure I saw my mom at least once a week. I had regrets with my dad. I didn't ever want to have them with my mom, or Grams for that matter. It was important to make time in your life for the people you loved. I'd learned that lesson the hard way. My relationship with Amber wasn't the only relationship I'd fucked up over the years.

She kissed me on the forehead. "Well, aren't you the sweetest. I missed you too." She was stalling and I wasn't sure why. Subtlety wasn't her forte, so the biting of the tongue she was doing struck me as odd.

The microwave dinged and she set the plate in front of me. Digging in with gusto, I savored the flavors as they exploded in my mouth. "Oh my god, this is sooo good!"

She patted me on the shoulder. "I'm glad you like it. We missed you at breakfast yesterday."

And so, it started. As good as the lasagna was, acid reflux was sure to be next on the menu. I hated the guilt trips.

"Theo missed you yesterday too. Your nephew is only three and he thinks you're the best uncle ever. You shouldn't take your anger with Amber out on him. You'll only ever have one sister."

I set my fork down. "Did you give her the same speech about me? She started the whole thing."

She waved her hand at me. "Yes. We had words, but it doesn't matter who started it. If one of you don't milk the cow, there ain't gonna be no cream."

My mom had a lot of crazy expressions, but this one was lost on me. "What the hell does that mean?"

"It means everybody else suffers. Me. Grams. Theo. You two need to put this to rest."

I rubbed at my temples. "Mom, I've tried. I know I've made mistakes. I've paid for them. I'm still paying for them. But Amber ruffles my feathers every time she gets a chance. I don't need her to constantly remind me. I'm reminded every day when I look in the mirror."

"Amber was out of line," she conceded, sitting down next to me. "I'm not happy with her either, but you know what the real problem is? Why it is you let her get under your skin."

She was poking at something. I just didn't know what. "Why?"

She took my hand over the table and cradled it in hers. "Because you haven't forgiven yourself."

Pain stabbed at my chest. Memories flashed through my mind. My anger faded and remorse took its place. Tears I wouldn't let fall welled in my eyes. "I can't."

"Yes, you made mistakes. Big ones. But the choice was ultimately Meredith's."

I pointed at my chest. "It was my fault. I should have been there. I made promises I didn't keep. I failed her."

She gripped my face between her palms. "It's been seven years. How long are you going to punish yourself? I can't stand seeing you like this. You deserve to be happy."

"Do you think she's forgiven me? Do you think she's happy?" I snapped. "I destroyed everything."

My mom held my hand again. "I'm sure she has regrets too. But do I think she made a voodoo doll of you and is sticking pins in it? Highly unlikely. She's moved on."

I relaxed back into the chair and sighed. "Maybe that's what bothers me the most. We were supposed to be together forever. We had dreams. She turned and never looked back. She moved on without me. How can I hate her and love her at the same time?"

"It's a fine line. Meredith was your first love and she'll always hold a special place in your heart. But your heart is big. It always has been, you just need to open it again. Let yourself be happy."

"I think I'm starting to."

Grams burst into the kitchen. "Go find my bikini, Betty! We're going to Tahiti. I'm gonna drink piña coladas and find me a young stud on the beach. Maybe do a little horizontal mambo." She rocked her hips back and forth.

146

There were so many disturbing visuals in that statement that I would have to bleach my mind. Grams was a hoot. On her deathbed, my ass. I'm not sure what got me more, the thought of her in a bikini or that she knew what the horizontal mambo was.

"How are we going to fit that in with our trip to Ireland?" My mom played along.

Grams referred to her pad of paper, flipping the pages. "Don't forget Italy and the Alaskan Cruise. It's going to be a busy year. Maybe Chase could take his new girl on a trip." She waggled her eyebrows at me.

And now it was time for the inquisition.

"We were just getting to that. Chase was going to tell me all about it," my mom said smugly.

I narrowed my eyes at her. "I was?"

"Uh-huh."

Grams scurried to the table and scooted her chair next to mine. "What's the 313?"

I burst out laughing. "You mean the 411. 313 is an area code."

She playfully swatted my chest. "313, 411, whatever. Give me the dirt."

"Yes," my mom prodded. "Tell us about Maggie."

"And her daughter," Grams added. "Don't forget that."

I pointed between the women on either side of me. "You two really need to get out more. Why is my love life so fascinating?"

"Because it's the first time you've mentioned anyone in forever. We want you to be happy."

I pulled my phone from my pocket and showed them the selfie I had taken of the three of us at the farm. "Does this look happy?"

They both peered at the picture I proudly displayed. Maggie, me, and Ella's toothless smile lit up the screen.

When I got to work, Zack called a staff meeting. All of us crowded into his office with questioning glances. Usually when Zack called us together, it wasn't for anything good. I racked my brain to think if anything had been amiss lately. Besides Draven and Layla's PDA, nothing came to mind.

Kyla and Tori, two of Rissa's best friends, squeezed into the back of the room and shut the door. Kyla, who was one of our contract designers, bumped me with her hip. "Do you know what's going on?"

I shook my head. "No idea. I hope Zack's not selling this place."

Layla looked worried. "What if he and Rissa are moving to California? It would make sense."

Draven chimed in. "He loves Forever Inked. I don't think that's it. He promised they were going to stay here."

Everyone's eyes swung toward the door when Brian, Layla's bestie and a longtime friend of the shop, entered. "Sorry I'm late." He kissed Layla on the temple, and she gave him a tight hug.

Now, I was really intrigued. He didn't even work here. *What the hell was going on?*

Zack cleared his throat. "No worries. You're right on time. I'm sure you're all wondering why I called everyone together today. Rest assured, it's good news."

That didn't make me feel much better. Good news to him wasn't necessarily good news for the rest of us.

Rissa gave him a playful slap. "You're making everyone nervous. Let me tell them."

Zack kissed Rissa on top of her mass of curls. "Of course, you're the boss."

Rissa clapped her hands together. "It actually is really good news. As you know my debut album is releasing soon and the music execs have planned a premiere party. They wanted to do it at some fancy venue in LA…" her smile got super wide, "but I convinced them to have it here. This is where I got my start, and this is where my friends are. It's going to be at The Locker on November 2, and you're all invited."

Excitement broke out in the small room. Everyone began talking at once and thanking Rissa for including us in the special event. I was so happy for her. She'd come a long way since I first saw her sing at The Locker.

When everyone quieted down, Rissa handed out the invitations and tickets that were printed on thick, fancy paper. "Attendance is by invitation only. You're all welcome to bring your significant other. Dress is formal. I'm really sorry about the late notice, but we had to keep the time and location a secret from the public, so please keep the details of the event to yourselves."

Draven spoke up, "Understood. But by formal, do you mean a tux?"

Zack laughed. "Yeah, don't worry I've got you covered. We're not exactly the tux wearing crowd, so I've already made arrangements. Clarissa and I decided to treat everyone to formal wear for the night, all you have to do is go in for a fitting. Ladies, Rissa has found a spectacular dress shop where I'm sure you will find something to your liking. The cost is on us."

I didn't want Zack and Rissa to pay for our attire, even if they could afford it. It wasn't a secret that Zack was wealthy. Like millionaire wealthy. And Rissa was going to be raking in the big bucks too. Despite their wealth, or maybe because of it, the whole idea made me feel like a cheap lowlife. I hoped everyone wasn't going to hate me for this. "Zack, although we appreciate your generosity, we can pay for our own clothes."

Grumbles of agreement echoed around me. Thank God I wasn't the only one.

Rissa answered instead. "Chase, we want to do it. If it weren't for the people in this room I don't know where I'd be. You were my friends when you had no reason to be, you supported me when I was trying to break into the industry, and you covered our asses when we went to California for a month. None of this would have been possible without all of you. Consider it our thank you. Please know that in our eyes it doesn't even come close to being enough."

Zack wrapped an arm around his beautiful wife. "We just want you to come and have a good time. No strings attached. I promise."

Well, I couldn't very well look a gift horse in the mouth.

Brian, who'd been very quiet, answered, "I think I speak for all of us. Thank you. I'm honored to be included."

"We're honored to have you as part of our family," Rissa said.

Zack scanned the room and laughed. "This is the most fucked-up family I've ever seen, but I'm glad it's mine."

Layla raised her fist in the air. "Hell yeah we are!"

As we exited the office, worries put to rest, Brian nudged me. "You bringing Becca?"

"Nah." I could already see the look on Maggie's face when I showed her the tickets. I winked at him. "I've got a new girl and she's going to freak when I tell her."

149

Chapter 18
Maggie

"I swear, Maggie, I didn't do it."

I sighed into the phone. "Seriously, Patty? It was either you or dad. And I know for a fact dad didn't cut my grass and bag all my leaves. Mom had him out shopping all day. She's on a redecorating binge."

"Again? I swear every time mom has everything exactly the way she wants it, she changes her mind," my brother said.

"Hey, it works out for us though when she hands down all the things she's tired of. But about my grass…"

"I've been in back to back meetings with clients all day. Even if I wanted to cut your grass, I wouldn't have had time. You know I've been working overtime trying to make partner."

That was the truth. Patrick worked at a corporate law firm. The competition was fierce, and he'd been busting his ass. "How's that going anyway?"

"I think I'm at the top of a short list. It's promising."

I was so proud of my brother, but he worked way too hard and put in way too many hours. I worried it would affect his relationship. "Did you ask Brian to move in with you yet?"

He groaned. "No."

Ella flitted into the room wearing her tutu and fairy wings. She spun in a circle and almost tumbled over but caught herself at the last second. Her tiara sat sideways on her head. "Whoa! That was a good one." She pointed her wand at me. "Is that Chase?"

She was a persistent little thing. I covered the phone with my hand. "It's Uncle Patty. Do you want to say hi?"

She practically ripped it out of my hand. "Hi, Uncle Patty! Did you know I'm going to be a fairy princess for Halloween? I gots glittery wings and a tiara and a wand. It's sooooo pretty."

I wasn't sure what my brother was saying to her, but she broke out in a fit of giggles. "I love you too, Uncle Patty. You're the bestest uncle ever."

Ella handed me the phone back and dashed off toward her room. "Well, you just made her day. Dinner on Wednesday?"

"Wouldn't miss it for the world. And Maggie, maybe it was the guy who sent you flowers."

I hadn't disclosed any information about my relationship with Chase. It was new. It was intense. I could barely deal with it myself, let alone tell my family. "Ummm." The words stuck in my throat.

"You don't have to say anything. But if it was him, maybe he's not a fucktard and you should hang onto that."

I felt the heat creeping up my chest. "Thanks, Patty. I think I might. And when I'm sure it's more than just a fling I'll let you meet him."

"Hey, there's no hurry. I dated Brian for a month before I introduced you. I get it. You're being cautious and I respect that. You're a good mom. Just make sure he's good to my princess."

Patrick had no idea how good Chase was with Ella. I wanted to think it was real, but there was a tiny bit of me that was holding back. It seemed too good to be true. It was hard to believe that one man could change my life so much. I was truly happy for the first time in forever. "He's… I'm just happy. He makes me forget all the shit and he makes Ella smile. I can't explain it."

"You don't have to. I can hear it in your voice. I think you have another call to make."

"What do you mean?" I feigned ignorance.

"Call the non-fucktard who cut your grass."

My brother was so eloquent. "I will. Love you, Patty."

"Love you too, sis."

I drummed my nails on the counter and looked at the clock. Chances were Chase was working. I didn't want to interrupt him during an appointment, but I couldn't let this go either. Before I could change my mind, I clicked on his contact and made the call.

It rang twice before he answered, "Hello, beautiful."

A giggle escaped my mouth. I didn't think I'd ever get used to his charming ways. "Are you my mystery maintenance man?"

"Why? You got other guys who want to mow your lawn?"

It was a clear sexual innuendo I eagerly played into. "You think my lawn needs to be mowed?"

He groaned. "Red, your lawn and bushes are trimmed perfectly. Did you call just to give me a hard-on?"

I giggled again. "No, I called to thank you. You don't know how much it helps. I was thinking I was going to have to put Ella on raking duty to get it done."

"I had some time this morning. Just thought I'd take something off your to-do list. I probably should have asked you first but…"

Chase was more than confident in the bedroom but second-guessed himself when it came to our relationship outside of it. Maybe I'd been too hard on him about Ella. Yes, he'd made a couple of blunders in the beginning, but he'd more than made up for it. Mowing my grass shouldn't have been something he worried about. I stopped him before he could apologize for something that needed no apologies. "You didn't have to ask. It was a perfect surprise. I really appreciate it. As a matter of fact, I'd like to show you my appreciation tonight."

"Hmmm. That sounds really nice. I should get off around eight."

"I'll be waiting."

After hanging up the phone, I called to my ballerina in training. "Ladybug!"

Ella bounded out of her bedroom, fairy wings and tutu still on. "Yes, Momma?"

I scooped her up and set her on the kitchen island. "I have a job for you."

She loved being a helper and smiled at me with her toothless grin. "What?"

"How would you like to make something special for Chase? He needs a thank you for cutting our grass and I think he would really like a card. Do you think you could make him one?"

"I'm great at making cards. Can I use markers?"

I lifted her off the counter. "Sure. Go get your art supplies and some white paper."

She dashed off to our extra bedroom. It was part toy room, part office. The room was a disaster on any given day, but that's what doors were for. I always promised myself one day it would get cleaned, but that day hadn't come yet. Most people had a junk drawer, we had an entire junk room.

Ella came back with markers, paper, glitter, and glue. She was diving in with full enthusiasm. I grabbed the glitter off the table. "We'll do this last." If I didn't, glitter would cover every surface of my kitchen. It was the gift that kept on giving. The custodians at school hated when I let the kids use glitter. No matter how many times they swept or vacuumed it kept reappearing.

My daughter scrunched up her nose at me. "But I had plans."

I ruffled her hair. "I'm sure you did. Don't worry, we'll get it all glittered when you're done with the picture."

That seemed to appease her. I folded the paper like a card and Ella got to work. As a bonus, it gave me time to fix dinner without interruptions.

Chase had barely made it through the door before his arms were wrapped around me. One hand cupped the back of my neck while the other was firmly on my ass. His lips pressed against mine and heat exploded between my legs. There was no way I'd ever tire of the way this man made me feel. It was intoxicating.

He broke the kiss and we were both breathless. "Hey, Red."

I pressed a hand against his chest. "I'm not Red yet. Someone is still awake. She's been waiting for you."

"You'll always be Red, whether you're in mom mode or Chase mode. I find both extremely sexy."

My heart swelled. Usually, mom mode won out. Being a single mom didn't always give me time to be a woman. The man standing in my entryway allowed me to be both. Being with Chase felt like I was finally finding some much needed balance. "The woman in me would like nothing more than to take you to bed, but the mom in me needs you to go talk to my daughter."

Chase smiled at me. "I don't want to disappoint her. Is it okay if I peek my head in her room?"

"She'd like that."

Chase headed down the hall and gently pushed her door open. "Are you awake, princess bug?"

Ella rolled toward his voice, the card she made him clutched in her tiny hands. "I've been waiting for you."

He crept into Ella's room, turned on the bedside lamp and sat on the edge of her bed. Chase pushed her hair off her face. "I'm sorry I made you wait."

"It's okay. Momma said you had to work," she said sleepily.

"I did, but I'm glad I got to see you tonight."

Ella straightened out the card in her hand. "I made you something for cutting our grass." She offered the card to Chase, a few pieces of glitter sticking to her cheek.

Chase carefully brushed the glitter from her face and inspected the card with a big, red glittered heart on the front.

"You made this for me?"

"Uh-huh. Momma helped."

"This is beautiful, princess bug."

"Open it," she prodded.

Chase unfolded the card. Inside was a picture she had drawn with the words *"Tank You Chase!"* Ella sat up tall and pointed to the picture. "This is you and this is Momma and this is me. And this is Not My Cat because he's your pet."

"I love it, princess bug. I especially like your curly, red hair." He pointed to another place on the card. "Who's this?"

"That's my puppy. I think when we're a family we should get one and his name can be Henry. He and Not My Cat can be friends. Cats and dogs aren't supposed to be friends, but I think they would be and then Not My Cat wouldn't be so lonely."

"That's a great idea and I think Not My Cat might like that. Thank you for the card. I'll hang it in my studio at work so everybody can see it." Chase kissed the top of Ella's head, "Good night, princess bug."

Ella wrapped her arms around Chase's neck and kissed him on the cheek. "Good night. Can you tuck me in?"

"Of course." Chase tucked the blankets around her like she was a little burrito. "Snug as a bug in a rug."

"A princess bug," she giggled.

"Yes, a princess bug." He tapped her on the nose. "Sweet dreams, baby girl."

"You too."

He turned out the light and backed out of her room. "Good night."

Ella's eyes drooped and she let out a big yawn. "Good night."

I couldn't erase the dopey smile that spread across my face. "Thank you," I whispered, as I quietly shut the door. Seeing the two of them together warmed my heart.

Family.

It was a concept in my life that had been lacking an integral element for a long time. Tonight, Chase filled in that missing piece with barely any effort at all. My head swam with thoughts of the three of us creating our own family and maybe adding to it in the future.

"No need. She's the sweetest."

I chuckled. "She has her moments."

He held up the card Ella made. "This was one of them." He opened it as we went to the kitchen. "Seems she has everything planned out." Chase pointed to the picture of the dog. "Henry?"

I grabbed him a beer from the fridge and handed it to him. "Don't even. I don't have the time or energy to deal with a dog."

He smirked at me. "Maybe one day? I love dogs and you have a great yard. Plus, it'd be a friend for Not My Cat. I'm thinking basset hound."

I grabbed my glass of wine off the counter and groaned. "And I'm thinking you're crazy."

Chase held his hands together in a praying motion and fluttered his eyes at me. "But they're so cute: short, little legs and long, floppy ears."

I smacked him on the shoulder. "Not you too. Talk to me again when you're willing to scoop dog poop out of the yard."

He puffed out his chest. "I can scoop poop. Actually, I'm an excellent pooper scooper."

I tilted my wine glass at him. "We can revisit this in six months. Right now, it's a hard no." The last thing I needed was a dog to take care of.

"You're no fun." Chase pouted. "And here I was thinking you were. I brought you a surprise and everything."

My ears perked up. "I can be fun. What is it?" I didn't see a surprise when he walked in.

He scrunched up his face. "I'm not sure dog haters are invited."

I poked him in the chest. "I'm not a dog hater. I'm a dog waiter. Big difference."

Chase grabbed me around the waist and pulled me down on his lap playfully, pressing kisses into my neck. "Yeah?"

"Yeah. What's my surprise?"

He reached into his back pocket and pulled out two tickets. "Want to be my date?"

I swiped the tickets from his hand and read the fancy writing on them. "Are you shitting me?" I tapped on the paper with my index finger. "This is here? And we're invited?"

Chase grabbed the tickets out of my hand. "I'm invited, but… I can bring a plus-one. I mean, my mom would be totally stoked to go or maybe Grams, but if you think it'd be something you'd like…"

"Are you kidding me?" I practically ripped the tickets back from him. "I want to go. The Rissa Black premiere party? I mean, I know she's like a normal person because I've met her, but still, it's a once in a lifetime." I inspected the tickets more carefully. "Formal attire? Does that mean you have to wear a tux?"

He laughed. "It does."

Popping up off his lap, I started to pace. "What am I going to wear?" I started mentally ticking off the contents of my closet. There were a couple of nice dresses I wore for weddings and special events, but nothing that would be suitable for a premiere party. What did one even wear for something like this?

Chase watched me in amusement. "You're cute when you're stressed."

I scowled at him. "I literally have nothing to wear."

"I like you in nothing. As a matter of fact, it's my favorite."

All of our nights included Chase that week. It was finally Friday. The one day a week Jeff bestowed his presence upon us. I didn't have the heart to ask Ella to keep Chase a secret anymore.

My relationship was none of his business. Lord knows I gave him plenty of chances to be part of my life. Jeff made it perfectly clear he wasn't interested in more.

And more is what I needed.

More than just a once a week visit with his daughter.

More than just an occasional fuck when it suited him.

More than just an obligation in his busy life.

Chase was my *more*.

The man who helped with homework while I cooked dinner.

Chase was my last glass of wine at the end of a long day.

The arms that wrapped around me in the middle of the night.

The kisses that set my soul ablaze, making me tingle from head to toe.

The release I needed from my carefully planned life.

Chase was everything I deserved, and Jeff had no say about it.

He would have to deal and that was the bottom line. When Ella left for dinner with her father, I kissed her goodbye and let the pieces land where they may. I was the queen in this messed-up chess game we'd been playing for years. Him thinking he was the king who held all the power was a delusion he'd have to get over. And my daughter certainly wasn't a pawn.

Shortly after Ella left, I heard Chase's truck rumble up in my driveway. It was the first time we had been truly alone all week and I planned on taking advantage of it. There would be no soft whispers or muffled moans. We had the house to ourselves and nothing was off-limits.

The mischievous twinkle in Chase's eyes as he entered my kitchen told me we were on the same page. Time alone was precious, and we wouldn't waste it.

"Have I told you lately how much you turn me on?"

My fingers grasped the front of his shirt. "You don't have to say anything. You show me every night."

Chase pressed his lips into my neck and ran his tongue along my collarbone. Every sweep was like fire on my skin. He lit a path down my chest as he unbuttoned my blouse. The fabric was thrown to the floor, leaving me in only lace and satin.

I tugged at the hem of his Henley. "I need this off."

Chase reached behind his neck and removed his shirt in a single motion. *Why was that so sexy?*

Both of us slid our jeans off and kicked them aside. We stood in the middle of the kitchen in nothing but our underwear. It was taboo. Something that would never happen with the threat of tiny footsteps interrupting us. It was the first time we had been intimate outside the confines of my bedroom.

Chase ran his finger along the side of my face. "Are you okay?"

"More than okay." With my hands on his hips, I made my confession. "I've never had sex in the kitchen."

His fingers played along my shoulder, caressing up my neck until they cupped the back of my head. "This kitchen or any kitchen?"

My experiences with sex were purely conventional: beds, couches, twice in the back seat of a car. That was it. My inexperience at the age of twenty-eight was humiliating to admit. I bit my lip and stared up at Chase through my lashes. "Any kitchen."

I was airborne in seconds, letting out a squeal as my ass hit the cool granite of the kitchen island.

He leaned his body over mine until my back hit the smooth surface. His arms caged me in on both sides, making me a captive to his seduction. "That's something that should be rectified immediately."

I felt something sticky on my butt cheek. "This is where I make Ella's lunch."

"That's what Clorox wipes are for." He smirked. "I promise we'll have it all sanitized before she comes home."

"I'm not worried about that." I lifted my hip from the counter. "But I think I just sat in jelly."

Chase leaned down to inspect the offended area. "You sure did." His tongue licked at my exposed cheek. "Grape, if I'm not mistaken."

"It's her favorite…"

Chase pressed a finger to my lips. "Grown-up time and no woman of mine is going to be deprived of culinary sex. What would you like? Italian sausage or Manwich?"

I giggled. "You're not even Italian and Manwich sounds like a ménage à trois. How about a frank and beans?"

He frowned at me. "Now that's just damn insulting." Taking my wrist, Chase placed my hand on his erection that strained against his boxer briefs. "Does that feel like just a frank?" He moved my hand lower to cup his balls. "And these are definitely more than beans."

He was absolutely right. Chase was way more than a frank and beans. I quirked an eyebrow up. "Wiener schnitzel?"

"No." He shook his head. "Just, no. You're not very good at this game. How about a five-dollar footlong?"

My nose scrunched up. "Sounds cheap and painful."

Chase placed his hands on my knees, blew out a frustrated breath and rolled his eyes to the ceiling. "Jesus Christ, Red." Then he leveled me with a hard stare. "Fuck it."

Chase left me alone on the island while he inspected my fridge. "What are you doing?"

He came away with a can of Reddi-wip that I had bought for our girls' night ice cream sundaes. "Fuck all the innuendos. I want Boston cream pie. Dessert it is." He unsnapped my bra and tossed it aside. The cold spray of the whipped cream hitting my nipples sent a shock wave down my spine. Chase lifted my hips, and my panties were thrown to the floor. He roughly pushed my thighs apart baring all of me. Before I had a chance to react, the same white cream covered the most intimate parts of me.

My cheeks burned. "Chase?"'

His tongue smoothed across his bottom lip. "So gorgeous, spread out for me like a feast." One finger ran through my slit and he popped it into his mouth, licking the whipped cream from the tip. "Sooo good."

Speechless, I bit my bottom lip. My muscles involuntarily clenched and my body shivered in anticipation. Clearly my body knew what was coming next even if my brain hadn't quite caught on yet. "Are you gonna…?"

Chase dropped to his knees and pulled me to the edge of the counter, dangling my legs over his shoulders. "No more talking. Let me enjoy my dessert." His mouth lapped at my pussy. Despite the sticky mess, I melted into the granite beneath me.

The man between my legs ate at me like I was the best thing he'd ever tasted. My back arched off the counter and my head dipped back in ecstasy. I don't know if he was doing something different or if it was the thrill of having sex in a normally forbidden place. I didn't question it. I just enjoyed the ride. My hands threaded through his hair and my hips bucked into his face. Chase made me feel unbridled and free. I didn't worry that his face was between my thighs. I didn't worry about the stream of incomprehensible profanity or the guttural moans that came from my lips. All I could focus on was how he made me feel and the shockwaves that traveled through my body.

When the last tingles of my orgasm left my toes, Chase finally came up for air. He wiped his mouth with the back of his arm. "Delicious. Best dessert I've ever had. And now for the cherries on top."

I wasn't sure what he was talking about until his tongue licked up my stomach and his mouth latched onto one of my nipples. He feasted and sucked the tip between his lips. Then he gave my other breast the same attention. Whipped cream coated his mouth and nose. I wiped it off with my finger. "You got a little something right there." I licked the sweetness off my finger and giggled.

He smirked at me. "Oh, you think that's funny?" Next thing I knew, he smashed our bodies together and kissed me passionately. We were both a sticky mess from lips to hips.

"Chase!"

He rubbed his nose against mine in an Eskimo kiss. "Now you got a little something right there too."

"You're so bad," I scolded.

159

"Only in the best way," he said, before he licked more whipped cream off me. Chase grabbed the dish towel from the counter and wiped between my legs. Then he pulled a condom out of our heap of clothes on the floor and rolled it down his hard length. "And since you couldn't decide what you wanted, I've decided for you. You're getting the Chase Deluxe with my secret special sauce." Tucking a stray strand of hair behind my ear, he whispered, "Guaranteed to satisfy and have you begging for more."

He didn't disappoint. The *Chase Deluxe* was my new favorite thing. It wasn't slow and sweet nor was it fast and wild. It was simply… perfect. His aqua eyes never left mine the entire time, connecting us in a way I'd never experienced before. The way he looked at me made me feel beautiful and desired. Sex with Chase was an addiction. He was like my favorite romance novel. At the end of each chapter, I felt totally satisfied yet craved to find out what would happen next, because there was no way it could get any better but somehow it always did.

I would never look at my kitchen the same way. Every surface was covered in sex and sin. The space was forever branded with our indiscretions and if I had my way it wouldn't be the last time.

When we both came down from our orgasms and blood finally returned to our brains, Chase swept a thumb down my cheek. "Now let's get you cleaned up." In one fell swoop, he scooped me up from the counter and carried me to the bathroom. Setting me down, he leaned into the glass shower and turned on the water, checking to make sure the temperature was just right.

I grabbed a clip from the counter and swept my hair up on top of my head to keep it dry.

Chase groaned, "Fuck, you look sexy as hell. I've got that whole hot teacher fantasy going on in my head."

"Hmmm," I tapped my lip with my red nail, "I'm not so sure it's a fantasy anymore. Seems we've turned that into a reality. What is it with guys and that fantasy anyway? I never quite understood it."

Chase groaned. "It's the illusion of sweet with a side order of sin. And trust me Red, you've fulfilled every fantasy I've ever had. I never knew it could be this good." Still naked as the day he was born, Chase pulled me into the shower and began to lather up my body.

I tried to keep my eyes on his, but it was impossible. I quirked my lips to the side as I stared down at his erection. "Seems I haven't completely fulfilled all your fantasies." My hand wrapped around his hard length and began to stroke him. It only seemed fair. He had brought me to pleasure several times, yet he'd only gotten to come once. I dropped to my knees to make sure tonight would be as memorable for him as it had been for me.

Chapter 19
Chase

Because spontaneity wasn't always possible, moments like these were even better. When I walked through the door tonight my dick did a full salute knowing we were alone. Alone time didn't happen often, so you bet your ass I was going to take full advantage.

The chance we'd get caught if her ex decided to cut his visit with Ella short only upped the excitement factor. It wasn't a feeling I'd had since I moved out of my parents' house. Even the few trysts in my studio at work hadn't given me the same zing.

I wrapped Maggie in a fuzzy pink towel that reminded me we wouldn't be alone for much longer. I poked my head into Maggie's room and checked the time on her alarm clock. We still had a half hour. "Why don't you get yourself together and I'll handle the kitchen."

She blushed. "Thank you." I watched as Maggie's ass swayed to her bedroom. She turned back to me, clutching the towel to her chest. "For everything. The shower. The kitchen." She bit the side of her thumb nervously. "For taking a chance on me. On us. For just being you. Thank you."

This woman.

She completely invaded my heart. Made me want to give everything to her when I'd

thought I had nothing left to offer. She made me want to be a better man. For her. For Ella. For both of them.

"Always, Red."

She gave me a shy smile and dropped her towel before closing the door behind her.

Damn!

I quickly tidied the bathroom and ran a towel through my hair before heading back to the kitchen to get dressed.

The space was a mess. Whipped cream and sex covered every surface. I got busy wiping everything down and used the Clorox wipes from under the sink to erase our debauchery from the cabinets and the counter. Once the evidence was gone, I tossed the towels and Maggie's clothes into the washing machine.

Bang! Bang! Bang!

I froze and stared at the front door. *The fuck?*

Maggie hurried from her room while pulling her arm through her sweater. "Shit! You might want to go hang out in my room for a minute."

If she thought I was going to leave her to open the door herself, she had another thing coming. I held her by the shoulders as she tried to squirm away to get to the door. "What the hell's going on, Red? Who is it?"

She pressed her lips together.

The banging came again.

"Maggie?"

She sighed. "If I had to guess, Ella told her dad about you."

"And?"

"He's not happy." Her body sagged. "Let me handle it."

I hadn't met the douche yet. I'd told myself I'd be civil to him for Ella's sake, but this first meeting wasn't exactly how I pictured it going down. "I'm not hiding in your bedroom like a pussy. He'll meet me eventually because I'm not going anywhere. Might as well rip the Band-Aid off."

"Chase," she protested. "I don't think…"

I wrapped my arms around her and pulled her to my chest. "I've got your back, Red. Always."

She stared into my eyes. "Okay. Let's do this, but let me lead. I know how to handle him."

I wasn't happy about it, but out of respect for Maggie, I agreed. He was a part of her life and I didn't want to make things any more difficult than they had to be.

Maggie unlocked the door and pulled it open with a smile pasted on her face while I stood solidly behind her.

The guy's fist was raised as if he were getting ready to pound again. Ella ran under his arm and wrapped herself around my legs in a big hug. "Hi, Chase! Did you and mommy have dinner while I was at McDonald's? My belly is soooo full. I had chicken nuggets and a chocolate milkshake," she chattered away.

I scooped her up in my arms. "We ate." It wasn't exactly a lie. "Did you have fun?"

"Soooo much fun. I climbed way up high on the playscape and crawled through the tubes, then I slid down into the balls."

Ella continued to talk a million miles a minute and I noticed not once did she mention the man who had taken her out. It was sad she was more interested in a Happy Meal than her father.

The douchebag who stood on Maggie's porch scowled at me. He looked like I imagined—an entitled, self-righteous frat boy, complete with a polo shirt, khakis and a combed-to-the-side hairstyle that gave him that boy-next-door vibe.

Maggie leaned into the side of the door, casually crossing her arms. "Hey, you're early. I didn't expect you for another twenty minutes."

He scanned Maggie up and down, scrutinizing her appearance. "Obviously." He clenched his teeth as he sized me up. "We need to talk."

I could already see where this was going. He was going to be a dick.

Maggie sighed, waving her hand in my direction. "Jeff, this is Chase. Chase, Jeff."

I stuck my hand out in an attempt to play nice. "Good to finally meet you, man." No need for the guy to hate me right off the bat.

Jeff crossed his arms over his chest, eyeing the tattoos on my arms with disgust. "Alone, Mags. Right the fuck now. This is about *our* daughter."

I didn't like the way he talked to her with a condescending tone. Ordering her around like he had a right to. I set Ella on her feet and kneeled in front of her. "Why don't you go play in your room for a few minutes while we talk to your dad."

She pecked me on the cheek. "Okay, Chase. I missed you."

I gave her a tight hug. "Missed you too, princess bug."

Ella ran off to her room and closed the door. *Smart girl.*

I stood to my full height and took a step forward to close the distance between us, crossing my arms over my chest to mimic dickhead's stance. "Are we going to have a problem here." I had a good three inches on him and probably outweighed him by at least forty pounds. I was lean, but solid. Working out five days a week had its perks.

"*We're* not going to have a problem," he pointed between the two of us, "because you're not part of this conversation. Ella's *my* daughter, asshole."

My jaw ticked. I was barely holding it together. This guy was a dickwad. Maggie should be thankful he never married her because she'd dodged a bullet for sure.

Jeff and I stared at each other in a Mexican standoff. He was trying to go all alpha dog on me, and I wasn't backing down. I should have, but everything about him pissed me off. Especially the way he tried to intimidate Red.

Finally, after a few tense moments of silence, Maggie put her hand on my chest in a gentle, calming matter. "I got this. We're just going to go on the porch." She gave me a weak smile. "Trust me."

It took everything I had to step back, but I had to believe this wasn't the first time Maggie had dealt with his shit. I wasn't Ella's father, and technically I had no right to intervene, but it killed me all the same. What kind of man was I to let Maggie step into the fire on her own?

Apparently, the kind that was a pussy and took two steps back.

I gave her a curt nod as she stepped out on the porch. She tried to pull the door closed behind her, but I grabbed it at the last second so it stayed open a couple of inches. Yeah, I might not have been standing beside her, but I wasn't going anywhere either. Whatever he had to say, I wanted to hear it. I wanted dickwad douchebag to give me a reason to knock him flat on his ass. I leaned closer to the door so I could eavesdrop like a curious child listening to his parents bicker.

"You don't have to be so rude," she started.

"I'm rude? Who the fuck is that guy? And why the hell is he hanging around my daughter?"

"I already told you. His name is Chase and he's my boyfriend. Is that a problem?"

Boyfriend. Take that dickwad.

He raised his voice, "Yeah, it's a fucking problem!"

"Stop right there! You've had your chance. Plenty of them. You made it crystal clear that you didn't want to be part of my life. What I decide to do is none of your business."

That's my girl. You tell him, Red.

"It sure as hell was my business when you let me crawl in your bed a few weeks ago."

Wait! What? He's lying. There's no way...

"And I told you that was the end of it. It shouldn't have happened then and it's never happening again. You can't just breeze in and out of my life when it suits you or your need to get your dick wet. I told you it was over."

"You've said it before, and you still let me in."

Well, fuck a duck.

"Not anymore."

"And what about my daughter?"

"What about *our* daughter?"

"You're going to expose her to some low-life dirtbag because you feel the need to get back at me?"

Low-life dirtbag? What the actual fuck?

Maggie tsked. "You're so self-centered. Me being with Chase has absolutely nothing to do with you. He's not a dirtbag. As a matter of fact, he might be the best thing that's ever happened to me. And your daughter... she loves him. He actually spends time with her and listens to her."

Take that, Mr. Douchey McDoucherton.

"Mags..." he pleaded.

Keep it coming, Red. Don't backdown now!

"Enough. You can be annoyed all you want, but you don't get to have a say. You gave up that right a long time ago. Maybe if you ever paid attention to your daughter, you'd see she was happy. And so am I. You'll always be Ella's father, and I would never try to take that away from you, but who I decide to date is none of your concern. Ella being happy and healthy is all you should be concerned about. And she is, so there's nothing to worry about. Now, I think it's time for you to go."

Good girl.

"We're not done talking about this, Maggie."

"Yeah, we are. Goodbye, Jeff."

Bye-bye dickwad.

Maggie came in and leaned back against the door. She let out a frustrated sigh. "I'm sorry."

I pulled her into my arms. "No. I'm sorry. Are you okay?"

She shook her head. "You have nothing to be sorry about. It was a long time coming. I should have already dealt with it."

I tilted her head back so I could look into her sad eyes. "I'm proud of you for standing up for yourself."

"Honestly, it felt good. I've wanted to do that for a long time. It feels final. Like I've finally shut the door on the back and forth. It feels... liberating."

I trailed my thumb along her jaw. "Tell me what you need. Do you want me to leave? Give you and Ella some time?" Lord knows it was the last thing I wanted to do but I was in uncharted territory.

She shook her head. "No, I want you to stay. I don't want to be alone."

"Are you afraid of him?" I asked, brushing a strand of hair behind her ear.

"Pfft...no, Jeff would never hurt me. His ego is wounded is all. For the first time in his life, he's realizing he's replaceable. He can't imagine me with someone else."

"Someone like me? A dirtbag." It shouldn't have bothered me, but it stung. I'd been called a lot of things in my life, but *dirtbag* had never been one of them.

"You were listening," she accused.

I shrugged my shoulders. "Just keeping an eye out for trouble."

"I've been dealing with his kind of trouble for years. He's more bark than bite, and he's jealous. Don't let what he said bother you." She stared down at her feet and shuffled uneasily, "So, you heard everything?"

I let out a ragged breath and ran a hand through my hair. "About you two sleeping together? Yeah." I didn't want to think she had cheated on me, but I needed to know. That first week or so we hadn't made any commitments, so I couldn't really be angry at her.

Maggie grasped my face between her hands, "It was before we met up at The Locker. I wouldn't do that to you. You have to know that."

I kissed her temple. "I believe you, but I don't want to stand in the way if you still have feelings for him. I want you to be happy. And I don't want to be an obstacle between Ella and her father."

"I am and you're not. Forget about Jeff. I know who I want and he's standing right here in front of me. Jeff will always be a part of my life and he'll be a part of yours if you decide this isn't too much for you. It's a lot, I know, but don't let him ruin what we've been building. We'll make this work."

Ella's feet pitter-pattered into the room. She propped her hands on her hips. "Are you guys gonna keep kissing or can we watch a movie now?"

I laughed. "What are we watching tonight?"

Ella spun around making her nightgown swirl out around her. "*Frozen*, of course. You haven't seen it yet and it's my favoritest." She held her hands up like claws. "Elsa has magic in her fingers."

I scooped her up. "Is that right?"

"Yep, and she's beautiful. Momma loves Elsa too, don't you?"

Maggie rolled her eyes. "Yep. Can never get too much Elsa around here."

Ella smiled her toothless smile. "See. It's the bestest."

"Yes, Chase is in for a big treat tonight," Maggie drawled sarcastically. "Why don't you two get settled while I get us some snacks. Popcorn or ice cream?"

"Chocolate ice cream with whipped cream on top." Ella hopped up and down on the couch.

Visions of Maggie spread out on the counter just an hour before swirled through my mind. I chuckled. "Yeah, Red, don't forget the whipped cream. It's my favoritest."

Her cheeks burned crimson. "I'll have to see if we have any left."

Ella held her hands together in front of her chest. "Please, Momma."

Knowing it would go over Ella's head, I couldn't help but add, "You know how much I like whipped cream on my dessert. It's like an addiction; once is never enough."

Maggie buried her head in the refrigerator searching for what was left of the tasty treat I'd sprayed all over her earlier.

Two hours later, I was surprisingly entranced by the movie. It was better than I expected and Ella serenading me with "Let It Go" was what topped the night. She was so dang cute with her theatrics that for a moment I forgot she wasn't mine. It felt like a family of three. And I liked it. Way too much. I'd been convinced for so long that I wasn't dad material and suddenly things were changing.

After Maggie put Ella to bed, we lay together wrapped in each other's arms. I'd changed over the past few weeks. Before Maggie, my idea of fun was a night out at the bar drinking with my friends and charming the ladies with hopes of taking someone home for a night of meaningless sex. Now, a night in, cuddled on the couch with my two favorite girls watching Disney movies was enough. It was more than enough. It was so damn close to perfect I was afraid to blink because I knew how easily it could all disappear.

My chest tightened with the thought. I kept my heart guarded for the last seven years. I didn't think it was possible to give it away again, because honestly, I didn't think there was anything left of it. I thought Meredith took my heart and soul with her on the day she left. I was resigned to letting her keep it because I didn't deserve that kind of happiness. Not after what I did.

But what if I was wrong? What if my heart was waiting for Maggie to fill it full again? What if she was the one who could make it beat inside my chest again?

I gazed down at Maggie's head resting on my shoulder as my arm wrapped around her waist. She was everything I never knew I wanted. It was on the tip of my tongue tonight to tell Maggie I loved her, but it was too soon. I'd only ever told one other girl I loved her, and it ended up destroying both of us. I feared saying the words aloud, afraid it would jinx the situation.

Instead, I kissed her temple. Maggie's eyes fluttered open. "Why are you still awake?"

"Just thinking about you." My thumb caressed her jaw in slow lazy strokes.

Maggie shifted to her stomach and propped her chin on my chest. "What about me?" Even without makeup and her red hair a wild mess of curls, she was beautiful.

"Everything. I want you to be happy. Are you happy?"

She smiled at me. "So happy. Are you?"

"Yeah, I'm happy, Red. It's been a long time since I've felt like this."

"Me too." Her hand glided across my chest as she traced my tattoos. "Tell me about these. You know my story. Tell me yours."

I lifted her hand and kissed her palm. "It's not a story I'm proud of. I'm not sure I can tell you everything. I'm not ready."

She traced over the black rose with the tip of her red fingernail. "Then just tell me what you can and maybe one day you'll tell me the whole story."

I took a deep breath. "I got my first tattoo when I was seventeen."

Maggie's eyes widened. "Seventeen? I thought you had to be eighteen."

"You do." I chuckled. "I nagged my mom relentlessly that summer. She thought it was a terrible idea and I would regret it, but eventually she signed the consent form. I hid it from my dad for two weeks. By the time he found out it was too late. He was pissed but there was nothing he could do at that point. What was done was done."

"And? Was she right? Did you regret it?"

"Eventually, but not because I didn't like it."

"Which one is it?"

I rubbed at my chest. "It's gone. I used to have Meredith's name right over my heart." Saying her name was like a punch to the gut. I never planned on telling Maggie about her, but it was out now. I knew she would have questions. Questions I didn't want to answer. She would never look at me the same way once she knew the truth.

Maggie frowned. "Is she the girl you were engaged to?"

"Yeah."

"Tell me about her."

"Why would you want to hear about my first love?"

Maggie tapped her fingers on my chest. "Because she's important to you. Isn't that enough?"

This girl.

"She *was* important to me, but she's my past and it doesn't matter anymore."

"Says the man who came face-to-face with my past tonight."

I scratched at my chin. "That's different. Jeff is still part of your life. Meredith hasn't been part of mine for years."

"Exactly, so telling me about her couldn't hurt."

She was so wrong because everything about Meredith hurt. I'd relived it in my mind a thousand times, picking at the scabs that hadn't fully healed. Speaking it out loud would cut me wide open. I'd gladly bleed out if it would change the past, but that was just wishful thinking. The only thing my past could do was take away my future with Maggie and I wasn't willing to risk this chance with her.

I gave her the abbreviated version that left out all the gory details. "I met her my junior year of high school. She was a year younger than me and had just moved here. She became friends with my sister and from the first time Amber brought her home, I was in love."

Maggie shook her head. "Wait! You have a sister? How did I not know this?"

I shrugged. "We're not that close. What happened between Meredith and me pretty much destroyed our relationship too. The only thing good between us anymore is her three-year-old son, my nephew, Theo."

She exploded a hand next to her head. "Mind blown! We'll get back to that later. Tell me more about Meredith. Was it love at first sight?" she asked dreamily.

Hearing her name come from Maggie's lips sounded so normal. Like it wasn't what haunted me for years on end and was the most natural thing in the world. "It was for me. She wasn't a cheerleader, but she came to all of my football games and was my biggest fan. She was a blond-haired, blue-eyed angel. I used to take her out in my Monte Carlo after every game. She was wild and beautiful."

"You should see your face right now. You were smitten."

I laughed. "Pretty much. After graduation I went to community college to get my degree in graphic design. She was way smarter than me. She went to OU and started nursing school. I eventually asked her to move in with me and proposed. I quit school to support us and got a job as a mechanic."

"Wow! You gave up your dreams for hers?"

I shook my head. "I never saw it that way. She was my dream. I'd do anything to take care of her and make her happy."

"Then what happened?"

"I fucked up," I admitted. There was nothing else to say.

"Did you cheat on her?"

"Never. The mistakes I made didn't include other women. She was it for me. I tried to be her white knight and ended up being the villain. She walked away and never looked back. End of story."

"Somehow, I don't think it is. Maybe one day you'll trust me enough to tell me the rest." Maggie tapped on the rose inked on my chest. "So, you got rid of her name and covered it up with this?"

I nodded.

"And the date below it?"

"My biggest regret. The day everything changed."

"Sounds like you're still punishing yourself. In the words of Elsa, maybe it's time to let it go."

If only it were that simple. "Unfortunately, life isn't a Disney movie. Some things are easier said than done." I needed to get out of my own head and there was only one way to do that. Only one thing could quiet the noise. I pulled Maggie to straddle my hips. "Enough talk. Ride me, Red."

I was disgusted with myself. I used Red that night like I'd used dozens of women over the years. With every pulse of her body over mine, the memories faded, and I gave myself over to the bliss of being inside her.

Chapter 20
Maggie

This was awkward with a capital A. I'd never had a girl posse. A best friend? Sure. But a whole girl posse? Never, but that's what I was part of today. There weren't any other words to describe it and I felt like an intruder in their tight-knit group.

When Chase told me I was going dress shopping with the girls for Rissa's premiere party I adamantly refused. Then Rissa called and wouldn't take no for an answer. Rissa Black. Even though I already met her a few times, I was still fangirling. It was hard to reconcile the sweet girl I'd met with the amazing voice on the radio. She seemed so normal. Beautiful, but normal.

No one in the dress shop knew who she was. After her coming-out in a couple weeks, I was sure all of that would change. She would no longer be an anonymous pretty face.

Rissa clapped her hands together. "Okay ladies, this is going to be fun. How often do we really get to play dress-up?"

The dark-haired girl I'd just met, Tori, piped up, "As little as possible. Give me a pair of jeans and I'm a happy camper."

Kyla, the blond I'd learned was one of the artists at Forever Inked, smirked at her friend. "The last time Tori wore a dress was her wedding."

"Not entirely true." She waved her hand between Kyla and Rissa. "I wore a dress to both your weddings."

Layla lifted the tag from a dress on a nearby rack and cringed. "Jesus Christ!"

Rissa smacked it out of her hand. "Nuh-uh. We're not looking at prices today, we're just having fun and getting whatever makes us look and feel fabulous. Zack is footing the bill for all his favorite girls."

I raised my hand like I was in school. "I still don't understand why I'm here. You barely know me."

Layla bumped me with her hip. "Because Chase is part of our fucked-up little family and now you are too. Just accept it. None of us can afford any of this glam except maybe Kyla and her hunky football playing husband."

I turned to Kyla. "Professional football?"

She tucked a strand of her blond hair behind her ear. "Tyler Jackson. He plays for the Detroit Lions."

I didn't know much about football or have time to keep up with sports. My face must have looked as blank as my mind felt. Tori rolled her eyes. "He's the quarterback."

I let that rattle around in my head. "Oh…ohhhh. So, he's famous too?"

Layla wrapped her arm around my shoulder. "Yep. But besides Tyler and Rissa the rest of us are just plain folks who can say we knew them way back when."

Kyla raised her hand like I had before. "Tyler's not famous."

Tori rolled her eyes. "Oh yeah? Remember that when we're sitting in those swanky seats at the games and people are crawling all over him to get his autograph."

"Okay, so maybe he's a little famous, but he's just Tyler to me."

"I'm not famous either," Rissa added. Then she let out a girly giggle. "At least not yet." Her excitement was contagious. We all started talking at once and congratulating Rissa on her debut album.

The ruckus we made earned us a sharp glare from one of the sales ladies. If she only knew how much money we'd be spending, she would have focused that glare somewhere else. Tori quieted us down. "Now, are we gonna try on some dresses or what? Because I have an awesome pair of jeans I could wear instead that Chris loves."

Rissa pointed at Tori. "Absolutely not! Look at us… we're a hot group of women and we're going to find dresses that make our men fall over their own feet when they see us. I think we should each pick out a dress for each other. We'll do a fashion show and choose the dresses each of you will wear." She clapped her hands enthusiastically and bounced on her toes. "Spread out and get shopping, ladies."

I let out the breath I was holding. This was the most stressful shopping trip I'd ever been on and it was going to take longer than I anticipated. I took out my phone and contemplated calling Chase. It was his first time alone with Ella. I hoped she wasn't being too demanding.

Layla squeezed my shoulder. "You okay?"

"Yeah. All of this," I waved my hand around the swanky store, "it's just a little overwhelming."

"I know. I want something that will give Draven a hard-on all night. I want him to look at me and think *Daaamn, I'm lucky*."

I giggled. "I've seen the way he looks at you. I'm pretty sure he already thinks that."

She shrugged. "A little catnip on his favorite pussy never hurt."

I opened my mouth to respond, but nothing came out. Roxy was blunt, but Layla's mouth was downright filthy.

She tapped the bottom of my jaw shut. "Don't worry. We're gonna put a little catnip on Chase's favorite pussy too." Layla sized me up. "You've got all the equipment, all we have to do is accentuate it. That man won't be able to keep his hands to himself." She thumbed through the rack. "What are you, a size six?"

"Sometimes an eight."

"It's those incredible boobs and perfectly round ass." She smirked. "You're going to look incredible."

I was almost afraid to see what she picked out. I would venture to say Layla was a little more adventurous than me. I quickly moved to another rack, perusing glittery white dresses. I would never wear white, except for my wedding. With my red hair and pale skin, it washed me out making me look ghostlike. I wasn't supposed to be shopping for myself, I was supposed to be looking for the other girls. The problem was I didn't really know them. Layla was dark and dangerous, and if I had to guess, black was her go-to color. Rissa on the other hand seemed pure as the driven snow. With her blond curls and tanned skin, she would be a knockout in white.

Like she was a mind reader, Rissa appeared and bumped me with her shoulder. "Thanks for coming out with us tonight."

I couldn't help but like her. Rissa had this aura around her that almost made her glow. "Thanks for inviting me." I shuffled uncomfortably from one foot to the other, "I appreciate the thought, but I'm paying for my own dress. I can't let you and Zack foot the bill for someone you barely know." I mentally calculated how much a dress from this shop would set me back. I had yet to see anything less than five hundred dollars and that was a hell of a lot more than the dress I saw online at Macy's.

Rissa pursed her lips. "Let me ask you a question. Do you love Chase?"

Love? Of all the things she could have asked me, this seemed out of left field. I felt the heat rising up my neck. I'd fallen in love with Jeff a long time ago and it got me nowhere. I was hesitant to give my heart away only to be disappointed again. I wanted to love Chase, and deep down I think I did, but I hadn't allowed myself to fully commit to the feeling. What if I told Chase I loved him, and he didn't say it back? I'd be right back at square one. Giving myself to someone who could never return the sentiment. Even if my heart told me otherwise, my head told me it was a bad idea.

"Okay, I can see you're freaking out about the L word, so let me rephrase. Does Chase make you happy?"

This I could answer. "Unbelievably so."

"And is he good to your daughter?"

"Better than her own father."

"And does he give you that fluttery feeling in your chest? Like when he's not with you, you feel like something is missing?"

I sighed. "All the time."

"Let me tell you a story. My mom died of brain cancer and my dad couldn't take the heartbreak. They were both gone by the time I was eighteen. I drove my dad's truck from Oklahoma across the country to New York to pursue music. That's when I met Zack's brother and we fell madly in love. We were going to get married and we had a baby on the way. Then he died too. I was all alone, and Zack convinced me to move here with him. We fell hard for each other, but as you can imagine it was a complicated mess and for a long time, we barely spoke to each other."

I chastised myself for ever feeling like my life was a mess. Rissa's life was like a bad country song, yet here she was spilling her guts to me. I felt like I was invading her privacy. This story was personal. More personal than our new friendship warranted. "You don't have to tell me…"

She held a finger to my lips to shush me. "Yes, I do. It's important to me." I silently nodded. "Anyway, I worked as a bartender at The Locker, and moved into one of the smallest, crappiest apartments in town. I was alone and pregnant and scared. I barely knew Layla or Chase. They were Zack's friends and I figured I'd lost them too. But I didn't. Layla would come to the bar and chat with me, but Chase… you know what he did? Every day, without fail, Chase would come to my apartment to check on me. Most days I would just give him a little wave through the window because I didn't feel like talking, but that never stopped him. Every morning he showed up on my doorstep just to make sure I was alive and let me know that someone cared. It helped get me through some really awful stuff. I never told anybody. Not even Zack knows about it and I don't think I'll ever tell him because that's between Chase and me. But what he did is a debt I can never repay. He's honest and true and loyal. So, let me do this. Let me do one tiny thing to try to pay Chase back for all he's given me."

It sounded just like something Chase would do. Like how he cut my grass every week without ever being asked. My eyes welled with tears and one rolled down my cheek at her sincerity. I quickly brushed it away. "Okay. Thank you. And to answer your question... yes. I'm undeniably and irrevocably in love with Chase." Admitting it made me feel vulnerable and a little terrified.

Rissa patted my hand. "Oh darling, I already knew that. I just wanted to make sure you did."

"Saw that coming from a mile away," Layla chirped in from over my shoulder.

I wiped at the corner of my eye with my thumb. "Do you think he loves me back?"

Rissa smiled sweetly, as if the answer should have been obvious.

Layla was a straight shooter, and I was beginning to think she and Roxy could be great friends. "Chase has some bad shit in his past. I don't know what it is, but I'm sure someone broke his heart. He's never had to beg for the company of women, but he doesn't get attached. He's always been casual and carefree. That's part of his charm. Most people think he's a manwhore, but I think he's just scared. Chase has got some serious insecurities. Since he's been with you, he's different. I've never seen him so devoted to anyone. That boy is head over heels crazy for you."

What Layla said made total sense. The story he told me about his ex confirmed it. Chase was scared, and he wasn't the only one. We'd both been burned. Being cautious was second nature to us.

Tori stepped out of the dressing room in a deep scarlet gown that reached the floor. Her dark hair tumbled over her shoulders in loose waves stopping just below her breasts. For a girl who loved jeans, she looked amazing except for the scowl on her face. "I can't breathe," she insisted.

"Stop being so dramatic," Kyla scolded. She set a pair of heels in front of Tori. "Put these on and try smiling."

"Seriously, you expect me to bend over? The seams on this dress will burst for sure."

Rissa let out a sigh and kneeled on the floor. "The seams are not going to burst. Give me your foot." Tori lifted one foot and Rissa slipped it in the sparkly shoe, then did the other. "Now go stand in front of the mirror and look at yourself. If you can't admit you look fabulous then we'll move to the next dress."

Tori walked awkwardly to the mirror and turned to the side. "It does make the girls look good." Then she patted her flat stomach. "I hope my belly doesn't decide to pop before your party."

My face must have conveyed my confusion. "She's pregnant," Kyla clarified. "And... so am I."

Tori spun around. "You bitch! Why didn't you say something?"

She shrugged her shoulders. "It's still early. I was going to tell you, but I didn't want to jinx it."

Tori ran as quickly as her snug dress allowed and threw her arms over Kyla's shoulders. "You're not going to jinx it. This is going to be amazing being pregnant together again."

My head snapped between the two of them. "Again? You both have kids?"

"Yep," Kyla answered. "I have twin boys and Tori has a daughter."

Rissa laughed. "Zack's chomping at the bit to have another one too, but I want to wait a year to see what happens with my career."

I looked at Layla. "What about you?"

Her eyes bulged out and she took a step back. "Nooooo, not me. I am nowhere near ready to have a baby." She patted the zipper on her jeans. "This IUD is staying firmly in place. We're just in the practicing part. Another year or so and we should be damn good at it."

"I have a feeling you're already good at it," I blurted, then threw my hand up over my mouth. I certainly didn't know her well enough to add my two cents.

Layla didn't seem bothered at all by my loose lips. She waggled her eyebrows. "That we are. That man is insatiable."

"Ticktock, darling," Rissa teased. "You're getting close to thirty."

Layla rolled her eyes. "Yeah, I'm practically ancient."

Rissa turned to me. "What about you, Maggie? Do you want more kids?"

177

The question was one I should have been ready for but stung anyways. "I always thought I'd have at least two by now, maybe three. But things just didn't work out the way I thought they would." I shrugged. "Ella would love to have a brother or sister. She seems to think Chase and I should get married and then poof, she'd have a sibling."

Kyla tugged down the zipper on Tori's dress so she could try on the next one. "Maybe you will."

I chuckled. "It's a little soon for that. Chase is still getting used to having Ella around. I don't think he's quite ready for marriage and a baby."

"Never say never," Tori shouted from the dressing room. "When you know, you know. I've known since I was sixteen that Chris and I would get married."

"True," Layla added. "I was never going to fall in love again and then Draven showed up. I tried to keep my distance but the electricity between us was undeniable."

"Confession time," Rissa said sheepishly. "I slept with Zack the night of his brother's funeral. We were both grieving and searching for something. That something turned out to be each other. We didn't mean for it to happen and it probably wasn't our best decision, but we couldn't deny the emotional connection." She shrugged her shoulders. "And look how it turned out."

"Not to mention Zack is a fine piece of ass." Tori smirked, as she exited the dressing room in another dress.

"Tori!" Kyla smacked her on the shoulder.

"What? I'm married, not blind. If I wasn't so devoted to Chris, I would have fucked him."

Rissa picked up a shoe and threw it at her playfully. "That's MY husband you're talking about!"

Tori dodged the flying high heel before it struck her in the hip. "He wasn't when I first met him. Besides, it was a compliment."

"All right ladies," Layla interjected. "I think we can all agree that the men of Forever Inked are all smokin' hot." She grabbed a strapless black gown off the dressing room door, "Although mine is the hottest." She stuck out her tongue in an immature gesture and hurried inside the dressing room, shutting the door just as another shoe collided with it.

I laughed out loud. It was a crazy group of girls, but I kind of loved them. All my apprehension about the shopping trip fell away along with my insecurities.

Chase and I might never get married and we might never have kids, but one thing was for sure… I was going to find a dress that brought him to his knees.

I slunk quietly into the house since it was much later than I'd intended on staying out. After dress shopping, the girls and I went for a drink. I couldn't remember the last time I had so much fun. They were loud and rowdy and a whole lot of inappropriate. Next time we went out I'd be sure to invite Roxy. She'd fit in just fine.

I laid my bag-covered dress and shoes on the chair, taking in the sight in front of me. An open pizza box sat on the kitchen counter with one piece left inside. Papers and markers were strewn across the kitchen table. In the center was a picture of Ella's mythical dog, Henry, and Not My Cat. She drew a heart over their heads with the words *"Beast Frends"*. I covered my laugh with my hand, then hung the picture on the fridge with lettered magnets we used to practice spelling. Obviously, we had a few more words to work on.

Toys were scattered across the family room and the television was left on, but that wasn't what stopped my heart. It was what was on the couch that made me take pause. Ella was cocooned in a blanket snuggled into Chase's chest, his arms wrapped protectively around her, both of them fast asleep. Chase's nails were painted a bright pink and a gold, plastic tiara covered in jewels sat askew on top of his head.

I quietly reached for my phone and captured the moment before sitting on the chair and watching them for a little longer.

This.

This was what I wanted.

For me.

For my daughter.

For both of us.

I pictured us as a family with Henry, Not My Cat and yeah… maybe a baby. It would be crazy. It would be chaotic. But most of all, it would be perfect.

Before the fantasy of what could be took over, I needed to put my little girl to bed. I tried to pry Chase's arms from around Ella, but he only squeezed her tighter.

I gently shook the man on my couch. His eyes fluttered open in sleepy confusion. I motioned to Ella. "I'm gonna put her to bed."

"I got her." Chase sat up, the tiara falling off, and held the back of Ella's head tenderly. She let out a contented sigh, snuggling into his shoulder. "Time for bed, princess bug."

I moved to the side, then followed them to the bedroom. Chase carefully laid Ella on her tiny twin-size bed. Pulling the pink blanket up around her shoulders, he tucked her in like a little burrito, the way my dad used to do to me.

Ella's eyes cracked open. "I love you, Chase."

"I love you too, baby." He kissed her on the head. "Sweet dreams."

My insides melted. It felt too good to be true. Too wonderful. Too perfect. This man was going to destroy me, because something this good couldn't possibly last.

But what if it could?

Chase followed me to the dimly lit kitchen and wrapped his arms around my waist pulling me in close. "Did you find a dress?"

I nodded to the bag laying over the chair. "Yes, and I had a lot of fun. I'm sorry I got home so late. We went for a drink after."

He chuckled. "Girls sucked you in, didn't they?"

I held up my forefinger and thumb slightly apart, peering between them. "A little bit."

"I knew they would. Crazy chicks with big hearts." He kissed me on the forehead like he did to Ella. "Can I see your dress?"

I bit my lip and shook my head. "We decided to keep the dresses a secret. You'll all get to see them on the night of the party."

"Not even a little peek?"

"Nope. Girl posse pact. You'll have to wait like the other guys." His blond hair was all tousled from sleeping on the couch. I ran my hand through it, then squinted it his face.

"What?"

"Are you wearing eyeshadow?"

He swiped the back of his hand over his eyelid and inspected the blue powder on his fingers. "Yeah. We were playing *Pretty, Pretty Princess.* She got carried away." Chase held up his fingernails explaining the pink polish.

My lips pressed together in an attempt to stifle my laughter. "She can be a handful. I'm sorry."

"It's all good. We were having bonding time."

I led him to the bathroom and sat him down on the closed toilet lid. "You're a good sport. I bet she had a ball." I took one of my makeup remover cloths out of the package and held it up. "Close your eyes." I swiped the cloth across each eyelid. "Where did she even find blue eyeshadow?"

Chase fluttered his eyelashes at me. "She said it matched my eyes. I didn't question it."

I sighed. "Another mystery to solve. That girl is full of surprises." I reached under the sink, pulling out cotton balls and nail polish remover. "Give me your hand."

Chase watched me rub the polish off each nail, making sure I got it off his cuticles too. "We watched *Frozen 2* and I have to disagree with you. There's definitely such a thing as too much Elsa."

"That, there is." I tossed the cotton balls in the trash can. "Let me make it up to you. I'll make you breakfast in the morning, my famous eggs and bacon."

His smile quirked up on one side, showcasing that damn dimple. "No sneaking out at six a.m.?"

"No, I want you to stay. I'm ready and I think she is too."

"Yeah?"

"Yeah."

Chase pulled me between his legs and kissed my stomach. "Then I have a better idea." He paused, as if debating his words. "Come to my mom's house with me for breakfast tomorrow. You and Ella. My mom makes a huge southern breakfast every Sunday: bacon, eggs, hash browns, pancakes… the works."

I was stunned. We hadn't done the whole family thing yet. It seemed like a big step. "You want me to meet your mom?"

"And my Grams."

"Do they know about…" I nodded to Ella's bedroom.

"Yes. And my mom has been itching to meet her. I can't make any promises that my mom won't spoil her to death, she's super excited to have a granddaughter."

A granddaughter?

And there went that fluttery feeling in my chest Rissa talked about, but instead of a single butterfly it felt like a whole swarm of them had taken up residency. Instead of fighting it, I succumbed to the feeling. "Breakfast with your mom sounds great."

There was no question in my mind. I had definitely fallen in love with Chase Montgomery.

Chapter 21
Chase

This was either the best or worst idea I've ever had. The jury was still out. I felt like a defendant waiting on a verdict. Not a good feeling. My nerves were basically shot, and we hadn't even arrived yet.

Maggie placed her hand over mine. "Are you all right? You seem a little nervous."

So much for hiding my anxiety. I squeezed her hand over the console of my truck. "I'm fine."

She raised an eyebrow. "Really? Because you don't seem fine. If you're uncomfortable with this, we can go back to that little pancake place we just passed."

My eyes darted to the rearview mirror, taking in Ella in the back seat who was oblivious to my distress. Her head bopped along to some song she was singing, that I'd never heard. Her arms and legs flailed around like she was in dance class. She was so excited when I told her about going to breakfast at my mom's this morning and wanted to wear a special dress for the occasion.

"I made her a promise. I'm not breaking it."

Maggie pointed to a grocery store parking lot ahead. "Pull over."

I stole a glance at the clock on my dashboard. "We'll be late."

"Pull over. This will be quick. I promise," she huffed.

I put on my turn signal and merged over, pulling into the busy lot. I was fucking this up and we'd only been in the car fifteen minutes. As soon as I parked, Maggie opened the door. "I need to talk to you." She hopped out and walked around the back of the truck.

"Where'd Momma go?"

"Sit tight, I'm going to check. Don't unbuckle your booster seat."

Ella frowned. "I hate this thing."

"I know, but we'll be there soon. Okay?"

She crossed her arms. "Okay, but only because mom says you're the boss now, too."

I chuckled. "We both know who the real boss is, don't we?"

"Yeah. You're like the assistant boss. You gotta listen to mom too."

"Only if I don't want to get in trouble."

She gasped. "Did you get a time-out?"

"Not yet." I opened my door. "Stay buckled."

"Aye, aye, captain." Ella saluted me.

I met Maggie around the back of my truck. "What's up?"

Maggie shuffled back and forth from foot to foot. "I get it if it's too soon. I really do. I mean I haven't exactly been rushing to introduce you to my family. It's only been a few weeks." She stopped to chew on the side of her thumb, one of her few nervous habits. "I don't want you to feel pressured… you know in case things don't work out."

I gently pulled her thumb from her mouth and kissed it. "You think I'm worried we won't work out?"

She shrugged. "Aren't you? I mean… Ella and I are a lot to handle."

"I'm not worried about us not working out. If I was, I wouldn't have suggested this. Let me tell you a secret." I gently took her face in my hands and caressed her cheeks with my thumbs. I didn't want her to doubt us.

Maggie placed her hands over mine. "What?"

"I haven't taken a girl home to meet my mom since Meredith. So, trust me when I say if I wasn't sure, then this wouldn't be happening."

She gulped. "Ever?"

"Never. I want you to meet my family."

"Then why are you so jittery?"

I inhaled deeply. "My sister. The last time I saw her, things got a little heated. I just don't want her taking it out on you. Or Ella."

Maggie scrunched up her nose. "She's just a little girl. I doubt your sister would do something like that."

"Well, she's basically a bitch, so I wouldn't put anything past her."

"I'm not worried and you shouldn't be either. We can manage it." Maggie went around to Ella's side and opened the door. "Come on, ladybug."

Ella hopped out of the truck like the expert she'd become. "Where are you going?" I asked.

She took Ella's hand and looked over her shoulder. "You'll see. We'll be back in five."

When we pulled up in front of the house I grew up in, the Bitchmobile was nowhere to be seen. *Thank God for small miracles.* I let Ella out of her seat and held her hand as the three of us walked to the door.

The smell of home greeted us as we walked through the house to the kitchen. My mom was at the stove frying bacon as Grams whipped up the pancake batter. They were so busy gossiping they hadn't heard us come in. I quietly leaned over mom's shoulder and gave her a kiss on the cheek.

She startled and swatted me with the towel in her hand. "Oh my goodness, you scared me."

"You knew we were coming; you should have expected it."

Grams opened her arms to me in her usual fashion. "There's my favorite grandson."

I stepped into her waiting arms, giving her a tight hug. "We go through this every time. I'm your only grandson."

"And therefore, my favorite," she sassed back.

Maggie stood in the entryway with her arms protectively over Ella's shoulders, who for the first time was acting shy.

My mom smiled warmly at them. "You must be Maggie." Then she crouched and bopped Ella on the nose with her finger. "And this pretty girl must be Ella."

Ella gave her an adorable toothless smile. "These are for you, Mrs. Chase's Mom." She held out the bouquet of daisies she and Maggie picked up at the grocery store.

My mom took the flowers and pressed her nose into the petals. "Thank you. They're very pretty and you can call me Betty."

"I picked-ed the ones with the mostest colors, Miss Betty. And my Momma said it's not polite to call grown-ups by their first name. She says it's dis.. dis…" she held a finger up to her chin and tried to think of the right word, "disrespectful and kids got to be nice to old people because…," she looked up at her mom and shrugged her shoulders, "because it's rude. Except for my mom's friend, Roxy. I can call her Roxy 'cuz she's not that old, but not at school. At school I got to call her Miss Sinclair, because you can't call teachers by their first name, only their last name or you go to the principal's office and nobody wants to go there because Momma says Ms. Jacobs is a whack job."

Maggie dropped her head into her hand and sighed, clearly not as amused as the rest of us with Ella's dissertation. "Ladybug, what have I told you?"

"It's okay, Momma. Miss Betty doesn't even know Ms. Jacobs, so she won't tell on you for calling her a whack job. Besides, Andy says snitches get stitches and I don't think Miss Betty is a snitch." Then she looked at my mom with big eyes. "You're not, are you?"

My mom winked at Ella. "Your secret is safe with me."

Ella looked back at Maggie. "See Momma, it's fine."

Mortified was the only word that seemed appropriate to describe Maggie's face. In contrast, Ella beamed with pride.

"I'm so sorry," Maggie apologized. I'm sure this wasn't what she imagined meeting my family for the first time would be like.

"For what?" my mom asked. "For her being honest? That was nothing compared to some of the things Chase said when he was her age. Children keep life interesting and that in itself is a blessing." She pulled Maggie in for a hug. "I'm so glad you two are here."

"Us too. Thank you for having us. Everything smells delicious. What can I do to help?"

Grams stepped forward. "You two can come here and give me a hug. I'm missing out on all the good stuff."

Realizing I'd been neglectful, I introduced them. "Maggie and Ella this is Grams."

Ella scrunched up her nose. "Mrs. Grams?"

"No. I'm Chase's grandma. You can just call me Grams."

Ella bounced her way over and hugged her. "I have a grandma too. Her name is Nanna, and she makes the bestest cookies. Do you make Chase cookies?"

She pushed one of Ella's red curls over her ear. "I did when he was little. Maybe one day we can bake him some together."

"Nanna says I'm a good helper." Ella looked up at her mom. "Did you hear that, Momma? Grams is gonna let me bake cookies with her."

"I heard, ladybug." Maggie gave Grams a tight hug. "It's so nice to meet you."

"The pleasure is ours. We've been waiting for Chase to bring you around."

185

I draped my arm over Red's shoulder. "Can't blame me for wanting to keep them to myself before you two sink your claws in. I can't have all the ladies in my life teaming up on me together."

Maggie playfully slapped my hand. "Oh, stop! We're not that bad."

"Hens," I teased. "All of you." I pointed at Ella. "And that one's the worst."

Ella pointed at herself. "Me? I'm not a hen."

"Yes, you!" I tickled her belly and lifted her to my hip. "You're the cutest one too."

She giggled and wrapped her arms and legs around me, pressing her cheek to mine.

My mom smirked at me from where she was arranging the daisies in a vase. My mom had been waiting years for me to move on. She wanted nothing more than for me to settle down with a nice girl, get married and have babies of my own. I didn't know if I was ready for all that, but I'd finally found a nice girl. For the first time in what seemed like forever, the future didn't seem like such a dark place. As long as I kept my shit together there was a possibility of more with Red.

Grams moved a chair over to the counter. "Ella, how would you like to help me stir the pancake batter?"

Ella climbed on the chair and pushed up her sleeves. "Stirring is my specialty. I'm just not so good with the eggs. The shells are tricky."

Maggie scrambled to help her, worry lines creasing her forehead.

Snatching her around the waist, I kissed her temple. "She's fine. This isn't Grams' first rodeo."

"So…" my mom interrupted, while turning the bacon in the frying pan. "Chase said you're a teacher. Dealing with little ones all day must be a challenge."

"It is," Maggie responded while keeping an eye on her daughter. "But it's also rewarding. They grow so much in first grade, by the end of the year, most of them are reading and writing like pros." She scanned the kitchen. "What can I do to help?"

"Sit down and take a load off. I imagine you rarely get time to relax being a single mom."

"Ain't that the truth." She plopped into a chair. "I'm not sure I'd know what to do with a whole day to myself if I ever got one."

I began taking plates and silverware from the cupboards, placing them around the large table that seemed ridiculous in size for just my mom and Grams. But my mom was all about family and one day she hoped to have every seat filled.

"Ever think about having more?" my mom asked.

I sighed. Here we go. *The Betty Louise Inquisition* was starting. She thought she was sly, but I knew exactly what she was doing; seeing how fast she could fill up those chairs around the table.

"At least one. Two if I'm lucky. Three if I'm really blessed." Maggie swiped the silverware from my frozen hand and continued placing it around the plates. "I've always wanted Ella to have siblings."

Two or three? It wasn't unrealistic or crazy by any means but just the thought had my heart racing and my brain spinning. It was fine for other people, but not the guy who'd already proven that he couldn't be depended on.

"A full home makes a happy heart." I could practically see the hope in my mom's eyes as she answered. "As a matter of fact, Chase, you'll need to put out two more plates. Amber and Theo are coming."

"Seriously?" I ground out.

"Yes, seriously. I wanted all my babies in the nest again. It's been a while."

I contemplated grabbing Ella and Maggie and making a mad dash for the door. "For good reason."

She waved a dish towel at me. "Now, don't go borrowing trouble. Amber promised to be on her best behavior and Theo misses you." When in doubt, she always pulled out the guilt card, tugging on my heartstrings for the little dude.

The anger I felt weeks ago rose to the surface. "One word. That's all it will take for us to leave."

Maggie placed her hand over mine. "We're good. If I can deal with Jeff, your sister will be a piece of cake."

I highly doubted that (a) my sister even knew what good behavior was or (b) Maggie was ready for the raging bitch Amber could be.

The front door opened and Theo ran to me, crushing my legs in a firm grip. "Uncle Chase."

"Hey, little man." I held up my hand. "Give me five." He crashed his hand against mine, "Ouch! You been working out?"

Theo flexed, showing me the nonexistent muscles under his sleeves. "I's big, Uncle Chase."

I lifted him high. "You sure are. Pretty soon you're going to be bigger than me."

He pointed at Ella. "Who's dat?"

Ella propped her hands on her hips, dripping batter from the spoon that was still in her grasp. "I'm Ella. Who are you?"

"Ella, this is Theo," I said, placing him back on the ground.

"Wanna see my toys?" Theo asked.

"Sure." Ella hopped down, leaving a trail of batter behind her as the two ran from the room.

Maggie swiped the spoon with supersonic reflexes, kneeling to wipe the drops from the kitchen floor.

"Wow! I knew women dropped at your feet, but this is a little ridiculous," the devil, otherwise known as my sister, drawled.

"Ignore her," I said, pulling Maggie to her feet. "She's barely house-trained. I wanted a dog, but we got her instead. I tried to put her on a leash, but my parents wouldn't allow it. They nixed the muzzle too."

"Nice." Amber crossed her arms.

Maggie tossed the dishcloth in the sink and wiped her hands on her pants. She reached one out to my sister. "You must be Amber."

Amber ignored her outreached hand. "And you must be Chase's latest plaything." She sized Maggie up with her eyes. "You're cute, but obviously naïve. Don't get too attached, Chase isn't much for sticking around."

It took everything inside me not to reach out and strangle my sister. Red didn't deserve her ire or her snotty attitude.

I was about to put Amber in her place when my girl cocked her head to the side. "Actually, I'm Maggie and that sweet girl playing with your son is Ella. And we're already attached to Chase because he's pretty amazing. So, I appreciate the concern, but it isn't needed." Maggie wrapped her arm around my waist and placed her other hand on my chest. "And I'm not naïve. Your brother is a great guy."

Amber brushed her long hair over her shoulder. "We'll see. Don't say I didn't warn you."

"Noted, but I'm a big girl, not some bimbo from the bar."

"Whatever. Where did Theo go?"

Maggie smiled sweetly. "He went to show Ella his toys."

Amber scurried off to check on the kids, giving us a much-needed reprieve. Only three minutes in and she already had my blood boiling.

Grams poured batter on the griddle in perfect circles. "You've got spunk, Miss Maggie. I think I love you already."

"Ummm... I probably could have handled that better."

"Nonsense. Amber's a tough one. She and Chase have been bickering for years."

"She needs to get over herself," I interjected. "She should be happy for me, but she can't even let me have that."

My mom, who'd been noticeably quiet, started grabbing the bacon from the pan with a pair of tongs and putting it on a plate. "I just want everyone to get along. Can you try for me, Chase?"

Was she kidding me right now? "I didn't do anything. She started in on Maggie without even giving her a chance."

"I know and I apologize for that. I'll have a talk with her."

"Yeah, you do that." I'd already seen how well it worked in the past.

Grams clapped her hands. "Food's ready."

Maggie helped bring everything to the table as I poured juice into the empty glasses and placed them on the table. Little feet thundered down the hallway and under my arm, causing me to splash some juice on the table. I quickly wiped it up with a napkin, smiling at the chaos that consumed our normally quiet kitchen.

"Slow down, munchkins!" my mom hollered.

"I'm so starved, Miss Betty." Ella clambered into a chair next to Red.

Maggie rolled her eyes. "You're not starved, ladybug. You ate a Pop Tart at home."

"Yeah, but just one. My tummy is still hungry."

Theo climbed into the chair next to Ella. "I wants to sit wit Uncle Chase and my new fwend."

I expected Amber to object, but she just shrugged her shoulders. Grams sat next to me and Mom next to Maggie. Amber took up residence between them, safely out of my reach.

Maggie placed a pancake on Ella's plate and passed them to me. I did the same for Theo, cutting it up and pouring syrup over the top.

Theo smiled up at me. "Bacon too, Uncle Chase."

I pounded on my chest. "Bacon is man meat. Makes you big and strong."

Theo giggled.

Ella held up her fork. "I want some man meat."

Everyone at the table snickered, including my stick-up-her-ass sister.

"What? Man meat is delicious," Ella insisted, cuing another round of giggles.

My mom passed the plate our way. "How about we just call it bacon?"

Ella shrugged, clearly not understanding what was so funny.

"You've got some learning to do," Amber said over the rim of her juice glass.

"It could have happened to anyone," I defended.

"Yeah, but it happened to you. Flippin' hilarious."

Ella gasped. "You said the f-word, Miss Amber."

"Hah," I pointed at my sister, "now you're in trouble."

She rolled her eyes. "Flippin isn't a bad word."

"But my mom says…" Ella started.

"Flippin flapjacks," Theo shouted.

Ella surveyed the situation. "Flippin man meat!"

Theo countered with, "Flippin' frogs."

"Flippin' farts!"

By the time they finished going back and forth everyone had lost it. Maggie tried to reel it in. "Okay, you two. That's enough potty talk. Eat your pancakes and bacon."

"Buzzkill," Ella murmured, before shoving a forkful of pancake in her mouth.

We finished breakfast without further incident from either the kids or my sister.

Before we left, Grams pulled me aside and hugged me tightly. "She's lovely. I hope to see more of Miss Maggie and that precious little girl."

I hugged her back. "I think I'll keep this one around for a while."

Grams pinched my cheek like I was a five-year-old. "If you're smart, you'll do more than that."

I rubbed at my offended cheek. "Yeah, well, nobody's ever accused me of being smart." That was the truth. Over the years I'd been the butt of more than a few jokes.

"Nonsense. You might have lost your way for a while, but that don't mean you're not smart. You just gotta find your compass and I'm pretty sure it's pointing at those two pretty, redheaded girls."

I saw the hope in my Grams eyes. She'd always been my biggest cheerleader. Even when I'd gotten myself in a heap full of trouble, she'd stood by my side telling me everything was going to be okay. I never believed her before, but this time I just might.

Chapter 22
Maggie

Halloween was without a doubt the worst holiday of the year for teachers, followed closely by Valentine's Day. The kids weren't focused on reading and writing, they wanted to skip right to the treats and parade. I'd learned over the years to just go with it. Stop fighting the tide and float along with the craziness.

The only thing that made this day bearable was the district's decision to finally... finally, make it a half-day. Three and a half hours was way more tolerable than seven.

"You ready for this?" Roxy asked, straightening her witch's hat. She looked damn sexy. Even though her costume was modest, the dress hugged her curves perfectly. Pair that with her striped hose and heeled boots and she was a walking felony.

"Are you trying to give your fifth graders boners? Every boy in your class is going to be walking around with a stiffy." Feeling frumpy, I looked down at my plaid shirt and the cowboy boots I'd worn to the farm. They still had a little mud on the soles. At least I thought it was mud. Could have been goat poop for all I knew.

Picking up a wad of material from her desk, she waved it in my face. "I'm wearing a cape during class, silly. There will be no prepubescent penises poking out in my classroom. That's disgusting."

I covered my ears. "Please don't ever say *prepubescent penis* again."

"You started it." She laughed as she threw the cape over her shoulders and fastened it in the front.

She had a point.

"I'm not taking off the cape until my lunch date."

"You have a lunch date?" This was new information. "I didn't know you were seeing anyone."

191

"Met him online. I figured since we had a half-day, it would be the perfect time to meet him in person. Casual, with minimal chance of him expecting me to bang him afterward."

"Smart. What's he do?"

"I'm not sure." She scrunched her lips to one side. "Something corporate? Honestly, I was too busy looking at his profile pics to care." She fanned a hand in front of her face. "Insanely hot."

"Corporate seems a little tame for you. Done with the bad boys for a while?"

She slumped back on her desk. "I don't know. I'm not getting any younger. I can't keep dating guys who can't string together three coherent sentences and whose only mode of transportation has two wheels. There's more to life than phenomenal sex."

I held up my hand. "Don't be hating on phenomenal sex, especially when I just started to realize how phenomenal it can be."

"Don't get me wrong. I still want the spank-my-ass, pull-my-hair, make-me-come-'til-my-vision-blurs sex. It's just not all I want. I'm pushing thirty and I need to start thinking about settling down. Start being a responsible adult."

It was all making sense now. There was only one reason why my highly spontaneous best friend was seeking out "responsible" dates online. "You talked to your mother again, didn't you?"

"Ugh! Yes! That woman drives me insane. There's a reason we barely speak. *If you keep giving away the milk for free, no one's ever going to buy the cow, Roxanna. You need to find a nice, dependable man, Roxanna. You should go back to church, Roxanna.* She's got my head all spun up."

"Remember who you are. Don't quit being you just to satisfy your mother. I need you in all your sassiness to keep guiding me in the right direction." I clasped my hands dramatically in front of my plaid-covered chest. "You're like my sexy, fairy godmother."

She playfully swatted at my hands. "Oh, stop! You're doing just fine. You've snagged yourself a hot man who curls your toes in bed and you're going to the Rissa Black premiere. If anyone should be jealous, it should be me."

"What?" I gasped. "You're jealous of me? That's a first."

Roxy tugged me by the arm. "Come on, smart-ass. Let the hell of Halloween begin. I wonder how many ninja's I'll have this year."

We strode toward the gym for morning pick up of our classes. "Not nearly as many as the number of Disney princesses I'll have. You should have seen Ella this morning. She was so hyped up. I can't imagine what she'll be like by lunchtime after she's crammed candy and cupcakes down her throat."

"Is Chase going trick-or-treating with you guys tonight?"

I settled the bulky cowboy hat on my head. "Yep. Gonna meet the whole family before we go out. I figured a quick dinner would be perfect since it won't give my brother time to interrogate Chase. I love him, but after Jeff left me high and dry, Patty's been overly protective."

She smirked. "Your brother is hot. Such a tragedy for women everywhere."

"Yeah, well, how do you think I felt crushing on his boyfriend? Now, that boy is haaawt. The two of them together are breaking hearts across the city."

"Truth. Mine included." Roxy stopped right outside the gym. "Do you think Patrick will be cool with Chase?"

"God, I hope so. I don't want anything ruining the night."

Thank goodness! The parade was the last part of this torturous Halloween school day from hell. Once we made our way down the street and back it would be time to pack up and send the little darlings home for their parents to deal with. Twenty-five first graders were a challenge on a regular day; on Halloween it was beyond challenging.

The thing I hated most about being a teacher at the same school my daughter attended was that I never got to volunteer in Ella's classroom. I knew she was fine and well taken care of, but while I was spending time with other people's kids, I didn't get to indulge in activities with my own daughter. I would have loved to attend the party in her room today, but it just wasn't possible.

At least during the parade, I could catch a glimpse of her. Kindergarten led the long line of students that marched down the sidewalk while parents and grandparents lined the street to take pictures of their children. I watched as Ella did a fancy twirl in front of my mom and dad who lived for stuff like this. She did a cheesy smile for the camera and then hurried to catch up with her class. At least she had them. Some of these kids had no one show up at events like this. And sadder yet, were the children that had no costume to wear to a Halloween parade. My daughter was lucky to have a family who adored her, and Chase was filling in the missing pieces that made her life complete.

As we approached the loop at the end of the street that marked the halfway point on our route, Joey tugged on the back of my shirt. "Ms. Malone, there's my mom. She's here! She's here!" The little pirate jumped up and down, he'd been so worried this morning that she wasn't going to make it to the parade.

I wrapped my arm around him as we continued to walk. "That's great, sweetheart. Where is she?" I'd only met her once, during Open House, but she was pretty memorable.

He pointed with his silver hook. "Right there! Across the street!"

My eyes followed Joey's outstretched arm. It was easy to find the buxom blond wearing a tight denim skirt and four-inch red heels, but it wasn't Joey's mom that captured my attention. It was who was standing next to her that I focused on.

You've got to be kidding me!

"Do you see her, Ms. Malone?"

"Yes, honey. I see her. You should give your mom a wave."

Joey started frantically waving his arms around. "Mom! Mom! I'm right here."

Several sets of eyes turned our way at the commotion Joey was causing, including those of the man standing next to the blond. *What was he doing here?*

I immediately began searching the front of the line where I had seen Ella. She was chatting with a miniature Cinderella, totally unaware of what was waiting up ahead.

We circled the loop and I began counting down.

Five.

Four.

Three.

Two...

"Daddy!" Ella broke into a sprint toward her father and jumped into his arms. He hoisted her up on his hip, both of them laughing hysterically. Ella's arms were animated with whatever she was saying, practically knocking off her bobby-pinned tiara. He placed her back on her feet and took her hand, swinging their arms between them as they continued the parade.

To anyone else their interaction would have looked totally normal and endearing. But not to me. It wasn't normal, and as much as I wanted it to be, it wasn't endearing. It was suspicious as fuck. *What the hell was he trying to pull?*

I wanted answers, but they would have to wait. My mind spun with implications as I tried to focus on my students and finish the parade with a plastered-on smile. But try as I might, the sight of my daughter holding the hand of the man who'd rarely gave us the time of day took up all the space in my brain. I led my class back to our room where the chaos of packing up treats for twenty-five little ones and handing them off to the correct parents would begin.

Roxy poked her head in my class. "You know about that?"

I ripped the stupid cowboy hat from my head and threw it on my desk. "Not a clue."

She gave me two thumbs-up and a grimace, "Good luck," and continued down the hallway.

We still had another twenty minutes left of the morning, but as always, the parents were anxious to get their munchkins home. I rushed around helping children stuff all their things in their backpacks, making sure treat bags weren't forgotten, and having parents sign their children out for the day.

All but five students had been signed out. Little Sarah Meyers sat at her desk dejectedly in her Tinkerbell costume. "My mom said she was gonna come today. She promised."

I kneeled next to her desk and ran my hands through her long, dark hair. "She probably had to work, sweetie. I'm sure she would have been here if she could."

Big blue eyes stared back at me and tears streaked down her cheeks. "My mom doesn't work. She forgot about me."

My heart broke for the sweet girl. I wrapped her in my arms. "Your mom didn't forget about you. Something really important must have come up. I'm sure she's really disappointed that she missed it." I knew the words that flowed from my lips were a lie, but what else could I say? Sometimes I forgot I was the only stable person in some of their little lives. Moments like these were the reason I continued on with my degree when I found out I was pregnant. If I could make a difference for one child, even if it was as simple as giving a much-needed hug, the job was worth it.

She wiped the tears from her eyes. "You think so?"

"I'm positive. She would have been here if she could. As a matter of fact, I bet she'll be waiting for you when you get off the bus. She'll be so excited to hear all about your day and see all your treats."

Lies and more lies fell from my mouth. I'd never met Sarah's mom. She hadn't shown up for Open House, nor had she returned any of the numerous phone calls I made in an attempt to discuss her daughter's lack of progress. More than likely, Sarah would be sitting here disappointed again next year. "Come on. Let's get you on the bus."

I called to the others who were waiting to go home. They quickly lined up and followed me like ducklings out to the buses. Once I had gotten them all safely on board, I noticed Cara Nelson, Ella's teacher, standing by the doors holding the hand of Spiderman. I quickly scanned the area. Surely Ella had come out with her teacher, but I didn't see her anywhere.

My feet moved lightening quick. "Where's Ella?"

"She went home with her dad."

"What?"

Taking in the panicked look in my eyes, she started to explain, "He signed her out twenty minutes ago. Was I not supposed to let her go?"

Deep breaths. Jeff was Ella's father; everything would be fine. "Of course. It just slipped my mind is all. Crazy day, you know?"

"Amen, sister." She held up the tiny hand that was grasped in hers. "I just have to call this one's parents. Someone always forgets to pick their child up on a half-day. It's not like we sent home five notices and did a robocall."

It was true, but I didn't have time to get into a discussion about it. "It's always something." I hurried back into the building, waving over my shoulder. "Enjoy the rest of your day."

Rushing to my desk, I pulled out my phone and called Jeff. When the line picked up, I didn't even give him a chance to talk. "Where are you? Do you have Ella?" My voice shook with worry.

"Calm your tits, Mags. We're in the parking lot."

I held a hand to my chest and sank into my chair. "Goddamnit, Jeff! You can't do stuff like that. You scared the shit out of me. Ella and I have a routine. You can't just take her without telling me!"

I could practically hear his eyes roll through the phone. "Are you coming out or what?"

"I'll be there in less than five minutes…" I'd barely gotten the words out of my mouth before the call ended. I stared at my phone in disbelief, *fucker just hung up on me.*

Roxy leaned against the doorway. "Everything okay?"

I grabbed my purse from the desk drawer and shoved my phone inside. "Yes and no," I huffed. "Jeff signed Ella out without telling me. He's pissed because I was upset. Can you believe it? *He's* pissed at *me*? He hung up on me!"

She hurried inside clearly concerned. "Where are they?"

I spun around looking for my travel mug. I could have sworn I left it on my desk this morning. "They're in the parking lot waiting for me, but that's not the point. He should have told me." The mug was definitely not on my desk, "Where the hell is my coffee cup?" Tears filled my eyes as my emotions caught up with me. I wasn't upset about the stupid cup. I was upset that for a few minutes I'd thought Jeff had absconded with my daughter. It wasn't logical. Jeff would never do that, but the thought of losing her for even a few minutes had put me in full-on panic mode. If I ever lost Ella…

Roxy grabbed me by the shoulders. "Take a deep breath. Ella is fine. Yes, what Jeff did was shitty, but the important thing is that your daughter is safe and waiting for you right outside those doors."

I wiped at the tear that ran down my cheek. "I know. He just scared me is all." I gave Roxy a tight hug. "Thank you for being here."

"That's what best friends are for," she said, hugging me back. Then she picked up my travel mug from the round table two feet in front of my face and shoved it into my hand. "Don't let Jeff ruin your night."

"I'll try." With my purse over my shoulder and mug in hand, I rushed from the room. Stopping in the doorway, I spun on my heel. "Hey, Roxy, good luck on your date and if he's cute… bang the hell out of him."

She laughed as I headed down the hallway. I heard her call after me, "I like what Chase has done to you."

Me too, Roxy. Me too.

Stopping at the double doors, I took another deep breath before confronting Jeff. I'd lost it with him on the phone, but I didn't need him to see me upset and flustered. I needed to pull it together. That man had already caused enough chaos in my life. This was just a little hiccup, that's all.

Pushing through the doors, I immediately saw Jeff leaned against his black BMW. Ella twirled in front of him, gabbing away. Despite his attempt to look interested, I could tell he was bored to death. In these moments, I was glad Ella was too young to pick up on his obvious body language.

When Ella saw me, she began to sprint across the nearly empty parking lot and for the third time today, my heart seized. "Ellanora Riley, what have I told you about parking lots?"

She stopped and looked both ways. "But there's hardly any cars."

I scooped her up, glad to have her safely in my arms. "It only takes one, ladybug, and Momma would be very sad if anything ever happened to you." I kissed her on the forehead. "How was your day?"

Ella talked a mile a minute as we walked to Jeff's car. "So much fun. We had chocolate cupcakes with orange frosting on top and we played pin-the-nose-on-the-pumpkin. I didn't do so good though, I stabbed him in the eye. But then we got to pass out our treats and Frankie gave us vampire teeth. I tried to scare Daddy with them, but he didn't get scared."

We stopped in front of Jeff and I set Ella down, never taking my eyes off him. "I think we were both surprised to see you here today."

He shrugged. "I saw it on the website, since you didn't bother to tell me about it."

I fumed. This was the man who had done as little as possible to be in our lives. "How ingenious of you. I didn't think you even knew the name of her school." I couldn't help but get a dig in of my own.

He crossed his arms over his suit jacket and tie. "Give me a break, Mags. You've worked here for years."

That was true, but in all the years I'd worked here, never once had he ever showed up or shown interest in my job. I matched his stance, crossing my arms and using all my self-control not to wrap my hands around his neck and squeeze. "Well, I'm glad you could come. You made your daughter very happy today. Next time, give me a heads-up so I don't worry when she disappears."

"She was totally safe. I had every right to check her out of school. I'm her father."

"I'm aware, however, it's called common courtesy."

Ella tugged on my elbow. "Daddy's coming trick-or-treating with us tonight."

I felt as if a bucket of cold water had been dumped over my head. This was so not happening right now. Chase was supposed to meet my family for the first time. Jeff being there was not part of the plan. I only had one question for Jeff. "Why?"

He smirked at me. He knew, dammit. Somehow, he knew this would put a monkey wrench in my plans. "Because Ella asked me."

"She asks you every year, and you're always too busy." Any other year, I would have been ecstatic. Was I supposed to believe that all of a sudden he'd decided to be a stand-up dad? He was screwing with me on purpose.

"And as luck would have it, this year I'm totally free. So of course, when Ella asked me, I said yes."

I was lost for words. Jeff and I glared at each other in a pissing contest I couldn't win. I would either disappoint Chase or my daughter. But when it came right down to it, there wasn't really a decision to make. My daughter would always win.

Ella's eyes ping-ponged between us. "Daddy can come, right?" If I hadn't already decided, her face would have done it for me.

I always promised myself that no matter what happened between Jeff and me, I wouldn't put Ella in the middle. She wasn't a pawn, and I wouldn't use her as one for selfish reasons. I'd seen it way too many times with the parents of my students. The sad part was the child always lost. I wouldn't do that to my own daughter. Jeff knew it too.

I crouched in front of Ella. "Of course, ladybug. It's going to be lots of fun."

"Yay!" She threw herself at Jeff and squeezed his legs. "I'll see you tonight, Daddy!"

He awkwardly hugged her back, smirking at me again. "What time?"

He'd manipulated me and was proud of it. He knew I would always choose Ella above everything else, but that didn't mean I had to make it easy for him. "We're leaving at five o'clock. Don't be late."

Chapter 23
Chase

"If you want to back out, I'd totally understand. This isn't what you signed up for."

I held the phone away from my head and stared at the screen, as if I could see Maggie's face through it. Yeah, nothing but black with the word *Red* staring back at me. Admittedly, hanging out with Jeff was definitely *not* what I signed up for, however, backing out would make me look like a coward and a chump. That's not the impression I wanted to give Maggie, or her family. And I wasn't going to let Jeff get the best of me either. There's no doubt that's exactly what that dickwad was trying to do. I cursed myself for feeling like I had to compete with that uptight asshole. "I signed up for being with you and Ella. Are you planning on abandoning me behind a dumpster or something?"

"What? No! It's...I didn't plan on Jeff being here tonight. He just showed up at school like it was a perfectly normal thing. It wasn't. He's never come trick-or-treating with us before, but when Ella asked if he could come, I couldn't tell her no. She gave me puppy-dog eyes and..."

I could tell she was just as conflicted about this turn of events as I was. "Red, stop. You don't have to justify to me. He's her father and although we didn't get off on the right foot, we can coexist. If he has a problem with it, then that's on him. I'll be fine." The words spewed from my mouth even if I didn't believe them. It showed maturity on my part even though it added another level of anxiety beyond meeting Red's family.

Maggie sighed on the other end of the phone. "You're pretty great, you know that?"

The last thing I wanted to do was spend my evening with Maggie's ex, but I wasn't going to let him dictate our relationship either. If we were serious about making a go of this, a little discomfort was well worth it. "*Great*'s a strong word, but I try. This doesn't have to be difficult."

"Then why do I feel like it already is?"

This was the real first speed bump in our relationship. The fantasy world we'd built with just the three of us was about to be tested. "It's not. It's just the first of many times we'll all have to get along. Honestly, I'm more nervous about meeting your brother." I tried to keep it lighthearted. "He doesn't moonlight as a UFC fighter or anything, right?" I knew her brother was gay, but that didn't mean the guy couldn't be built like a brick house.

Maggie's beautiful laugh carried through the line. "No. I told you he's a lawyer. Patty's too pretty to get his face messed up in a metal cage."

"Good to know. What time should I be there?"

"Whenever you can. Everybody's coming at three-thirty, but I told Jeff not to come until five, when trick-or-treating starts."

"I'll see you soon, Red." I blew out a frustrated breath and left my studio in search of Zack. I wanted to cut out early today, but if he needed me to stay longer I would. I desperately needed a shave and shower. Since I wasn't sneaking out of Maggie's house at the ass crack of dawn anymore, I didn't want to monopolize the one bathroom in the house and disrupt their routine. Having a sister, I was well acquainted with the morning rituals of women and their endless need for time in front of the mirror. Instead, I spent my mornings making coffee and fixing breakfast for my girls.

I found Zack in his office talking animatedly with Rissa, who was perched on his desk, running both hands through his hair that now stuck up in every direction. Zack was usually calm, cool and collected, so seeing him flustered was highly entertaining.

"I don't know, sweetheart. Can't we just bring her with us?" Zack asked his wife before I could make my presence known.

I knocked on the doorframe, afraid of being caught eavesdropping on their personal conversation.

When Zack returned from New York with the beautiful Rissa in tow I was immediately attracted to her. She was adorable. Smart and witty, with the face of an angel and a voice to match. Zack was a goner from the start. Even a blind person could have seen how perfect they were together, and so I relegated myself to the dependable friend-zone.

Rissa smiled at me sweetly. "Come in, Chase. Please tell Zack that the premiere party is no place for a baby. Tori's mom offered to babysit Alexandria since everyone else we trust will be at the party. Zack's having a difficult time letting go."

That was no surprise. Zack exerted protectiveness over everything in his life, his daughter and wife being at the top of that list. I proceeded with a caution I'd learned was necessary when asked my opinion about either of them. "I think you should listen to your wife. She wouldn't do anything to put Alexandria in harm's way. You two deserve to enjoy the night."

Zack cocked an eyebrow at me, clearly not thrilled with my two cents.

Rissa beamed. "See? It makes perfect sense. I knew Chase would be on my side."

The scowl on Zack's face told me that not only was he not convinced, but he was annoyed we had ganged up against him. I smoothed it over with something he couldn't refute. "Besides, by tomorrow the cat will be out of the bag about the premiere and the paparazzi will be out in full force. You don't want your daughter's face splashed across the front of every magazine and social media page from here to California, do you?"

"Definitely not." He let out a defeated sigh. "Fine. I'll concede, but I'm calling to check in every hour. Make that every half hour."

Rissa leaned across the desk, planting a kiss on his cheek. "I wouldn't expect anything less."

Zack visibly melted. He was helpless against the girl who'd stolen his heart. Before Rissa, he'd been just as lost as me. It was amazing what the right woman could do.

"Did you need something?" he asked gruffly.

My hands delved into my pockets. "Just wanted to know if it was cool if I take off early."

He leaned back in his chair. "You never leave early. What's up?"

"I'm taking Maggie and Ella trick-or-treating. You know the holiday where parents willingly allow their kids to take candy from strangers and everyone seems to think it's okay?" When put that way, it seemed a little fucked up.

He laughed. "I'm familiar with the tradition. Thankfully, Alexandria's too little to realize it's Halloween."

Rissa smacked his shoulder playfully. "Don't even think about denying our daughter the traditions of childhood. You know you'll never be able to tell her no."

He crossed his arms over his chest. "We'll see."

I held out an index finger and circled it with the other. "You're a big talker, but she's already got you wrapped around her little finger. Every time she blinks those big green eyes and smiles, you cave, and she can't even talk yet."

Rissa giggled softly into her hand.

Zack eyed both of us with disdain. "I'm not that bad."

I flopped into the worn leather chair across from his desk. "You kind of are."

"Whatever," he huffed. "It's not a sin to love my daughter."

My hands went up in surrender. "Didn't say it was. I've got the same problem and Ella's not even mine."

"So, how's that going?" Rissa asked, sitting in the chair next to mine.

"Which part?"

"All of it."

I shifted uncomfortably. Talking seriously about women wasn't my thing. Usually, I threw out a cheesy one-liner about how hard I was to resist or how women couldn't help but fall at my feet. Maggie deserved more than a flippant response. She wasn't some random chick I picked up at the bar. Well, she was, but I knew she'd be more than that the first night she walked out of my apartment. Somehow, in the short amount of time we'd spent together, she'd wedged herself into my heart. "Would it be crazy if I said she was the one?"

Rissa laid her hand on my knee. "Not at all. We can all see how much you care about her. Have you told her yet?"

"She knows I care about her," I answered sheepishly.

She rolled her eyes. "I meant have you told Maggie you love her?"

I looked to Zack for reinforcement.

He leaned forward on his desk, clearly not letting me off the hook. "Well, have you?"

There was no getting out of this. These two were more tenacious than my parents when I got caught with my hand down Meredith's pants. "Not yet."

"Why not?" Rissa asked.

I shrugged. "It's too soon, isn't it? I don't want to disappoint her. You know it's just a matter of time before I fuck up."

Now Zack rolled his eyes. "We all fuck up. I fucked up. Draven fucked up. Layla fucked up. Hell, even Rissa's fucked up before."

She shot him a death glare.

"Sorry, sweetheart. The truth's the truth. You're damn close, but even you aren't perfect." He focused back on me. "My point is, we all mess up. And when it happens you gotta be man enough to admit it and then fix it. That's what love is. So, you gotta ask yourself, is she worth you groveling when you do fuck up? 'Cuz it won't be pretty."

Zack was right. I didn't know anyone who hadn't made mistakes, yet they'd been able to still figure it out. Except for Meredith and me. Some fuckups were too big to fix. But Maggie wasn't Meredith, and this was a fresh start. I'd asked Maggie to jump with me, but it was my feet that were still firmly planted on the ground. She'd broken every one of her self-imposed rules about relationships for me. I'd let her jump into the deep alone because I was afraid of some future catastrophe where I let her down. She was waiting for me, treading water, until I fully committed. I was already fucking up, but this I could fix. No groveling required. "Yeah, she's worth it." I slapped my knees and stood, ready to give Maggie what she'd clearly already given me…all of her. She deserved all of me, not some half-baked version with an inferiority complex. "About tonight?"

Zack waved me off. "Get out of here. I'm closing shop until Monday. If the paparazzi do show up, I don't want them hanging around here. This is supposed to be our safe place."

"Thanks, man. For everything."

Rissa hugged me tightly. "Don't you know we love you? We'd do anything for you."

I hugged her back and waggled my eyebrows at Zack over her shoulder. I loved pushing his buttons when it came to his girl.

Zack launched a pen at my head. "Thin ice, man. Get your own woman!"

This sucked. I couldn't shake the nerves. There was a lot at stake tonight. I wanted to charm Maggie's parents, be cool with her brother, and keep myself from knocking her ex flat on his ass. Easy peasy. Shouldn't be a problem at all. I checked my hair in the rearview mirror and tucked the gift I brought for Ella under my arm.

As I approached the house, I wondered if I should knock on the door. I'd become accustomed to just walking in, but with her family here, I wasn't sure if it was appropriate. They might not know we were at that level yet.

The door flew open and Ella came running down the sidewalk, saving me from making the decision. "Chase! You're here!" She jumped into my arms, wrapping herself around me.

I propped her up, careful not to smash her fairy wings and carried her toward the door. "Hey, princess bug." Her face was done in full makeup and glitter I knew Maggie would never allow any other day of the year. "You look beautiful. I like your sparkles," I said, wiping a bit off her neck.

"Momma said I could wear it today because I'm a fairy princess and I gots to have glitter 'cuz that's what makes fairies magical."

"She's absolutely right." I set Ella on her feet just inside the door and handed her the wrapped gift. "Happy Halloween."

"For me?" she gasped as she ripped off the orange paper covered in jack-o'-lanterns. "It's Not My Cat!" Ella hugged the stuffed tabby cat to her chest. "I love him! Thank you! I'm gonna go make him a bed in my room." She sped into the house with the cat in tow. It was amazing how the littlest things could bring the biggest smiles.

Brushing the excess glitter from my shoulders onto the porch, I remembered the card Ella made me. Let's just say glitter is the gift that never goes away. It seemed to pop up in my apartment in the most random places. I exerted extra effort to keep as much of it on the porch as possible and as an added benefit delay the inevitable of meeting the fam.

Maggie appeared in the doorway. "They don't bite."

"I was just…"

She placed a finger over my lips. "I know what you were doing. Come in. They're all quite tame and trained. I promise."

"I wasn't stalling," I insisted.

"Of course you weren't." She picked a speck of glitter from my cheek and held it up on her finger for me to see. "You had a little something on your face."

I captured her mouth with mine and gently coaxed her lips open with my tongue. She melted into me as I held the back of her head and proceeded to kiss her in a way that was definitely not family friendly. She tasted like chocolate and red wine. "Mmmm. You started drinking without me."

"Liquid courage," she explained. "I've kept you a secret for a while now and well…this is big for me."

"I promise to be on my best behavior," I assured her.

Maggie threaded her fingers through mine and pulled me through the door. "It's not you I'm worried about."

"Oh. My. God. This is the guy you've been dating?" her brother yelled out.

Surprised wasn't even the right word to describe what I was feeling when I saw not one, but two familiar faces. All the tension drained from my shoulders. This was going to be a piece of cake. I walked right to Maggie's brother and pulled him in for a bro hug, giving him a hearty pat on the back. "What's up, man?" I repeated the gesture to the other guy standing in the kitchen. "How's it going, Brian?"

Maggie stood there speechless; her mouth held wide open at our friendly greeting. Finally, she pointed between the three of us. "Wait a minute, you guys know each other?"

"Brian is Layla's best friend. I've known him for years. And Patrick is Brian's better half, so, yeah. We've all hung out together."

Patrick rolled up his sleeve, revealing the scales of justice inked on his forearm. "Chase did this for me."

She slumped against the kitchen counter. "All this anxiety for nothing? How come you didn't tell me you knew my brother?"

I shrugged. "You said his name was Patty. I never put two and two together."

Patrick scowled at his sister. "That's a family thing. Nobody else calls me Patty."

Brian swirled the wine in his glass. "Isn't this an interesting turn of events. Here Patrick was ready to give you the third degree and now it's not necessary. There goes my entertainment for the night."

Reaching into the fridge, Patrick pulled out a bottled beer and handed it to me. "Don't think I won't still kick your ass if you don't treat her right. Maybe if Maggie hadn't been so secretive about her new man…"

"Stick a sock in it, *Patty*. It's not like you were forthcoming when you started dating Brian," Maggie chastised her brother.

"Wait!" Brian pointed at himself. "You kept *me* a secret?"

Patrick narrowed his eyebrows. "Yeah. Didn't you keep me a secret?"

"Hell no! Layla and I sat around drinking wine and eating ice cream while discussing our love lives. I'm an open book."

I stared at Maggie and her brother. "Looks like you all have some issues."

"We don't have issues," Maggie argued. "It's called keeping your nosy brother out of your business." She jabbed him in the chest.

Patrick grabbed her offending finger. "She's the nosy one."

"Issues." Brian chuckled.

Tiny feet pitter-pattered down the hallway. Ella jumped into the kitchen, baring long plastic teeth at me. "Grrrrh!"

I clutched my chest and fell to the floor. "Save me! There's a vampire in the house."

Ella climbed onto my chest, pulling the teeth from her mouth. "It's just me, Chase! Did I scare you?"

"So much! I thought you were going to bite me."

She giggled. "I wouldn't bite you. I just wanted to scare you."

Maggie held out her hand for the spit-covered teeth. "That's enough scaring people. You already got Uncle Patty and Uncle Brian too."

Ella reluctantly dropped them into her hand. "Darn it! I was just having fun."

Maggie wrapped the teeth in a paper towel. "Go wash your hands. Nanna and Papa will be here any minute with the pizza."

"Yay! Pizza!" The vampire teeth were quickly forgotten as she rushed off to wash her hands.

Patrick reached out to pull me from the floor. "You're good with her." It felt less like a simple gesture and more like an approval.

"She makes it easy," I said, accepting his outstretched hand.

"That she does. Girl's had me wrapped since the day she was born. It's too bad her sperm donor doesn't see it. Guy's a total fucktard."

Maggie threw the vampire teeth at his head. "I told you not to say that. I don't want Ella overhearing you."

Total fucktard, Brian mouthed to me.

Maggie, who missed nothing, elbowed him in the gut. "And you're not any better."

I knew there was a reason I liked these guys. Seemed our dislike of Jeff was one more thing we had in common. I couldn't wait to see the look on Jeff's face when he saw how well I got along with Patrick and Brian. It was going to be priceless.

"Helloooo," a feminine voice sang from the front door.

"Nanna!" Ella raced to the door with her new Not My Cat tucked under her arm. She led Maggie's parents into the tiny kitchen, which was feeling smaller by the minute.

Her mom was a petite woman with bright blue eyes, shoulder-length red hair and freckles across her nose. There was no doubt the genetics in Red's family were

207

strong. It was like looking at one of those age progressed photos. No one would be able to deny the three generations of women standing in the kitchen were related.

Maggie's dad was a tall, stocky man with a full white beard and piercing gaze. I took the stack of pizza boxes from her dad. "Here, let me help you with that." I set them on the counter and held out my hand. "I'm Chase. Nice to meet you."

He gripped it in a firm shake. "Craig. Glad to finally meet the man Maggie's been dating." He squeezed a little harder than necessary and leaned in. "What are your intentions with my daughter?"

Shit! I'd thought it would be her brother I had to worry about. His question was valid, but I was too blindsided by his forwardness to answer. "I…umm…I…"

Maggie's mom pushed him aside. "Craig, leave the poor guy alone. You're scaring him."

Her dad gave me a solid slap on the back. "Relax, Maureen. I'm just messing with the boy."

I hadn't been called a boy in years, except by my mom and Grams. I wasn't sure if I was reading him right, but I got the feeling I was definitely going to have to prove myself to Maggie's dad. I couldn't blame him. When Ella started to date, I'd be the same way.

Whoa!

That thought popped into my head from nowhere. I'd have to shelve it for now and analyze it later.

Maggie's mom hugged me around the shoulders. "I'm Maureen and I'm so happy to finally meet the man who's had my daughter all smiles." She sent her husband a scathing look. "Ignore my husband. He can be a little overbearing." Still holding my arms, she leaned back as if inspecting me and tilted her head to the side. "You're very handsome. You'll do just fine."

Turning on the charm, I winked at her. "You're not so bad yourself. I can see where Maggie gets her good looks from."

She blushed just like I'd seen Red do a hundred times. "Oh, please. There's no need to flatter an old lady." Maureen fluffed her hair with one hand. "Although, I *was* quite the looker back in the day."

I chuckled. "I'm sure you were."

Maggie clapped her hands together as if she were conducting her class of first graders. "Okay, that's enough of the introductions. There are plates and silverware on the counter. Everybody, dig in." She began opening pizza boxes and pulled a salad from the fridge.

Patrick and Ella were first in line. He whispered in her ear as he prepared her plate, setting them both up at the table. Brian pulled up a chair on the other side of Ella. She clearly adored both men. Maureen and Craig joined them with their own plates full of food.

Red was still flitting around the kitchen, obviously flustered. I sidled up behind her, wrapping my arms around her waist and setting my chin on her shoulder. "What's wrong?"

"You weren't supposed to flirt with my mother," she hissed.

I grinned like a Cheshire cat. "I wasn't flirting. It's called being charming. I want my woman's mom to like me."

She turned in my arms. "Well, it worked. You're in like Flynn. But don't think that shit's going to work with my dad. He'll see right through it. He respects actions not words."

"Oh, ye of little faith. Besides, I have every intention of proving I'm good enough for his daughter."

Maggie patted me on the chest. "Just stop flirting with my mom. You're laying it on a little thick." She pointed to the open box on the counter. "This pizza's got less cheese than you."

The next hour went seamlessly. I toned down the cheese and settled into comfortable conversation with Maggie's family. Her dad was a lot of bark, but so far, I'd managed to keep from getting bitten. He seemed genuinely interested in my work as an artist, even if he asked personal questions about my income and future goals. My goals were a little sketchy, but I did have them. Someday I planned on finishing my degree in graphic design. I had the talent, I just needed to learn the business end of the profession. I always thought I had more time. My life had fallen into a comfortable pattern, but Craig's questioning got me thinking more about my future and the kind of life I wanted to provide for Maggie. She was the inspiration I needed to get my ass in gear and make good on the goals I'd set for myself.

A knock on the door interrupted our raucous laughter.

Craig looked at his watch. "It's a little early for trick-or-treaters, isn't it?"

Maggie pursed her lips. "That'd be Jeff. He's going with us."

The air in the room shifted as Craig stood from the table and threw his napkin on his plate. "I'll get it."

"Daddy's here?"

Maggie took Ella by the hand. "Come on, ladybug. Let's get the pizza sauce wiped off your face and touch up your makeup." They disappeared down the hall.

The tension was thick. "What's going on?"

"Craig hates Jeff," Brian answered. "Maybe there will be entertainment after all."

"I take it you and Dad didn't know?" Patrick asked his mom.

She held a napkin to her mouth and shook her head. "I should intervene."

Patrick put his hand on her shoulder. "We got this." He motioned for Brian and me to follow him.

The three of us, each of good size and stature, formed a formidable wall behind Craig as he opened the door.

Jeff's hand froze mid-knock when he saw us all standing there. The look on his face was better than priceless. As my mom would say, he looked like someone had not only pissed in his bowl of Cheerios but stomped on the whole damn box.

Jeff's throat bobbed. "Craig. Didn't know you were going to be here tonight."

Craig casually crossed his arms across his chest. "I'm always here on Halloween. You'd know that if you were around more often. As a matter of fact, I'm here for Thanksgiving, Christmas, Easter, and birthdays too. You know, all the important events in my granddaughter's life."

Daaamn! Maggie's dad was brutal. I almost felt bad for the guy, but then again, he'd brought this on himself.

Jeff shoved his hands in his pockets. "I work a lot." It was a flimsy excuse for his absence in Ella's life.

Craig clapped him on the shoulder. "That's right, you're a career man. Busy, busy, busy. As I recall you were busy working the night Maggie went into labor, though you weren't too busy to get her pregnant. Had plenty of time for that."

If I had any chance of getting along with Jeff, I had to throw him a lifeline. Guy was drowning. He didn't know it yet, but I was his best shot at survival right now. I stepped forward extending my hand. "Come in. We were just finishing up dinner."

He grasped my hand with uncertainty. "Thanks. Maggie didn't say anything about dinner."

"It was a *family* thing," Patrick answered.

"There's a few pieces of pizza left if you're hungry." I motioned toward the kitchen. "Feel free to make yourself a plate."

It might've stung now, but hopefully being nice to him would pay off in the long run.

Chapter 24
Maggie

By the tenth house Jeff was checking his watch. Thankfully, my parents and brother had stayed at the house to pass out candy. If my dad were witnessing this, he would have had steam coming out his ears. His tolerance for Jeff was minimal at best. This whole experience was awkward enough without my father making snide remarks.

Ella skipped down a driveway to meet the three of us where we were waiting for her. She carefully readjusted the stuffed cat under her arm as she reached into the sparkly, pink pumpkin that held her candy. She pulled out a large Hershey bar, almost dumping the entire contents. Chase caught the pumpkin before it crashed to the ground. "Look! It's a biggie!"

"You know this would be a lot easier if you'd let go of that cat." Jeff tried to take it by the tail, but Ella wasn't having any of that.

She yanked it back, hugging the cat protectively to her chest. "No, Daddy! I love him."

Jeff rolled his eyes. "All right, let's go to the next house."

There was a long string of dark porches ahead of us. "How far to the next house?"

"Looks like we have to go to the corner and cross the street," I answered.

"But it's so far," she complained. It'd been a long, busy day for her.

"Wanna ride on my shoulders?" Chase offered.

That got her attention. "Can I?"

"Yep." Chase grabbed her by the waist and lifted Ella up over his head. "Hold on tight." Chase secured Ella's legs over his shoulders while she wrapped her hands around his forehead, nearly taking out his eye with the pumpkin in the process.

"Here, let me hold that." I took the pumpkin from her hands.

"Well, aren't you guys cute?" Jeff said sarcastically.

I held a hand up in his face. "Don't start."

Chase put his hand on my shoulder. "It's fine." He looked up at Ella. "Are you having fun, princess bug?"

"Yes! Halloween is the most excellent holiday ever, except for Christmas because Santa comes, and I get lots of presents." In her excitement she let go of Chase's head and wobbled backward. Chase tightened his grip on her legs and caught Ella before she fell. "Whoa! That was a close one." She giggled.

"You're going to drop my daughter," Jeff insisted.

Chase, bless his heart, pressed his lips together and took a deep breath through his nose. "I'm not going to drop her. I wouldn't ever let anything happen to her."

How he was maintaining such calm, I didn't know. If I were him, I would have lost it a long time ago.

After we crossed the street, Chase set Ella back on her feet. There were several houses in a row that were lit up for the holiday. The first house was covered in cobwebs and had a coffin sitting on the porch. Eerie music played and strobe lights illuminated the smoke coming from a fog machine. A large group of older children screamed as they ran away from the house.

Ella stopped in her tracks and hugged the cat tighter to her chest. "I don't think I wanna go to that house."

Jeff put his hands on his hips. "Why not? The other kids are going there."

She twisted her lips to the side. "It's scary. I'm not gonna go."

Jeff kneeled in front of her. "What if Daddy went with you? Would you go then?"

It was one of the few times he actually seemed empathetic. I was happy for Ella that he was finally stepping up to the plate.

She looked up at him with big eyes. "Will you hold my hand?"

"Sure, baby." He held out his hand for her. She took ahold and hugged the cat to her chest tighter. I passed him the plastic pumpkin and they took off toward the door.

I kept my eye on Ella but spoke to Chase. "You know she's going to sleep with that damn cat tonight, right?"

"Probably."

"It was super sweet for you to get it for her." Seeing Ella was safe, I finally gave Chase my full attention. "Thank you for being here tonight. It means a lot to her."

He laced his fingers through mine. "I wouldn't be anywhere else. I love spending time with both of you."

He *loved* spending time with us. My conversation with the girls flitted through my head. Did he love me? I so desperately wanted to take this to the next level. Chase had been a blessing coming into our lives. He'd filled the empty place in my heart I'd given up on filling. He wasn't selfish or arrogant, if anything, he'd sacrificed so much to be with us. Nights reading bedtime stories and doing homework had to pale in comparison to the life he'd been living before us. But the best part was Chase made me feel as if it was the only thing he wanted to do. I'd never had a man make me feel that way. Jeff at his best, fit me into his busy schedule. I had never been his priority. I'd never been cherished or adored.

"Thank you for putting up with Jeff. He's really not a bad guy, he's just… self-absorbed."

"Your dad hates him." He smirked.

I rolled my eyes. "There's a lot of history there. I don't think my dad will ever forgive him for what he put me through. He doesn't understand why I tolerate Jeff, but I won't break Ella's illusion of what she thinks her father is. We've never been together, so she doesn't know any better. One day she'll figure it out and that'll be on him."

Chase stroked my cheek with his thumb. "You don't have to explain. I get it, I really do."

And that was another reason I'd fallen for this man. He didn't make me feel guilty for indulging Jeff's selfish behavior. Instead, he made everything easier by accepting my complicated life.

Ella and Jeff returned with matching smiles. "How was it?"

"It wasn't scary at all. The lady was really nice, and she called me cute."

"Our girl was a trooper," Jeff confirmed.

If nothing else, Ella was spending quality time with her father and I had to give Jeff credit; he was actually acting like a dad.

Chase left early Saturday morning. He'd counted off a list of tasks he had to accomplish before this evening, including picking up his tux. As silly as it sounded, it felt like we were getting ready for prom and I was the giddy girl who couldn't wait to see him all dressed up. Only underneath that tux wouldn't be a boy. I was acutely aware of his broad chest, washboard abs, and tapered waist. Chase was all man.

It was ridiculous that I was so nervous about tonight. It wasn't every day I got to attend a premiere party. This was a first and probably a last. It was also the first time Chase and I would be out alone in what seemed like forever. Most of our nights included a rambunctious six-year-old. We still managed to have sexy times, but they required us to sneak around in my own home. We always had one ear open for tiny footsteps.

Tonight we were spending the night at Chase's apartment. Tonight we would truly be alone. Tonight I was going to lay my heart on the line with him and hope he didn't squash it in the palm of his hand.

The last time I'd given my heart away hadn't worked out so great. I should have seen the signs, but I was too blinded by love. Love that hadn't been reciprocated.

I hadn't allowed myself to fall again until Chase walked into my crazy, chaotic life. I had no doubt he cared about me, but I wanted it all. The fairy tales that Ella's favorite Disney movies were made of. The white knight that would rescue me from loneliness. A man who wanted to build a life with me and wouldn't bail at the first sign of trouble. A forever love who'd still stand by my side thirty years from now and still make butterflies take flight in my stomach from a simple kiss.

The question was, did Chase want the same things? With me? A forever and always?

I was almost ready. My hair cascaded over my shoulders in soft waves I normally wouldn't have the time to create. It took a head full of hot rollers and a lot of patience. My lashes were long and dark, complementing the smoky shadow that took hours of watching YouTube to perfect. A deep red gloss across my lips finished the look.

All I had to do was slip on my dress. I carefully unzipped the garment bag, revealing a turquoise beaded gown that made my own heart stop. It was too much: the glitz, the glamor, and definitely the price tag. Everything about it screamed sultry sex, but at the insistence of the girls, I ended up bringing it home.

I shimmied into the dress and carefully zipped up the back. Slipping on my silver, strappy heels, I appraised the woman in the mirror. The wide straps of the dress gave way to a deep V that showcased the girls, revealing plenty of cleavage but not so much that I was afraid of having a wardrobe malfunction. The gown

214

hugged my hips, giving me curves I often forgot I had. The icing on top of the cake was the slit in the skirt that ran halfway up my thigh. It was both classy and sexy.

Attaching the diamond studs to my ears that had been my grandmother's, I took one last look at myself and went out to the kitchen where my mom and Ella were waiting before heading out for a sleepover. Ella let her stuffed Not My Cat fall from her arms, holding him only by the tail. "You look like a princess, Momma."

"Thank you, ladybug. Do you think Chase is going to like it?"

"I think he's going to kiss you." She giggled.

I bopped her on the nose with my finger. "I hope so."

My mom inspected me from head to toe. "You look gorgeous, Maggie. Chase is going to more than kiss you. As a matter of fact, you'll be lucky if you leave the house when he shows up. Or maybe it would be lucky if you didn't."

My eyebrows shot up. "Mom!"

She shrugged innocently. "Just keeping it real. I don't know how he could resist you." She pushed a stray curl behind my ear. "This looks good on you."

I smoothed the fabric of the dress down over my hips. "Chase's friends picked it out for me. It's a little much, but I couldn't say no."

She gently clasped my face between her hands. "The dress is beautiful, but that's not what I meant. Happiness looks good on you. Ever since you started dating that boy, you've been glowing. It does my heart good to see you like this."

"He makes me so happy, Mom. Sometimes, it seems too good to be true. Like any minute the bubble will burst, and I'll be back to reality."

"That's nonsense. You deserve every bit of this happiness. Tonight don't worry about being a mom or doing laundry or checking papers. I want you to enjoy being the woman you are. You are bold and beautiful and fierce. Own it. And if your night lingers into the morning, enjoy that too. I have nowhere to be tomorrow."

My eyes misted. "Yeah?"

"Yeah." She smiled up at me. "Now the two of us are going to get out of here before your date shows up."

"But I want to see Chase," Ella grumbled.

My mom grabbed Ella's Elsa backpack off the chair. "They'll take lots of pictures, honey."

I squatted down and hugged Ella goodbye. "Be good for Nanna."

"I will."

"I'll see you tomorrow." I kissed her chubby cheek, leaving a lipstick print behind.

Once they left, the nerves set in again. I loaded up my silver clutch with the essentials and brought my overnight bag to set it near the door. This was it. So much was on the line for me tonight. I wanted to take our relationship to the next level and saying those three little words I'd been holding back would either move us in the right direction or have him tucking tail and retreating.

A quick rasp of knuckles on the front door alerted me to his arrival. I opened the door and drank him in. The way his shoulders filled out the tux and showcased his trim waist, it had obviously been tailored just for him. His face was clean shaven, showing off his rugged cheekbones, and his hair was styled back with a little gel, giving him an air of refinement. Gone were the boyish good looks and the careless appearance that first drew me in. The man in front of me looked so sophisticated and devastatingly handsome that he could have walked out of the pages of GQ. I wasn't sure which I liked better, but both were mouthwateringly delicious. "You clean up well. You look hot."

Chase's mouth quirked up on one side in his signature smirk, the dimple popping on his smooth cheek. His aqua eyes raked me over, a deep growl erupting from his throat as he stepped through the doorway and wrapped an arm around my waist, tugging me into his body. "And you look like a dream. Every dirty fantasy I've ever had come to life." His free hand slid up my neck and cradled the back of my head. "You're gorgeous, Red. I'm not going to be able to let you out of my sight tonight. Every woman will want to be you and ever man will want to fuck you."

His filthy words trapped the breath in my throat and made my sex clench. Maybe my mom was right and we'd never leave the house. It wouldn't be the worst thing that could happen.

Chase lowered his mouth to mine, capturing my lips in a soul-searing kiss that had my head swimming with desire. *Damn, this man.* A little whimper escaped when his tongue delved in and twisted with mine. Fire raced through my veins, making me unsteady. If it hadn't been for his arm anchoring me to him, I would have melted at his feet.

He eased back and wiped the smeared lipstick from my mouth as a contented sigh fell from my lips. "Wow. You're going to make walking out that door tonight hard."

He lifted his hips and pulled me in tighter, pressing his erection into my belly. "Yes, extremely hard. If Zack and Rissa wouldn't be totally devastated by our absence, I'd strip you naked right here in the hallway."

I pressed both hands to his chest to create a little distance. "Yes, Rissa would never forgive me if I kept you from missing her big night. We'll have to restrain ourselves until the after-party."

He chastely pecked me on the lips. "Ummm… the party of two I'm very much looking forward to." His grip on me released and his hand slipped into his pocket, producing a black velvet box. "I bought you something special, but you look so beautiful tonight I'm not sure you need it." He flipped open the box revealing a delicate silver chain with a single diamond pendant.

A hand flew to my lips in an effort conceal the gasp. "Oh my god! It's gorgeous."

"Turn around."

I turned and held my hair up, allowing him to clasp the necklace in place. I glanced down between my breasts and let my fingers slide over the jewelry. "It's stunning."

Chase lifted my chin. "Yes, you are." He checked his watch. "We need to go. Layla and Draven are waiting for us."

I retrieved my clutch from the coffee table and Chase grabbed my overnight bag. His hand went to the small of my back as we left the house. "We're picking them up?"

We continued down the front walk to the driveway. A black stretch limo took up most of it. "Yep. Zack wanted us to arrive in style." The chauffeur hurried to open our door so we could slip inside. "Fancy digs, huh?"

I settled in, running my hand along the soft leather seat. "I've never been in a limo."

Chase frowned at me. "Prom date didn't get a limo?"

I shook my head. "Nah. He borrowed his dad's Cadillac. Trust me, it was better than the mint green Dodge Aspen he drove. The car was supposed to be classic, but it was a piece of crap."

He chuckled. "If you were my girl back then, I would've sprung for the limo." He reached for the bottle of champagne, pouring us each a glass. He held his glass up to mine. "To us."

"To us," I repeated.

We'd barely been in the limo fifteen minutes when it pulled into the back lot of Forever Inked. I remembered Chase saying Draven and Layla lived in the apartment atop the shop, but I hadn't really given it much thought.

The back door opened, and Draven led Layla to the limo with an arm protectively around her waist. She was gorgeous. I'd already seen the black strapless sequined dress, but done up with her hair in a fancy twist and colorful tattoos adorning her skin, she was even more breathtaking. And Draven... well crap, he looked dark and foreboding as always. I swear the man was made out of stone. Even in her four-inch heels, he towered over Layla. Together they looked like a portrait of sin and ink.

The door opened and they slipped inside the limo, the space immediately shrinking to half its size. Draven eyed our glasses. "Couldn't wait for us?"

Chase smiled at him as he lifted the glass to his lips again. "Let's not pretend like you two haven't already downed some whiskey shots."

Layla took the champagne bottle from the ice bucket and handed it to Draven. "You know us so well."

Draven lowered the divider and spoke to the chauffeur. "Drive us around for twenty minutes before pulling up front." The Locker was only a stone's throw from the tattoo shop. We had time to burn before we were expected to arrive at the event. Draven raised the divider again and poured their champagne into the glasses Layla held up. "You're not even going to recognize our little hole-in-the-wall. Rissa's record label went all out. I snuck a peek earlier today. The Locker is all decked out. Fancy-schmancy shit."

"Rissa went through hell to get where she's at. No one deserves it more than her." Chase's adoration for the woman was evident. The way she talked about him; the feeling was mutual.

A quick trip around the city and the limo was pulling up in front of the bar. Draven was right, the front had been fancied up, complete with a bright marquis bearing Rissa Black's name, banners featuring giant photographs of the rising star, and spotlights. Lots and lots of spotlights. Tons of people stood behind the barricade that lined the red carpet, trying to get a glimpse at what was going on. I gulped. "We're supposed to get out here?" I leaned over Chase and pressed my face to the glass. "But we're nobodies."

Layla waved her hand at me. "We may be chopped liver to everyone else, but not to Rissa. We're her people."

I stared at the photographers waiting to snap pictures of us. I knew this event was going to be fancy, but this was over the top. "Who in the world would want a picture of me getting out of a limo?"

Draven cracked a rare smile and nodded to Chase. "I can think of one person."

"My woman's hot. I'm gonna frame it and hang it over my bed," Chase joked back.

"Seriously, Maggie," Draven continued, "the fact that were unknown only makes us more interesting to the paparazzi. You look gorgeous. Let them wonder who you are. Walk in there like you own the place."

I touched the diamond around my neck and rubbed it between my fingers. "All right."

Chase knocked on the window to alert the chauffeur we were ready. The door popped open and Chase stepped out, straightening his jacket. Lights began to flash as the photographers encroached on our space. Chase reached his hand to me. I clasped it and swung my legs out, careful to not give anyone a naughty show. With my hand firmly in his, Chase and I headed to the door. People shouted at us, asking who we were. Chase and I just smiled and posed for pictures, pretending we were somebodies.

A second round of shouts and camera flashes rose up as Draven and Layla exited the limo. They played the game even better than us, treating the crowd to a kiss I wasn't sure would qualify as PG-13. When they had their fill, Draven and Layla met us at the door where security checked their list and admitted us entrance.

Draven was totally right. *Fancy-schmancy* didn't do the inside justice. The whole bar had been transformed into another world. A high-tech stage with a grand piano, guitars and a drum set took up one corner of the bar. The tables, draped in black and gold, had been moved along the walls to create an open space where people dressed to the nines were mingling and swaying to the light music that was pumped in. Waiters walked around serving champagne and hors d'oeuvres. Bright lights were strung around the room, showcasing promotional photos of Rissa. The theme was soft and pure, with a distinct dark edge to it. A strange combination that oddly worked. Rissa's country roots mixed with the rock influence that colored her songs.

Chase wrapped his arm around my waist. "Really looks great, doesn't it? You can barely tell it's the same bar where we met."

"It does. What time are Rissa and Zack getting here?"

He checked his watch again. "About a half hour. How about we step to the bar. Draven and Layla are already there."

"Sure." I nodded.

I admired Chase from the back as I followed him. Not only were Draven and Layla at the bar, but also Tori and Kyla with their husbands. Introductions were made and I settled into my comfort zone. I knew these women and they had accepted me into their inner circle. The guys discussed football, while us girls picked over the crowd searching for someone famous. Layla had assured us that more than one A-list celebrity was on the guest list.

Tori tapped me on the arm. "Isn't that Penny Stillwater?"

I tried to look nonchalantly over my shoulder. "Yep. And I'm pretty sure that's Randy Stevens standing next to her."

Kyla popped her head between us trying to get a better look. "Where?"

Layla slyly shifted Kyla to the left. "Right there by the stage. Try not to be so obvious."

Kyla huffed. "I can't help it. I'm too short."

Layla glanced at her feet. "Yeah. You need higher heels."

"Oooh, by the door! That's Mara Whitfield," Tori whispered. "I read she's dating Dean Thomas."

I hadn't seen my brother and Brian yet, but they had to be here somewhere. I craned my neck to get a better view of the bar and spotted them in the corner chatting up a couple of women who probably assumed they were straight. I let out a little giggle at the rude awakening they were going to get.

The girls and I continued to gossip until the lights dimmed and Rissa's debut song, "Broken Wings", started to play. Chase clasped my waist from behind, placing a soft kiss on my cheek. "She must be here."

The attention of everyone in the room turned toward the doors as a smiling Rissa entered, waving and blowing kisses to her guests. In the white halter dress I chose for her, she was glowing. She abruptly turned, searching for Zack and pulling him to her side. It was obvious he wanted her to bathe in the spotlight, to relish this moment in time, for her to be the center of attention, but she wasn't having any of that. From the first time I met her, I knew she and Zack were a team. She attributed her success to him, and he adored her. They were a small-town power couple being thrust into the limelight. Although Rissa had admitted she was nervous about tonight and the attention she was going to garner, she handled it with confidence and grace.

When I looked at Zack and Rissa, I saw pure, unwavering love and trust. That was the kind of relationship I wanted with Chase. There was no doubt that I loved him. I just wondered if I could trust him completely with my heart.

Chapter 25
Chase

My date was hot. And although it was her looks that had first drawn me to her, led me to bringing her home, she was so much more than a pretty face with a sexy body. No, Maggie Malone, my Red, was a beacon of light that drew me in and refused to let go. She was honest, giving, kind, and too sweet for words.

She had taught me to trust again. To open my heart and bury the demons that plagued me for the last seven years. She'd shown me what unconditional love was and gave it with no stipulations or promises of more from me. But all I could think was more is what she deserved. Maggie deserved someone who would be her life preserver when she felt like she was drowning in the deep waters of life. Someone to hold her up when she felt like it was too much. Someone she could depend on.

Since Meredith, I'd refused to jump. I'd been content wading in shallow water where I didn't need anyone and no one needed me. It was safe there. Void of complications and real commitment. But Maggie? She was complicated and I found myself getting deeper and deeper in her waters until my feet no longer touched the bottom. Her world was a deep and alluring ocean I'd been drawn to from day one. I'd struggled at first, learning the ebb and flow of her life. I'd sputtered and made mistakes, but Maggie was always there. Not condemning me for them but offering a lifeline to try again and float back to the surface. To be a part of her and Ella's life in a way that was both meaningful and intrinsic.

No, I hadn't cannonballed in, but I'd gotten there just the same. I was in deep and it felt amazing.

I held Maggie close, swaying around the dance floor, my hand clasped in hers as the night wound down. Rissa had just finished performing a set that left everyone awestruck by the raw power of her voice. Many artists needed the magic of a recording studio to polish their sound, with Rissa it was natural. She could make the crowd go wild with enthusiasm or have them blinking back tears with her emotional and soul-crushing sultry voice. Her last song had ripped open my heart. It was about her journey with Zack and the emotional scars they had overcome to be together, but it had felt like she was singing directly to me, putting a healing balm on my wounds from the past. Encouraging me to not give up, to take chances, and to live again.

I lowered my lips to Maggie's ear. "Are you ready to get out of here?"

She simply nodded.

I think we were both ready to move on to the next part of our night. Our limo was waiting out front, having already taken Draven and Layla home and come back for us. We slipped into the back and Maggie leaned her head against my shoulder. "Tonight was wonderful. Thank you for inviting me."

I kissed the top of her head. "There's no one else I would have rather shared it with."

Within a few quick minutes, the limo pulled up behind Forever Inked. Maggie crinkled her nose in that cute way she and Ella shared. "I thought we were going to your place. What are we doing here?"

"I wanted to show you something first." I took her hand and hauled her out of the car, in through the back door and up the stairway. I unlocked the door at the top and led her onto the roof. It was a special place for those of us who worked here. A place where you could come to think and clear your head. With the lights strung around the rooftop, the stars in the sky and the sights of the city blazing in the background, it was also romantic as fuck.

Maggie spun around, taking in the view. "Wow! This is breathtaking. You can see everything from up here."

I wrapped my arms around her waist from behind and nuzzled into the soft valley between her neck and shoulder. "I've never brought anyone up here before."

"I'm the first?" she whispered.

"Yeah, Red, you're the first. You're the only one I've ever wanted to share this with."

She turned in my arms, wrapping herself around me. "Thank you. Thank you for choosing me."

I caressed the side of her face with my thumb, tracing the delicate features of her jaw. "There was no choosing. You captured my heart from that first night. You were all I could think about. I'm in love with you, Maggie."

Her eyes glistened with unshed tears. "I'm in love with you too, Chase. I have been for a while. I was just too afraid to tell you. Afraid I would ruin it and you'd go running."

"I'm not going anywhere. The only place I want to be is with you." I pressed my lips to hers in a kiss that was more than a kiss. It was a promise. A promise to stay. A promise to be the man she could depend on. A promise to protect her. A promise to love her. So many unspoken vows wrapped in a single moment. "I love you, Maggie." Saying those three little words on this rooftop meant so much more than if I'd said them the first time while tangled in the sheets. I wanted her to know I meant it. That it wasn't some careless expression spilled out in the dark while I was buried deep inside her. I was trusting her with my heart and my soul.

"Take me home, Chase. Take me home and make love to me. Let me show you how much I love you."

Maggie stood before me in the dress that had been nothing but a tease all night. It showcased all of her perfection. Soft curves, swelling breasts, round ass, and that slit in her skirt that gave me a peek of her long legs hidden underneath. She was stunning, but there was nothing more I wanted than to shed her of the glitzy material and sink deep inside my woman.

My woman.

The woman who lured me out of my safe place and proved my past didn't have to dictate my future.

The woman who'd convinced me that I was more than my mistakes.

The woman who'd been unforgettable from that first night.

Maggie tugged on the lapels of my jacket. "Say something. You're making me nervous."

"Mmmm. I'm just thinking about how lucky I am to have you, and all the things I want to do to you."

The moon glinted off her dress and cast her face in shadows, highlighting her perfect cheekbones and delicate features. "Like what?"

"Like getting you out of this dress and into my bed." I growled as I kissed along her neck. My fingers deftly worked the zipper at her back, the sound echoing in the otherwise quiet room. My cock hardened even more with the anticipation.

Maggie took a step back, pulled the straps down her shoulders and let the dress pool at her feet. Covered only in a scrap of turquoise lace and her red hair that fell in soft waves over her round, full tits, she was the most beautiful thing I had ever seen.

I pulled at the tie secured around my neck and tossed it on the chair. "You are stunning." Cradling her face in my palms, my lips descended upon hers, soft and gentle. Maggie was made to be cherished, to be worshiped, to be loved. She deserved nothing less and I planned on doing all of those things tonight.

Cherishing her.

Worshiping her.

Loving her.

Maggie mewled as our tongues tangled together in a slow dance that was picking up pace. "You have too many clothes on." She tugged at the buttons of my shirt, trying to release them but getting nowhere fast.

I helped with the buttons, shrugging the shirt down my arms as she went to work on my pants. Never once did our lips relinquish their connection. Our actions became needy and lust fueled in our quest to surrender to everything we felt with our bodies and our hearts.

My pants fell to my ankles and we toppled back onto the bed, still ravaging each other. Her hands tangled in my hair, pulling at the longer strands as I struggled for a better position.

I kicked my legs with no success and groaned. Maggie pulled away from the kiss. "What's wrong?"

"I'm stuck." I sighed.

She gave me a curious look, cocking her head to the side.

Talk about ruining the perfect moment. "In my pants. They're stuck on my shoes."

Her face broke into a smile that turned into a giggle, and finally hysterical laughter.

I rolled to my back and threw an arm over my head. "Laugh it up, Red. I was trying to put my moves on you and be romantic."

She wiped at the tear falling down her cheek as her body shook with uncontrollable laughter. "I'm sorry. It's just... it's just funny." She snorted and laughed harder at her faux pas, her body continuing to shake.

I couldn't help but laugh too. "Did you just snort?"

She struggled to take a breath. "Yes!"

I grasped her chin, forcing her face to mine, as her laughter subsided. "You're fucking adorable, you know that?"

"I just ruined the moment, didn't I?" she wheezed.

I shook my head and motioned to my ankles. "No, but the problem persists."

Maggie propped herself up on her elbows. "You better handle that Rico Suave."

"Just the pants or the socks and shoes too? I hear naked men wearing black dress socks is a total turn on to the ladies," I joked.

She tapped a finger to her lips. "Decisions, decisions. If only you had those sock garters that old men wear. My grandpa used to walk around the house with them and his boxers on. I'm quite sure my grandma found it sexy and that's why they've been married fifty years."

I scrunched up my face. "Ewww…did you just reference your grandparents having sex? Way to deflate a man's boner."

She shrugged her shoulders. "Okay, not the visual I was going for, but if it wasn't for them, I wouldn't be here."

"True." I rolled my eyes. "But let's keep the sexy senior citizen talk out of our bedroom."

She pouted playfully. "Awwww… you're going to be a sexy senior one day and I can't wait to see you in sock garters."

I clamped a hand over her mouth. "Never. We shall never speak of this again. Put that whole demented idea right out of your head. Promise?"

I felt her lips quirk up under my hand. "Promise," she mumbled.

The moment was gone, and I still needed to get out of my stupid dress shoes. I scooted to the edge of the bed, untying my shoes, and removing them and the damn socks. I wiggled my toes and slipped the pants off my ankles.

"Better?" she asked.

"Much." I hung my pants and jacket over the chair along with Maggie's dress.

She bent her knees and held one sexy foot out to me. "Take off my shoes?"

I grabbed her foot and placed a tender kiss on her ankle. "Nope. These hooker heels are staying on."

She gasped. "Do you have a hooker fetish?"

I kissed my way up to the inside of her knee. "No, I have a *you* fetish." I kept kissing up her leg to the junction of her thighs, nipping at her clit through the flimsy material that covered her pussy. "And these sexy panties that you claimed you didn't have, need to come off."

I hooked my fingers in the sides of the turquoise material that barely qualified as panties and peeled them down her legs. Maggie lifted her hips. "They're new."

"Did you buy them for me?"

She bit her lip and blushed. "Yes."

I held them to my nose and inhaled her scent, sweet and musky and uniquely her. My dick must have smelled it too because he sprang back into action and saluted the ceiling. I tucked the panties into my nightstand drawer.

Maggie narrowed her eyes at me. "What are you doing?"

"Keeping them for later." I motioned toward my dick. "Seems he has a *you* fetish too."

"Are you going to... you know?" she asked, clearly picking up on my insinuation for future use of her panties.

"Maybe." I spread her legs apart and kneeled between them. "Now, where were we?" My hands skimmed down her thighs as I leaned forward.

"You were kissing me," she whispered.

I leaned closer, boxing her in with my arms, our faces inches apart. "Yes, I was, wasn't I?"

She nodded.

"Let's get back to that." I pressed my lips to hers and ran my tongue along the crease. She opened and our tongues tangled, getting right back to where we started. Needy little moans escaped from Red as her hands wound into my hair, the lust kicking into overdrive. My cock rubbed against her pussy. He wanted in, but I needed to slow this train down. My cock would have to wait because there were several stops on the way to the love shack. I had every intention of doing exactly what I planned earlier.

Cherishing her.

Worshiping her.

Loving her.

I kissed along her jaw and up to her ear, whispering, "I love you, Maggie. I want to show you how much."

"I love you too, Chase. So much." She shivered as I kissed along her shoulder and down between her breasts. I circled my tongue around one tight nipple and sucked the peak into my mouth. Maggie arched her back as goose bumps broke out along her flesh. I took her into both my hands, squeezing and kneading her tits as I lavished her nipples with gentle strokes of my tongue and light nips of my teeth, sucking them until she moaned my name over and over.

"What are you doing to me, Chase?"

"Cherishing you."

I kissed down her body to her soft belly. Maggie wasn't a stick with a flat stomach and hipbones that jutted out. She had curves I loved. She was all woman. She was perfectly imperfect.

I ran my tongue over her soft mound and down through her pussy. Her smell and taste were intoxicating. I'd quickly become addicted to everything that was Maggie. My hands slipped under her round, perfect ass and lifted her to my face. I had to get closer. I ate at her with reverence. Her pleasure was my only concern. My tongue worked her clit like it was my mission. I'd learned quickly what made Red come. I knew how to take her to the edge and then back away. How to build her anticipation. How to build her orgasm 'til she was begging me for it.

She squirmed on the bed, one hand fisted in my hair and the other fisting the sheets. "What are you doing to me?" she asked again.

"Worshiping you, Red. Giving you everything you deserve."

"Make me come, Chase. Please," she begged.

I took her clit between my lips, giving it a slow, long, hard suck to push her over the edge and into ecstasy.

"Oh god… shit, baby…it's so intense…I'm gonna...ahhhh!" Maggie's eyes rolled back, her head thrashing from side to side. I kept at her clit until she came down and her body stilled. "Oh my god, oh my god... Jesus Christ, Chase," she panted.

I crawled up her body and kissed her, letting Red taste herself on my lips. "That was beautiful. You're so beautiful when you come for me."

"Make love to me, Chase. I can't wait any longer."

"I plan on it, Red. All I want to do is love you." I reached for the condoms in my nightstand.

Maggie grabbed my wrist. "Wait!"

"I can't, Red. I need to be inside you."

She gulped. "I want you inside me and only you. I'm on the pill. I don't want to use a condom."

Well, fuck me! The last time I hadn't used a condom had been with… It felt like sacrilege to even think her name while Maggie lay naked before me and I could taste her on my tongue.

I knew she was on birth control. I'd seen the pills in her bathroom cabinet. "Are you sure? What if…"

She nodded and bit her lip. "I'm sure. I've never had sex without a condom. I'm clean. What happened with Ella was... the condom broke."

I scrubbed my hands over my face. Jeez, was she really worried I thought she wasn't clean? She'd probably had sex with less than five guys in her life. I, on the other hand, had sex with that many women in a week when I was at the height of my manwhoring. It was the reason I got tested regularly. When you're spreading the love, you don't want to be spreading anything else either. I caressed the side of her face with my thumb. "I wasn't worried about that. I'm clean too, but this is a big step. Are you sure?"

She rubbed her thumb over my hand. "I'm positive. I want this with you."

I couldn't tell her no. I wanted it too. It somehow felt like a seal on the words we'd finally said tonight. The consummation of a promise we'd vowed to each other. "Gonna make love to you now, Red." Caging her in with my forearms, I slowly slid the tip inside her. She was so wet, and the feeling was incredible. I pushed into the hilt and savored it. Savored the feeling of nothing between us. Like heaven wrapped around my cock. "Jesus, baby. You're killing me. Feels so goddamn good."

Maggie dropped her head back and let out a sigh. "Don't stop."

"I'm just getting started, Red." I kissed her forehead, then pulled back and gently pushed in again. And again. And again. It wasn't fast. It wasn't hurried. It was... something I hadn't done in years.

I wasn't a making love type of guy. Yes, I liked things to be sensual. I wanted a woman to get the same pleasure I did. But I never felt anything inside. My heart was never part of the equation. It was simply an act between two consenting adults as a means to a happy ending in the form of orgasms.

But, if I was being honest with myself, it had always been more than that with Maggie. From our first night together, my heart had flickered to life. It had started to beat again for someone besides myself. And now my chest felt so full, I thought it might burst from the love I felt for this woman.

I pulled her leg up around my hip and pushed in deeper, rotating my hips. I couldn't get deep enough inside her. I wanted to consume her, let her know that no one would ever love her like I did. I wanted to be closer, so close I couldn't tell where I ended and she began.

"Fuck, Chase. You feel amazing." Her back arched and she grabbed onto my shoulders Her nails digging into the skin sent little pricks of pleasure down my spine.

I couldn't get close enough to her. "Come here, baby." I scooped my hands under her shoulders and lifted her from the mattress and onto my lap. Her fingers ran through my hair as I buried my head between her breasts. She rode me slowly as I pushed up into her. So tight and so wet. So perfect, I was sure this was as close to heaven as I'd ever get.

She gently tilted my head back and peered down into my eyes. "I love you, Chase. So, so much."

The air shifted as something deeper took ahold of us. A connection that pulled us together and threatened to never let go. It was the moment I knew she was the one I had been waiting for. That every mistake I'd made, every decision gone wrong, every price I'd paid had had a purpose. That bumpy and twisty road led me to Maggie. Without the bad there would have been no good. And god, I needed the good she brought to my life.

I held her tight and pumped my cock into her pussy, deeper and harder. No way was I letting her go. "Come for me, Red. I want you to come while I'm inside you."

She pressed her hips forward, increasing the friction on her clit. "I'm so close. I'm gonna…" Her head dropped back, and a string of incoherent words fell from her lips as her pussy convulsed around me. I pumped in harder and faster chasing the high. It didn't take long 'til my muscles tightened, and tingles started at the base of my spine shooting out in every direction as I came long and hard into her body. I pulled her hips down on my cock until every last drop had been released.

Falling back on the bed, I pulled Maggie with me and held her to my chest. "That was…"

Maggie put her finger to my lips. "Everything. That was everything I've ever wanted and more."

"Yeah." I ran my fingers through her long red locks. "You make me feel things I never thought I'd feel again. I love you so damn much."

She snuggled into my chest. "Don't let me go, okay?"

"I won't"

Never. I was never letting her go.

Chapter 26
Maggie

"Mmmm…that feels so good." Chase massaged the shampoo into my hair. Last night had been perfect. I couldn't remember a time I had felt so complete or so cherished. We'd made love and then fucked into the early hours of the morning. Yes, there was a difference and yes, I loved both. It was everything I had hoped for and more.

I woke to breakfast in bed—me being the breakfast in Chase's bed, although he made bacon, eggs, and coffee too. After leisurely waking up, he wanted to shower together, something we never got to do at my house unless Ella was gone and even then, I was nervous we'd get caught.

"Turn around, Red."

I did and Chase rinsed the lather from my hair. He squirted some conditioner between his hands and ran them over my head. We continued washing each other in silence, our hands and lips teasing one another.

I rubbed my hand over his cock. "I should be exhausted, but I just can't get enough of you."

His fingers slipped between my legs. "The feeling's mutual. I can't stop touching you." Chase pulled my back to his chest and continued playing with my clit as he squeezed my breasts. "Lean your head back on my shoulder and relax. I'm gonna take care of you. Always."

I closed my eyes and enjoyed the bliss of Chase's hands on me, focused purely on my pleasure. My legs began to shake as the pressure between my legs began to build. It started slow, coming in gentle waves that increased in intensity until I was hit by the power of a tsunami. I could feel myself being pulled under by wave after wave, my mind void of everything but what my body was feeling. The bliss that consumed every part of me. My knees went weak. Chase held me to his body as I reemerged from the dissociative state and clambered back to shore.

Chase whispered in my ear. "Where'd you go, baby?"

"Heaven. I'm pretty sure that's what heaven feels like."

"I'm not done with you yet. Lean against the wall and stick that luscious ass out for me."

I did as I was told, splaying my hands against the wall and arching my back.

"So fucking beautiful." He wrapped one arm around my waist while the fingers of his other hand twined with mine. He entered me slowly, making love to me while the warm water cascaded over our bodies.

It was the perfect ending to a perfect morning.

"How was the grown-up party?" Ella asked, kicking her legs in the back of Chase's truck. "Was it boring?"

Chase smirked at me, as he held my hand over the console. "Nah, princess bug, it wasn't boring."

Knowing Ella was going to inundate us with a barrage of questions, I glared at Chase. "It was a little boring."

"Pfft! If you call dancing all night boring." He squeezed my hand and pressed his lips together to suppress a smile.

"I like dancing! I'm really good at it and Miss Heather says I'm getting better and better and I barely fall on my butt anymore because I'm a practicer and Miss Heather says practice makes perfect! Was there balloons? I like balloons too!"

I took a deep breath. "Yes, ladybug, there were balloons. But we were there for Miss Rissa. Do you remember her from Chase's work?"

"Yep. She's nice and she's got long, yellow hair."

"That's her. She's got a song on the radio and she sang for us last night."

Ella gasped. "Just like Elsa! Did she look like Elsa?"

Chase tapped on his chin. "Now that you mention it, she did look a little like Elsa."

"One day, Momma said she's gonna take me to Disney World so I can meet the real Elsa, cuz that's where she lives. All the princesses live in a big castle and there's magic. Andy at school says magic isn't real, but I think he's lying. Do you believe in magic, Chase?"

I gave him a pointed look, wondering what he was going to say to the six-year-old in the back of his truck who believed in fairies.

He caught Ella's eyes through the rearview mirror. "I didn't used to, but I do now. Magic definitely exists, princess bug. You should believe whatever your heart tells you."

It was the perfect answer. I squeezed his hand with affection. The way he interacted with my daughter melted my heart.

Ella crossed her arms over her chest. "I knew Andy was full of phony bologna."

I turned in my seat to face my daughter. "Andy talks too much. You shouldn't listen to his nonsense." That kid was trouble with a capital T. He'd already put too many ideas into her head. I was dreading Christmas, hoping he wouldn't ruin Santa for her. That was one illusion I wanted Ella to keep as long as possible. "What did you do at Nanna's house?"

She held up her fingers counting off all the things. "First we made brownies and Nanna let us eat them with ice cream on top. Papa had two and Nanna scolded him about his col...coltest..."

"Cholesterol," I provided, while rolling my hand forward for her to continue.

"Then we watched a silly movie about cats and dogs that were spies, but Papa fell asleep in his chair and he snored so loud we could barely hear the movie. Nanna let me put a blanket on his head and he did big snorting under there but then he fell back asleep and" she clapped her hands together, "Boom! It was quiet again. Can we see Not My Cat today?"

Well, that was an abrupt transition. I couldn't help but giggle and Chase chuckled too. "You know he doesn't live at my apartment, right, princess bug?"

Ella rolled her eyes like she was exasperated. "I know, but maybe we could check if he's there. I bet if I put treats out, he would want to play with me."

She clearly had a plan. I quirked an eyebrow at Chase.

He shrugged. "Why the hell not?" He flipped on the blinker and changed lanes, heading back toward his apartment.

Ella pumped her fist in the air. "Yay! And also, you said a bad word, Chase."

He glared at her through the mirror. "My bad. And also, I've heard you say worse."

I loved that he was calling Ella out on her potty mouth that she'd picked up from me.

She gasped and blinked her eyes innocently. "Who me?"

"Yes, you, little lady."

"Only at the gas station and at home. Not at school though."

"How about we practice not saying those words at all."

Ella threw her hands in the air. "Why the hell not? Nobody cares."

This time neither Chase nor I could contain our laughter. She was going to be a handful when she got older. "Because you're six, Ella. Just try not to say bad words, okay?" I reasoned with her.

We pulled into Chase's apartment complex. Ella unbuckled and practically jumped from the vehicle before it was parked. Chase leaped out after her and plucked her from the ground by the waist. "Hold up. You have to wait for us. You're going to give your mother a heart attack jumping from the truck like that."

Truer words couldn't have been spoken. My heart was already beating out of my chest. My worst nightmare was anything happening to my baby.

Chase threw her over his shoulder and skipped up the steps while Ella squealed in delight. Once inside, she raced to the slider and threw it open. Disappointed by the empty balcony, she started calling, "Not My Cat, where are you? Come here, little fluffy butt! Not My Cat, I loves you!"

I let out a frustrated breath. "She's going to be totally crushed if that cat doesn't show up."

Chase reached into the cupboard and pulled out a can of tuna. "Maybe not. Let me work my magic. He and I are dude-bros. I know what pussies like."

I slapped a hand over my mouth. "You did not just say that."

He kissed me on the forehead. "I did, and I didn't hear you arguing last night. But seriously, that cat is a sucker for a good meal."

Chase took the open can of tuna out to the balcony, while Ella shook the bag of treats like a mad woman. Now they were both calling for that damn cat. I couldn't see this ending up any other way than a very disappointed little girl who was going to sulk all night.

I was about to end the torture, when low and behold the striped tabby jumped onto the railing and down onto the balcony. Well, son of a pup, color me surprised! I never in a million years would have thought that cat would show up on demand.

After helping himself to a good meal, Not My Cat let Ella pet him head to tail. Then, she sat in the chair and Chase put the cat on her lap. He settled in and soaked up the affection my daughter was giving him. The cat's eyes closed, and he looked extremely comfortable.

Careful not to disrupt them, I crept onto the balcony, "Ellanora Riley, I think you might be a cat whisperer."

She smiled up at me with her toothless smile. "He likes me, Momma."

And just like that, I fell deeper in love with Chase for making my sassy child just a little bit happier.

Monday morning, we woke to a drizzly, dreary day. Ella and I were both dragging ass and although I would have been happy to call both of us into school absent, it wasn't really an option. For one, I didn't have sub plans ready. And two, I wouldn't be setting a good example for my daughter.

"Ella, please brush your teeth so we can go!" I yelled down the hallway on my way to the kitchen. Chase handed me a cup of coffee, which I drank down greedily. Although mainlining caffeine would have been faster, I was appreciative. "You're a life saver."

He shrugged. "I do what I can. I have a late appointment tonight. Do you still want me to come over?"

I took another long drink from my mug. "Is that even a real question? All I can think about is snuggling back in that bed with you."

He wrapped his arms around me. "Just snuggling?"

"Meh. Maybe some other stuff too if I'm in the mood."

Chase threw his head back and laughed. "Yes, I'm sure getting you in the mood will be quite the problem."

I gave a teasing shrug. "You never know. I could be totally wiped out."

"I can think of a few things that might energize you."

Ella ran into the kitchen. "I'm ready!" She was a mismatched mess of colors and patterns that made my eyes want to cross. I didn't have the time or patience to argue with her, so it would have to do.

She shrugged into her raincoat as Chase picked up her backpack and handed me a to-go cup. "Let's get my two favorite girls off to school." He then grabbed an umbrella by the front door and led Ella out to the car. After getting her buckled into her booster, Chase tossed the umbrella on the floor by her feet and kissed her cheek. "Have a good day."

"I love you, Chase!"

"Love you too, princess bug."

He closed her door and leaned into the driver's side. "Love you, Red."

The words swirled around my head and settled in my chest, making it ache in the best way. There was something about hearing them outside the bedroom that made them more real and meaningful. "Love you too. See you tonight."

"I'll be late," he reminded me with a kiss.

"I'll be waiting."

He closed the door and stepped back from the car, unfazed by the light rain. I checked over my shoulder, ready to back out, when I caught Ella huffing hot breath on the window. My dad had scolded Patty and me, as kids, about writing on the windows. And since it was inevitable that we turned into our parents, it was now a pet peeve of mine too. Harsh words sat on the tip of my tongue as Ella stared at Chase and drew a heart on the window. The words died on my lips as Chase pushed his nose to the window and drew a heart back.

Every time I thought I couldn't fall deeper in love, this man did something to prove me wrong. My heart melted into a puddle.

Pushing my pet peeve aside and taking Ella's lead, I steamed up my own window and drew a heart. Chase's finger ran through the droplets on the glass, forming a large lopsided heart around mine. Water rolled down the window, distorting the shape.

It was perfectly imperfect.

Chapter 27
Chase

Layla leaned into my studio. "You have a visitor."

My next appointment wasn't due for an hour. I was just putting the finishing touches on the sketch of the wolf for the tat. "He's early. Tell him to have a seat in the lobby and I'll be with him in ten."

She stepped inside and shut the door. "I don't think it's your appointment. Doesn't look the type."

"How do you know?"

She raised one shoulder. "Just a hunch. Asked for you by name though and he doesn't look happy."

Now my curiosity was peaked. I rolled my stool over to the door and cracked it open. *What the hell? This was not on my to-do list today.* Taking a deep breath, I rolled back and leaned my arms on my knees, dropping my head.

"You know him?" Layla asked quietly.

I met her curious eyes. "Yeah. That's Maggie's ex."

She scrunched up her nose. "What's he doing here?"

"No idea," I answered with a shake of my head.

"You want me to get rid of him?"

All I'd have to do was say the word and he'd be gone. Layla had a gift for being bitchy when she wanted, and I knew she'd do me a solid. "Nah. If he's lowering himself to coming here, it must be important. This isn't exactly a golf course."

"You want me to get Draven?" she asked.

I quirked an eyebrow at her and chuckled. "Why? You think he can take me?" I was a lover, not a fighter. I hadn't punched anyone in the face in years and even then, it was in self-defense.

She threw up her arms. "I don't know! We're in uncharted territory here. I've never known you to have a beef with anyone. Everybody loves you."

"Apparently not everybody." I stood and pecked my friend on the cheek. "I'm good. I can handle my own shit."

She didn't look convinced. "If you need anything just holler."

I ushered her out the door. "Thanks, but I got it." I was a hundred percent positive she was going to inform Draven, and probably Zack too, of the current situation. I should have been insulted she had so little faith in me, but I knew her concern came from a place of love. My friends always had my back and I had theirs. That's what families did for each other.

Jeff glanced at his watch as he paced back and forth in the lobby. I approached him with a confident swagger. I may be a *low-life dirtbag*, but we were on my turf and that gave me the upper hand.

When Jeff saw me, he looked at his watch again. "Finally! I've been waiting forever."

I crossed my arms and leaned casually against the front desk. "You should have made an appointment. You're a businessman, Jeff. You know how businesses run. If you want to see someone, it's best to make an appointment."

He scanned the tattoo parlor as if it were a cesspool. Zack ran a clean shop, never failing a health or safety inspection. Forever Inked was the top-rated tattoo shop in the tri-county area. People came from all over for the inking expertise we offered, including a long list of local celebrities and athletes. Zack had built this business from the ground up on nothing more than his determination and reputation. So, although it wasn't a country club, Forever Inked was a point of pride for this community. Jeff's lack of appreciation and ignorance of the talent it took to work here did nothing to diminish the business.

"I'll keep that in mind, but I'm here now," he snapped.

I liked seeing Jeff here, out of his comfort zone. Something about it gave me a zing. A feeling of confidence. I pushed off the desk and looked at my nonexistent watch. "What do you know? I have twenty minutes before my next *appointment*." I had longer, but fuck if I was going to give him any more time than that.

He smirked at me in a way that didn't quite feel right. The cat that ate the canary look. "I won't even need that long."

"Then by all means, come in." I motioned to my studio. There wasn't a proper table or desk for us to sit at. Just two rolling stools and an adjustable, leather tattooing chair. This was a workspace not an office.

Jeff surveyed the room with disdain and settled on one of the stools. I took the other stool, keeping the tattooing chair between us.

His eyes bounced around taking in the artwork on the walls. "You're talented."

I wasn't sure if that was a compliment or just an observation. Didn't really matter to me. I leaned back against the counter and crossed my arms. This guy was full of shit and I could smell it a mile away. He'd rubbed me wrong from day one. "I'm sure you're not here to talk about my work. What do you want, Jeff?"

He pinned me with an arrogant glare. "I want you to stop seeing Maggie."

There it was. The reason for this little visit. A laugh rumbled up from my chest. One that was part disgust and part incredulous. "And why the fuck would I do that?"

His jaw twitched in aggravation. "Because she's mine. Always has been."

This guy was a real piece of work. Maybe he was able to push his weight around in the corporate world, but not here. I wasn't impressed or intimidated by him. The only reason I was even entertaining this little impromptu meeting was for Maggie and the promise I made her to play nice with her ex. Because of Ella, he'd always be a part of her life, but that didn't mean I was going to lay down and let him walk all over me.

"From what I know, Maggie gave you plenty of opportunities to claim her and all you did was string her along. You dangled a carrot in front of her, making her think she could have a future with you. And now that she's realized that carrot was nothing more than shit on a string, you want to piss a circle around her like a dog? What even makes you think she'd want you back?"

Jeff steepled his fingers, tapping the tips together. "Maggie wants a family. She wants to be married and have another child. I'm Ella's father, so I'm the perfect candidate."

Everything he said was true. He was the perfect candidate. But he'd held her at bay for seven years and toyed with her emotions. "She doesn't love or trust you."

He quirked an eyebrow. "Not yet, but she will. Mags has loved me since college, that doesn't just go away."

"I think you've misjudged the situation. Maggie's moved on. With me. And I'm not willing to let you play with her heart just because someone's taken away your favorite toy. If you cared about her at all, you'd give her a real chance at happiness. And again, I ask, why the fuck would I stop seeing Maggie?"

A calculating smile crept up his lips. I didn't like it. At all. "Because you love her. Because you want to see her happy. Because you love Ella."

Something was not quite right here. I was ready for this little face-to-face to be done. "All you've done is provide reasons I should stay. I hope to God you're not an attorney because you're closing argument sucked."

Leaning forward, Jeff took a folded piece of paper out of his pocket. His fingers played along the edges as he spoke. "Oh, Mr. Montgomery, that wasn't my closing argument. That was my opening statement. A chance for you to do the right thing. But I can see your going to be difficult. This," he said as he opened the paper and slammed it down on the tattoo chair between us, "is my closing argument."

My eyes shot to the paper and my heart fell out of my chest. I could feel the color draining from my skin and the blood whooshing in my ears, drowning everything else out but the memories.

Red and blue lights flashed in the rearview mirror.

This was the last thing I needed tonight. I promised Meredith I would pick up Chinese food on the way home. I was already running late because of this errand.

I pulled into an empty parking lot, the patrol car following. I hadn't been speeding. I needed to get pulled over like I needed another hole in my head.

Shifting my Monte Carlo into park, I rolled down the window. My hands were on the steering wheel. My dad had taught me well. Keep your hands in sight. Yes, sir. No, sir. Don't give them a reason. I'd never been in trouble with the law, just a speeding ticket back in high school.

The cop approached alongside my car, shining a flashlight inside. "You've got a taillight out."

I breathed a sigh of relief. "I'm sorry officer. I'll get it fixed right away."

I wasn't surprised about the taillight on this piece of shit Monte Carlo, but I should have been smarter. I should have checked it before going out tonight.

He grunted, "License and registration," and continued to shine the light in the car as I pulled my license from my wallet. I handed it to the officer then reached to the glovebox to get the registration. As soon as the compartment opened, a brown paper bag fell to the floor. I gulped down the anxiety creeping up my throat as I located the paperwork.

His light fell on the bag. "You dropped something."

My fingers landed on the registration and insurance paperwork. "I'll get it later." I handed them to the officer and waited while he looked everything over. I was sweating bullets and my jaw tightened. I needed this guy to leave so I could get on with my business. It was a fucking taillight for Christ's sake.

Bright light flashed in my face. "You all right? You seem a little nervous."

No shit I was nervous. I squinted into the beam. "Yeah. I'm just... my fiancé's pregnant and she's waiting for me to bring her food. She gets hangry if I keep her waiting." It was the perfect excuse. Everyone knew pregnant girls liked to eat.

I thought I'd get some sympathy in the situation, but the guy never cracked a smile. He looked at my license again. "You're a long way from home, Mr. Montgomery. Where's your fiancé live?"

Immediately, I realized that using Meredith as an excuse was stupid. I was driving the opposite direction of home. My brain went blank. I couldn't think of a goddamn thing to say. "Ummm..."

"Step out of the car, Mr. Montgomery."

I got out and casually put my hands in my back pockets. My palms were sweating, and it was as good of place as any to wipe them off.

"Have you been drinking tonight?"

"No, sir." I was smarter than that. No way would I have been drinking tonight.

A second patrol car pulled up. Backup had arrived. It seemed a little overkill for a broken taillight, but it wasn't the fucking taillight I was worried about.

The two had a silent exchange that included a nod toward my car. The second cop shined his flashlight through the windows, sweeping the interior of the car in slashing motions. When he got to the front passenger side, my stomach bottomed out. He opened the door and lifted the paper bag from the floor mat. I watched as he opened it and nodded to the cop in front of me.

Meredith was never going to forgive me for this. I promised her and I broke her trust. All for a payday that was never going to come.

I was quickly flipped around and forced face-first into the hood of the car, my hands splayed out on the warm metal. The cop dumped the contents of the bag onto the hood in front of me. I knew it was full of weed. What I didn't know was the bag also contained several small packets of white powder. I'd been transporting cocaine.

Motherfucking sonofabitch!

My arms were wrenched behind my back. "You have the right to remain silent..."

My stomach bottomed out and I felt an overwhelming need to puke. Nothing could have prepared me for this.

Jeff tapped my mug shot on the rap sheet in front of me. "I'm going to assume Mags doesn't know about this or your boss for that matter. Drug possession and possession with intent to sell." He let out a low whistle after reciting the charges.

He'd not only threatened my relationship, but my job as well. My only shot was to act like it wasn't a big deal. I waved my hand at the paper. "That's ancient history. I was convicted of simple possession and it was reduced to a misdemeanor. I served my time and moved on. It was a stupid mistake I made as a kid. That's not who I am." Yes, I had served my time, but I lost everything while I did. It was a big deal. Just not in the way Jeff thought.

He tapped a finger to his lips. "Something tells me Maggie wouldn't take this so lightly. Can you imagine if her teacher friends found out she was dating a drug dealer?"

I clenched my fist around the paper, crumbling it into a ball. "I wasn't a drug dealer."

He continued as if I hadn't spoken. "I wonder what a judge would think about a drug dealer living in the house with my daughter or, God forbid, becoming her stepfather."

I slammed my hands on the leather chair between us. "What do you want Jeff?"

"I already told you. Stop seeing Maggie."

"And if I don't?"

"Then I'll take Maggie to court and fight for full custody of Ella."

He was bluffing. No way would he be that vengeful. "You'd never do that. It would kill Maggie."

He crossed his arms and leaned back, clearly pleased with himself. "Are you willing to take that chance? Because I will do everything in my power to protect my daughter."

When Jeff walked in this morning, I expected him to puff up and beat on his chest. But this...I wasn't even close to being prepared for it. "I would never do anything to hurt Maggie or Ella."

"Then walk away. If you really care about them, do the right thing." He strolled to the door, his hand on the knob. "I may not be a lawyer, but I know how to close a deal. I always get what I want." As if an afterthought he added, "Oh, and I think it'd be best if we kept this little meeting just between us. Maggie's happiness depends on it." Asshole had the audacity to wink at me on his way out.

I sat and stewed after he left. *What in the fuck just happened?* Having my past shoved in my face was an ultimate low. I worked hard to put it behind me and in an instant, it resurfaced to fuck with my life again. I was supposed to just give Maggie up? Give Ella up? For the first time in years, I was truly happy and in five minutes my entire world had been turned upside down.

No way would I let him take Ella away from Maggie. I would never stand between a mother and her child. I'd done that once. I wouldn't do it again.

Rage like I'd never felt before surged up inside me. My fists clenched and unclenched trying to get it under control, but all I could see was red. I could feel myself being handcuffed again. Being controlled by someone else. Being left with no choice but to face the consequences of my mistakes.

"Motherfucker!" I swiped everything from the counter in one fell swoop. Bottles of ink flew against the wall and crashed to the ground, splattering on every surface. Pens and paper scattered around the room. My breath came short and fast. I felt like a bull ready to charge as I stared blankly at the mess.

"Chase? Are you all right?"

My head snapped up to Layla. "No! Not even a little bit." She'd been my friend for a long time, and didn't deserve my anger, but I couldn't control it. I scooped up the crumpled paper from the floor and pushed past her.

Once in Zack's office, I slammed the door behind me. Might as well get this part over with first so I could move on with the rest of my fucked-up life. I was tired of the lies and walking on eggshells. If he fired me, it'd be five years down the drain, but at least I wouldn't be living a lie and there was some solace in that.

Despite my grand entrance, Zack calmly looked up from his computer. "Problem?"

I hadn't really thought this out. I was acting mostly on impulse and being an asshole wasn't going to do me any favors. Sucking in a deep breath, I uncrumpled the paper and tossed it on his desk. "I lied to you on my application."

He picked up my rap sheet and inspected it.

Waiting for his reaction, I tapped my foot nervously. We were friends, and I was a damn good artist, but Zack was my boss first and foremost. This tattoo parlor was his baby. He wouldn't let anyone, or anything destroy it. I was a liability, and I knew it. My days at Forever Inked were numbered. If I had to guess, I'd bet my days left here were zero.

Zack was taking his time, making me sweat. It was unnecessary when I already knew my fate. "I'll go pack up my shit."

"Why in the hell would you do that?" He held the paper up and shook it at me. "I already knew about this."

What. The. Fuck?

I collapsed into the chair across from him. "How?"

"You didn't think I would hire you without a background check, did you?"

For the second time today, I was knocked for a loop. "Actually, that's exactly what I thought you did."

Zack reached into the file cabinet behind him and pulled out a manilla folder. He laid it flat on the desk and began to read. "Chase Crawford Montgomery. Parents are Crawford and Elizabeth Montgomery. You have a sister named Amber. Played football in high school and was a wide receiver. Attended Macomb Community College to get a graphic design degree. Got engaged to your high school girlfriend and dropped out of college to support her. Worked at an auto mechanics shop. Arrested for possession of drugs with intent to sell. The charges were reduced to simple possession and you served six months with early release for your cooperation in bringing down the police's intended target. You were nothing but a pawn in their game and paid the price. Upon release, you moved back home and apprenticed at a top-notch tattoo parlor that just so happened to be my biggest competitor."

My entire life was reduced to a file folder. He was missing some important details, but for the most part it was accurate. Scarily so.

"But you know what I find most interesting in this report?"

I slumped down in the chair. "I'm afraid to ask."

He tapped on the file. "You had a 3.87 GPA and scored a 1420 on your SAT, yet you let everyone around here think that you're dumb as a box of rocks."

Ouch! That hurt. "I wouldn't say a box of rocks," I grumbled.

"Whatever. You get my point. Why is that?"

"School was never my problem. Decision-making was. I'm impulsive, think with the wrong head and wear my heart on my sleeve. Even my best intentions end up having dire consequences. It's easier to be what people assume I am." All of this was riveting but it still didn't answer my question. "So, knowing all of *that*," I waved at the file, "why in the hell did you hire me?"

Zack closed the file and locked eyes with me. "Chase, you are one of the most talented people I've ever met. Your work is second to none. When I read the private investigator's report and the details about your case, I knew you needed a second chance. Not once have I ever regretted hiring you."

I was overwhelmed and thankful, even if it still didn't make sense to me. "Why risk it? I lied on my application."

Zack spread his arms out wide. "This place, Forever Inked, was my second chance. I dropped out of Yale, enlisted in the Marines, and was for all intents and purposes disinherited by my father because I was such a huge disappointment. My grandfather helped me make this place happen. He gave me a second chance and I vowed to pay it forward. Layla showed up with a suitcase and a social security card that barely had the ink dried. She had no background. I knew she was running from something. And just like you, I've never regretted hiring her. Draven's family is organized crime. The only reason I asked him to come here was because I knew he needed an out. Rissa was lost and alone with only her dreams. All she needed was someone to believe in her. We're all a little fucked up, but this place," he pointed at his desk, "is our second chance. We decide who our family is, and we support each other. If anything, that's what makes me proud to own this place. Yes, I love that we're a talented bunch of motherfuckers and it's a successful business, but I'm more proud of the family we've built."

Emotions caught in my chest. I never realized the leap of faith Zack had taken in hiring me. I swallowed down the feelings I didn't know how to reconcile. "If all of that's true, then I don't think I've ever properly thanked you. Thank you for taking a chance on a screwed-up kid. And just for the record, I never did drugs. I didn't know I was transporting anything more than weed. I figured what was the harm in making a few extra bucks if it meant I could take better care of my fiancé. She worked hard as a nursing student and I wanted to prove I could provide for her. I was young and stupid, and in the end, I lost her anyway. I could barely take care of myself, let alone someone else."

"Everyone makes mistakes. You're a good guy, Chase. You're hardworking, easygoing and have one of the biggest hearts I've ever seen. Sometimes that bumpy road we travel is what leads us to our true destination. You've got Maggie now and seem really happy."

Just hearing her name reminded me why I'd come in here in the first place. I groaned. "I don't have Maggie. I don't have shit."

"Visit with the ex didn't go well?"

Of course Layla would have told him. "He's using that," I pointed to the rap sheet, "against me. Said he'll fight Maggie for custody of Ella if I don't back off."

"Seriously?"

"Seriously. I won't do that to Maggie. I won't let her be dragged to court. Even the threat of losing Ella would destroy her."

Zack straightened in his chair. "I have a good lawyer. You can fight him."

He was a fixer, and I appreciated his offer, but this couldn't be fixed. "You have the evidence in front of you. No judge in his right mind would choose me over Jeff. Maggie's a great mom. I won't let him try to take that away from her."

"So, what are you going to do?"

Defeated, I stood and buried my hands in my pockets. "Whatever it takes to make her happy."

Chapter 28
Maggie

I stared at my phone disappointedly as I stuffed another bite of salad into my mouth.

"Staring at it isn't going to make him reply faster. The man has a job. You know that, right?" Roxy bumped my shoulder with her arm as she took her lunch from the microwave.

Flipping my phone over and setting it on the end of the long table in the teacher's lounge, I let out a sigh. "I'm aware. It's just…"

"You're so in love you can't help yourself," she supplied. "I get it. You have this whole hearts-in-your-eyes thing going on. Must have been some weekend."

Understatement of the century. Possibly the millennium.

I stabbed at the lettuce in my bowl. "It was. And I'm not just talking about the premiere party, which was fabulous by the way."

Roxy chuckled as she set her food on the table between us. "I'm sure it was more the after-party."

My relationship with Chase wasn't a secret by any means, but I didn't need *everything* out in the open. Teachers were notorious gossips. Give them a shred of information and pretty soon the entire staff knew all your business plus a few little tidbits that had been added along the way.

At one time, I was guilty of being part of the gossip train, but that was well before my life became the subject of it. Everyone knew I had a new man in my life. Ella shared stories about Chase and Not My Cat during circle time and it had taken on a life of its own since then. I wasn't upset with Ella. I couldn't blame her for being excited, it was just one of the hazards of working where your child went to school.

I leaned over the table, trying to keep our conversation semi-private. "You know those three little words I was hemming and hawing about saying? Well, he said them first. Everything about this weekend felt different. Just… more."

"Maggie, I don't mean to burst your bubble or anything, because clearly you're happy, but it's been less than two months. Don't get ahead of yourself."

I rolled a cherry tomato from one side of my bowl to the other contemplating her words. Roxy was right. I knew she was, no matter how much I didn't want to admit it. Our relationship was still fairly new.

"I'm sorry." She put her hand over mine. "I should keep my mouth shut. I don't know what I'm talking about. Chase is a great guy and who knows, maybe he's your white knight and you'll ride off into the sunset together. Lord knows I wouldn't know a white knight if he stabbed me with his sword, and trust me, I've been on the receiving end of plenty of swords." She wiggled her eyebrows at the implication.

My body shook with laughter. I could always count on Roxy to lighten the mood, even if she was the one to put a damper on it in the first place. "I understand where you're coming from. Jeff strung me along for years and yes, I got hurt. He was never the father or the man I wanted him to be. Giving up on him was the best thing I ever did for myself. Chase has been more involved in our lives in two months than Jeff has in seven years. If you could see him with Ella, you'd understand. Everything is so easy with Chase. Gah…I'm so in love with him."

"You go girl!" Cara, Ella's teacher, shouted from the end of the table. The room filled with suppressed giggles.

Heat crept up my neck and into my cheeks as I almost face-planted into my salad.

Roxy shoved my shoulder. "Cat's out of the bag." Then she turned to the group of gossiping teachers and pointed at me. "Our girl here is getting the good dick and he's a hot piece of ass."

Loud, raucous laughter erupted from the women.

"Roxy!"

"What?" she asked innocently. "It's the truth."

More laughter ensued, along with some hoots and hollers. Staci, one of the third-grade teachers piped in, "I wish I was getting the good dick. I haven't had sex in weeks."

Cara held up her fork. "I second that!"

"Me too!" chorused around the small room.

Now we were all laughing. Matt, the only guy on the teaching staff, stood and tossed the rest of his lunch in the trash. "And that's my cue to leave. You girls are crazy." He left the lounge, letting the door slam behind him.

Staci shrugged. "I guess he's not getting the good dick either."

My alarm blared at five-thirty the next morning. I rolled over to wrap my arms around Chase only to find the sheets cold and empty.

When I got his text last night I was disappointed. *My appointment is running later than I thought. I don't want to wake you up so I'll talk to you tomorrow. I love you.*

I'd texted back my own *I love you* and got nothing in response. When I tried to call him it went immediately to voicemail. By now, I should have been used to the odd hours he worked. It wasn't the first time he'd opted to go directly home instead of coming here, but somehow I thought it would be different now.

Maybe Roxy was right. Just because we'd said the words, didn't mean he was moving in or we were planning a wedding. That was all a silly fantasy I'd built up in my head. In actuality, nothing had changed except for the words we'd exchanged. Life would go on as normal and maybe in a few months we'd talk about moving to the next level.

Feeling better about Chase being absent from my bed, I shuffled into the kitchen to start the coffee maker then headed to the shower. The warm water pulsed against my stiff muscles and eased away the tension. All my worries swirled down the drain with the suds and water, leaving me clearheaded and ready to get on with my day.

After getting myself ready, I woke Ella and ushered her into the kitchen for breakfast. I set a bowl in front of her and filled it with Froot Loops. She rubbed her eyes groggily. "I wanted pancakes."

"We don't have time for pancakes, ladybug. Eat your cereal while I go pick out your clothes."

"Chase makes me pancakes."

I rolled my eyes. "Yes, I know, but he's not here this morning so you'll have to be satisfied with Froot Loops." Ella had gotten quite spoiled in the last few weeks. We both had. I didn't have time in the morning to make fancy breakfasts, but lately Chase had been our morning chef while I ran around like a chicken with my head cut off.

You'd think I'd have a better handle on morning time, but I'd yet to master a routine. It was much easier before Ella was in school. My mom would come over in the morning and then take Ella back to her house in the afternoon. All I had to worry about was myself. Now I was packing two lunches, preparing breakfast, picking out clothes and combing her unruly curls. All before seven-fifteen. My mornings were a whirlwind.

When I came back to the kitchen, Ella's bowl of cereal had been abandoned and instead she was busy scribbling with a red marker on a piece of notebook paper. "You haven't finished your breakfast. What are you doing?"

She smiled up at me with a big toothless grin. "I'm writing Chase a note."

Curious, I moved closer to see what she had written. Big red letters covered the page. *Can you make me pancakes?* She drew a giant heart and colored it in with the marker. At the bottom she'd signed her name, as if he wouldn't know who it was from.

"Why don't you put it on the fridge and finish eating."

Ella hopped off the chair taking the note with her. As soon as she picked up the paper, I immediately saw her mistake. And mine. Sharpies were a strict no-no in this house. The ink had bled through the paper, imprinting her message on my kitchen table. I grabbed some wipes from under the sink and rubbed at the spot, but the ink had already soaked into the light colored wood.

It was too late to worry about now, I needed to get her dressed and her hair combed. "Two more bites, ladybug, and then you need to get dressed."

She shoveled two spoonfuls into her mouth and sped down the hallway with her nightgown floating out behind her.

Ten minutes later we were in the car headed to school for another day. It seemed odd not to have Chase here, but then again it wasn't that odd at all considering it had been just Ella and me for the past several years. It confirmed how much I'd come to depend on him in our short time together. Feeling a little morose, I shot him off another text even though I was sure it would be hours before he saw it. *I miss you!* It was basic and didn't come off too needy, although that was exactly what I was feeling.

When we pulled out onto the main road, Ella broke the silence in the car. "Is Chase coming back over tonight?"

"Without a doubt, ladybug. He'll be here."

Inside my gut twisted and I wondered if I had just lied to the girl who was my whole world.

Chapter 29
Chase

Light filtered in through the blinds and seared my eyeballs behind my lids. I curled to the side and immediately regretted it. My head throbbed. Groaning at the intensity of it, I sluggishly checked the time. It was already after ten. Two little pills sat on my nightstand along with a bottle of water. I greedily swallowed them down and rolled to hang my legs off the bed.

What the hell happened last night?

I remembered leaving work after my appointment and heading directly to the bar. I didn't go to The Locker for fear of running into anyone. Instead, I'd driven to a little hole-in-the-wall called Winners. It was ironic. I was far from a winner. As a matter of fact, it would have been more appropriately called Losers. The dark lighting and hard rock cover band had fit my mood perfectly. It was a haven for local bikers and other unsavory characters. I was one of the few guys there without a beard or a leather cut. I had no interest in them and their interest in me was even less. It was a perfect place to drown my sorrows and figure out a plan.

When Maggie had texted, I felt the knife in my chest twist. I had no idea what I was going to tell her or how I was going to let go of the best thing that had ever happened to me. After my third shot of tequila I was no closer to an answer. No matter what I decided it was going to crush Maggie, but the pain would be less than if Jeff tried to take Ella from her.

I should have told her about my arrest from the beginning. I'd meant to, but the deeper we got, the further down I pushed my past. I should have known it would come back to bite me. All I had wanted was a chance to be happy. I would have told her eventually. The longer I kept the secret, the easier it became to pretend it didn't exist.

After the fourth shot, I'd called Becca. She knew my past and wouldn't shove it in my face. I needed my friend and her advice. After she showed up, everything got a little hazy. I remembered her arm over my shoulder as I spilled my guts. My heart had bled out on the bar top.

What I didn't remember was how I got home. That thought was a little disconcerting. It'd been a long time since I'd blacked out from drinking.

Last night, I'd been a chickenshit. I should have told Maggie the truth. I should have confessed my sins and manned up. But I wasn't ready to see the look of disappointment I knew she'd give me. I wasn't ready for the rejection. And I sure as hell wasn't ready to put Maggie in a position no woman should ever be put in.

In the light of day, nothing had changed. It was still an impossible situation that could only have one outcome.

No more Maggie.

No more Ella.

I had to let them go.

I pushed to my feet and headed for the kitchen, wearing only my boxer briefs. At least I'd had the good sense to get undressed before crawling into bed last night. Yay me! I made one good decision in my haze of drunkenness.

As I stepped into the front room, my already nauseous stomach fell to the floor. "What the hell are you doing here?"

Wearing one of my T-shirts and only her panties, Becca held out a mug of coffee to me. "Well, good morning to you too, sunshine."

Of all the things I thought would happen today, finding Becca in my kitchen half-naked wasn't one of them. I racked my brain, trying to remember what happened last night but came up empty. As if the situation with Maggie wasn't bad enough, this made it so much worse. I wasn't a cheater, except the evidence standing in front of me told me I was.

I cautiously took the cup from her hand. "What happened last night?"

She chuckled. "You don't remember?"

Taking a sip from my mug, I let the hot liquid scald my throat. "Clearly not."

"You don't remember calling me?"

"Yeah, I remember that, but everything else is a little fuzzy. Did we... sleep together?" The mere thought of cheating on Maggie made me want to throw up.

Becca tapped her nails on the counter. "I should fuck with you, but you just look too damn pathetic. We didn't sleep together. By the way you were pounding back tequila shots, I'd have been surprised if you didn't have whiskey dick."

Usually, the mention of whiskey dick would offend me, but in this case I was relieved. I motioned to her lack of clothes. "Then why are you wearing my shirt?"

She sighed and shook her head. "Because after I wrangled your ass into my car and drove you home, you vomited all over me. Super classy, by the way. Plus, I wanted to make sure you didn't drown in your own puke. It would be a tragic way to go."

I leaned on the counter and rested my head in my hands. "I'm sorry and thank you."

Becca rubbed her hand up and down my back. "That's what friends are for. You'd have done the same for me, although I hope I'm never that pathetic on a Monday night."

"Hardy-har-har. Where are your clothes?"

"In the dryer. I'll take you to get your truck when they're done." She slid my coffee across the counter toward me. "In the meantime, drink up. You want breakfast?"

I settled into a chair at the table. "I could eat."

"I figured." Becca scrounged around in my fridge and pulled out half a dozen eggs. "It's slim pickings in here."

"I've been spending most of my time at Maggie's."

She cracked a couple of eggs in the pan. "You wanna talk about that?"

I ran a hand through my hair. "No. Yes. I don't know." I could talk this around in circles all day. It wasn't going to change a thing.

"Thanks for clearing that up. I almost forgot how concise you are."

I gave her a hard glare. "Remind me why we're friends again?"

She held up the spatula like a microphone. "Reasons Becca and Chase are friends. Number one, everything is easy between us. No stress, no pressure. Number two, you can call me when you need someone to pick your drunk ass up from the bar. And number three, the sex was phenomenal." She ended her performance with a little bow.

I groaned. The last thing I wanted to be reminded of when Becca and I were both in our underwear was us having sex. It felt like cheating even if it wasn't.

As if sensing my discomfort, she pointed the spatula at me. "Whoa! Don't get your panties in a twist, I've got a new man now. I wasn't implying anything." She cocked a hand on her hip. "I swear I told you about him last night."

And this is why even though I cared about Becca, we could never be together. If she had anything besides air between her ears, she would have remembered I was practically incoherent last night. "Your eggs are burning."

"Yikes!" She quickly spun around and flipped the eggs in the pan. "Anyhoo, I think you should just be upfront with Maggie."

"I can't. She'll end up hating the father of her child and what good would that do?" None. Ella would pay the consequences and be torn down the middle. I couldn't be responsible for that.

There only seemed to be one answer.

I knew what I had to do and the thought of it made me feel sicker than the tequila shots I drank last night.

Chapter 30
Maggie

Normally, my phone stayed tucked away in my purse during school hours, but not today. The uneasiness that had sunk into my stomach last night hadn't diminished. If anything, it had intensified as the minutes ticked away.

One unanswered message was nothing. Several was something. Something that was gnawing away at me. I reread the messages I had sent Chase during the day.

Maggie: I miss you!

Maggie: What time are you getting off work tonight?

Maggie: Will I see you later?

Maggie: Please call me.

Maggie: Did I do something wrong?

It had started innocent enough, but each subsequent message sounded a little more desperate. I never wanted to be *that* woman. The one who was needy and clingy. I'd made that mistake with Jeff and all it did was push him further away.

I turned my phone back over on my desk and sighed.

"What's wrong, Ms. Malone?" In my daze I hadn't even seen Joey standing at my desk. The little bugger was sneaky and perceptive as hell.

"Nothing, sweetheart. Everything is fine," I assured him. I might have been crumbling inside, but that wasn't my students' problem. They deserved a hundred percent from me.

Sarah crept up next to Joey. "You look sad. Did somebody die? I was sad when my dog died."

I smiled, "No, nobody died, and you know I don't have a dog." God, I must have looked worse than I thought.

"Did someone make fun of you? Bullies are mean, but you got to kill 'em with kindness." Joey flashed me a toothless grin.

255

Seemed someone had been listening. There was a little satisfaction in that tidbit. Sometimes I forgot that these kids cared about me as much as I cared about them. I was the adult. It was my job to console them, not the other way around. I crouched in front of the two tiny people. "I'm just fine. There's nothing for you two to worry about." I gave them each a tight squeeze. "Now go meet me on the back carpet. We're going to do something really fun with math today."

They both ran off to the back of the room as I instructed the rest of the class to follow. It was time to put on my happy face.

A ding from my desk pulled my attention. I tentatively turned my phone over and read the message. The pit in my stomach instantly turned into a dark abyss and I was sure the salad I ate for lunch was going to reappear in the most volatile way.

Chase: I'll be over at 5. We need to talk.

This wasn't good. It wasn't good at all.

Pins and needles. I felt them on the back of my neck, the base of my spine and the soles of my feet. It was an uncomfortable prickling feeling that had me wanting to crawl out of my own skin.

In my experience, never did the words *we need to talk* translate into something good.

As a kid, it meant that I had got caught breaking the rules and was going to be punished. As a teacher, it meant that someone had complained about the way I disciplined their child. As a parent, I said it to Ella when her pet fish died. But said by the man you were sleeping with... that was something I wasn't prepared for.

The clock ticked toward five o'clock. The best I could do as a parent was spare Ella from whatever this was going to be. I took my tablet to her room and set it on her bed. "You know that new game you like?"

She nodded her head. "The one with all the princesses?"

"Yep. You've been such a good girl lately; I think you deserve a reward." I clicked into the game. "Do you remember your password?"

"Uh-huh. It's *ladybug*." She smiled up at me.

"That's right. I want you to stay in your room for a little bit, okay?"

Ella was already pressing on the screen and picking the dress and hair for her princess. "Okay."

I exited her room closing the door behind me. At least that was taken care of.

I fidgeted around the kitchen, wiping the counter, and going through a pile of junk mail. Why did it seem like time crept by when you were waiting for something ominous? I threw all of Ella's toys into the basket in the corner and fluffed the pillows on the couch.

The rumble of Chase's truck drew my attention to the window. I wiped my hands on the front of my yoga pants and walked to the door. The last time I was this nervous I'd been waiting on the results from a little white stick. The longest three minutes of my life.

I threw open the door and plastered a smile on my face as Chase came up the walkway running a hand through his already tousled hair. "Hey."

He chastely pecked me on the cheek. "Hey, Maggie." Maggie. Not Red. It was the kind of kiss you'd give your grandma, not your girlfriend.

"You coming in?"

He shoved his hands in his pockets. "I can't stay."

I frowned. "Oh, okay. What's going on?"

"We need to talk." The dreaded words fell from his lips and sank into my soul.

I pulled the door closed behind me and sat on the step of the porch. "You're breaking up with me, aren't you?" I could pretend I didn't know what was happening but denying it would just prolong the inevitable.

He sat down beside me and wrapped an arm around my shoulder, pulling me into his side. "You deserve better than me."

I let out a very unladylike snort as my eyes welled with tears. "You're really going to be so cliché? *It's not you, it's me.* Just be honest."

Chase stared out into the setting sun, his face impassive. "Be real, Maggie. I work in a tattoo parlor. I'll never be able to provide the life you deserve. I'm not cut out for this. Dance classes, slumber parties, and princess movies? Do you really think that's who I am?"

I pulled away in disgust, my sadness turning to anger. "Are you fucking serious right now? Did I just imagine the last couple months? Because if that's not you, then you're one hell of an actor. What was this weekend about? Just a bunch of pretty words and lies to see how gullible I was?"

"Don't do this, Maggie. That's not what it was. Don't make this harder than it has to be. I never wanted to hurt you."

I stood and faced him, planting my hands on my hips. "Hah! You never wanted to hurt me? You were the one who pursued me. I told you from the beginning this

257

wasn't a game. You made me fall for you, but worse you made that little girl fall in love with you. She didn't need another man in her life to push her aside." My heart was cracking right down the middle and bleeding out into my chest. I should have known better than to believe that someone could love us. The tears fell down my cheeks for the man I fell in love with and the daughter I knew was going to be heartbroken.

Chase cupped my face between his hands and pressed his lips to mine. His tongue tangled with mine in a gentle caress and I had no choice but to fall into him. For a minute I thought it was just a bad dream, a nightmare born out of my own insecurities. But when his watery aqua eyes met mine, I knew I was wide awake, and the kiss was nothing but a goodbye.

"I love you, Maggie. Trust me when I say this is not what I wanted, but for once in my life I'm trying not to be selfish here. I'm trying to do what's best for both of you. You're better off without me."

I pulled out of his embrace, the tears falling faster down my face. I unclasped the diamond pendant from around my neck and slapped it into his hand. "You're a liar, Chase Montgomery. You're nothing but a coward. We could make this work, but you're too afraid to try."

A tear dripped down his chiseled cheek. "Goodbye, Red."

There was nothing I could do. I wouldn't beg him to stay. If I learned anything from Jeff, it was to have some self-respect. I'd done enough begging in my lifetime to know that it wouldn't make a bit of difference.

I stood there paralyzed and watched him walk away. Time stood still and the moments we spent together flashed through my mind. All of it had been an illusion. Something I had wanted so badly I created a fairy tale in my own mind.

The front door flew open and Ella ran toward him. "Chase! Wait!" I tried to grab her arm, but it slipped right through my fingers. She crashed into Chase's legs, holding on to that damn stuffed cat he'd bought her. "Where are you going?"

Chase scooped her up and held her to his chest. "I have to go, princess bug. I'm not going to see you for a while, okay?"

I wrapped my arms around myself, trying to hold it together at the sight of them.

"Why?" she asked innocently. "Don't you love us anymore?"

He squeezed her tighter. "I love you very much," his voice hitched.

"But not my mom?"

"I love her too, but I gotta go." Chase set Ella on the ground and moved quickly to his truck. She tried to follow, but I snatched her hand to keep her from running after him. Ella shouted, "Chase, don't go!"

He started his truck and pulled out of the driveway, leaving us nothing but a view of his taillights. I lifted my daughter into my arms and carried her into the house as she cried on my shoulder, big heaving sobs leaking from her chest. No matter what I was feeling, I needed to be strong for the little girl that was clinging to me. I ran a hand through her messy curls. "Shhh. It'll be okay. I got you and I'm never letting go."

"I miss him already." She sniffled.

"I know, ladybug. I know," I consoled her.

Damn him for breaking our hearts!

Chapter 31
Chase

Breaking my own heart was one thing. Breaking the hearts of the people I loved the most was on a whole other level. Watching Maggie was hard enough, but listening to Ella's wail, begging me not to go, damn near ripped me apart.

It was all I could do to keep walking, because once I turned around, I would have caved in an instant. I would have told her the truth, consequences be damned. I would have been selfish and tried to keep them.

My only salvation was knowing that I had allowed one of the women I loved to keep her child.

I didn't want her to see me this way, but I owed her an explanation. Clad in an orange jumpsuit with my hands cuffed in front of me, I was led into a room furnished with only a few tables and chairs spread throughout. Meredith sat on one side of the table, her eyes red and puffy, looking as exhausted as I felt. Having her see me like this was excruciating. Seeing the pain in her eyes was worse.

The words I had prepared stuck in my throat as she stared at me across the table, a tear running down the side of her face. "I'm sorry." It was totally inadequate. I'm sorry *was what you said after forgetting to transfer clothes from the washer to the dryer or accidently sitting on her sunglasses. This... this was way beyond an* I'm sorry.

She wiped the stray tear away. "Tell me it's a lie. Tell me what they're saying isn't true."

I stared at her face, unable to say the words she wanted to hear. In the five years we'd been together, I'd never lied to her. I cherished her, adored her, would do anything for her. It was the last one that got me. I dropped out of school so I could get a job. My part-time gig on campus wasn't cutting it. I needed real money if I wanted to support Meredith the way she deserved. I thought working as a mechanic would pay the bills, but we were still scraping by. When the opportunity arose to make a little more cash, I jumped on it. Every time I made a run, I knew it was wrong, but my desire to provide for Meredith outweighed my guilty conscience.

"Say something, Chase."

The admission was thick on my tongue. "I did it. I didn't know there was cocaine in the bag. I thought it was just weed."

Her sadness turned to anger. "Oh my god, Chase! How could you be so stupid? They're charging you with possession and intent to sell. Do you know what that means?" I stared at her blankly. Yeah, I knew what it meant. Frustrated with my silence, she continued, "Do you? Years! You're going to be locked away for years."

I'd talked with my lawyer earlier. He'd hinted at a possible deal. "It might not be that bad. My lawyer said…"

"You have a lawyer? Who are you? People like us don't have lawyers."

"My dad…"

She held up a hand to stop me. She wasn't interested in what I had to say. If I weren't so ashamed of my situation, I would have been pissed, but it's hard to be pissed at the girl you love when you're wearing a wardrobe courtesy of the county jail and handcuffs.

"Just stop, Chase. You promised me you quit running jobs for your asshole boss. We didn't need the money that bad. We were fine."

We weren't fine. Meredith wasn't getting paid for her nursing clinicals and she didn't have time for a job. I did what I had to do, shady or not, to keep us afloat. I didn't hear her complaining when I paid for her new stethoscope or the scrubs she needed. Why couldn't she understand, everything I did, I did for her. The ring on her finger should have been proof enough.

I thought when she graduated and got a full-time job, things would get better. But then we got pregnant and the pressure to provide for her doubled.

My jaw clenched. "I didn't know about the cocaine. I did it for you. For us. It was stupid, but it was a mistake. My intentions were good."

She laughed, actually laughed in my face. "Your intentions? Look where your intentions have gotten you. That's the stupidest thing I've ever heard. You're selfish! I love you, Chase, but I can't be with you. I'm moving out of the apartment and in with a friend. When you get out… if you get out… don't call, don't text, don't contact me at all."

Panic surged. "You can't do that. We're having a baby. I need to be there."

She pushed her chair back and stood from the table. "Yeah, well I guess you should have thought about that before you decided to be a drug dealer. You promised me, Chase. You promised me you'd be there. You promised me I wouldn't have to do this alone."

She was right. I had promised her. "When I get out..."

"There won't be any baby. I'm getting an abortion."

What? I tried to stand, but a beefy guard pushed me back in the chair with his hand on my shoulder. "No! You can't do that!"

"I can and I will. Goodbye, Chase." *She walked to the door and never looked back.*

"Meredith, stop! Please! I love you!"

She walked out of my life. That was the last time I ever saw her. I never called. I never texted. I never tried to contact her in any way.

I was out of jail in six months with only a possession charge. I testified against my boss at the auto shop. Come to find out he'd been on their radar for over two years. I was a pawn in a game. An easy target. The feds had been watching the shop. My arrest was nothing but a power play on their part. A way to get the evidence they needed to bring down a whole honest-to-God drug ring. What I thought was a little weed, turned out to be a whole lot more. I made a plea deal and came home with my tail between my legs.

My dad died of a heart attack while I was locked up. Grams had moved up from Alabama to help hold the pieces of our family together. Amber barely talked to me.

I was ashamed of what I'd done and retreated into my own little world, back to the room that held the dreams of my childhood on the walls. Going back to school wasn't an option for me, so I applied for an apprenticeship at a local tattoo parlor. It was there I learned the art of inking my designs on skin. It wasn't my intended career path, but I was good at it and that was something.

For the first time ever, I considered breaking my last promise to Meredith. I wondered what became of her. Was she married? She was beautiful, surely a woman like that wouldn't be single anymore. She probably married a doctor and had a couple of kids by now. I wondered where she lived and if she was even in Michigan anymore.

Sitting on my balcony with a beer in my hand and Not My Cat laying at my feet, I clicked into Facebook. Layla stalked people all the time on FB, checking out our clients and getting the nitty-gritty. For her it was entertainment. For me it was morbid curiosity.

My finger hovered over the search button. "Should I do it?" I asked the large tabby. He rolled on his back, stretching out and showing me his teeth with a big yawn. He wasn't concerned about my distress. "I'm not sure if that was a yes or a no. I'll need something more." Not My Cat flipped to his feet and hopped on my lap, letting out a loud meow. I rubbed his fluffy head. "Is that a yes?" Another meow.

I typed her name in the search engine and she popped up immediately. Part of me had hoped the search wouldn't give any results, then the decision would have been made for me. I took a deep breath, closed my eyes, and tapped on her name.

Her profile pic popped up and it took my breath away. She was as beautiful as ever, sitting on a beach with her blond hair blowing in the breeze. It made me think of the times she would stick her head out the window of my car and scream into the wind. That was when our only worries were where the next party was at and where we were going to sneak off to afterward.

Before scrolling to her posts, I clicked in the *About* section. The first things listed, were all things I already knew: where she was from, what high school and college she attended. She lived in Livonia now and worked in a hospital there. After all these years apart, she lived less than an hour from here. If she wanted to see me, she could have and that thought hit me hard. Suspiciously missing from her profile was Meredith's relationship status.

I knew her posts would give me the most information. A peek into her life without me. It felt wrong. Sure, I had checked out a few other girls' profiles before, but this was different. I wasn't checking out a potential hookup. I was going to get a glimpse of what I lost.

Meredith's last post was from a week ago. *Rough day today. Nothing says therapy like egg rolls.* It was a picture of her take-out container opened up showing the food inside. To say I was disappointed would be an understatement.

I scrolled to the next one. *Feeling really good today. Cade and I spent the day finding the perfect pumpkins. So fortunate to spend this time with my favorite guy.* Again, no picture of her, just a field full of bright orange pumpkins. Good. I didn't want to see her *favorite guy* anyway. Even though I had no right, jealousy flared.

I should have stopped. My question was answered. Meredith had a man in her life, and she was happy.

A glutton for punishment, I scrolled down. My jaw clenched. Definitely not what I was expecting. *Love this girl! Couldn't ask for a better friend or support system. Don't know what I'd do without you!* It wasn't so much the caption, but the picture that had my blood boiling. Meredith was wearing a hat and had her arm wrapped around another woman. Not just any woman, but Amber. The post was dated two months ago. My freaking sister had been in contact with Meredith this whole time and never said a word to me. Un-fucking-believable! All the guilt she'd laid on me about losing her best friend was nothing but a lie.

Seeing Amber with Meredith was shocking, but the next post blew me away. It was dated six months ago. *Cade's first fish! Such a proud mama!* Meredith had her arm around a boy about Ella's age. He was holding up his fish like a trophy, clearly proud of himself. But it wasn't the fish that caught my attention. It was the unruly blond hair and piercing aqua eyes.

It couldn't be! There was no fucking way!

Pushing Not My Cat off my lap, I ran into my apartment and pulled the picture of my dad and me from the shelf. I was young, maybe six or seven, and holding up a fish. I held the picture next to my phone. The similarities were uncanny. The eyes. The hair. Even the toothless smile. They were identical.

She never had the abortion. I had a son!

I had no proof he was mine except the evidence before me.

I always wondered if the baby had been a boy or a girl and what he or she would look like.

Emotions overwhelmed me as I sank into the couch, both pictures clutched in my hands. So many emotions.

Regret over the mistakes I made that led to this.

Sadness for the time I'd lost with my son.

Anger at Meredith for not telling me the truth.

Hatred aimed at my sister for her betrayal.

Fear, because I had no idea how to be a father.

Anxiety that Meredith wouldn't let me be a part of Cade's life.

Cade.

I had a son named Cade.

Not My Cat jumped up on the couch beside me. "I have a son," I told him. He rubbed into my side and began purring. "I know. It's kinda great, isn't it?" He purred louder.

I pulled out my laptop and got to work. I had to find where they lived. I would go there and grovel at Meredith's feet if I had to. I wasn't going to lose any more time.

If I could find Maggie by internet, surely, I could find Meredith. It couldn't be that hard.

Maggie.

Fuck!

She would know what to do. She was a great mom, but I couldn't call her. I'd burned that bridge already. How would I explain that I didn't know I had a child? How would I explain about my fucked-up past?

I couldn't depend on Maggie as a crutch. It wouldn't be fair. I needed to be a man and face this alone.

My fingers flew across the keyboard. It didn't take long for her address to pop up on the screen.

I put the tabby back outside and grabbed my keys. I had no idea what I was going to do, but I had to see him. I had to see where they lived.

Putting the address into my GPS, I followed the turn by turn directions until my truck sat across from Meredith's house in the dark. It had taken me forty-five minutes. It was barely anything at all. I'd have driven hours to see him.

The small ranch-style home sat on a quiet street in a nice neighborhood, a white Equinox parked in the driveway. The front blinds of the house were open, offering me a view into the brightly lit room. I could see Cade sitting on the couch watching TV, chomping on an apple, and wiping his mouth with his pajama sleeve. I wasn't sure how much time had passed since I'd parked, but I could watch him for hours. I was about to call it a night when Cade walked to the window and looked out. There was no way he could see me in the dark, but I felt his gaze, nonetheless. The apple dangled by his side as he placed his other hand on the glass. I pressed my palm to the truck window feeling the undeniable connection between us.

After a few minutes, Meredith scooped him into her arms and closed the blinds.

Tomorrow.

Tomorrow I would get my answers.

Chapter 32
Maggie

I let Ella sleep in my bed last night. I'd clung to her as much as she'd clung to me. Both of us needing the comfort and reassurance that we would be okay. We were broken, but we would heal. We would make it through this storm together.

I looked in the mirror at the woman who was reflected back. Her eyes were puffy and red. I stayed awake long after Ella had conked out, staring at the ceiling, and replaying the last several days in my mind. I searched for anything that would have led to him walking away without a valid explanation.

I was drained. There was no way I was going to make it through this day putting on a happy face and the performance of a lifetime for twenty-five little people. I'd never last. The mere thought of it was exhausting.

So, I did the only thing I could think of and called Roxy. "This better be an emergency," she grumbled groggily.

"It is," my voice quivered. "I need you to pick Ella up for school."

"What's wrong? Are you sick?"

I couldn't get into this with her now. She'd have to forgive me for lying. "I don't feel well at all." It wasn't a complete lie. My stomach was nauseous, my head hurt, and I felt like a Mack truck had run over my body. And most importantly, my heart was broken. I'd say that qualified as sick.

"Shit, honey. Okay. You get Ella ready for school and I'll come get her."

"Thank you." I hung up and wrangled Ella from my bed. She was exhausted too, but I needed time alone today. Going to school was what was best for her. Routine and something to keep her mind busy. I needed it too, but I just couldn't do it.

"How come you're in your robe, Momma?" Nothing slipped past her.

"Roxy is gonna take you to school today."

Ella rubbed her eyes. "You're not going?"

I ran my fingers through her wild curls. "Not today, ladybug."

"Can I stay home too?"

"Nope. You're going to make turkeys today with Miss Nelson. Doesn't that sound like fun?"

"I like making turkeys. Miss Nelson always lets us use glitter."

I smiled down at her even if I was feeling anything but happy. "Then let's get you ready."

Forty-five minutes later I had Ella's backpack over her shoulder and ready for school.

"You look awful," Roxy stated the obvious.

I wrapped my robe tighter around myself. "Pretty much feel like it too. I might need you tomorrow."

She held a hand to my forehead. "You don't feel like you have a temp."

Brushing her hand away, I dismissed the amateur diagnosis. "I think it's something else." *Like my heart being ripped from my chest.*

"Okay, well, get some rest and don't worry about Ella."

I gave her a tight squeeze. "Thank you. You're a life saver."

After they left, I curled back into bed with phone in hand. I scrolled through all the pictures Chase and I took over the past several weeks. I scrutinized each one searching for something I missed. Some sign that everything wasn't as perfect as I thought it was. All I saw was that damn dimple and his piercing aqua eyes. We looked happy. We were happy.

What went wrong?

I racked my brain trying to think of something that would have told me he was unhappy. I guess I was so caught up in my own bliss that I missed all the signs. But as I looked through the pictures again, there were no signs.

After a morning of hosting one of the biggest pity parties ever, I decided a hot shower might make me feel better. I scrubbed my skin roughly, trying to rid myself of Chase. The way he kissed my lips. His tongue gliding down my neck. His teeth nipping at my breasts. His hands holding my hips. His cock pushing deep inside me.

It was impossible. Every inch of my skin had been branded by his touch.

I pounded my fist on the shower tile and let out a guttural cry. "Why? Fuck you, Chase! Fuck you for making me fall in love with you!" I collapsed in a heap and sobbed on the shower floor. Nothing made sense. I'd given him everything, let him into our lives, let my daughter fall in love with him. And it wasn't enough. I wasn't enough for him. The tears came fast and hard as I let out everything I'd been holding in. The sadness, the pain, the anger, the betrayal. I let it swirl down the drain.

I replayed his words in my head. *You deserve better than me. I never wanted to hurt you. This is not what I wanted, but for once in my life I'm trying not to be selfish here. I'm trying to do what's best for both of you. You're better off without me.* None of it made sense.

When I stepped from the shower and wrapped the towel around myself, I realized that even if I could wash away the sadness, pain, anger and betrayal, there was one thing I couldn't get rid of. Love. It made my heart swell and left a gaping hole in my chest simultaneously.

I didn't imagine what we had together. It was real. My life wasn't better without him. Since he'd become part of my life, I felt alive again. I felt wanted and desired. I felt like I had someone to share the load. We were a team by day and lovers by night. I couldn't think of anything more perfect.

My realization didn't make my chest ache any less, if anything, it was worse.

The urgency to talk with Chase consumed me. My heart beat double time as my finger pressed on his contact. The line rang and rang before going to voicemail, *This is Chase. You know what to do.* Just the timbre of his voice sent a wave of warmth through me.

I hadn't planned out what to say if he didn't answer. Hell, I hadn't planned what to say if he *did* answer. I was a complete and utter mess. I spewed what was in my heart and didn't care if I sounded pathetic. "I miss you, Chase. I don't know what this is about, but whatever it is we can work it out. I don't deserve better than you. You are exactly what I've always needed. Please don't give up on us. If you still love me, please call."

He may have given up, but I hadn't.

There was nothing left to do but sit and wait.

Chapter 33
Chase

This was the moment of truth.

I watched as Meredith put Cade on the bus this morning. No one else had come or gone from the house.

My knuckles rapped on the door and I cracked my neck as I waited anxiously for it to open. When it did, I took a quick inventory of Meredith's appearance. Her blond hair spilled out beneath a colorful scarf tied around her head. She was thinner than I remembered and looked tired, like she hadn't slept in days, but was still the pretty girl who once thought I hung the moon. It didn't matter. I wasn't here to rekindle an old flame. I was here because she had something that belonged to me.

She stared at me in surprise. "Chase?"

There were so many things I wanted to say to her, but I stuck with the most important one. I held my phone in Meredith's face showing her the picture I'd stumbled upon. "Is he mine?"

If she was shocked, she didn't show it. Instead, she nodded and swung the door open wider. "We should talk."

Talk? Yeah, we had a shit ton to talk about, starting with why I didn't know I had a kid. I calmed my temper and sat on the couch my son had been on last night. My hand rubbed along the fabric trying to absorb him into my skin. The house reminded me of Maggie's. Toys were strewn about, books on the coffee table, markers and paper piled next to the TV. Being here was twice the torture I'd anticipated.

"You lied to me."

Meredith eased into the chair across from me. "I did, but you lied to me too."

She was right, but this was different. I lied for a few months; she'd lied for years. I nervously ran a hand through my hair. "I made mistakes, Meredith. Big ones. There was a lot going on. We were barely scraping by and you were pregnant.

I never wanted to hurt you. All I wanted to do was be able to take care of you. Take care of us. Yes, I jumped into something that seemed like easy money and it's the biggest regret of my life. It cost me everything. I lost you and I lost my son, who I didn't even know existed until yesterday." I pointed at her, letting everything I'd been holding in for the last twenty-four hours come out. "You told me to let you go. Not to call. Not to text. You told me you weren't having the baby. I thought I owed it to you to let you walk away after everything I'd put you through. I held up my end of the bargain. But you shit all over it by keeping this from me. You said you weren't keeping the baby."

She nodded, accepting my words. "I was so mad at you, Chase. Everything we were building together was shot to hell in one night. I trusted you and you broke my trust. I needed to move on. The only reason I was keeping the baby was because of you. I wasn't ready and you were gone."

"And?" I prodded. There was more and I needed to hear it.

"I went to the clinic. They did an ultrasound, and I heard the baby's heartbeat. It wasn't 'til then that I fully understood the gravity of what we created together. I couldn't go through with it."

I felt so many things. I wished I would have been with her when she heard our son's heartbeat and was relieved that she didn't go through with it. "Do you know how long I've felt guilty? Not just about what I did, but the fact that I'd taken our baby from you. That if it hadn't been for my bad decisions, how different our lives would have been?"

She shifted uncomfortably. "I couldn't be the woman who waited on the sidelines for years while her fiancé was in prison."

"I never went to prison. It was county jail, and I was out in six months."

Meredith dropped her head and stared at the floor. "I know. But by then I'd already started a new life. I couldn't take the chance that you'd fuck up again."

She was full of shit. Before then, I'd never given her a reason to doubt me. "Because that's all I was to you? One giant fuckup? That's not true and you know it."

"You went to jail, Chase. What was I supposed to think?"

"You could have had some faith in me. I wasn't a drug dealer and I've never done drugs. Yeah, I smoked weed a few times, but so did you." I stabbed myself in the chest. "I'm not a bad guy. I loved you more than life itself. I gave up school for you so you could have everything you needed."

"I never asked you to."

I threw my hands in the air. "Well, that's just great! Did you ever love me?"

"You know I did. Things just started moving really fast and I wasn't ready for marriage and a family."

"God, Meredith, I was so in love with you. I would have done anything for you. All these years I haven't been able to have a relationship because I was still stuck on you, so afraid of getting hurt again or hurting someone else. I've blamed myself for years. I take full responsibility for what I did, but you…you cheated me out of years with my son."

Meredith buried her head in her hands. "I'm so sorry. I don't want you to hate me, Chase. I fucked up… bad."

Despite how angry I was at her I'd never been able to stay mad at Meredith for long. When we were teenagers all it took was one tear and I was toast. I hated seeing her cry. She was my biggest weakness and the cause of my greatest downfall. And although everything inside me was torn up I could never hate her. "Who does he think his father is? What have you told him?"

She shrugged one shoulder. "I told him you lived far away, and he seemed to be satisfied with the explanation."

Every answer Meredith gave me frustrated me more. I ran both hands through my hair, undoubtedly making it stick up in every direction. One side of Meredith's face quirked up into a semi-smile. What she could possibly find funny at a time like this was beyond me. "What?" I snapped.

"I'm sorry. It's just that some things never change. You always did that hair thing when you were irritated. I guess it's good to know you're still you."

"Lots of things have changed since we were together. I'm not the same man."

"I know, but I'm hoping that somewhere underneath all that anger is the boy I once loved," she said sheepishly.

I wasn't sure what that meant. I never thought I would see Meredith again. I never thought I'd be sitting here in her house. I never thought we'd be having this conversation.

It was so much to process. My brain hadn't caught up to everything that transpired in the last twenty-four hours. I didn't know where we went from here. I didn't know if Meredith and I would have any type of relationship and I didn't know how to be a single dad.

There was only one thing I knew for sure. "I want to get to know my son. I want to spend time with him."

Meredith adjusted the scarf covering her head. "There's been a lot going on in our lives. Please give me a couple days, so I can prepare him. I want to talk to him first."

What was a couple of days when I'd waited years? I had to tell my mom she had another grandson. And Grams. This was going to change all our lives. "Friday. No longer, Meredith." I stood from the couch and headed toward the door.

Meredith followed, clutching at me. "I'm sorry, Chase. Please don't hate me."

I looked at her small fingers wrapped around my arm, fingers that had been threaded through mine more times than I could count, fingers I'd brought to my lips and kissed, fingers that had brought me pleasure. Noticeably absent was any ring on those fingers and I wondered what had happened to the one I gave her. "I could never hate you, Meredith. All I ever did was love you."

Chapter 34
Maggie

"Today is the last day," Roxy said Friday afternoon.

I pulled the ties of my robe I'd been wearing for three days tighter, wrapping myself inside its protective barrier. "I know."

Roxy crossed her arms and tapped her foot. "Ella told me Chase hasn't been around. That you guys had a fight."

"It wasn't a fight," I insisted. "He just," my eyes welled with tears, "broke up with me. I don't even know why. He won't return my calls or my texts."

Her rigid stance softened. "Why didn't you tell me?"

"You warned me about getting involved too fast. I had this whole fantasy built up in my head and I wanted it to be true more than I've ever wanted anything. I just didn't want to hear you say, 'I told you so'."

She frowned. "Oh, honey."

"I don't know what to do. I can't think straight. I can't eat and I can't sleep."

Roxy folded her arms around me. "The first thing you're going to do is get out of that damn robe, brush your teeth and comb your hair. Then you're going to forget about him for a while. You're a kick-ass mom and an incredible woman. A man doesn't define you. You were fine before Chase and if he can't figure out how amazing you are, then you're better off without him. Give yourself the weekend to straighten your crown and on Monday, act like the queen you are."

"I miss him." I sobbed into her shoulder.

She ran her hand through my hair like I was a child. "I know you do, but you've been through worse. You've practically raised Ella by yourself. You're stronger than you think."

"Will you stay for a few. I haven't been a good mom the past few days and I just need a little more time for myself." I pulled my robe up over my nose and sniffed. "I need a shower."

Roxy turned me by the shoulders and marched me to the bathroom. "Take your time, but not too long." She smirked at me. "I have a date."

I lifted a brow in question. "Corporate guy?"

"Let's just say he's not as straitlaced as I thought." She tapped me on the ass. "Now go!"

I shuffled into the bathroom and scrutinized myself in the mirror, a bad habit I'd developed over the past few days. I looked tired. My eyes had dark circles under them, and my skin was pallid.

After a quick shower, I dried my hair and applied a little makeup, just enough to make me look alive.

When I finally emerged, dressed in clean clothes, Ella and Roxy were on her phone watching puppy videos and giggling.

"You look better, Momma," my daughter said.

God, even my daughter knew I was having a breakdown. "Thanks, ladybug. I feel better."

Roxy tucked her phone into her purse. "One-hundred-percent improvement." She tapped on her nonexistent watch. "Time for me to fly. I've got a little freshening up to do myself. I've got to get ready for dessert."

I could see the gears in Ella's head turning. "You can't have dessert before dinner."

She patted Ella on the head. "I can if I'm lucky."

I playfully smacked Roxy on the shoulder. "Oh my god! Get out of here before you corrupt my daughter any more." I gave her a tight hug. "Thank you. For everything."

"That's what best friends are for." She squeezed me back.

"Wait." I ran to the fridge, pulled out the can of whipped cream, and shoved it into her hand. "Enjoy your dessert." At least one of us should have a good night.

She shook the can and squirted a stream into her mouth, making it look filthy. "Things just got infinitely better."

"Can I have some?" Ella bent her head back, sticking her tongue out.

Roxy shrugged. "Why not?" She squirted a stream into her mouth.

Ella licked her lips and rubbed her tummy. "Whipped cream is delicious. It makes everything better."

My friend's face quirked up into an evil grin. "It certainly does." She gave us a little wave and left for whatever debauchery she planned for the evening.

274

I kneeled in front of Ella. "I'm sorry I've been so out of it the last few days. I'm going to do better."

"It's okay, Momma. I know you're sad, but Chase will come back."

I didn't know if it was healthy to indulge her misconceptions, but I wished I had her optimism. "How do you know?" I asked, curious as to where her head was at.

She threw her arms out as if it were obvious. "Because he loves us, and we love him. He'll come back."

If only it were that simple. I wanted to capture her innocence, put it in a bottle and hide it in a place where no one would ever be able to steal it away. But I knew one day her heart would be shattered just like mine. One of the hardest parts of being a mom was knowing I wouldn't always be able to protect her. I didn't want to dim her light, so I settled for a less than perfect response. "Maybe, ladybug."

A sharp knock on the door interrupted our quiet moment.

"Daddy's here! I gotta go get my cat!" Ella squealed as she ran off to her room.

I didn't want to see that damn stuffed animal, but I couldn't tell her no. I sighed and opened the door for the man I had no desire to see. "Hey."

He hiked a thumb over his shoulder at the empty space in my driveway. "No date tonight?"

Leave it to Jeff to pick at the open wound that had just started to scab over. "Not tonight." I left it at that. He didn't need nor deserve any details about my personal life.

Ella appeared at my side, hugging the tabby to her chest. "Hi, Daddy!"

"Hi, sweetie." He picked Ella up, set her on his hip and kissed her cheek. That was the most affectionate I'd seen him with her in a while. Aside from Halloween, he usually acted as if being with his daughter was more of an obligation than a privilege. He tugged on the cat's ear. "How 'bout we leave this here tonight?"

She hugged it tighter. "I love him and he's hungry too."

I waited for Jeff to throw a fit and demand she leave the cat behind.

He surprised me by letting it go. "All right. Does he like chicken nuggets?"

Her face practically glowed. "Uh-huh. With barbeque sauce."

"Of course he does." Jeff tapped her on the nose. He focused back on me. "You wanna come with us, Mags?"

My eyes bugged out of my head. It'd been years since I'd gone to dinner with the two of them. Funny how only months ago we'd been able to share a bed but not a meal. It really put the dysfunctionality of our relationship in perspective. I didn't

275

know what kind of game he was playing, but I had no intention of being a willing participant. "I don't think so. McDonald's really isn't my thing."

"We could go somewhere else."

Ella held up a finger. "Only if they have chicken nuggets."

Jeff rolled his eyes. "Obviously. You want Momma to come to dinner with us?"

She pressed her hands together. "Please, Momma."

It was a new low for Jeff to use my daughter against me. How was I supposed to say no to that? If Chase were still around it would have made my choice easy. Spending time with Jeff would have felt like cheating. But Chase wasn't around, and it was just dinner. It wasn't like we were cracking open the wine when we got home. Yeah, there would be absolutely no wine tonight. Or any night.

"Come on, Mags. It's food. You need to eat."

"Since when have you cared about me eating?" My hackles were up. Trusting Jeff had gone out the window long ago.

He hiked Ella higher on his hip. "Maybe I didn't always show it, but I've always cared. Just come to dinner with us."

"Fine," I relented. I grabbed my purse from the kitchen counter and followed them out to Jeff's black BMW.

We ate at Applebee's, surrounded by families with moms that were too tired to make dinner after a long week. I'm sure we looked just like any other happy family. Nothing could have been further from the truth. Jeff and I weren't a couple and hadn't been since before Ella was born. The only time he gave me the time of day was when he wanted to warm my bed.

The conversation was strained. I didn't want to reveal any tidbits about my personal life and luckily Ella hadn't brought up Chase's sudden disappearance from our lives. Jeff droned on about how he was climbing the corporate ladder and really making a name for himself. I guessed all those early mornings he'd snuck out of my bed to play golf were really paying off.

Ella pointed at her empty plate. "Can I have dessert, please?"

I looked to Jeff. He was paying for this shindig, not me.

"Of course, sweetie." He motioned to my water. "You want a glass of wine?"

I internally laughed. Some things never changed. "Yeah, I don't think so. Water is fine."

He shrugged. "Suit yourself."

Ella reached for the dessert menu in the middle of the table. "I want the big brownie with whipped cream on top."

Jeff flagged down our waitress and she returned with the decadent treat within minutes. Ella scooped up the whipped cream. "This is so yummy. Next time I'm going to have dessert first like Roxy."

Jeff glared at me while Ella sucked down the sticky sweetness. I shrugged. "What?"

"You know what I think of her. She's a bad influence."

I rolled my eyes. "Whatever. You don't like anyone I hang out with."

"I just want you to set a good example for our daughter." He scoffed.

My blood started to boil. I knew this dinner was a bad idea. Jeff and I could barely be around each other anymore without insulting one another. "You mean like the example you've shown her of how a man should treat a woman?"

I expected a quick retort or a smart-ass comment. I didn't expect him to reach across the table to pick up my hand. His thumb ran gently across my knuckles. "I know I've been an…" he glanced at Ella who was more interested in her dessert than us, "a jerk, but I'm going to do better."

I slid my hand out of his grasp and into my lap. "That would be nice." It was true. I wished that there wasn't always so much tension between us. We had a lot of years ahead of us: birthdays, holidays, graduations, and one day, hopefully many, many, maannny years from now, Ella's wedding. We were going to be thrown together in social situations. It was inevitable. It would also be nice to not want to strangle him all the time.

I was quiet on the way back to the house, staring out the window, contemplating my evening. Going to dinner with them tonight was a surprise but not totally unpleasant, which in itself was a pleasant surprise. Isn't this what I always wanted? It seemed like too little too late. How convenient that Jeff decided to step up his game when my life was falling apart. He didn't need to know what was going on in my personal life. He'd forfeited that right a long time ago.

One step in the right direction didn't erase all the wrong steps he'd made over the years. If I'd learned anything, it was not to get excited over something as mundane as dinner.

Jeff drummed his fingers on my thigh. My head snapped in his direction at the unsolicited touch. "You all right, Mags?"

"Yeah."

"Is Chase working tonight?"

"Yes." I lied.

He nodded his head. "Thanks for coming to dinner with us. I think Ella liked seeing us get along."

Jeff and I rarely fought, but we weren't overly friendly either. Except when wine was involved, then we were like two teenagers in the back seat of a car for the first time, all hands and lips and no common sense. I studied him, trying to figure out where this was going. "Probably."

"We should try to do things together more often. For Ella's sake."

I narrowed my eyes. "We'll see."

When we pulled into the driveway, I got out and slammed my door. All I wanted to do was put on my pajamas and tie that stupid robe back around me. I wasn't in the mood for the emotional back and forth he put me through.

Jeff and Ella met me on the porch. He gave her a quick hug and kiss goodbye, setting her inside the door. She ran off to change for bed, leaving the two of us alone. He cocked his head at me. "I liked spending time with you, Mags."

"It was tolerable," I deadpanned.

He chuckled. "God, you're tough."

I crossed my arms over my chest, not seeing any humor in the situation. "I've had a lot of practice. Good night, Jeff." I expected a snarky response.

He just stuck his hands in his pockets and backed down the sidewalk. "Good night, Mags."

I watched as his taillights faded away.

Not having that glass of wine at dinner was the only good decision I'd made tonight.

Chapter 35
Chase

I just needed to see her.

That's how I found myself parked across from Maggie's school this morning. Her car wasn't in the parking lot, so I waited. The crossing guard gave me a strange look.

I guess a guy sitting alone in a black truck across from a school full of children had suspicious written all over it. Yeah, it wasn't creepy at all.

Just as I was about to leave, a little red car darted into the parking lot. Roxy jumped out and pulled Ella from the back seat. The two of them rushed into the building without a backward glance.

I waved at the crossing guard and pulled out into traffic, making a detour on the way to my mom's. I drove by Maggie's house and her car was parked in the driveway. I'd reread her texts a hundred times. Listened to her voicemails over and over. Everything in my heart told me to go to her, but Jeff's threat fresh in my mind, was all it took to keep driving. *It was better this way*, I reminded myself.

I pulled into my mom's driveway. All I could think about yesterday was how I was going to tell her about Cade. And her daughter's betrayal.

The phone call to Amber when I left Meredith's was brief and brutal. *I know about my son and your friendship with Meredith. You. Are. Dead to me.* I didn't stay on the line long enough for her to give me some lame excuse or flimsy explanation. Her betrayal cut the deepest. My sister was my blood. She should have told me.

I used my key and entered the quiet house. Grams sat at the kitchen table, her hands wrapped around a cup of coffee while reading a magazine. She looked up at my sudden appearance. "You're here early. Coffee's hot."

I bent and kissed her cheek. "Thank you." I poured myself a cup and sat across from her. A sense of calm washed over me. This woman had always been my

279

biggest supporter no matter how much I fucked up. She was the one who'd encouraged me to follow my passion for art. When I'd been released from jail, she welcomed me with open arms, no questions asked. She told me to follow my dreams, whatever they were. I floundered for a while with no direction. Then one day I walked by a tattoo parlor and found myself applying for an apprenticeship position. No judgment.

Grams cupped my face with one hand. "Your heart looks heavy."

I bent my head, willing away the tears that threatened. I'd been so consumed with being angry that I hadn't let the gravity of my situation sink in. "It is."

"Want to talk about it?"

I nodded.

My mom stuttered when she walked in the kitchen, her robe wrapped around her. She looked from me to Grams. "What's going on?"

I took a deep breath. "I need to talk to you two."

She eyed me with worry, no doubt expecting the worst. I'd disappointed her before. I didn't blame her for being concerned. She poured coffee in her mug and sat down. "Are you okay?"

I nodded.

"Did something happen with Maggie?"

This wasn't what I was here to talk about, but I couldn't lie. "I broke up with her."

My mom crinkled her forehead. "Why?"

I looked up at the ceiling. "My past. Maggie's ex threatened to take her to court for custody."

Grams took ahold of my hand. "What did Maggie say?"

"She doesn't know. I won't make her choose. She deserves better."

Mom squeezed my other hand. "Don't you think Maggie…"

I cut her off. "No. For once in my life I'm not going to be selfish."

Always intuitive, Grams said, "There's more." She wasn't asking. She knew.

"Yeah." I took my phone from my coat pocket, pulled up the picture of Meredith and Cade and set it on the table. "I have a son."

My mom swiped the phone into her hand. Her eyes filled with tears. "Oh. My. God." She passed it to Grams.

Grams stared at it lovingly. "He looks just like you."

"How?" my mom asked.

I gave her a pointed look.

"Well, obviously I know how, but I thought…" She shook her head.

"Me too," I said. "All these years I've left her alone and then when everything happened with Maggie, I got sentimental and looked Meredith up. This is what I found. I tracked her down and showed up on her doorstep two days ago. I'm going to meet Cade today."

"His name is Cade?" Grams held a hand to her chest as she looked at the picture of my son.

"I have another grandson," my mom said.

I could see the reality sinking in. Telling them made my discovery ten times more real. I had a son, and I was going to meet him in a few short hours. "I'm scared. I don't know how to be a dad. He doesn't even know who I am."

Grams patted my hand. "You're smart. You'll figure it out. You're good with Theo and Ella adores you. I believe in you. You'll be a great dad."

They encouraged me more and I filled them in on the details I knew. "There's one more thing."

My mom blew out a ragged breath. "I'm afraid to ask."

"Amber knew." I showed them the picture of Meredith and Amber.

Mom's hand raised to her mouth to cover the shock. "Well, Christ on a cracker."

Yeah, that about summed it up.

"Come in." Meredith opened the door, her sweater hanging loosely on her thin frame. Cade hugged her leg, hiding himself behind his mom. She prodded him forward.

Nothing could have prepared me for the first time I met my son. He was so beautiful. His blond hair was a little disheveled and his aqua eyes were as piercing as mine. He had on a Detroit Lions sweatshirt and a pair of jeans, bare feet hanging out the bottom.

I got down on one knee in front of him and smiled. "Hey, buddy. My name is Chase."

He moved a little closer. "You're my dad."

"Yeah, I am. I've waited a long time to meet you."

"Are you leaving again for work?"

I cast a glance at Meredith. Tears filled her eyes and one fell down her cheek. There were worse lies she could have told him. "I'll still have to work, but I'm going to be around. A lot."

He pointed to the arm behind my back. "What's that?"

I'd stopped on the way and bought the same cat I gave to Ella on Halloween. I thrust it at him. "I got this for you. I hope you like cats."

He took it and ran his hand over the tail. "I like dogs, buts cats are cool."

I felt like a failure already. I didn't even know if my own son was a cat or dog person. There were a million other things I didn't know either: his birthday, his favorite color, or what he liked on his pizza.

Meredith gave him a little nudge. "What do you say, Cade?"

"Thank you." His eyes rolled up and he scrunched his mouth to one side, like I'd seen Ella do a hundred times. His gears were turning. "What do I call you?"

This was uncharted territory for both of us. I shrugged a shoulder up. "You can call me Chase or Dad. It's really up to you." I didn't want to make this situation more stressful than it needed to be for him.

"Can I think about it?"

I ruffled his hair, savoring the feel of the strands through my fingers. "Sure, bud."

"You want to see my room?"

I looked to Meredith. "If it's okay with your mom."

She waved us on. "Of course."

Cade grabbed me by the hand and led me to his room. I took it all in. The blue walls, the plaid curtains, the bedspread with footballs on it, the stuffed animals piled on top. It was small but cozy.

I picked up a picture I knew well, from his dresser. I had the same one in my apartment. We looked so young. The black dress had fit Meredith's body like a glove. I remembered wanting to leave prom early so I could strip her out of it.

Cade stared up at me. "Mom said you used to be her boyfriend. Did you love her?"

I hadn't expected the tough questions to come so soon. "I loved your mom very much. We were together for a long time."

"She said you played football."

I sat down on his bed and he crawled up next to me. The whole situation felt surreal. "I did. Do you like football?"

"Uh-huh. I played flag football this year, but the season's over. Want to see my jersey?"

"I'd love that."

Cade scrambled off the bed, pulling the blue and white shirt from his bottom dresser drawer. He held it up. "I'm number 17 and my name is on the back." He turned the shirt around and my heart swelled.

In big, bold letters it said MONTGOMERY across the back. She'd given him my last name. Meredith hadn't tried to completely erase me from his life and for that I was thankful. "I was number 17 too when I played ball."

Cade smiled up at me. "Mom picked my number."

"She did, did she?" *Interesting.*

"Yep. She said it was her favorite. Did you score a lot of touchdowns?"

"I had a few." I chuckled. "I started playing when I was ten and then through high school. Your mom came to all my games when we were together. Cheered me on at every game."

"Did she…kiss you when you got a touchdown?" he asked sheepishly.

"Occasionally," Meredith said, leaning against the doorjamb with her arms crossed while watching us.

I ruffled Cade's hair and whispered in his ear, "It was more than occasionally."

He giggled. The sound was like music to my ears. A sound I thought I'd never hear, but the best one I'd ever heard.

"Secrets already?" Meredith chided.

I shrugged. "Making up for lost time."

Cade jumped off the bed. "You ever play Madden?"

"It's been a while." I couldn't remember the last time I'd sat down to play a video game. Probably back in college.

"You wanna play? I'm really good."

"Sure, but I've got to warn you, I used to be pretty good myself."

"Not as good as me." He raced from his room tossing out the challenge.

Cade set everything up on the big screen in the front room, picking his team and roster.

I chuckled as I sat on the couch next to him. "Your team is stacked, dude."

He grinned up at me. "Scared?"

"Not a bit," I said, lining up my team.

We spent the next hour in a fierce competition. The kid was good and could smack talk with the best of them.

When his wide receiver ran into the endzone, he tossed the controller to the floor and threw his arms in the air. "Touchdown!"

I shook my head in defeat. "Rematch."

"Another day," Meredith said from behind the couch. "It's getting late."

"Awww, Mom! Can Dad come back tomorrow?"

Dad. My son just called me Dad.

"That's up to him."

"I'll be back," I assured him. "If it's warm enough maybe we can toss the ball around."

"Cool." He wrapped his arms around my neck and squeezed. "See you tomorrow, Dad."

I hugged him a little tighter than necessary, relishing the weight of him in my arms. "I'll see you tomorrow, Cade. Why don't you go brush your teeth while I talk to your mom."

He ran off leaving me alone with Meredith. "I'm going to need more time with him. A lot of time."

She bit her bottom lip like she used to do when she was nervous. "I know. You're good with him, Chase."

It was an unexpected compliment. "You should have had faith in me. I've lost so much time with him. God, Meredith, I don't even know my son's birthday."

She looked at the floor. "January 5."

I sucked in a deep breath. "I got out in December. I was out, Meredith. I could have been there. I *should* have been there."

She put her hand on my chest. "I know. I made a lot of mistakes too. I let my anger get the best of me. I can't change what I did, no more than you can change what you did, but if we want this to work, we're going to have to leave the past behind and move forward."

She was right. All the bullshit between us was water under the bridge. The only thing that mattered now was getting to know my son and being a part of his life.

Given this chance, I wasn't going to waste it.

Chapter 36
Maggie

Chase still hadn't returned any of my texts or calls. During one of my weaker moments, I'd driven by his apartment, but his truck was nowhere to be found. It was like he'd dropped off the face of the Earth.

I called Forever Inked this morning. Admittedly, my behavior was becoming stalkerish. Layla said he'd been out all week. When I asked why, all she said was something personal had come up. *Something personal?* That was vague with a capital V. In other words, *it wasn't any of my business.*

I thought Layla and I had somewhat become friends, but I should have known her loyalty lay with Chase.

So, girls' night? And promises to do it again? That wasn't happening. I wasn't part of the girl posse. I was a guest and my invitation had been revoked. Those women were Chase's friends, not mine.

I stared at the dress Rissa bought me, the one that cost a week's pay, and now hung uselessly in my closet. Every time I walked by the damn dress, I could hear it mocking me. *Sure fooled you, Red. Guys like him don't want girls like you.* I'd built up the fantasy that quiet nights at home with a six-year-old would be enough for a man like Chase Montgomery. I should have known from our first night that it was fleeting. I should have followed my instincts and accepted the one-night stand for what it was. Instead, I let him suck me in and believed it was real.

It wasn't a secret that Chase had been with lots of women, yet I thought I'd be the one to change him. It was foolish and immature. It was clear from the night I saw him with all his friends at The Locker that I didn't fit in with his crowd. They were edgy and fearless, I was conservative and cautious. We were polar opposites. Pieces of two different puzzles that didn't fit together. Like fitting a square peg in a round hole.

I shoved the dress in the back of my closet. Out of sight, out of mind. I didn't want to keep it, yet it couldn't be returned since I'd already worn it.

I knew what I had to do to ease my conscience about the dress. It would be a big hit to my checking account, but it was the right thing to do.

"I'm ready, Momma." Ella appeared in my doorway dressed in pink tights and a black leotard. Dance class started in thirty minutes. We'd have just enough time to make a quick pitstop.

I threw her hair up in a puffy ponytail. "It's cold outside, ladybug. Put some sweats on and then we'll get out of here."

She zoomed to her room, doing as she was told. Ella could be a handful, but most of the time she was easygoing. She gave my life purpose and was the reason I hadn't totally crawled into a hole over the past few days. I didn't have time to wallow or feel sorry for myself. I had responsibilities and if nothing else, I would be a good mother.

When we pulled up in front of Forever Inked, my nerves got the best of me. I shouldn't have been there, but it was the right thing to do. In and out. Easy peasy.

"Are we here to see Chase?" Ella asked from the back seat.

"Chase isn't working today, but I have to give something to Miss Rissa. We'll be really quick, I promise. And please don't run around inside. It's not really a place for kids and I probably shouldn't have even brought you." This was a bad idea. What was I thinking bringing a child into a tattoo parlor? It would be different if Chase were here, but he wasn't. Jeff would probably wring my neck if he knew.

"Can I have a Slurpee if I'm good?" she negotiated.

I sighed. "Yes." Whatever it took, I didn't care. I just wanted this to go smoothly.

Ella held my hand as we walked through the door. I expected to see Layla, but Draven was behind the front desk. Every time I saw him, I got intimidated. Maybe it was his size or the way his hair was pulled tight into a manbun or the tattoos that covered his arms, but most likely it was the scowl that marred his pretty face. It softened when he saw I had Ella with me. Maybe it was a good thing I'd brought her after all.

"Hey, Maggie." Then he got down on one knee in front of my daughter. "Hey, short stack."

She stared up at him. "Hi, big-man-who-I-don't-remember-your-name."

He let out a hearty laugh and held out his hand to her. "Draven."

She giggled and put her little hand in his big one, shaking it up and down.

I held up a hand. "Hey. Before you say it, I know Chase isn't here. I came to see Rissa or Zack."

He cocked his head to the side curiously. "Rissa's not here, but Zack's in his office," he said, hiking a thumb over his shoulder.

I held out my hand for Ella. "Is it okay if I take her back there?"

"Or she can stay with me. I've got a brand-new pack of Sharpies with her name on it."

I glanced down at Ella. "I'll stay here," she said.

My daughter was braver than I was at her age. Hell, sometimes I thought she was braver than I am now. It was a good thing.

I brushed my thumb over her cheek. "I'll be quick." Before I turned the corner, I already heard Ella giggling again. These were good people, but they weren't my people.

Zack's door stood open at the end of the hall. I gave a courtesy knock and stepped inside. He looked up from his computer. "Hey."

"Hi. I was actually looking for Rissa but," I reached inside my purse and pulled out the envelope, "can you give this to her. Tell her I said thank you." I placed it on his desk.

Zack picked up the envelope as I turned to walk out the door. The faster I could get out of there the better.

"What is this?" He held up the check.

I swallowed down the lump caught in my throat. "It's for the dress. And the shoes. It's the right thing to do." I quickly headed back to the front of the shop.

"Maggie, wait!"

I froze.

He held the check out to me. "Clarissa won't want this. There weren't any strings attached to the dress. Just because you and Chase…" He didn't have to finish. We both knew how that sentence ended.

I ignored his outstretched hand and smiled at him weakly. "There's always strings attached, Zack. Let's not pretend Rissa and I will still be friends now that they've been cut. I'm glad I met you all; you're good people. No hard feelings."

He frowned. "Chase may have cut the strings, but he wasn't holding the scissors. Take care, Maggie."

I didn't know what the hell that meant, and it didn't matter. I didn't have time for cryptic words or mind games.

When I got up front, Ella held her arm up for me to see. "Draven drew me a princess cat." Sure enough, a cartoon cat with long eyelashes, a crown and jeweled collar adorned her arm. It was super cute, and I could tell Ella loved it.

I pinched her chubby cheek. "We'll have to wash around it in the tub."

"I gave Draven a tattoo too," she said proudly.

Draven held his arm up. It was covered in intricate designs that nightmares were made of, but right between the Grim Reaper and a viper, in the crook of his elbow, sat a pink cat with big ears and crooked whiskers.

This gruff, scary man let my daughter draw on him in pink Sharpie. "Thank you." I gave him a hug. "You'll make a great dad one day."

He winked at me. "I'm ready, just trying to convince Layla."

Ella and I hurried out to the car and off to dance. Our little detour had us running behind a few minutes. We pulled in the parking lot with only a minute to spare. Once we were inside, Ella yanked off her sweats, put her ballet shoes on, and plopped onto the floor next to another aspiring ballerina.

I settled into the chairs outside the large viewing window with the other parents. Just to torture myself, I checked my messages again. There weren't any. I tucked my phone away promising myself I wouldn't check it again until dance class was over.

It was one more promise I made to myself that I couldn't keep.

"I'm going to kill him."

I'd just gotten Ella to sleep and was already relaxing with a glass of wine when my brother showed up on my doorstep with Brian in tow. The two of them made my kitchen feel infinitely smaller, especially with the waves of anger Patty was emitting.

I grabbed them each a beer from the fridge and leaned against the counter. "You're an attorney. You know better than to put voice to a threat. Who told you anyway?" The best defense with my brother was always a good offense.

Patty twisted the top off his beer and took a long draw from the bottle. "Not the person I should have heard it from."

Brian put his beer back in the fridge, pulled a wine glass from the cupboard, and held it out to me. I filled it halfway. He cocked his head and I filled it to the brim with Merlot. "I heard it from Layla."

Of course he would have. It didn't escape me how ironic it was that all our lives were interconnected. Patty was dating Brian. Brian's best friend was Layla. Layla had worked and been friends for years with Chase. Chase broke up with me. And it got back to Patty. It was one big frustrating circle. I wanted to wallow alone, but it was impossible. "She called you?" I asked.

"No." Brian shook his head. "She mentioned it over coffee this morning, assuming I already knew. You could have told us."

"I didn't want to talk about it. What'd she tell you?" I was hoping Brian could give me some answers.

"All she said was you and Chase broke up and didn't offer any details. I tried digging, but she clammed up tighter than a straight guy's ass," he said with a frown.

"That's why we're here." My brother slammed his empty bottle on the table. "I want to know what the hell is going on. You guys looked happy at the premiere. What happened?"

I shrugged. "I don't know."

"What do you mean you don't know?" I jumped at his abruptness and annoyed tone.

My eyes welled up. "I don't know, okay? We didn't have a fight. He's never been anything but good to me. Then, bam! He broke up with me out of nowhere, giving me some *it's not you, it's me* line. I don't know what I did wrong!"

Brian wrapped me in his arms when it should have been my brother consoling me. "Hey, you didn't do anything wrong. Chase has always been a free spirit. It was my only concern when I saw you two together. He's a good guy, but he doesn't commit."

Patty growled at Brian. "Is he fucking someone else?"

I cringed. I didn't want to think about Chase having sex with another woman.

"Why are you looking at me?" Brian huffed.

"He's your friend."

"Friend of a friend," Brian answered. "Besides, he's your friend too."

Patty scoffed. "Friend of a friend of my boyfriend."

My head was starting to hurt. "Stop it, you two! This isn't helping. It doesn't matter whose friend he is." I held my arms out wide. "He didn't want *this*. Toys piled in the corner, nights watching Disney movies, a six-year-old who loves ballet, and a woman who has to work her Friday nights around her ex's visitation schedule." I let it out, giving Chase every excuse I could think of, because I wasn't mad at him. I was mad at myself for believing a man like him could want a woman like me. "What man in his right mind would sign on for this? I was stupid to think it would last. Even Ella's own father didn't want us."

When it came right down to it, that's what hurt the most... the rejection. I'd tried over the years to form healthy relationships with men. As soon as they found out I had a child, they ran. And who could blame them? If Jeff didn't want me then how could anyone else?

"Maggie..." Patty didn't finish his thought, just gave me a look of pity that matched Brian's.

It practically broke me. Jeff didn't want me. Chase didn't want me. I didn't need anyone to feel sorry for me.

Not my brother and not Brian.

I didn't need their pity because the truth of the matter was, I already felt sorry enough for myself.

Chapter 37
Chase

Tossing the football around with my son was better than anything I could have imagined. The air was crisp, but the sun was shining. There was no telling how many more days we would have like this before the weather turned to freezing temperatures and snow.

For a little guy, my son had an arm like a cannon. All he needed was some coaching. I'd never been a quarterback, back in the day my body had been built for speed. I was the guy catching the pass, not throwing it, but I knew the basics from my years of play.

I jogged over to Cade. "You know how to do a three-step drop?"

He shook his head. "What's that?"

"It helps you get some power behind your throw." I squared up his shoulders and showed him the footwork. He mimicked my steps and let the ball soar. I charged across the yard catching the ball with ease and cradling it to my chest. "How'd that feel?"

"Awesome!"

"Coming back at you." I lobbed a pass to him that landed right into his outstretched arms.

Meredith slipped out the back slider in her bare feet and a heavy sweatshirt draped over her body. "Time to eat, boys."

Cade ran past her into the house, leaving me on the deck with his mother. "You didn't have to cook for me."

She rolled her eyes. "Don't flatter yourself. I had to cook dinner for my son anyway."

"Our son," I corrected.

Meredith pulled the sweatshirt tight around herself. "He likes you being here."

"I like being here with him. I have a lot of time to make up for."

She looked into the empty backyard, zoning out. "I hope you mean that. He's going to need you."

"I'm not going anywhere, Meredith."

She attempted to smile. "Good. Let's eat before it gets cold."

I followed her into the kitchen, checking out the house on my way. There were lots of framed pictures of Cade. A few of them with both Cade and Meredith. Noticeably missing from the photos were any men. A boyfriend or husband. I hadn't asked her, but I assumed she would have someone in her life. A girl like her couldn't have been single for long. But the more I looked around, the more I realized there wasn't a single indication that a man spent time here.

I made a mental note to ask Meredith about it later, because it was important. I needed to know if another man was part of my son's life. If so, I'd have to be okay with it and try harder than I did with Jeff to get along. I now understood Jeff's jealousy of me and what made him tick. The difference was he'd left Maggie voluntarily. I was just a stupid fuck and the rest was history. I didn't leave her by choice. Meredith had every right to move on.

Seeing her after all these years was different. She was still gorgeous, but the flame wasn't there anymore. I still cared about her. How could I not? She was my first love and the mother of my child. Maybe one day we could forgive each other for the mistakes we'd made, but right now my focus was Cade.

Meredith placed the casserole dish with chicken, roasted potatoes, and green beans in the center of the table. I sat next to Cade and watched as she scooped a helping on Cade's plate and cut his chicken for him.

"Smells good," I said, stabbing a piece of chicken with a fork and moving it to my plate.

"My mom's a good cook."

I smiled at him. "I remember. She used to cook for me a lot."

Cade looked between the two of us. "Were you guys ever married?"

I watched as Meredith pushed the food around on her plate. I took that as my cue to answer. "We were engaged. Do you know what that means?"

"Uh-huh. It means you gave her a ring and you were gonna get married."

I nodded. "We were."

"What happened?" Who knew so many questions could come from such a small person? I should have expected it. Ella was full of questions too. She and Cade were practically the same age and would have gotten along great. But since I'd ended things, they would probably never get that chance.

I didn't want to lie to my son, but I couldn't tell him the whole truth either. "I made a lot of mistakes. Your mom ended the engagement because I did things I shouldn't have."

"If you weren't married, then how did I get here?" he asked with wide eyes.

And the questions kept on coming. Meredith was no help. She kept pushing her food around, taking tiny bites and refusing to make eye contact.

Cade was too young for the birds and the bees talk, so I tried to explain the best I could. "Well, sometimes when two people love each other very much they have a baby. That's how we got you."

He gave me a toothless smile that reminded me of Ella's. "Because you loved each other?"

I reached my hand across the table and ran my fingers over Meredith's knuckles. "Yeah, we did."

"Excuse me." Meredith pushed away from the table and scurried down the hallway, closing herself behind a door.

Cade didn't seem to be bothered by his mother's behavior as he scooped a spoonful of potatoes into his mouth. We sat quietly for a few minutes. I didn't know what to say. Apparently, the memory of the two of us together upset Meredith. Another casualty of my bad decisions.

The unmistakable sound of retching carried down the hallway. Great! I'd made Meredith so upset she was actually puking at the thought of us together. I looked between Cade and the door in the hallway, unsure what to do. Should I go to her or pretend I didn't hear the awful sound?

"It happens all the time," Cade said, as he popped another bite of chicken in his mouth.

That wasn't normal. When we were together, the only time Meredith had thrown up on a regular basis was when she was pregnant. Was she pregnant again? My forehead furrowed. "What do you mean?"

"It's the medicine. It makes her sick," he said matter-of-factly.

"What medicine?"

He shrugged. "I don't know. Auntie Amber takes her to get it."

My sister? What the hell did she have to do with this? Meredith was awfully thin. I wondered if she had a drug problem, although I couldn't see my sister taking her to a drug dealer.

293

My curiosity and concern got the best of me. My chair scraped over the floor and before I knew it, I was outside the bathroom door. My knuckles tapped on the wood. "Meredith?"

"Go away, Chase." Her words came out strained and lacked conviction.

If she thought I was going to leave her alone, she didn't remember a thing about me. The knob turned and I peeked my head inside. She was hunched over the toilet and tears silently rolled down her face. "Are you okay?"

She flushed the toilet and leaned back against the tub. I remembered finding her like this the night she showed me a little white stick with a plus sign. "Are you pregnant?"

Meredith wiped at her face. "Not even close."

Prescription bottles littered the counter. I began reading the labels. Percocet. Lorazepam. Morphine. Ativan. Xanax. Zofran. I only knew what half of them were used for. I sat down next to her on the floor. It was the most intimate we'd been in years. "Cade said this happens all the time. What's going on?"

Her head dropped back, and she stared at the ceiling, the tears running down the side of her face and into her hair.

"Meredith?"

"Why do you care, Chase? We're not together."

"And you think that means I don't give a shit about you?"

She shrugged a shoulder.

"I know it's been a long time, but I think you know me a little bit better than that."

"Promise me you'll take care of him. I haven't talked to my parents in years. I don't want them raising him."

I heard what she said but the words weren't computing. "You're his mom."

She let out a long, slow breath. "I have cancer, Chase. I think I'm dying."

"No." Everything was starting to click into place. The tiredness in her eyes. Her loss of weight. The scarf on her head. The throwing up. The pill bottles.

"The doctors say the chemo is working, but I'm not so sure. I'm so damn tired."

Of all the things she was going to tell me, I didn't think it would be this. My arm instinctually wrapped around her shoulders and I pulled her to my chest, holding her there as the tears soaked into my shirt. I'd just found her again. It didn't feel fair that she could be so easily ripped away for a second time. I wasn't in love with her anymore, but I did love her, and Cade needed his mom.

I grasped her chin and forced her to look at me. "You're not dying. Do you hear me? I won't let you. Whatever you need, I'll do it."

She smiled up at me, but it didn't quite reach her eyes. "Thank you. We should talk after Cade goes to bed. He knows I'm sick, but I've tried to shelter him as much as possible." Meredith squirmed out of my arms and stood in front of the mirror, wiping the mascara that ran down her cheeks. "Time to put on my happy face."

I couldn't help but wonder how often she'd said those words to herself. Living alone and taking care of our son while going through chemotherapy couldn't be easy. It was a living nightmare.

In that moment, looking at the woman I used to love, I pledged to do everything I could to help her through this.

Because there were no choices. She would make it through this.

Chapter 38
Maggie

Another week had come and gone and still not a word from Chase. I must have been a masochist because I couldn't let go of the shred of hope that he would call or text or something. But every day there was nothing. No sign that he thought about me at all. It was depressing to think I was that forgettable, that easy to let go of.

I had no idea what he was doing. Was he out drinking with his friends? Was he picking up some woman like he'd done to me? Was he holding her close and pushing deep inside her? It was these images that were driving me crazy.

I'd thought he loved me. He told me he did, but maybe they were just words muttered in the heat of the moment. I hadn't told a man I loved him since before Ella was born. Those words meant something to me. When I said them back, I didn't do it lightly.

"Daddy's here!" Ella's voice drew me out of my Chase-induced haze. Still in my skirt and blouse from work, I went to open the door for Jeff.

His eyes appraised me up and down. "You look nice."

I rolled my eyes. Compliments from Jeff always had an ulterior motive. "You don't need to butter me up. Just ask what you want to ask."

"Are you going out tonight?"

My social calendar was none of his business but pretending to have a date when I didn't was stupid and childish. He'd figure out soon enough that Chase and I weren't an item anymore. Honestly, I was shocked Ella hadn't already let it slip. "Not tonight."

Jeff picked Ella up. "Want Momma to come to dinner with us again? That was fun, wasn't it?"

Her face broke out into the biggest grin. "Please!"

Not again. Last Friday, I was weak. My resolve was stronger now.

"Orrrr…" Jeff drew out, "we could order pizza and stay in."

Ella punched a fist into the air. "Yay! Pizza!"

I crossed my arms in irritation. "What about your chicken nuggets?"

She rubbed her belly. "I like chicken nuggets, but I love pizza. Can we get cheesy bread too, Daddy?"

He pecked her on the nose. "Of course. Your mom loves it, even if she won't admit it."

True.

Jeff pushed through the doorway and sat at my kitchen table, pulling out his phone to place the order.

"Just make yourself at home," I said sarcastically. I was planning on a quiet night reading the new romance novel I'd downloaded. If I wasn't having sex anymore, I figured I could at least indulge in some mommy porn.

After placing the order, Jeff went to the cupboard and pulled out two wine glasses.

I don't think so!

I quickly plucked them from his fingers and returned them to the cabinet. I didn't know what he was trying to pull, but we were not going down that road again. Instead, I shoved a can of diet Coke in his hand. "I'm not drinking with you."

"Relax, Mags, it's a glass of wine not tequila."

He knew I rarely drank liquor. Wine was my weakness. It made me do stupid stuff and I'd reached my limit with stupid lately. "Why are you here, Jeff?"

"It's Friday night. I always come to see Ella on Friday."

How daft could he be? I planted my hands on my hips. "I mean, what are you doing in my house?"

Jeff popped the top of his can and took a long sip, testing my patience even further. My toe tapped furiously while I waited for his response.

Finally, he set the can on the table. "Look Mags, we used to do stuff like this all the time. I know you're pissed because I was rude to your boyfriend, but I think we can call a truce. I can get along with him if he can get along with me. We're all adults."

I wasn't going to correct him on the boyfriend matter. He didn't need to know my heart was broken and I was crumbling inside. He didn't need to know another man had rejected me. He didn't need to know in a small way I was relieved not to be spending the evening alone.

"Fine," I huffed.

"What does that mean?"

"It means exactly what I said. Fine. We'll sit together and have pizza, but I have things to do tonight. If you want to stay here to visit with Ella that's fine, but don't expect me to hang out with you all night." It was a total lie, but he didn't need to know it. I didn't have a damn thing planned but I would find a way to keep myself busy. Hell, I'd scrub the bathtub if it meant not getting looped into whatever game he was playing.

He shrugged. "Suit yourself."

Lately, all Jeff liked to do was argue with me. I was shocked he conceded so easily.

The pizza arrived quickly and the three of us sat down to eat. Ella put her cat in the empty chair at the table, giving me another reminder that Chase was missing. I yearned for the moments we used to spend as a "family". Again, another part of my fantasy.

Ella chatted the entire meal about the turkey project they were working on at school. "We got to use real feathers instead of paper like Mrs. Murray's class. They had to draw their feathers, but ours are soft and fluffy. And we got to use big googly eyes." She held her fingers up around her eyes to demonstrate.

"What color feathers did you use on your turkey?" Jeff asked.

She ticked them off on her fingers. "Pink, purple, blue, green, red and yellow."

Jeff laughed. "Sounds very colorful. Do you think I could hang it on my refrigerator when you bring it home?"

Ella clapped her hands together. "Yes!"

A part of me was disappointed that I wouldn't get to keep the first turkey she ever made at school, but that was selfish. Jeff should get some of her projects. I still had her jack-o'-lantern, with its crooked eyes and sharp teeth, stuck to the front of my fridge.

After packing away the leftover pizza and cleaning off the table, they wrangled me into a cutthroat game of UNO, which Jeff and I rigged to make sure Ella won. It was probably bad parenting on our part. Ella needed to learn how to lose gracefully, however, I didn't want her to deal with another disappointment.

She'd still been asking about Chase and seemed to be under the illusion that he had to go away for work. I didn't tell her that and I didn't remember Chase saying it either. It was something she had created on her own. I didn't have the heart to correct her and hoped that eventually she would stop asking.

It was time for me to excuse myself and let Jeff fend for himself with his daughter. Ella flopped down on the couch and turned the television to *Animal Planet*. "Look, Daddy, puppies! Can we get one?"

I looked at Jeff and smirked. "That's my cue to leave."

"Daddy?"

"Help me out here, Mags."

I gave them both a little wave. "You're on your own. Enjoy the rest of your night."

I hustled down the hall into my room, closing the door behind me and locking it for good measure. Taking a deep breath, I leaned back against the door and closed my eyes. Having Jeff here was weird. For years I thought we belonged together. I thought that was the life I wanted. If anything, the last couple of months had shown me I was wrong. I didn't want to settle for less than I deserved. Chase had shown me what a real relationship was like. What it was like to feel desired and cherished.

Until he bailed.

On the upside, seeing Jeff spending time with Ella and interacting with her was amazing. It was good for her. I always wanted Jeff to be more involved. Maybe it took having another man in my life for him to appreciate his daughter more. Whatever the reason for his change in behavior, I was thankful.

Now, I was hiding out in my bedroom thinking about the two men in my life. The man I used to love, who pushed me aside for seven years, was suddenly showing interest and I no longer cared. The man I did love was avoiding me like the plague. I couldn't win. This was so fucked up.

I face-planted onto the bed and let out a muffled scream into the comforter. Instantly, my nose filled with the familiar scent of cologne. Every day I told myself I was going to change the sheets, but I couldn't bear to do it.

I didn't want to let go of the little piece of him I had left.

Chapter 39
Chase

I sat in the chair next to Meredith and held her hand.

"Take a deep breath," the pretty, brunette nurse said.

I watched as Meredith sucked in a generous breath and closed her eyes. The nurse stuck the large needle into her port and taped it in place. "You're all set, sweetie. We'll get started in a few minutes."

Meredith managed a half smile. "Thank you, Stella."

"First name basis?" I questioned.

"We tend to bond when I feel like they're holding my life in their hands."

I couldn't believe I was sitting here in a hospital room with Meredith. I thought we'd be doing this when our child was born, but that never happened. Instead, I was holding her hand and assuring her she wasn't dying minutes before they started pumping poison into her body.

Life was strange. I was sure my life was on one track when I proposed to Meredith. We were going to get married, have a baby, and live happily ever after. Only one of those things was right.

Instead, I spent six months behind bars, Meredith had the baby without me, and I spent the next several years bedding woman after woman because I didn't want to cause of, or the recipient of, that kind of pain again. Then I met Maggie and it happened anyway.

The nurse returned and started the medicine that was supposed to cure Meredith. I watched the yellow liquid from the bag go down through the tube and into the port in her chest. She patted Meredith's other hand. "This will run a couple hours. I'll be back to check on you."

Meredith pulled the blanket up on her lap and smiled weakly. "I'll be here."

"So… when did this all start?" I wanted to know everything. Seeing as we were sitting in a hospital, this seemed like the logical place to begin.

"Summer. I went for my annual and my doctor found a lump. After that it was a mammogram, a biopsy and lumpectomy. Everything moved really fast."

I squeezed her hand. "I'm sorry."

She quirked an eyebrow. "For?"

"Everything. Being stupid. Leaving you alone. Not being there when you needed me."

"I forgave you a long time ago, Chase. I wasn't faultless either. I put a lot of pressure on you. You shouldn't have dropped out of school."

"I wanted to take care of you. I was shortsighted, going for an easy fix instead of sticking with the plan and making it work." I picked at the nonexistent lint on my jeans. "Do you have someone in your life? Another man?" Curiosity was killing me. It wasn't my business, but I needed to know. If she had someone, where was he?

"You really want to talk about this?"

I gave her my dimpled smile she used to love. "You're a captive audience right now. No better time than the present."

Her lips twisted to the side. "I did have someone. Adam and I were together for two years. He proposed to me last Christmas."

I didn't want to think about Meredith being with someone else, but I always knew she wouldn't stay single. I looked at her naked finger. "What happened?"

She motioned to her body from head to toe. "This. After my first chemo session, he told me he couldn't deal with it. My hair started to fall out and I had to get a wig." She touched the scarf on her head with blond strands cascading out underneath. "He couldn't stand watching me throw up and be sick. He didn't want to watch me die. Said it wasn't what he signed up for."

"Sounds like a douche."

She chuckled. "Yeah, I guess he was."

"So, who's been helping you?"

Meredith looked down at her lap. "Amber. She's been a godsend."

"I kind of hate her right now." The fact that she kept all of this from me pissed me the fuck off.

"It wasn't her fault. I swore her to secrecy. She was only doing what I asked her to do. You should hate me, not her."

I shook my head. "I could never hate you. It's easier to hate my sister."

She squeezed my hand. "Try to forgive her. She's really good to Cade. He loves his Auntie Amber."

"It's gonna be hard, but I'll try for you and Cade."

"Thank you." She glanced at the clock. We still had a long time until she was finished for the day. "So, turnabout is fair play. Amber said you have a girlfriend. What's she like?"

I couldn't help the smile from turning my lips upward. "Amazing. Maggie's a first-grade teacher and she has a daughter almost Cade's age. Both have gorgeous red hair and Ella's got the cutest darn freckles. For the first time since you, I was really happy."

"Was? What happened?"

"It's a long story."

She held up the tubing running into her body. "Time is something I have a lot of."

I told her the whole story from beginning to end. How we met. Connecting with her daughter. Rissa's premiere party. My visit from her ex. And how I had to let her go. When I finished, Meredith asked only one question. "Do you love her?"

Talking about this was awkward. I ran a nervous hand through my hair. "More than anything."

"So, fight for her. One thing I know about you is when you love, you love with your whole heart."

"I don't understand. Why are you encouraging me?" The last thing I expected Meredith to do was push me toward another woman.

"Because I want you to be happy. And if I don't make it through this, I want Cade to have a woman in his life, someone to be his mom."

I lifted Meredith's hand and kissed the back of it. "You're his mom and you're not going anywhere."

Chapter 40
Maggie

Jeff spent more and more time at our house. He'd increased his visits with Ella to twice a week and called her every night. I wished he'd shown this type of commitment for the last six years. Better late than never, I supposed.

He was attending Thanksgiving with us at my parents' house. It was Ella's idea, and my dad was putty in her hands. He was willing to suffer through Jeff on one of his favorite holidays for the sake of his granddaughter. It wasn't my dad I was worried about though. Patty and Brian were my bigger concern. If my dad hated Jeff, there wasn't even a word to describe what my brother felt.

The men sat around the dining room table with Ella, while my mom and I brought in the food. My dad loved Thanksgiving and my mother doted on him, cooking all his favorites: turkey, mashed potatoes and sweet potatoes, squash, green bean casserole, carrots sweetened with brown sugar, corn, biscuits, and her famous stuffing. She prepared enough food for a small nation, but I knew Patty and I would both be going home with care packages that would feed us for days.

"Everything looks delicious, Maureen." Jeff had always been more successful schmoozing my mom than my dad.

"Thank you, Jeff. It warms my heart having my whole family here."

My brother coughed into his fist and I swear I heard *bullshit* slip from his lips. I picked up my glass of wine and took a sip, giving him a glare and imploring him to behave in front of Ella. Yes, I was drinking wine tonight. It was a holiday and after the last few weeks I thought I deserved it, regardless if Jeff was driving us home or not. Nothing was going to happen.

"Maggie tells me you've been spending a lot of time with my girls," my dad said not so subtly, as he filled his plate with all the goodies on the table.

"Yeah, work has let up a little bit. Figured I'd spend the extra time with Mags and Ella." It was flimsy reasoning at best. It wasn't a matter of his work schedule. If he'd wanted to be with us, he would have been.

As if Patty read my mind, he piped in. "Must have been hard working that much for the last six years. I'm a lawyer and I still find time to spend with Brian every day."

I gave my brother an internal round of applause.

"When you care about someone enough, it's not that hard to fit them into your life," Brian added. I wanted to reach across the table and kiss him.

"Well, I'm here now. That's what matters." I couldn't blame Jeff for feeling ganged up on, but he'd brought it on himself.

"Is that so?" my dad asked.

"Yes. I want us to be a family."

I choked on my wine. "Excuse me?"

Jeff reached over Ella and rubbed my shoulder. "It's what you've always wanted, Mags. I'm ready to make that happen."

"Holy shit!" That came from my brother.

"Patrick!" my mom scolded.

Patty motioned to Jeff. "This is crazy!"

I scooted my chair away from the table. "Jeff, can I talk to you a minute in the other room?"

"Where are you going?" Ella asked.

I kissed her on top of her head. "Mommy and Daddy need to talk about a few things. I'll be back in a minute."

Jeff followed me into my childhood bedroom. I clicked the lock behind us. "Explain yourself!"

Jeff rubbed his hands up and down my arms. "There's nothing to explain. I want us to be a family. I love you and Ella. Move in with me."

I must have been in an alternate universe, because I swore he just asked me to give up our home and move in with him. "Are you out of your mind?"

"I know this is unexpected…"

"Unexpected? Unexpected is when garbage day is on Wednesday and they come on Tuesday. That's unexpected. This is…" I didn't even have the right words to describe it.

"Perfect," Jeff finished. His arms wrapped around my waist, pulling me closer and pressing his lips against mine.

I pushed hard at his chest, putting some much-needed space between us. "What in the world are you doing?"

"Kissing my girl. You've always been my girl, Mags. Let me make an honest woman of you."

I took two steps back and held my hand up to stop him from coming any closer. "Number one, that was cliché as hell. Number two, did you just ask me to marry you?" I wanted to make sure I wasn't misunderstanding him.

Jeff dropped to one knee and pulled out a ring with a huge diamond in it. "Maggie Malone, will you do me the honor of being my wife?"

All these years and now he was asking? This was exactly what I wanted. What I dreamed about. My old self would have said yes in a heartbeat. I should have been over the moon with joy.

"No."

Jeff blinked and shook his head as if he hadn't heard me correctly. "I'm sorry, did you just say no?"

"I'm not going to marry you, Jeff."

He stood and dropped the ring back in his pocket. "Why not? I thought this is what you wanted from me."

"It was. I tried for years with you. I practically begged you to give us the time of day, but we were so far down your priority list we practically fell off. I was willing to take the crumbs you offered us. But, you know what I learned? I learned I deserve better than to be second or third best. I learned I deserved to be someone's priority. I learned I didn't have to settle. I'm glad you're spending more time with Ella and being a father, but I don't want to be your wife. I'm not in love with you, Jeff."

I opened the bedroom door and headed back to the dining room. I felt a sense of freedom. For so long I let Jeff walk all over me, but no more. I would rather be alone than be the doormat he treated me as.

Jeff's footsteps stomped behind me and I prayed he wouldn't make a scene. The whole purpose of leaving the room was to protect Ella from this insanity. She didn't deserve to see us fight. She deserved to have two parents who loved her, and we owed it to her to show each other some respect.

Just as I reentered the dining room, Jeff lost it. "It's because of him, isn't it?"

I didn't want to feed into his goading, so I leaned against the doorway and played stupid. "Who?"

"You know damn well who I'm talking about! That lowlife, Chase Montgomery!"

Now I was pissed.

Yes, Chase broke my heart and left us without a backward glance, but I could honestly say in all our time together he never said a cruel word to me or gave me any indication that he wasn't a good person. Chase, before our demise, was one of the sweetest guys I ever met. "First of all, you don't know anything about Chase and secondly, my relationships are none of your business."

Before I knew it, Patty and Brian were standing guard behind me, just itching to step in if needed. Brian leaned in close. "You go, girl."

Jeff inched closer, undeterred by my brother and his partner. "I know plenty about Mr. Montgomery and it is my damn business. If you thought I was going to let a guy like that hang around my daughter you're out of your mind."

The last few weeks played out in technicolor in my mind. Chase's abrupt breakup. The phone calls and texts that weren't returned. Jeff's sudden interest in taking me to dinner. Him spending more time at our house and the extra phone calls. This wasn't simply coincidence. There was something bigger at play.

"What did you do?"

"I did what I had to do."

My blood began to boil. All this time, I thought it was me Chase didn't want, when Jeff had been pulling the strings the entire time. Zack's cryptic words echoed in my head, *Chase may have cut the strings, but he wasn't holding the scissors.*

"What the fuck did you do, Jeff?" I screamed.

My mom escorted Ella into the kitchen and I was thankful. She didn't need to witness this shit show. My dad put his hand on my shoulder in a show of support. He was letting me handle this but would intervene in a heartbeat. All three of the men behind me would.

Jeff angrily pointed his finger at me and spewed venom. "You think Chase is a good guy, Maggie. He's not! You're so fucking naïve. The guy has a rap sheet, Mags. All I had to do is threaten to take Ella away from you and the guy folded like a cheap house of cards. He knew he wasn't good enough for you. You're the only one who hasn't figured it out yet." He opened his wallet, took out a folded sheet of paper and shoved it in my face. "That's your precious Chase Montgomery. He's a fucking criminal."

I unfolded the paper and Chase's mug shot stared back at me. The words were too blurry to read through my tears.

"Get the fuck out of my house!" my dad roared.

"Why? Because I'm the only one here who didn't have the wool pulled over my eyes? Because I care who Mags lets stick their dick in her? I'm the bad guy?"

My dad's hand tightened on my shoulder. It took everything he had not to pummel the shit out of Jeff. My whole world flipped upside down in a matter of minutes. "Leave!" I screamed.

"I'm taking my daughter with me!" Jeff yelled back.

My dad charged at Jeff, pushing him out the door. "The fuck you are! Get the fuck out!"

"Better get an attorney, Maggie. This isn't done! I'll be seeing you in court!"

My knees shook as I clutched the paper to my chest. It was too much. The room started to spin and blood whooshed in my ears. *The proposal. The truth about why Chase left. The paper clutched in my hand.* My legs began to wobble. *Jeff was going to take my daughter.* My brother's strong arms held me tight as I collapsed on the floor.

"Maggie?"

I sobbed into his chest. "I can't lose my daughter."

Chapter 41
Chase

"I'm nervous. Your mom hates me."

I looked at Meredith. She was exhausted. The last round of chemo had been a killer. Or maybe it was always that way, but it was my first experience with it. I'd been staying in her guest bedroom, helping the best I could. I was there when the nausea hit, rubbing her back and wiping down her neck with a wet washcloth. I let her sleep for hours while I helped Cade with his homework and made sure he had dinner. I called her doctor when the pain was unbearable. I did her laundry and washed her sheets. I took Cade to school and picked him up afterward. But most importantly I held her hand and assured her she wasn't dying. That the world would be a darker place without her. There was nothing worse than feeling helpless in a situation you couldn't control.

"My mom doesn't hate you."

"You and Cade should have come without me," Meredith insisted.

I kissed her on the forehead. "There's a lot to be thankful for this year. I want you to be here."

"Okay." Meredith looked scared to death, but if she could take on cancer, my mom would be easy as pie. All my mom had been able to talk about was her new grandson and finally getting to meet him.

The aroma of turkey filled the house as we walked in. Cade held my hand tight and Meredith stayed two steps behind.

As soon as we entered the kitchen Cade let go of my hand and rushed toward my sister. "Auntie Amber!"

Amber wrapped him in her arms giving him a huge hug. It was bittersweet. On one hand, Cade had a familiar face here to make him feel more comfortable. On the other, it was a stark reminder of the secret my sister had kept from me. She'd had years with my son and I'd only had weeks.

My mom held a hand in front of her mouth and tears filled her eyes. "He looks just like you," she whispered.

I kissed her on the cheek. "I know." There was a certain amount of pride in creating another human being. Every time I looked at Cade, all I could think was *I did that*. I might not have been the poster child for great dads, but had I known, I would have been there from day one. I planned on being there for the rest of them.

Mom held out her arms to Meredith. "Come here, sweet girl."

Meredith stepped into my mom's embrace. Her shoulders shook as she held on tight. "You must hate me."

My mom held Meredith's face in her hands. "There will be none of that. We've all made mistakes. How could I possibly hate you when you've given me such a precious gift." When we were younger, Meredith had a rocky relationship with her own parents and my mom more than willingly took her in as her own. That connection was still there.

"Cade, come meet your grandma," Meredith called to our son.

He looked to Amber for reassurance. She nodded, encouraging him to come over. I kneeled in front of Cade. "This is your Grandma Betty. She's my mom."

He stuck his hand out. "Nice to meet you, Grandma Betty."

My mom laughed. "So polite, but in this house we hug." She wrapped him in her arms and was struggling to let him go. I knew the feeling well.

"Can I get one of those," Grams asked. I didn't mean to leave her out, it was just a lot for Cade to take in.

"It's okay," I assured him. "That's my grandma and she's the best grandma in the world. You can call her Grams."

They hugged each other and Grams pulled two chocolate chip cookies from the counter and handed them to him. "Why don't you go share these with Theo in the other room."

At the mention of Theo's name, Cade perked up. I hadn't thought about it, but it made total sense that if Meredith and Amber had been friends all this time, Cade and Theo would know each other. They both had a relationship with the son I'd just recently become acquainted with.

Amber and Meredith talked quietly in the corner. I hadn't said a word to my sister yet. I was still pissed as hell at her and she wouldn't be getting my forgiveness anytime soon.

My mom clapped her hands together getting our attention. "This is nice having my whole family under one roof." She looked between my sister and me. "Now if my two children would quit pretending the other didn't exist the day would be perfect."

"Too soon, Mom." I went to the family room and sat down with Dave, Amber's husband, to watch football. The boys played with Legos on the floor, each building some type of contraption with wheels. The end of the first quarter was winding down, the Lions leading the Bears by three.

Dave and I weren't close, mainly because he traveled a lot for work and was barely around. "Did you know?" I asked him.

He shook his head. "I knew they were friends and Amber was helping her. I didn't know you were Meredith's ex. In my defense, I came into the picture well after everything went down."

"I'm really…" I glanced at the boys, "…mad at Amber. I don't know if I can forgive her."

"I get that. Amber feels bad about it. Said she regretted not telling you."

She felt bad? Really? "How would you feel if you missed seven years with Theo?"

Dave sighed. "Sometimes I feel like I am. I travel too much and I know it. One day he's going to be a teenager and want nothing to do with me and I'll have no one to blame but myself."

I cocked my head. "Why don't you do something to change it then?"

"I've been looking for a new job, but the pay cut will be a huge hit."

"Money won't buy back the time you're missing with your son. Don't waste the time you have with him. Once it's gone you can never get it back."

Dave scratched his chin and contemplated my words. "So, Meredith? You two back together?"

Now that was the question. I thought when I saw her all the old feelings would come rushing back. I had a fantasy for a long time that if I ever saw her again, I'd beg her to take me back. That she'd forgive me, and all would be right with the world.

We'd spent the last few weeks together and made our apologies. Relived our youth through the memories we shared. She was the first girl I made out with in the back of a car. We lost our virginity to each other. I gave my heart to her without a second thought and never asked for it back. We loved and we lost. I regretted how I hurt her, destroyed us. We both made decisions that changed us forever.

When I held her hand it was soft and warm, but the spark was gone. The flame had been extinguished by time. I cared about her still. We would always be a part of each other's life, connected by Cade, but we decided to keep the past in the past where it belonged.

Who knows? Maybe if we'd stayed together we would have married only to get divorced down the road. Grams was a big believer in destiny and fate. She believed in a higher power and that everything happened for a reason.

My reason was Maggie. She was the one I couldn't erase from my mind or heart.

And Ella. I couldn't help but think that she and Cade would have gotten along great. Cade was in first grade, just eight months older. He'd make a great big brother and Ella would have driven him crazy with her dream of being a princess.

"Chase?"

I realized I'd spaced out. "Yeah?"

"You and Meredith?" Dave asked again.

"Nah, we're friends but we're not together."

Chapter 42
Maggie

Ella was tucked tight in my arms, asleep in the queen-size bed that took up half the space in my childhood room. She had so many questions and I didn't have any answers. *Why was Daddy yelling? Why was Papa so mad? Why was I crying?* How could I explain any of it to my daughter when I barely understood it myself? I failed tonight as a mother.

This was not the Thanksgiving any of us planned on. My dad insisted Ella and I spend the night for fear that Jeff would show up at my house. I'd never been afraid of Jeff before, but what happened today made me unsettled, made me question and rethink everything that happened over the last few months.

When I started dating Chase, I knew Jeff was jealous and part of me relished in that fact. I wanted him to be jealous. To know that someone else found me desirable. To make him feel like he had lost his chance. Never in a million years did I think it would evolve into this.

I didn't expect the proposal. I didn't expect his confession about Chase. And I certainly never expected him to fight me for custody of Ella. My boring, simple life turned into a clusterfuck in a matter of a few months.

The light knocks on the doorframe shook me from my personal pity party. My brother leaned against the entryway with his arms crossed. "She asleep yet?"

"Yeah. We both had a good cry."

"Can I talk to you in the kitchen?" He motioned with his head.

"I'll be there in a minute." I slowly slipped my arm out from under Ella, careful not to wake her, and pulled the blanket over her small body. Kissing her on the head, I whispered, "Love you, ladybug."

My family—Dad, Mom, Patty, and Brian—sat around the table waiting for me. My dad motioned to the empty chair. I slipped into it, dropping my head to the table. "What is happening to my life?" This whole day had been exhausting.

My mom rubbed my back gently. "Want some tea?"

"That would be great. Thank you." My mom didn't deal with conflict well and making me tea kept her busy.

My dad cleared his throat to get my attention. "Let me start by telling you how proud I am of you."

I laughed. "You're kidding me, right? I got pregnant in college with a guy who ditched me, the man I chose to replace him with ended up being a criminal, and now Jeff wants to fight me for custody. There's not much to be proud of. I've made a mess of everything."

My dad kissed my cheek. "Let's take those one at a time. First of all, not a day goes by that I'm not proud of you. I couldn't have asked for a better daughter. Was I happy that you got pregnant in college? No. However, you could have dropped out, but you didn't. You finished and have done an amazing job supporting yourself and raising our granddaughter. Even though it was unexpected, I can't imagine our life without Ella in it."

My mom placed a mug in front of me. "You're a good mom, Maggie. We're extremely blessed to have you as a daughter."

I sipped my tea, letting the warmth travel down my throat and into my queasy stomach. "Well, one out of three ain't bad. Things are still a mess."

Brian uncrumpled the paper Jeff shoved at me and flattened it out on the table. "Let's talk about this."

I stared at Chase's mug shot. "Seems self-explanatory."

Brian tapped on the rap sheet. "Something doesn't add up. I've known Chase for years and I've never once heard a thing about this. I wouldn't put it past Jeff to Photoshop it."

I wanted Brian to be right, but it was wishful thinking. "If that were true, then Chase would have called his bluff. He would have told me."

Brian shook his head. "I don't know. One thing I do know about Zack is that next to his wife and daughter, owning that tattoo shop is the most important thing in his life. It's his baby. He wouldn't hire someone who had a felony if it put his business at risk. There has to be more to the story."

My mom sheepishly raised her hand like we were in school. "I liked him."

I rolled my eyes. Of course she did. Chase charmed the hell out of her with his stupid smile and dimples.

Ignoring our mother, Patty took the paper from Brian. "We have investigators at the firm. Let me make a few calls and do some digging."

"I can't afford an investigator." Christmas was coming and money would be tight. With the way things went tonight, I didn't know if Jeff would make his child support payments or not. I hoped he wouldn't punish Ella because he was mad at me, but if I'd learned anything tonight it was that I couldn't trust Jeff.

"Just let me handle it, Maggie," my brother insisted.

"What happened tonight? One minute we're having dinner and the next all hell broke loose," my mom asked.

I sat back in my chair and crossed my arms. "You're going to love this. Jeff asked me to marry him. He had a ring and everything."

Everyone started talking at once, expressing their disbelief and shock. Never in all the years since I'd gotten pregnant had Jeff ever indicated he wanted us to be together. Until tonight.

My dad quirked an eyebrow. "I assume you told him no."

"Damn right I did. I told him I deserve better."

Brian started a slow clap and everyone joined in. "It's about time."

"Do you think he'll really fight me for custody of Ella?" Out of everything that happened tonight it was the only thing I was worried about. Losing my daughter would destroy me.

"I think Jeff's jealous and pissed off," my dad said. "If he wants to go to court, bring it. There's no way any of us would let that happen. He doesn't have a leg to stand on. He's been a part-time dad at best for the last six years. I don't want you to worry about Jeff."

"He's a fucktard," Patty muttered.

"Patrick!" my mom scolded.

I laughed the first real laugh all night. "Mom, he's right. Jeff is a total fucktard."

Chapter 43
Chase

I watched Cade like a creeper as he sat in front of the coffee table drawing a picture of us playing football in the yard. He'd definitely inherited his art skills from me. If the pictures Ella drew were any indication of what was age-appropriate, Cade's skills far surpassed it. It made me a proud papa to know even though I'd been absent for the first seven years of his life, he still had parts of me. In the nurture verses nature battle, nature had won out. He was artistic and could throw one heck of a spiral.

Meredith bumped me with her shoulder. "You don't have to babysit me, you know. I'll be fine."

The last few days were good. Meredith had been up moving around the house and cooking again. The nausea subsided and her energy was back. I wrapped an arm around her shoulder. "I know. I just can't stop looking at him. You did good."

"We," she corrected. "He's got all your best qualities."

My phone chirped notifying me of a text message. Seeing Red's name, I quickly stuffed the phone back in my pocket.

"That thing has been going off all day. Are you going to read any of those messages?"

I shrugged.

"Is it your girlfriend?"

"She's not my girlfriend anymore. She deserves someone better than me. I'm a complication she doesn't need."

Meredith held her hand out. "Give me your phone."

"Why?"

She wiggled her fingers. "Just hand it over."

I reluctantly placed it in her palm.

She tapped into my messaging app. "Red? Cute." She read through the messages from Maggie. "This woman has been texting you for weeks and you haven't replied once."

"I don't see a point. We can't be together. I figured she'd forget about me after a while." I refused to give Jeff a reason to carry through with his threat. I loved Maggie too much for that to happen.

Meredith handed me back my phone. "I think you should read her messages, especially the ones from today."

"Why?"

"Quit being a stubborn ass and just read them." She sidled up next to Cade. "Give your dad a hug. He's going home."

"I am?"

"Yes. Go home and get your girl. Give yourself a chance to be happy."

After hugging Cade and promising him to come back soon, I sat in Meredith's driveway with the heat blasting in the cab of my truck. Leaving Cade was hard. I'd been spending most of my time at Meredith's, but she didn't need me like she had the first few days after her chemo. It wasn't healthy to be spending so much time with her, and if I was being honest, she was probably sick of me. It was nearly impossible to pull myself away from my son and being here helped me to fill in the gaps of everything I'd missed. I had my own apartment and a job I needed to get back to. Zack had been amazing about flexing my schedule and giving me time off, but I had to get back to something that resembled normal.

Normal?

So much in my life changed so quickly, I didn't even know what normal was anymore.

I glanced at my phone, pondering if I should read Maggie's messages or not. My finger hovered over her name indecisively. *Why the hell not?* I quickly tapped her name before I could change my mind.

Red: I know what Jeff did.

Red: Please call me so we can talk.

Red: I haven't given up on us. Have you?

She knew. How much?

I could text her back like a chicken. Or I could call her, but then I wouldn't be able to see the expression on her face when I told her everything. I should have told her about my arrest record when we started dating, but I didn't. No matter what happened between Maggie and me, whether she wanted to be with me or not, I wouldn't keep secrets from her anymore. I would tell her everything about my arrest, Meredith, and my son.

I pulled out of the driveway and made the almost hour drive to Maggie's house. It was after nine and Ella would be asleep. A smart man would have called first, but my past actions showed I couldn't always be trusted to use the best judgment.

Standing on her front porch, I knocked on the door and shoved my hands in my pockets, to both keep them from fidgeting and keep them warm. Since Thanksgiving, the temperature had dropped significantly, and I could see my breath. I was about to knock again when I saw Maggie peek out the side window.

The door crept open and Maggie's hand rested on her chest. "You scared me."

I was already fucking this up. Of course she would be scared. Who knocks on someone's door at nine-thirty at night on a Wednesday? This guy, that's who. It was pitch black outside except for the few Christmas lights hung on the porch. Being here without calling first was more evidence of my poor decision-making skills. "I'm sorry."

"It's all right. I thought you were Jeff is all."

"Do you want me to leave?" I hadn't planned this out well. Again, my impulsivity got the best of me.

She frowned. "Are you kidding me right now?" She held open the door. "Come in, stranger."

I smiled at her use of the word *stranger*. It was her big hang up when we first got together. I hadn't been here in a month. I missed the way it smelled, the toys scattered about and the beautiful woman in front of me. I stepped inside, slipped my shoes off, and sat on the couch.

Maggie curled up on the opposite end and tucked her knees to her chest, wrapping her arms around her legs protectively. "I've missed you." I hurt her and for that I was truly sorry.

I leaned forward, resting my arms on my legs. This conversation was harder than I thought it would be. There was so much to say, and I didn't know where to start. "I've missed you too, but I couldn't stay."

"Because of what Jeff did?" she asked, setting her chin on her knees.

"Yes. I should have been honest with you from the start. My past," I shook my head, "I'm not proud of it. I was young and dumb. I made shitty decisions and I didn't want you to think less of me. When Jeff showed up at my work and threatened to take Ella away from you, I didn't have a choice but to let you go. I would never ever put you or Ella at risk."

"Tell me about your arrest," she said.

"Meredith and I were engaged," I started. "She was pregnant."

Maggie's eyes widened, but she didn't say a word. She let me tell my story and so I did. I told her about the weed and the coke, the arrest, Meredith leaving me and every other little detail until the day I walked out of county jail six months later. The only thing I left out was Cade. It didn't seem right to lump him in with my indiscretions, because I would never consider Cade a mistake. "I'm not a bad person, Maggie. I made a lot of awful decisions and I've been living with the guilt and consequences ever since."

She reached out her hand to me and I took it, threading our fingers together. "I'm sorry you've been carrying that burden. None of us are perfect. We all wish there were things in our past we could go back to change. It's how we deal with the aftermath that shows our true character. When Jeff showed me a picture with your mug shot, I was devastated that I could have made such an error in judgment, but deep down I think I knew you weren't the person he was portraying you to be. That wasn't the man I knew."

"But I am."

"It wasn't the whole story though." Maggie bit her lip. "Promise you won't be mad at me?"

Was she joking? Sitting here on her couch felt like a second chance I didn't deserve. "What could I possibly be mad at you for?"

"My brother had someone look into your case. I knew the truth before you told me, I just wanted to hear it from you."

I was so confused. "Why bother? It changes nothing. You and Ella deserve…"

"To be happy," she answered. "Before Ella was even born, I wanted to be with Jeff. I wanted him to make us his family. And then you came along, and you showed me how empty my life had been. You made me a priority, you made me feel desired, and you made me imagine a future that made me happy. That's why when Jeff proposed on Thanksgiving, I told him no. He wasn't part of the future I imagined."

"He proposed?" I was shocked, although I shouldn't have been. I knew Jeff planned to pursue Maggie, but damn, that was fast.

She nodded. "I should have known something was off from the beginning. All of a sudden, he started asking me to come to dinner with him and Ella, calling and dropping over unexpectedly." Maggie gave a self-deprecating laugh. "I thought he was actually stepping up to the plate as a father. I didn't realize how far he would go to snake his way back into my bed."

I had no right to ask, but I had to know. "Did he? Snake his way into your bed?"

Maggie smiled coyly. "No. I think it pissed him off, especially when he realized I was still in love with you." She crawled onto my lap and held my face between her hands. "I love you."

I grabbed her hips, pulling her closer. My lips pressed against hers and I felt like I was home. "Yeah?"

"Yeah."

"I only left because I didn't want Jeff dragging you to court because of me. I couldn't make you choose. I didn't want to do that to you."

Maggie pressed her hands against my chest, creating unwanted space between us. "Chase, he's threatened to do it anyway. I don't know if he'll follow through, but if he does, I want you by my side."

"He's doing it because of me."

"No. He's doing it because of him. He doesn't like losing and he knows he's lost me. I won't let him win. I won't let him determine who I love. If Jeff decides to take me to court, we'll fight. I'm not afraid of him."

I gripped her hips tighter. I'd gladly stand by her side if that's what she wanted, but this conversation was far from over. "I want to be honest with you. There's one more thing you need to know."

Chapter 44
Maggie

There's one more thing you need to know.

The words seemed ominous. My mind spun with the possibilities. The worst of which was he had slept with someone else. We were apart for a month, so it's not like it would be cheating, but still. I didn't want to think of him being with some other woman- whispering dirty words in her ear, stripping off her clothes, or pushing deep inside her. It wasn't a secret that before we got together, Chase was quite the ladies' man. It was very possible he sought comfort in the bed of some floozy from the bar.

Was it something I could get past? I wasn't sure.

I stiffened my back preparing myself for the bomb Chase was about to drop on me. "What do you need to tell me?"

Chase lifted me from his lap and set me on the couch beside him. "I looked up Meredith."

Oh!

His ex. The one woman in his life he'd been in love with. They were engaged. Were going to have a baby together. Build a life together. First love dies hard, I knew that from experience. It'd taken me years to get over Jeff. My only comfort was knowing it wasn't some random woman, although maybe it would have been easier.

I swallowed the lump in my throat. "Okay. And?" I wasn't sure what else to say. I needed more information.

"She never aborted the baby." Chase pulled out his phone and showed me a picture. "I have a son."

That was the last thing I expected him to say. My hand came up to cover my shock. "Oh my god!" I took the phone from him to study the picture of Chase and his son. They had the same shaggy blond hair and the same aqua eyes. No one would ever be able to dispute they were father and son. "What's his name?"

Chase's face broke into the widest smile. "His name is Cade and he's amazing. He plays football and he's artistic like me. He'll be seven in January, so just a little bit older than Ella. I've been spending a lot of time with him. It was love at first sight."

"That tends to happen. When I was pregnant with Ella I was scared to death, but once they placed her in my arms I fell in love." I pretended to look at the picture a bit longer than necessary as I decided to broach the most important question on my mind without coming off jealous or needy. "How are you and Meredith getting along?"

"Great, actually. I was really angry at her for keeping Cade from me but we've both made mistakes and have decided to leave them in the past."

I nodded. "That's good. I'm happy for you, Chase." *Was it good?* I wasn't sure what it meant for me.

He brushed his hands down his jeans in a nervous gesture. "Meredith has cancer, Maggie. I went with her to chemotherapy and have been helping her out a lot. She thinks she's dying, but I refuse to believe it. She only has two more treatments left. I can't believe now that I've finally found her, I could lose her all over again."

Could he have tugged at my heartstrings any harder? Not only was Meredith his long, lost love, but they had a child together and she had cancer. No woman could compete with that even if she wanted to. What kind of woman did it make me to even want to compete with her? The right thing to do, would be to back away gracefully and accept that Chase had found someone else. So, why was it so hard?

It hadn't gone unnoticed that when I just told Chase I loved him he didn't say it back. So, I asked the one question I wasn't sure I wanted an answer to, yet had to know. "Do you love her?"

Chase ran a hand through his hair, a clear sign he was stressed or flustered. "I wasn't sure I could forgive her, but yes, I love Meredith. Always have."

I nodded and handed his phone back. "You deserve this. I'm sorry about all the texts and phone calls. I just thought that…," I shrugged, "maybe we still had a chance, but I can see how happy you are."

He cupped the side of my face and ran his thumb along my cheek. I soaked in the feel of him touching my skin, knowing it would be the last time. I wanted to engrain Chase into my memory, so I could hold on to it when I lay alone in bed at night.

"What makes you think we don't have a chance?" he asked.

Despite my best effort to stop it, my eyes filled with tears. "You're in love with another woman. I won't compete with her. I won't be something on the side for you."

"You could never be something on the side, Red. You're everything. I love Meredith, because she's the mother of my child and I care about what happens to her. But I'm not *in* love with her anymore. I'm in love with you, Maggie Malone."

The tears fell down my cheeks. "You're in love with me?"

"Undeniably. What I did to Meredith is my biggest regret. You are my greatest redemption. I wandered around lost for so long, but with you I found my purpose. You make me feel complete. You are the missing piece that makes me whole. Wherever you are is where I want to be. So, if you'll still have me, I'd like to come back home."

I fell into his chest, wrapping my arms around him, "I love you, Chase. Don't ever leave me again."

He held my head to his chest. "I'm never letting you go."

I breathed in his cologne and sighed. He was *my* home.

Chase pulled out the necklace he gave me the night of the premiere and fastened the pendant around my neck. "This belongs to you. It's my promise to be the man you need me to be."

My fingers brushed over the diamond. "You already are."

A loud gasp had us both turning toward the bedrooms. Ella stood there in her nightgown, her cat hanging by its tail. "You came back!"

"Yeah, I'm back, princess bug."

Ella ran and jumped into his arms, hugging him so tight I thought she might strangle him. "I told you, Momma!"

"Yes, you did, ladybug," I said, as I ran my fingers through her hair. Seeing the two of them together made the misery of the last month melt away.

Chase sat Ella on the couch between us. "I'm sorry I was gone so long. How did you know I'd come back?"

She smiled up at him with her toothless grin. "Because you love us."

Chapter 45
Maggie

Meredith and I sat in a semi-private room. It was decorated in muted colors that were supposed to be calming, but they looked cold and sterile to me. There was a picture of a rainbow on the wall with the words *The greater your storm, the brighter your rainbow*. I wondered if other people who sat in this room found it uplifting, because I didn't. Places that needed inspirational quotes were generally depressing in my experience.

Meredith relaxed back into the blue recliner and closed her eyes. I sat in a folding chair in the corner, just taking everything in. This whole place was so quiet, even my thoughts were too loud.

Meredith and I got to know each other over the past few weeks, but I really didn't know why I was here.

I was nervous when I first met her. Meredith was the woman Chase once loved and she was beautiful. They had a child together. They had history. He had every reason to be with her, so my insecurities were on high alert.

But then I met her, and she hugged me so tight I thought she was going to crush me. She was strong for such a tiny thing. "I'm so glad to meet you," she'd said.

And with that, my insecurities washed away. We'd spent Christmas together, letting the kids get used to this new dynamic. It was nice to not have the awkwardness that existed when Jeff and Chase were in the same room.

Jeff and I were still on shaky ground. I barely spoke to him, and when I did it was clipped and full of resentment. He made it clear he was pissed Chase and I were back together. I made it clear I didn't care what he thought. Jeff assured me he had no intention of taking Ella from me, but he did file for more visitation time. It was his way of trying to exert control over me and the situation. I wasn't happy about it, but there wasn't much I could do. I hoped in the long run it would help build the relationship Jeff and Ella should have had from the beginning.

Chase wasn't quite as optimistic as me, but he tried for Ella. Maybe in time we would all get along, but I wasn't holding my breath for any Kumbaya moments.

The sound of footsteps pulled me from my thoughts. A nurse pulled back the curtain and smiled brightly, "Good morning, Miss Meredith. Big day today."

Meredith smiled back, but it didn't reach her eyes, "Last treatment, Stella. I get to ring the bell, right?"

She held up her hand for Meredith to high-five. "That's right, girl! You ready to get this over with?" She was way too chipper, but I supposed she had to be to do this job every day.

"So ready. Lay it on me," Meredith said. She reclined the chair back and pulled her collar to the side, so the nurse could access her port.

The nurse cleaned the area with an alcohol swab. "Take a deep breath," Stella instructed.

Meredith closed her eyes and breathed deep.

"One, two, three, done." The needle was inserted, and the nurse asked Meredith a plethora of questions.

I squirmed in my seat. This felt way too personal for me to be here. It made me uncomfortable, as if I were invading Meredith's privacy.

Stella started the medication and patted Meredith's hand. "I'll be back in a bit to check on you."

"You all right?" I asked.

"Every time I come here, I think the anxiety will be less, but it never is." She sighed.

"Last time though, right?" I gave her a weak smile.

She shrugged. "Maybe. Maybe not."

I pointed at where Stella had left through the curtain. "But she just said…"

Meredith reached for my hand and I took it. "Yes. Today is supposed to be the last day. I go for a PET scan in a month. That'll tell me if the chemo worked or not. If it didn't, then there will be more treatments."

I squeezed her hand "I'm sorry." I was so out of my element. I'd never had anyone close to me go through cancer treatments. I didn't know the ins and outs.

"You're probably wondering why I asked you to come with me today," she said.

"Kind of. Not that I mind being here, but I was wondering why you didn't ask Chase or Amber."

She thought about her answer for a moment. "Did you know I almost decided to not have Cade?"

Okay… so we were moving into ultra-personal territory. Not where I thought this was going at all. "Chase told me."

"I wasn't ready to be a mother and with Chase being gone…" She shrugged. "But then I went to the appointment and once I saw the ultrasound, I couldn't do it. I wasn't ready, but not a day goes by that I regret having Cade. He's brought me so much happiness."

I sat up a little taller in my chair. "I'm not judging you," I assured her. "When I found out I was pregnant with Ella, I was scared and alone. The thought of having an abortion crossed my mind more than I'd like to admit. But like you, I'm glad I made the choice to keep her."

Meredith and I weren't that different. We'd both been young when we had our kids. We both knew the struggles of being a single mom. Maybe that was why I immediately liked her. We were kindred spirits.

She smiled at me. "I had already planned on contacting Chase before he showed up on my doorstep. He just beat me to it. I guess you could call it fate or kismet. I kept putting it off even though I knew I had to tell him about Cade. But the longer you keep a secret the harder it is to tell the truth, you know?"

Actually, I didn't know. I'd never kept Ella a secret. Jeff had chosen not to be part of our lives. We'd raised our children alone for two very different reasons.

I wondered why she was telling me this. Maybe she wanted Chase back. It made sense. "What made you change your mind about telling Chase?"

Meredith picked up the tubing that ran poison into her body in the name of healing, "This. Everything changed when I found out I had cancer."

I didn't know what to say, so I said nothing. I couldn't imagine how she felt. Anything I had to say would have seemed insufficient.

"What Chase and I had together was magical. He was my whole world and he spoiled me rotten, giving into my every whim. He was loyal to a fault. He quit school so I wouldn't have to get a job. I was selfish and I let him give up his dreams for mine. I put too much pressure on him. What he did was as much my fault as it was his."

I couldn't help myself, I had to ask, "Are you still in love with him?"

Meredith sighed. "I'm in love with the idea of what we had. Part of me will always love Chase."

Everything in me seized. If she had an opportunity for happiness, wouldn't that be the best gift I could give her. "Are you asking me to step aside? Do you want a second chance with him?"

"No. I can see how happy he is with you."

I breathed a sigh of relief.

"The first time I saw him with Cade I got butterflies in my stomach. He was a natural. Despite how mad I was at Chase, I always knew he'd be a good dad."

"He's pretty great with Ella too." I remembered our first few weeks together. "He stumbled along the way, but he was a fast learner. Ella adores him."

"He's easy to love."

"Yes, he is," I agreed.

Stella poked her head in the room. "How's everything going? Can I get anything for you ladies?"

Meredith gave her a thumbs-up. "I'm fine. Thank you, Stella."

Stella looked at me. "I'm good too. Thanks."

Meredith waited until Stella was gone to continue. "I don't know how long I'm going to be around," she admitted sadly.

"You're not going anywhere," I said. It might not be the truth, but any other answer was unacceptable. I refused to believe she wouldn't make it through this.

Her eyes welled up. "My woman's intuition tells me otherwise. That's why I wanted to talk to you alone today."

Pressure built in my chest. "What can I do?"

Meredith squeezed my hand. "I'm so glad Chase found you. I've watched you with Ella and Cade. You're a great mom."

Again, I was lost for words. "Thank you," was all I managed.

"I wanted to ask you to do me a favor."

Whatever she asked, I wouldn't be able to deny her. "Anything."

Meredith's eyes filled with tears. "When I die, I want you to take care of Cade."

Now I was crying. "You're not dying."

"I might be, and I need to know Cade will have a mom that loves him. Someone that will kiss his scraped knees. That will tuck him in at night. That will go with him to buy flowers for his first girlfriend and dance with him at his wedding. I don't want him to miss out on anything because I'm not here."

The tears poured down my cheeks. "How about this?" I bargained. "I'll love Cade as if he were my own no matter what, but as long as you're here, we do it together. He'll have two moms that love him unconditionally. Deal?"

She nodded. "Deal. Thank you."

"You're very welcome." I leaned in, careful of the tube connected to her chest, and gave Meredith a tight hug.

We were both crying messes when we released each other. Today hadn't been about solidifying a friendship. It was about forming an unbreakable bond. Not for us, but for the ones we loved.

And an unspoken promise I hoped I'd never have to keep.

Epilogue
Chase
6 Months Later

"Are you nervous?" I asked Cade.

"Nah, I'm cool. Are you?"

"A little." I shrugged, turning to look at him in the back seat. He'd gotten so big that the booster was a thing of the past. Ella was already harassing Maggie about when she could get rid of her booster seat as well. The two had become thick as thieves and I wasn't sure yet if it was a good thing or a bad thing.

He stared at me with eyes that matched my own both in color and the mischief they held. "Don't worry. You got this, Dad." It should have been worrisome that my kid had more courage than I did, but he'd been raised by a great mom, so I chalked it up to that. One day this kid was going to break hearts. If he was anything like me, he was going to be good-looking and charming. I felt bad for the girls already. They had no idea what was in store for them.

I held up my fist for him to bump. "You ready?"

He knocked his small fist into mine. "Yep."

"Got your box?"

"Yep." He tapped on the small black box sitting in his lap. "You got yours?"

I held it up for him to see. "Are you sure you're okay with this?"

"I'm good with it, Dad. Maggie's really nice. She bought me all that cool art stuff."

I ruffled his hair. I wished life was as easy as he made it out to be. The two of us got out of my truck and headed into Maggie's house. Well, my house too. When the lease ended on my apartment Maggie suggested I move in. I thought she would want to wait because of Ella, but she said I spent so much time there anyway it made sense. I accepted Maggie's offer because, let's face it, wherever she was is where I wanted to be. No more going back and forth or packing a bag.

Meredith and I didn't have a formal visitation schedule, but Cade was spending every other weekend with us. It wasn't nearly enough, but it never would be. Maggie insisted he have his own room, so we moved Ella's toys from the spare bedroom to the basement to create a playroom for the kids. She let Cade pick out his own bedding and décor. He was definitely making it his own.

When we walked in, Henry, our three-month old basset hound, trotted over to us, tripping on his ears that dragged on the floor. Cade fell to his knees, stuffed the box in the pocket of his hoodie and ruffled the dog's ears. "Hey, buddy." Henry licked his face with a ton of enthusiasm and even more slobber. He was a happy pup and watching my son with him made me an even happier dad.

It took an enormous amount of convincing to get Maggie to agree to adopt the adorable hound. The kids and I had to practically make a blood oath taking full responsibility for Henry. She could pretend she didn't like him, but I knew otherwise when I found them sleeping on the bed together the other night with Henry's head resting on Maggie's stomach and her arm wrapped around his tiny puppy body. She loved that damn dog as much as the rest of us.

As for Not My Cat, he was curled up on the back of the couch, his tail wrapped tightly around his bulky body and his ears perked up, always on alert even when snoozing. When I'd decided to make the move to Maggie's, it bummed me out to end my five-year relationship with the little dude. Ella begged me to bring him home and I had the painstaking task of explaining he wasn't our cat to take, hence his name. However, as he watched me load the last of my boxes into the truck, I made him a one-time offer.

"You coming or you staying?" He wound himself between my legs, rubbing his lean body against my calves while purring. I scratched him between the ears. "I know you're a free-range cat, so if you want to stay, I'll understand, but I'll miss our bro time together." I looked like an idiot talking to a cat that clearly wasn't going to answer back. Leaving him was harder than I thought it would be. After some more petting by me and purring by him, it was time to say goodbye. "Catch you on the flip side, cat dude." I let out a somber breath and made the short trek to my truck that was loaded and ready to go. As I opened the door, Not My Cat leapt up inside, securing his place in the passenger seat. I assumed when I started the truck, he'd freak out and try to escape. Instead, he let out a bored yawn showing me all his teeth and curled up on the leather, closing his eyes. I ran my hand along his back. "Yeah, I kinda love you too."

Not My Cat came and went as he pleased, always returning when his belly growled, or he needed a safe place to nap. I had no doubt he'd been making the rounds, charming the neighbors with his feline good looks, coaxing them out of both treats and affection. When we brought Henry home, the tabby gave him a swift smack on the nose with his paw, effectively telling the goofy hound who's the boss. Henry hadn't gotten the message yet, but the two of them had been peacefully coexisting even if it meant Not My Cat perched in the highest places possible, far away from Henry's puppy antics.

"We're in the kitchen!" Maggie's voice rang out into the hall.

Cade and I left the slobbery dog to follow behind us as we set off in the girls' direction. Montgomery men might have been easily distracted, but we always got the job done and today's mission was of utmost importance.

The kitchen looked like a bomb had gone off… a gigantic flour bomb. Both my girls were covered from head to toe in white powder, as well as the counter and the floor.

Cade skidded to a halt. "Whoa!"

"What in the world happened in here?"

Maggie used her pinky to push some strands of hair away from her face, smearing even more flour across her cheek. "We were making chocolate chip cookies and the bag of flour started to tip off the counter," she started.

"And luckily I caught it," Ella finished, slapping her hands together, while standing on the chair.

Maggie rolled her eyes. "Luckily," she said sarcastically. "It was like a giant white volcano."

This wasn't at all how I planned this to go down, but it was perfect. Perfectly crazy. Perfectly chaotic. Perfectly us.

I stepped in front of her and brushed the flour from her cheek with a tender caress of my thumb.

She raised an eyebrow, as if reminding me we had an audience. I wasn't shy about public displays of affection. I kissed her often, many times in ways that exceeded the PG rating Maggie insisted on in front of the kids. I wanted the world, including our children, to know how much I loved her. That she was the center of my world.

But now wasn't the time for passionate kisses that would make her toes curl. Now was the time for honesty and devotion. I kissed her sweetly on her smudged cheek. "Thank you."

"For what?" she whispered. "The cookies were a bust."

"I'm not talking about cookies. I'm talking about this." I motioned at the mess around us. "This wonderful, crazy, chaotic life you've given me. I wouldn't want to share it with anyone else." I took the black box from my pocket, dropped to one knee on the flour-covered floor, and popped open the box containing the diamond ring that had belonged to Grams. A gift she had insisted I give to the woman who had made me whole again. My redemption amongst a sea of regret. "Miss Maggie Malone, will you marry me? Will you be my forever partner in this life we've created together? Share my hopes and dreams, and stand by my side no matter what the future brings us?"

Maggie fell into my arms. "Yes, yes! A thousand times yes!"

I slipped the diamond on her finger and gave her a definite PG-13 kiss, tongue and all.

Ella tapped Maggie on the shoulder from her perch on the chair. "Can I see, Momma?" Maggie held her hand up for Ella to inspect. She clasped her hands together tightly. "It's so beautiful! You got a princess ring, Momma."

I nudged my head at Cade. It was his turn.

Cade took the box from his pocket and popped it open in front of Ella's face. "Ella, will you be my sister?"

She looked back and forth from the heart-shaped necklace to Cade's face, resting her tiny fists on her hips. "I'm not kissing you, Cade Montgomery. I'm only six and I gotta keep my options open."

Maggie giggled into my neck. We were in trouble. Ella was going to be a handful when the boys started coming around.

Cade pushed the box into her hands. "Ewww! I don't want to kiss you. I'm asking you to be my sister not my wife."

Ella reluctantly took the box from his hands. "Okay, but don't try no funny stuff, mister."

I saved Cade from the torture Ella was raining down on him by taking the necklace out of the box and clasping it around her neck. "This is to remind you that no matter where I am, you're always in my heart. I might not be your real dad, but I'll always take care of you and protect you."

Ella wrapped her tiny arms around my neck, hugging me tight. "I love you, Chase."

"I love you too, princess bug."

"Group hug," Maggie announced. The four of us huddled together with our arms wrapped around each other. "I'm so lucky to have such wonderful men in my life."

"What about me?" Ella asked.

Maggie gave her an extra tight squeeze. "You were the first love of my life, ladybug."

"Dad, can I take Henry outside?" Cade asked.

I ruffled his hair. "Go for it, buddy." He'd been a trooper and done his job well.

"I'm coming too!" Ella squealed as she jumped off the chair.

The two flew out the back door in a flurry with the basset hound nipping at their heels, all big paws and floppy ears. Not My Cat meandered over to the door, stretched lazily and released a loud meow. I let him out too. I doubted he wanted to play and was more interested in exploring the wild and trying to finagle treats from the neighbors.

I walked back into the kitchen in time to catch Maggie staring at the ring on her finger. When Grams gave it to me, she told me how my grandfather had proposed to her when she was only seventeen and although she was young, she knew he was the one. She said she hoped the ring brought us a lifetime of happiness just as it had her and my grandfather. I didn't want to take it, but she'd insisted it would make her the happiest grandmother ever, especially since she was dying soon, which I knew she wasn't. Grams would live at least another twenty years. After all, she had all those trips from *The Price is Right* to take.

"What are you thinking about?" I asked.

She reached out her arms to me and I stepped into them. "How lucky I am to have you in my life."

I held Maggie tightly. "I think I'm the one who's lucky. And Cade. He doesn't have just one terrific mom, but two."

"Mmmm. I think he's pretty terrific too, just like his dad."

We stayed locked in each other's embrace a little longer, savoring our time alone. Moments like this were few and far between lately. When we separated, I looked around the wrecked kitchen. "What can I do to help?"

She laughed. "Start looking for bigger houses."

Since I'd moved in and Cade had stuff here too, plus the addition of two pets, the house was a little cluttered and a lot lived in, but it was our home, and it was filled to the brim with love. "Nah, I like this house and it has a great backyard. It's perfect for the four of us."

"It is," she agreed. "But… where are we going to put the crib?"

I cocked my head because surely I hadn't heard her correctly. "I'm sorry, the what?

"The crib," she said, patting her flat stomach.

My mouth quirked up on one side. "You're pregnant?"

I saw the worry in her blue eyes. She bit her lip and nodded. "Are you upset?"

Was I upset? A year ago, the only person I had to be concerned about was myself and I was content, but I wasn't truly happy.

Then I met Maggie and she challenged everything I believed I deserved. I learned to love again, to trust, to believe in myself. I found a woman who accepted all my broken parts, helped put them back together and loved me with her whole heart. Her daughter adored me, and I couldn't imagine my life without the sassy little girl with the wild red curls. She was my daughter too.

I mended my relationship with Meredith, who proved she was a badass by battling cancer and winning. It'd been the fight of her life, but she was officially in remission and for that I was thankful. Although Meredith and I would never be together again, she was still an important woman in my life, as a friend and the mother of my son.

I discovered I had the coolest kid ever. He was the best thing to come out of the mistakes I made, because he definitely wasn't one of them. I may have missed the first part of his life, but I'd spend the rest of mine making up for it.

I took Maggie's face in my hands. "I'm not upset. Actually, I think I'm the happiest man alive. We are already so blessed, but this baby might be what ties us all together as a family. I missed so much with Cade and you practically raised Ella alone. This is our chance to experience everything in a whole new way. I want to be there for every doctor's appointment, I want to buy you pickles at ten o'clock at night, and I want to hold your hand during every single moment."

"I'd like that, but I'm scared. Is it too much too fast? Two kids, a wedding, a new house, and a baby? It's a lot."

I smoothed out the wrinkles on Maggie's forehead. "It is a lot. But you know what we have going for us?"

"What?"

"Each other. I asked you when we first started this to jump with me. Now I'm not only asking you to jump but to let me be your life jacket."

"You'll keep me afloat?"

"When life starts to be too much, I'll keep *us* afloat. Trust me?"

She smiled. A real one that touched her eyes. "Yes."

"So, you want to marry me?" I asked her again.

"I really do." Her smile widened.

I spread my palm across her stomach. "And you want to have a baby with me?"

"I really, really do."

I picked Maggie up and spun her around our disaster of a kitchen. "So, let's do this. All of it."

Another Epilogue
Maggie
3 Months Later

It was the fastest wedding in the history of planning weddings. I wanted to be Mrs. Maggie Montgomery when the school year began and my baby bump started to show, not Miss Maggie Malone. I had a history of doing things a little bit backward, and although I again fell into that pattern with Chase, I felt confident in our decisions and where our life was headed. Because never in my life had I ever felt happier or more completely adored.

That's what Chase did to me.

He was my partner in crime during crises, my shoulder to lean on when life got crazy, my laughter in the midst of tears, my last glass of wine at the end of a long day, and my lover who never stopped worshiping me in the bedroom.

I'd say I had a pretty good life. A damn spectacular life.

Today was just making it official.

"Are you ready, sweetheart?"

I smiled up at my dad as I looped my arm through his. "I've never been more ready for anything in my life." It was a warm August day. The sun sparkled off the sequined bodice of the gown Roxy and my mom helped pick out. The sheer satin of the skirt gently flowed to the cobblestones beneath my feet, effectively concealing any evidence that I was pregnant. It wasn't a secret, however only our closest friends and family knew we had a baby on the way. I thought my dad would be disappointed that again I'd done things out of order, but he simply smiled and told me he was ecstatic I finally found someone who respected and cherished me. Also, he was totally excited about being a grandpa again.

"Songbird" by Fleetwood Mac began to play. My dad kissed me on the cheek before we started our walk down the floral-lined path that led to the gazebo where

335

my future husband waited for me. Chase's friends and family sat on one side of the aisle and mine on the other.

I hadn't lost my girl posse. They'd been cheering us on silently from the sidelines, waiting for Chase to realize what they already knew. That he was undeniably and irrevocably in love with me. That love was worth fighting for.

As I passed all the wonderful and supportive people in our lives, I couldn't help but think about how fortunate we were. If it weren't for our family and friends, I don't know if Chase and I would have found our way back to each other.

I zeroed in on the man I loved. He gave me a smile that dimpled on one side and his aqua eyes pierced my soul. He was my home, and I was headed right to him.

My maid of honor, Roxy, stood to one side with Ella. Zack, Chase's best man, stood to the other side with Cade. We had the cutest flower girl and ring bearer ever and they were excited to be part of the ceremony. Ella tottered back and forth on her feet while Cade kept pulling at his bow tie.

As I got closer, Chase took my hand in his. "You are stunning," he whispered.

Toasts were made, the cake was cut, the bouquet had been tossed. We were finally to the part of the night where I could relax in my husband's arms. Yes… it felt amazing to say. Chase was my husband, and I was his wife. When I had Ella, I'd wanted nothing more than to get married and have a family. I was crushed when Jeff rejected me. But It wasn't the right time or the right man. Life had other plans for me.

Something unexpected.

Something passionate.

Something spectacular.

Chase held me tight as he spun me around the dance floor. "What are you thinking about, Red?"

I smiled at him because I couldn't stop smiling today. "How much my life has changed in a year and what a wonderful and unexpected surprise you were in my life."

He ran his thumb along my cheek in the way that always made me melt. "I feel the same. I had resigned myself to being alone, but then you came barreling into my life."

I laughed. "I didn't barrel into your life. If I remember correctly, I ran out on you."

"Twice." He chuckled. "But I couldn't get you out of my head. Everything about our first night together was unforgettable."

"Our *first* first night together or our *second* first night together?" I asked coyly.

His hand on my waist skimmed down my back and squeezed my butt. "Both. You gave me no choice but to chase you."

"So, the Chase was on." I laughed again, thinking I was funny.

He waggled his eyebrows at me. "The Chase was turned on, just like I am right now." He pressed his erection into my stomach. "Would it be awful to leave our own wedding early?"

"So awful."

He groaned.

"We can't leave. All our friends are here. What will they think?"

"They'll think I'm fucking my wife," he whispered in my ear.

Now, it was my turn to groan.

He scanned the crowd dancing around us. "You think Draven won't drag Layla out of their wedding early?"

They were getting married next month. The way Draven and Layla practically had sex with their eyes, I was surprised it took them this long. "I think he'll probably pull her into the coatroom for a quickie," I said honestly.

Chase's eyes sparkled with mischief.

"Don't even think about it," I warned. "Our children are here."

"Fine," he huffed. "But I have plans for you later."

I put my hand on his chest. "I should hope so." I nodded over my husband's shoulder to Roxy. She was dancing with corporate guy. His name was Nate and they'd been together since Halloween. "Did you see the way Roxy nearly hip checked our daughter to catch the bouquet?"

"Yeah. Ella was pissed too." He laughed. "You think Roxy will marry Nate?"

"I don't know. He seems too straitlaced for her, but maybe she's ready to settle down." Roxy and Nate were polar opposites, but Roxy swore he was a freak in the sheets, so maybe not. She was happy and that was all that mattered.

337

Everyone seemed happy tonight. Zack held on to Rissa like she was his dying breath. Brian and Patty were having drinks at the bar. My parents danced like teenagers at the high school prom. Chase's mom was chatting it up with Meredith and Amber.

Chase still hadn't forgiven his sister, but with a little prodding they were working on their relationship. It was going to be a slow process. Amber's betrayal was the wound that cut Chase the deepest.

And Grams... she shocked us all by bringing a plus-one from the senior center. She was adorable all dressed up and on a date.

I rested my head on Chase's shoulder. This whole day had been a magical fairy tale right out of Ella's Disney movies. I wore a beautiful gown, married my prince and found my happily ever after. It couldn't get much better than this.

I felt a little tug on my skirt. Cade stood there with hopeful eyes. He held his hand out to me. "Momma Maggie, can I have this dance?"

My heart burst. I took ahold of his little hand. "It would be my honor to dance with you, Cade Montgomery."

Ella wasn't far behind. She held her arms out. "Will you dance with me Daddy Chase?"

He swept her up into his arms. "Of course, princess bug. I was just going to come find you, but I was afraid your momma might get jealous."

"You were?" She lit up.

"Yep."

Ella scrunched up her nose at me. "Are you jealous, Momma?"

"Nope, ladybug. I've got the most handsome dance partner right here." I nodded to Cade.

He beamed up at me.

When I said things couldn't get much better?

I was wrong.

This, right here. The four of us together? This was better.

Chase carried me over the threshold of our hotel room. I couldn't help but giggle. It was silly, but also super romantic.

He tossed me into the middle of the king-size bed. It was soft and poufy, and I giggled again. I propped myself up on my elbows and bent a knee on the bed. "So, Mr. Montgomery, you made me some promises tonight."

He slipped his tux jacket off his shoulders and tossed it on the chair. The tie came unfastened next. "Yes, I did." He tugged at his shirt, pulling it from his pants and began to unbutton it from the bottom. "And I plan on following through with every." *A button popped.* "Single." *Pop!* "One of them." *Pop!*

I bit my lip. God, why was he so sexy? He was teasing me, and I liked it. The anticipation. A shiver of desire ran down my spine and tingled between my legs. "I'm so ready."

Chase held up his hand. "But first, I have a gift for you."

I frowned. "I didn't know we were doing gifts. I didn't get you anything." I'd been so busy planning the wedding that I hadn't thought about buying presents. I felt like that was something we should have discussed.

"Look at you, all spread out on the bed for me, Red. You are my gift. I couldn't have asked for anything more than everything you are."

"I should have gotten you a present," I mumbled.

He put a finger to my lips. "Shhh. It's not that kind of gift."

When he started to slide his shirt off, my mouth watered. It didn't matter how many times I saw him shirtless, it always turned me on. I sat up straighter. "Oooh, I like this gift."

Chase straddled my legs, and I was a little confused. I didn't know how I was supposed to get out of my dress when I was trapped underneath him.

His shirt fell away and his right side over his hip was covered with gauze. He slowly peeled the tape off and lifted the gauze away. "I had Zack do this while you and the girls were getting your hair done this morning."

I ran my hand over the fresh ink on his side. A tree was tattooed into his skin. The thick trunk of the tree had our names in a heart carved into it. The branches spread out reaching to his back and stomach. "You put my name on your body?"

He nodded.

"You know that's forever?" I asked, brushing my finger over our names.

"I'm aware."

"That doesn't scare you?"

Chase leaned forward, caging me in with his arms. His lips pressed gently against mine. "I'm not scared. I meant every word I said today. I'm in this forever. 'Til death do us part."

It was a little morbid but romantic. "I love you so much."

"Mmmm…love you too, Red." He pressed his lips to mine once more and pulled back. "You haven't seen the rest. Look at the branches."

I squinted my eyes, taking in the details of the branches and leaves. Cade's name was interwoven into one of the branches. Ella's name was on another, along with a ladybug.

Chase was claiming Ella, much like he claimed me. My heart swelled. This man. This man never stopped finding new ways to make me love him.

My fingers brushed over the kids' names. "It's beautiful. I can't believe you did this."

He lifted my chin, gazing into my eyes. "It wasn't a hard decision."

There were three more branches left blank. One was for the baby I was carrying. But there were two more. Two. "There's empty branches. More than one," my voice hitched.

"I don't want to put limits on us or our future. If we only have the baby growing inside you right now, I'd be fine with it. But if we decide we want more, that's okay too. And if I need to have more branches added, so be it."

My eyes about popped out of my head, "Slow down there, Casanova. Let's see if we can handle one more before you go planning an entire team."

Seeing the concern in my eyes, he smirked at me. "All I'm saying is that wherever life takes us, I'm ready."

I relaxed and relished in this gift Chase was giving me.

I was ready too.

Whatever life had in store for us, Chase and I would do it together, with laughter and love. Together, nothing was impossible. Our future was wide open, and I couldn't wait to see where the journey took us.

Thank you so much for choosing to read *Regret & Redemption.* If you enjoyed the story, please consider leaving a review. Even a sentence or two is super helpful and greatly appreciated!

Want to read more about the Forever Inked crew? Check out the rest of the Forever Inked Novels.

Books 1~ Tattooed Hearts: Tattooed Duet #1 (Zack & Rissa)
Book 2~ Tattooed Souls: Tattooed Duet #2 (Zack & Rissa)
Book 3~ Smoke and Mirrors (Draven & Layla)
Book 4~ Regret and Redemption (Chase & Maggie)
Book 5~ Sin and Salvation (Eli & Roxy)

Keep Reading for a preview of *Sin & Salvation*.

Sin & Salvation

Eli

I couldn't stand another day in my father's house, so when Zack, my new boss at Forever Inked, offered me the apartment above the tattoo parlor, I jumped on it. The rent was reasonable, and it couldn't have been closer to work. It was super clean, with exposed brick walls, hardwood floors, streamlined furniture, linens in the closet, and a fully equipped kitchen. All I had to do was buy food, and it was move-in ready.

I set my duffel bag on the floor and leaned over the island to sign the lease. "This is perfect."

Zack looked at my bag. "You travel light."

I scrawled my name across the line and tossed the pen on the counter. "I'm a minimalist. Years in the military taught me to only carry what I need."

"What branch?" he asked.

"Navy. Did four tours as a SEAL." That was my past, but it defined the man I grew into.

"Impressive." Zack pointed a finger at his chest. "Marines. Two tours. That life makes you grow up real fast. Seen shit no one should ever have to see."

"You ain't kidding. Saw a lot of fucked-up shit. After four tours, I couldn't do it anymore. Needed something a little more civilian."

He reached out his hand to me. "Well, we're happy to have you on board. My artists have all got families now, and we were getting a little thin. It'll be good to have some fresh blood around here. And truth be told, I like having someone living in this apartment. Feels like an extra layer of security."

I gave his hand a firm shake. "I'm happy to be here and this apartment is a blessing. It couldn't have worked out better."

The door opened and Chase, who I'd met yesterday, walked in carrying a large box. Following behind him was another guy and two women, all carrying an assortment of boxes into the apartment.

"Zack, I'm glad you're here," Chase said. "Good news. I got a renter for the apartment." He set the heavy box on the floor. "Isn't that great?"

Zack scratched his head in confusion. "Small problem. I already rented it to Eli."

"Fuuuuck!" Chase groaned. "Roxy needs a place to stay because Nate the Great cheated on her. I figured this place would be perfect since it's been empty for months."

A woman with long, dark hair stepped from behind the others and gave a little wave. "Hi, Zack."

I stared at her. There was no fucking way. The braces were gone, and she was a lot curvier, but how many women could possibly be named Roxy. Her vibrant blue eyes confirmed it; they were stunning with her dark hair. She was the whole reason I got sent to Georgia, and you didn't forget a girl like that. I cursed her name for years, blaming her for the normal teenage life I'd been robbed of.

"Well, this is a clusterfuck." Zack ran his hands through his hair, clearly frustrated. "Eli needs a place too. He just signed the lease."

Roxy's face dropped. Her attention turned to me as if she just noticed my presence. Her eyes squinted in an expression I remembered well. She looked me up and down, studying me like a science project. I wasn't the same gangly seventeen-year-old boy anymore. I'd grown up too; I was taller and wider, with a body built by the military. I could tell when it finally clicked, as her expression turned from confusion to surprise. "Elias?"

My arms instinctively crossed over my chest. "It's Eli now."

Zack looked back and forth between us. "You two know each other?"

Roxy's face broke into a huge grin. "We used to…"

I cut her off. "We used to know each other." Those days were long gone, and I didn't need her getting any stupid ideas. She was wild and reckless. That wasn't me anymore.

The red-haired woman standing in the entryway clapped her hands together. "Well, isn't this a happy coincidence. There's two bedrooms. Maybe you could both live here."

It was a terrible idea.

I needed another complication in my life like I needed another hole in the head, and Roxy had complicated written all over her. She was a whirling dervish who left chaos in her path.

Zack blew out a breath. "That could work. I'd cut the rent in two and you could each pay half. It's up to Eli though. He already signed the lease."

Roxy looked hopeful, but when I didn't say anything, her face fell. "It's okay. I'll just stay in a hotel until something else comes along." She picked up her box from the floor and turned toward the door. "Come on, guys. Next stop, Holiday Inn."

She was really going to live at the Holiday Inn? Something deep inside me twisted. I loved her once, surely, we could get along for a few months. Besides, I was going to be so busy between work and visiting my father that I'd rarely be here. "Wait!" The word came out of my mouth before I could stop it.

Roxy turned back and cocked her head at me.

"On one condition," I said. Now I sounded like my father, who had conditions for everything. "It's a temporary arrangement. You need to keep looking for someplace else to live. Until then, you can stay here, but I'm taking the master bedroom." *Fuck.* I sounded like a prick. Maybe the apple didn't fall too far from the tree after all.

She chewed on her bottom lip. "I'd really appreciate it."

"Then it's a done deal," I said gruffly. There was no sense in giving her false hope that we would be together again.

"Are you sure?" Zack asked.

I gave him a curt nod.

He picked up the paperwork from the counter and tore it in half. "Stop by my office downstairs for the new lease agreement and keys."

"Let's get your stuff into your room," Chase said, leading the way to the second bedroom.

Roxy paused as she passed me and put her hand on my arm. "Thank you, Elias. You don't know how much this means to me."

My skin tingled under her touch, the same way it did when we were kids. "It's temporary," I reminded her.

"Of course."

I watched in amazement as the small group made several trips up and down the stairs and piled box after box in her room. She had a lot of shit.

What in the hell had I gotten myself into?

Roxy

Maggie and I huddled in the corner of my new room. "You know him?"

"He's the preacher's son," I whispered.

Her eyes went big. "The one who did that thing with his tongue?"

"That's the one. I haven't seen him in almost fifteen years."

"Sweet Jesus!" she gasped. "He's gorgeous. Broody, but gorgeous."

I started pulling shoes from a box and tossing them in the closet. "He's bigger than I remember, and he didn't used to be so gruff." I pulled out a red stiletto and rummaged through the box for its missing partner. "I don't think he's very happy I'm here."

Maggie frowned. "How could he not like you? Everybody likes you. What did you do to him?"

I ignored her question and kept searching for the other red shoe. If I left it behind, I was going to be pissed.

My best friend grabbed my wrist. "Roxy, what did you do?"

I let out a huff. "Nothing. We never even had a fight."

"Then why does he hate you?"

"We got caught having sex in his dad's office." I shrugged my shoulders. "It was my idea. He probably blames me for getting him sent to Georgia."

"Shit. You don't have to stay here if it's going to be uncomfortable. You can come back to our house. We'll make it work," Maggie offered.

I finally found the other stiletto at the bottom of the box. *Thank goodness*. Those shoes cost a fortune. I held up both shoes and pointed around the room with them. "All my stuff is already here. You heard him, *it's temporary*. It's not ideal, but I can handle a broody man for a few weeks. Might even be less."

Maggie rested her hand on my shoulder. "Good luck. Maybe he'll soften up and you guys can rekindle that old spark."

I looked through my open bedroom door just in time to see Elias leaving the apartment, the door slamming behind him. "I'm not sure that's in the cards for us, but maybe we can at least be civil. I'll lie low for a while and try not to poke the bear."

"I hate to tell you this, but I think you already poked him." She held up her hands in claws and growled.

More like I stabbed him with a ten-thousand volt cattle prod.

Don't miss **Sin & Salvation** and the whole Forever Inked crew!

Books 1~ Tattooed Hearts   Tattooed Duet #1 (Zack & Rissa)
Book 2~ Tattooed Souls   Tattooed Duet #2 (Zack & Rissa)
Book 3~ Smoke and Mirrors (Draven & Layla)
Book 4~ Regret and Redemption (Chase & Maggie)
Book 5~ Sin and Salvation (Eli & Roxy)

Want to be the first to learn book news, updates, and more?
https://www.subscribepage.com/sabrinawagnernewsletter

Not My Cat

Yes… Not My Cat is real! He started coming to our house several years ago. After a couple months of coaxing, we gained his trust. Now he stops by almost daily for cuddles and treats. He has become an integral part of our family. I am not under any illusion that we are the only ones he visits, but we are honored and blessed that he chose us to be part of *his* family.

Song List on Spotify

Regret & Redemption

Seein' Red~ Dustin Lynch
Shape of You~ Ed Sheeran
Home~ Daughtry
I Knew I Loved You~ Savage Garden
Who I Am With You~ Chris Young
I Do (Cherish You)~ 98°
Back At One~ Brian McKnight
I Could Not Ask For More~ Edwin McCain
This I Promise You~ *NSYNC
Good Morning Beautiful~ Steve Holy

Listen and Enjoy!

Acknowledgments

Thank you for choosing to read **Regret and Redemption**. I loved telling the story of Chase and Maggie. Although it was something I really wanted to do, it took me over two years to complete it.

When my younger sister got cancer, I decided that life was too short to not do what I wanted with it. It was then that I started writing. I had a story in my head and began to put it on paper. Once I finished Smoke and Mirrors, her cancer got worse. I put my life and writing on hold to help her and her family through their most difficult times. And although she fought hard, my sweet sister lost her battle. I grieved for a long time and tried to put the pieces of her family's, and my own, life back together. And then the pandemic hit, and nothing was normal. I was still teaching elementary school, and as we all know, virtual teaching was a stressful disaster for everyone involved. So, I quit. I decided to focus on myself and the things that made me happy, because as I said before…life is too short. I stopped wasting my time and energy on the things I no longer loved and began writing again. And that was when this book, that was half written, got its second chance and finally came to life.

I somehow wanted to incorporate the journey I took with my sister, but that much grief would have made for a very sad love story. It was through Meredith that I could touch on the emotions involved when a woman faces the prospect of leaving her young children motherless. It is real and scary and one of the worst things a woman will encounter in her life. I hope I did Meredith justice in the few short chapters that were hers. And although Meredith survived, my heart goes out to all the families that weren't so fortunate.

To my husband~ I could have never done this without your love and support. Thank you for affording me the opportunity to do what I really love. Not many people get the chance to quit their job and pursue their passion. For that I will be forever grateful. Also, technology scares the crap out of me, and you've been a patient saint walking me through all my mishaps and frustrations. Thank you for believing in me!

To Linda, Ari, Missie, and Deb~ You ladies are the best beta readers anyone could ask for! You've supported my journey and given me pep when mine was all gone. Your suggestions, critiques, and encouragement helped me in ways you'll never understand. Your constructive criticism improved this book so much and helped make it into something I'm proud of. I could never thank you all enough for your help!

To Jill~ You've been a great friend! We have learned so much together. We went through so many photos and ideas as I put in my two cents about each of them. I truly value your friendship, patience, and artistic talent. You continually rise to the challenge even when you don't always see my vision, and again you came up with something amazing. Thank you for the beautiful cover of *Regret and Redemption*... I absolutely love it!

To my readers~ Thank you for supporting me in this journey. There are thousands of books that you could have chosen to read, and I am honored that you chose mine. Please spread the word and leave a quick review on **Amazon** and **Goodreads** if you have enjoyed this book. Without you, writing would still be a dream.

About the Author

Sabrina Wagner lives in Sterling Heights, Michigan. She writes sweet, sassy, sexy romance novels featuring alpha males and the strong women who challenge them.

Sabrina believes that true friends should be treasured, a woman's strength is forged by the fire of affliction, and everyone deserves a happy ending. She enjoys spending time with her family, walking on the beach, cuddling her kittens, and great books. Sabrina is a hopeless romantic and knows all too well that life is full of twists and turns, but the bumpy road is what leads to our true destination.

Want to be the first to learn book news, updates and more?
Sign up for my Newsletter.

https://www.subscribepage.com/sabrinawagnernewsletter

Want to know about my new releases and upcoming sales?
Stay connected on:

Facebook~Instagram~Twitter~TikTok
Goodreads~BookBub~Amazon

I'd love to hear from you.
Visit my website to connect with me.

www.sabrinawagnerauthor.com

Made in the USA
Monee, IL
28 February 2023